INSATIABLE

THE PHOENIX CLUB
BOOK EIGHT

DARCY BURKE

Zealous Quill Press

For my amazing and inspiring daughter

Some of Kat is based on her, and I'm thrilled to give an autistic heroine a happy ever after.

Quinn, thank you for teaching and loving me, and making me prouder than I could ever imagine. I love you, Bunny!

INSATIABLE

Society's most exclusive invitation...

Welcome to the Phoenix Club, where London's most audacious, disreputable, and intriguing ladies and gentlemen find scandal, redemption, and second chances.

After Miss Kathleen Shaughnessy is seen kissing a gentleman in a Gloucestershire garden, she's sent to London to avoid scandal. She doesn't, however, plan to abandon her research of mating rituals, and she knows the perfect person to provide assistance: her brother's best friend, Lord Lucien Westbrook, who is renowned for helping others.

Disdained by his haughty father, Lucien runs the Phoenix Club, an inclusive community where no one is ostracized or overlooked. It's also a secret rendezvous for the Foreign Office, where important connections are made, and information is passed—until a scandal ricochets through the club and threatens Lucien's position with his superiors.

As Lucien works to maintain control of the club, his best friend's sister seeks his personal expertise and assistance with researching the "science" of mating. He can't possibly say yes, but the more time he spends with the genuine and captivating Kat, the weaker his resistance. He's soon battling his desire for her as well as the powerful forces who wish to push him out of his club. When Kat is thrust into real danger, Lucien will stop at nothing to protect the woman who has stolen his heart.

Don't miss the rest of *The Phoenix Club*!

Do you want to hear all the latest about me and my books? Sign up at Reader Club newsletter for members-only bonus content, advance notice of pre-orders, insider scoop, as well as contests and giveaways!

Care to share your love for my books with like-minded readers? Want to hang with me and see pictures of my cats (who doesn't!)? Then don't miss my exclusive Facebook groups!

Darcy's Duchesses for historical readers
Burke's Book Lovers for contemporary readers

Want more historical romance? Do you like your historical romance filled with passion and red hot chemistry? Join me and my author friends in the Facebook group, Historical Harlots, for exclusive giveaways, chat with amazing HistRom authors, and more!

CHAPTER 1

London, February 1816

"*I*...would like to participate in the Season." Kathleen Shaughnessy perched on a chair in the drawing room of her brother's house, her hands folded demurely in her lap and her gaze fixed placidly on her brother and sister-in-law who occupied the settee opposite. She knew her request would shock them, but that wasn't why she was making it.

Her sister-in-law, Cassandra, or Cass as Kat, and most other family and friends called her, spoke first. "You would?"

"You're surprised," Kat said.

Cass's dark brows arched briefly. "Given how vehemently you opposed attending nearly every Society event you were invited to last Season, yes, I'm surprised."

Ruark, Kat's older half brother and the Earl of Wexford, narrowed his blue eyes at her. "Why do you want to participate in the Season?"

Kat expected his skepticism. He knew her better than almost anyone and was well aware of her aversion to large social gatherings, because he cared to. She was not an easy person. Or so her mother told her.

There was no way she could tell him the truth, that it was the best, if not only, way she could conduct her research. What better place to observe human mating rituals than the London Marriage Mart? Actually, in the past, she *would* have told him precisely what she planned, but she'd learned that could get her into trouble. Besides, Ruark was married now with a child on the way, and she wouldn't involve him in her schemes.

Schemes? That was something her and Ruark's mother would say.

It was good their mother wasn't here, that she'd allowed Ruark and Cass to take Kat in. Nothing Kat did was what her mother wanted or hoped for. Kat was far too interested in wildlife and documenting her observations in both writing and drawing. Mother would say, "You'll never find a husband doing that." To which Kat would respond, "Then I won't find a husband."

Lifting a shoulder, Kat tried to appear indifferent while answering Ruark's question as to why she wanted a Season. "It will make Mother happy."

A sharp laugh bolted from Ruark's throat. "That is *not* why you're doing this, so don't try to sell me that nonsense. Have you decided to wed?"

That seemed the best answer, and if she said yes, hopefully, he'd let the issue rest. "I'm considering it."

"That is quite a change," Cass said. Now *her* gaze had turned dubious.

Kat threw up her hands. "I thought it would please you that I wished to join the Season, but if you're going to interrogate me and be suspicious, then perhaps I shouldn't bother."

Ruark waved his hand. "No, it's fine. It's quite good, in fact. You're right that our mother will be pleased, especially since we had to convince her to let you return to London with us."

"I don't understand why she required persuasion," Kat said. "My reputation in Lechlade isn't exactly pristine." That was because she'd moved on from observing the mating rituals of wildlife to humans and conducted an experiment in which she'd kissed a gentleman who was betrothed. Since he was already spoken for, Kat had deemed him the perfect research object. She certainly didn't want to *wed* anyone.

However, despite Kat's careful planning to kiss him in the dark garden at the assembly, they'd been seen. Mother had whisked her away from Gloucestershire before scandal could bloom. Not that it hadn't taken root—indeed, while the gentleman was now wed to his bride, Kat was still not entirely welcome by everyone back home.

"It's not ruined either," Cass pointed out. "But I do understand why you prefer to be here."

Kat loved London. After the "scandal," her mother had dragged her here in order to marry her off. Instead, Kat had spent last Season with Ruark and his new wife, Cass. "There are endless entertainments," Kat said. As well as a much higher likelihood of conducting her research more anonymously.

"Do you want to be presented to the queen?" Ruark asked. He looked to Cass. "Does she need to be?"

"Ideally, but it's not completely necessary," Cass replied. "Your mother ought to come for that, but I can act as sponsor."

Kat's insides somersaulted. "Must I? I don't feel a need to meet the queen." She offered them what was probably a tepid smile. Alas, it was the best she could muster. The thought of garbing herself in a ridiculously old-fashioned costume and curtseying to the queen was vastly unappealing in every way.

"If you're invited to do so, you'll have no choice, I'm afraid," Cass said sympathetically. She was the best sister-in-law Kat could have hoped for. She was kind, witty, and incredibly supportive of Kat's...quirks. She didn't care that Kat didn't enjoy dancing or shopping for clothing or that she adored museums and bookstores. She also didn't harangue Kat if her fingers were stained from sketching or writing. "But we'll do our best to keep you from drawing notice."

"That means you'll need to be on your best behavior," Ruark said. "No clandestine meetings in gardens with gentlemen who are already betrothed." His tone wasn't one of scolding but of pleading.

Kat looked him in the eye. "I promise I will be a model of grace and propriety."

"Then I suppose we must go shopping," Cass said, smiling. Unlike Kat, she loved to visit the modiste. And the milliner. And everything in between.

"Must we?" Kat already knew the answer.

"I'll have the modiste come here." Cass gave her an understanding smile. "Would that make you more comfortable?"

Again, Kat appreciated her sister-in-law's kindness. "Yes, thank you."

"We've been invited to a soirée tomorrow evening," Cass said. "Do you want to come with us?"

So soon? Kat had thought she'd have a few days to acclimate herself to the idea of being amongst crowds of mostly simpering people. While she wanted to do this for the sake of research, she also knew she'd be uncomfortable, at least some of the time.

"If you tire early, we can send you home in the coach,"

Ruark offered. He knew Kat could grow weary of social events, especially large ones.

"Then yes, I'll go with you." Kat would make sure she was ready. She glanced toward Cass. "Surely I have something to wear that will suffice?"

"More than likely. If not, my maid may be able to alter something of mine."

"Really?" Kat was a couple of inches taller than Cass's five feet and four inches.

"Stenby is a master with a needle," Cass assured her with a smile.

"That's settled, then." Kat started to rise, but the butler came in and announced they had a visitor—Lord Lucien Westbrook.

"Send him in, Bartholomew," Ruark said.

Kat pressed herself back into the chair. If the guest had been nearly anyone else, she would have left. However, she liked Cass's brother. Everyone did.

Lord Lucien was nearly thirty, two years older than her brother, Ruark, with dark hair, thick brows, and captivating sable eyes. Kat didn't use that description—captivating— lightly. She employed it for certain animals she studied, those with an aura of confidence and demonstrable intelligence. It was sometimes difficult to gauge those attributes in a goat or a cow, but not impossible. Kat was nothing if not a patient and thorough observer.

It did not take patience to assess Lord Lucien. At first glance, he was aggressively attractive and charming. There was simply no ignoring the magnetism he possessed— everyone could sense it. If one couldn't, they ought to make sure they were still breathing. Tall and white, he possessed alluring laugh lines around his eyes and mouth that lured all he encountered into his orbit. She tried not to fixate on the latter of his features and failed. Ever since the abysmal kiss with Hickinbottom, she'd focused on men's mouths—well, *some* men's mouths—and wondered if any of them could perform better. Or perhaps it was just that Kat hated kissing. She rather assumed that was the case, since every woman she'd asked about kissing had told her how thrilling it could be.

Could be.

And that was why Kat needed to conduct more research. So, it was perfectly fine that she was staring at the contour of Lord Lucien's lips, at how the lower was slightly plumper than the upper. She licked her own lower lip as if to determine whether hers might be the same.

One of Lord Lucien's brows ticked slightly up, his gaze fixing on hers for a fleeting moment. Had he noted her attention? Did that matter? Some would say yes, but Kat didn't care about such things. She *did* have a good reason for studying him, and she'd tell him so if necessary.

Because she was inspecting him, she noticed something she hadn't seen before—a faint pucker between his brows. Was he troubled about something? She'd presumed he was impenetrable to worry.

"I apologize for intruding," Lord Lucien began, "but I'm afraid I need to speak with Wexford." He gave his sister an apologetic glance.

"Phoenix Club business." Cass pressed her lips together. "That I cannot be privy to."

"Or me, apparently," Kat added, not that she cared. Lord Lucien owned a popular membership club, and while it was probably the one place in London where Society gathered in which she felt most at ease, it was still typically full of too many people. But then she was only allowed to visit the weekly assemblies on Fridays during the Season because she was not a member and those were a crush.

As a young unmarried lady, she was not allowed membership. However, if she became a spinster, it seemed she could garner an invitation. *If* the membership committee deemed her appropriate. Or something like that. Kat didn't follow the specifics very closely, not like Cass and her friends did. Her closest friend, Fiona, was married to another of Lord Lucien's friends, Lord Overton. He was also involved in the club, as was Ruark. Which was why Lord Lucien was here. While Kat didn't follow gossip or Society happenings, she was aware that there was some sort of scandal surrounding the club.

That had to be the source of Lord Lucien's consternation.

"Forgive me," Kat said, pinning her gaze on Lord Lucien. "Is something amiss with the club? I'm afraid I'm not up on the latest news." They'd only just returned to London about ten days ago after spending the holidays and the entire month of January in Gloucestershire.

"It's, ah, complicated," Lord Lucien said.

Kat ticked her head to the side and narrowed her eyes. "Are you trying to say I wouldn't understand? Or that you'd rather not share the particulars?"

"I would never insult your intelligence, Miss Shaughnessy," he said quickly—and earnestly. "I rather assumed you would find this, dare I say, boring?"

He knew her that well? Perhaps he was also an excellent observer. He rose in her esteem. "Typically, yes, but I know how much this club matters to my brother and to Cass. And to you, I'm sure."

He laughed softly. "Yes. It is of critical import to me. Unfortunately, there are problems." He flicked a glance toward Ruark. "But I'm certain we'll overcome them."

Ruark frowned. "Did something else happen?"

Lord Lucien made his way to a chair angled near the settee where Ruark and Cass sat and lowered himself to the edge of the cushion, as if he didn't plan to stay long. Or was, himself, on edge. "Evie left town today. She and Gregory are traveling to Oxfordshire where they will wed."

Cass's eyes sparked and her mouth rounded before spreading into a happy grin. "Truly?"

"Yes, and I convinced her to remain at the club."

"Good," Cass said firmly.

Evie—rather, Mrs. Renshaw, as Kat knew her—managed the Phoenix Club and was a close friend of Lord Lucien's. Kat now recalled that she was the reason for the club's current notoriety—or at least part of the cause. "Again, I haven't paid close attention," Kat said. "Why did you need to convince Mrs. Renshaw to stay?"

Ruark exhaled. "It's a somewhat unseemly story. I'm sure Lucien would prefer we didn't discuss it now. Cass can explain later."

"Well, that makes me feel like a bothersome child," Kat muttered. She rose. "I shan't burden you with my presence, then."

"Don't be like that," Ruark said, scowling. "You'll lose interest halfway through the story. This isn't the sort of thing you give two figs about."

That was true, so why was Kat even asking? "You're right. I suppose I was just trying to be supportive." Her mother often told her she should take an interest in other people's concerns, and once in a while, Kat remembered to do so. She started toward the door, stopping at Lord Lucien's chair. "I'm sorry you're having trouble with your club. I'm sure things will improve." She offered him a smile before leaving the drawing room.

Kat climbed to the second floor, where her bedchamber was located, her mind quickly moving on from Lord Lucien and the Phoenix Club and returning to the matter foremost in her mind—her research. Tomorrow, she would attend the soirée and begin.

She'd start with observations as she normally did. However, she acknowledged the fact that she needed to once again insert herself in the investigation, just as she'd done back home in Lechlade. She'd make sure that this time there was no possibility of getting caught.

Closing the door behind her after entering her chamber, she went to her desk and opened a drawer to remove the most recent book she'd acquired. She retreated to the cozy chair near the hearth where she kicked off her slippers and sat, curling her feet beneath her in the manner that would draw her mother's disapproval. *"Kathleen, you'll ruin your gown!"*

Kat hardly thought wrinkles would ruin a garment, but that never stopped her mother from insisting so. Pushing thoughts of her mother from her mind, Kat opened the book, *A Lady's Guide to Matrimonial Duties.* It contained mostly boring information about how to manage a household and behave socially, but there was a chapter on "Wifely Duties" that was pertinent to her research. It was, unfortunately, shorter than the rest of the chapters, but included several pages on how to be attractive to one's husband and how to submit to him in the bedchamber. There were even a few illustrations.

The drawings were somewhat vague: a man and a woman embracing, lying together in bed, and finally, the man atop the woman as she stared up at him. The descriptions were more detailed as far as what was happening with certain body parts, but even they were lacking…something.

Something indescribable. Something Kat would have to experience for herself.

∼

*L*ucien settled back in his chair despite the tension squeezing him from within. He glanced toward his sister and hoped she couldn't see it. His agitation was from more than the problems with the club. A good portion of it was due to their bloody father. He and Lucien had always had a contentious relationship, but today, it had reached a new level of discord. While Lucien was typically able to shrug their interactions away, today's would stay with him for quite some time. And he simply couldn't think of it as just another quarrel.

"I'm glad you persuaded Evie to stay at the club," Ruark said, interrupting Lucien's thoughts, which he appreciated. "Not just because she belongs there, but how would you run the damn place without her?"

"That was not a small consideration." Lucien snorted. "It wasn't easy to get her to agree, but Gregory helped."

Cass smoothed her skirt. "I'm so pleased they are to be wed. When she returns to London, she'll be Lady Evie. Unless..." Cass hesitated. "Will she still go by the name Evie?"

Evangeline Renshaw wasn't her real name. She'd been born Mirabelle Avenses in France during the Terror. Her mother had fled to England with Evie and her older sister and a maid, leaving behind their father, who'd been imprisoned. "Yes. The biggest news of the day is that her father has been found. After he was released from prison, he made his way here to find his family."

Both Cass and Ruark leaned forward, their expressions rapt. "Extraordinary," Ruark said in his Irish lilt, his blue eyes piercing with intensity. "How did that happen?"

"There's a group here that works to reunite families separated in the Terror." Lucien hadn't been aware of them until today when Evie and Gregory had come to tell him the news on their way out of town. Lucien wasn't going to tell Cass that their father was part of that group, that he'd helped to bring Evie and her father together because Lucien still couldn't believe it was true. Their father, the Duke of Evesham, didn't help anyone unless it served his self-interest. His actions raised the question of what he would gain.

Cass put a hand to her chest. "Evie must be overjoyed. I'm doubly thrilled for her—she's found her father *and* she's to be wed. I do hope that makes up for the scandal."

The scandal was Evie's past, that she'd been a courtesan before reinventing herself as widow Evangeline Renshaw and becoming the manager as well as a patroness of the Phoenix Club. She'd been Lucien's mistress before he'd founded the club. When she wanted to retire, he'd offered her a job managing the club and suggested she leave town, then return as someone new. Someone who would have the respect of Society. So, she'd become a widow whose fictional deceased husband had been an old friend of Lucien's.

"I don't think anything can do that." Lucien was still so angry that her secret had been exposed. All because a selfish, sniping member of the club—Lady Hargrove, another of the patronesses—didn't like that her suggestions for members and other matters were usually ignored. She'd uncovered Evie's past and had delighted in every detail being published in several newspapers.

"The gossip will fade," Cass said with a confidence Lucien didn't share. "Her marriage to Lord Gregory will help."

"I hope you're right."

Cass's brow furrowed, her sherry-colored eyes clouding. "Who are you? Where is my optimistic brother who can fix anything?"

Lucien exhaled, but it didn't dispel his frustration. "I can't fix this. Everyone knows about Evie." The scandal had been publicized two days ago.

"And they know about you," Ruark said in a low tone. "That you were her keeper."

"I don't care that they know that about me. You can't think that matters? The news that I kept a mistress is neither surprising nor interesting, nor would it prompt people to resign from the club."

"Have they?" Cass asked, her features creasing with worry.

Lucien nodded. He didn't want to get into things too deeply, especially in front of Cass, who wasn't part of the membership committee. Indeed, she'd only been a member since wedding Ruark. The club didn't allow unmarried women unless they were firmly in their spinsterhood. That was one aspect Lady Hargrove had complained about. She found it unseemly that any unwed women were allowed at all. Hell, the entire notion of a membership club that included women was seen as unseemly by a great many people, and that was why the Phoenix Club wasn't for everyone. If someone couldn't support a diverse membership that included working men, unwed ladies, and all other manner of people who weren't welcome at other membership clubs, they didn't belong in Lucien's club.

Lucien's club.

He thought of it as his. Everyone recognized it as his. But the truth was that it didn't belong to him. He only owned a minority share, and the majority, owned and controlled by the bloody Foreign Office which also employed Lucien, had the final say over the membership. The two anonymous members of the committee were their representatives, which was why they were unknown to the rest of the committee. Those remaining members were Lucien's friends: Tobias Powell, the Earl of Overton; Dougal MacNair, the Viscount Fallin: and Ruark, plus Evie and the club's bookkeeper, Ada Hunt, who was now Lady

Warfield after marrying Lucien's friend and fellow soldier, Max.

Ruark gave Lucien an encouraging look. "Those who resigned can't be people we wanted anyway."

They weren't, in fact. They were people the Foreign Office had invited because they gave credibility and prestige to the membership roll.

Lucien was worried, however, that the departure of significant numbers of members would prompt others to leave—people they *had* chosen.

Cass rose, her attention on Lucien. "I am optimistic, even if you aren't, that this will improve the club in the end, and this scandal with Evie will pass. I'll leave you alone to talk, because I can see that you want to speak with Ruark."

"Thank you." Lucien gave her a grateful but fleeting smile. His siblings meant everything to him, though he and his older brother, the heir, had only managed to find a closer relationship within the last year. And now Constantine was a father, which had completely softened his harsher edges, *and* Lucien had been spared from being the spare.

Cass closed the door to the drawing room as she departed. Ruark stretched his arm across the back of the settee. "The number of resignations... It's bad? Are we bleeding members?"

Bleeding... Lucien winced inwardly at that. The image dredged up memories—one in particular—of his time as a soldier in Spain. He shoved those away to the dark recesses of his mind where he'd mostly forgotten them. It was best that way.

"It was a dozen yesterday." Which was more than Lucien had anticipated. "I expect double today as people likely gathered and discussed the matter last night."

Ruark's brows arched. "At the club?"

"There was hardly anyone *at* the club last night," Lucien

said sardonically. "I assume they discussed it wherever they were. It is the biggest gossip of the moment."

"We stayed in last night, so I can't offer any insight." Ruark grimaced.

Lucien waved his hand. "I'm not asking for that. But I would appreciate you keeping your ears and eyes open going forward. I need to be able to mitigate this damage—if I can."

"There are far more people who love the club and what it stands for than don't. There is no other place where so many, myself included as a horrid Irishman, feel not just welcome but wanted. Inclusion and the idea of being *chosen* are almost primal in their effect."

Ruark wasn't wrong about that. Part of the reason Lucien had started the club was precisely for those sentiments. He'd often felt like an outsider because of the way his father favored his brother and sister.

"The anonymous people on the membership committee will not be happy that these members they suggested are fleeing en masse." Lucien was already provoking their anger by refusing to expel Evie, which they'd demanded he do.

"Perhaps it's time you expel them from the committee," Ruark said darkly.

"I can't." Nor could Lucien tell Ruark the reason why. "They were…instrumental in the founding of the club. I may decide they should go, but I haven't yet arrived there."

The one person who knew that the Foreign Office was involved with the club, but not that they actually owned it, was Dougal MacNair, the new Lord Fallin. Dougal had also been a soldier in Spain, and he'd spent the last several years working in England as an agent for the Foreign Office. Until he'd left last year after becoming heir to his father's earldom —and he'd also married.

They'd both been recruited in Spain, but Lucien's appointment had come much sooner. He'd spied during the war until he'd been involved in a terrible incident. His friend Max had gone mad and retaliated against a squadron of soldiers for their brutal assault and murder of his betrothed. Lucien had covered up Max's actions by planting a letter on the dead soldiers to prove they were involved in espionage. They'd both been wounded and sent back to England as heroes.

Lucien's injury hadn't been bad enough to warrant discharge, so he'd wondered if someone had somehow learned the truth of what happened. Back in England, Lucien's work for the Foreign Office had included reviewing reports and overseeing domestic assignments, such as the ones Dougal undertook.

Then someone from the Foreign Office had approached Lucien about finding a place where people of varying backgrounds could gather and where Foreign Office business could be conducted in secret. Lucien had already begun thinking of starting a different kind of membership club that catered to the less welcome in Society. The mix of members and guests at the club would be the perfect situation for people to blend in and go unnoticed. So far, it had worked exactly as they'd conceived it.

But now the club was at the center of Society's attention, feeding its hunger for gossip. The Foreign Office didn't like that, and so the anonymous members had insisted Lucien expel Evie. Pushing her out would distance the club from the scandal. In hindsight, Lucien wondered why they hadn't asked him to leave too. Perhaps because all of London saw the Phoenix Club as his, and his departure would only increase the cacophony of the rumor mill.

"I wish you didn't feel beholden to them," Ruark said, referring to the anonymous members.

Lucien wished he wasn't beholden to them *or* the Foreign Office. He also wished he could tell his friends the full truth, but the Foreign Office was explicit in their instruction that *no one* must know of their ownership and involvement.

But someone else *did* know. Earlier that day, Lucien had gone to see his father, swallowing his pride and disdain for the man, to ask for a loan to buy out the Foreign Office. The duke had warned Lucien when he'd opened the club to never come to him asking for money if it was failing. But Lucien had no other choice, and the club *wasn't* failing. It just wasn't under his control. He didn't want anyone to tell him who could or couldn't work at or belong to *his* club. And it was, without question, *his*, even if he didn't own the entire bloody thing.

Lucien was not surprised his father had refused to lend him money. However, he'd been shocked when his father had calmly told him he could not buy out the Foreign Office. When Lucien had pressed him about how he knew about that, he'd only answered vaguely, that he was a meddler, like Lucien.

They were *nothing* alike.

And how the hell did he know about Lucien's deal with the Foreign Office?

"Lucien?" Ruark queried softly.

Blinking, Lucien refocused on his friend, who was staring at Lucien with concern.

"My apologies. I had a rather disappointing interview with my father earlier."

"Is there any other kind?" Ruark asked with a smirk. He and the duke had been at odds before Ruark and Cass had wed. The duke hated that his daughter had fallen in love with an Irishman. Eventually, he'd come to accept Ruark, realizing it was a gift that his daughter had found love. Or so Cass had said. Lucien couldn't believe their father would be that sentimental.

"No, there is not," Lucien said, shaking his head.

Normally, he could joke about his relationship with his father, but not today. "What I need for you—and Cass—to do is to try to keep the membership intact. If you hear of anyone who is considering leaving, convince them to stay. And spend as much time as you can at the club. The first assembly is in less than a fortnight, and if it isn't well attended, I fear how it will affect the club."

Ruark nodded. "I understand. We'll do what we can. Cass is quite popular, as you know."

"Yes, as is Con." Their brother circulated in a different circle and hadn't initially been a member of the club. Only through he and Lucien growing closer last year had that come about, and Lucien was glad to have him. "In fact, I should speak with him as soon as possible. He possesses the status and prestige to convince those members who might think of leaving because they fear for their reputation to stay." Keeping those people would allow Lucien to argue to the anonymous members that retaining Evie wasn't a detriment and that the club would still operate as it always would, as the Foreign Office expected and needed it to.

"You truly want those people to stay? Can't say I'll miss the Hargroves, for instance."

"I do want some of them, but you're right, there are a number who can go. Indeed, those who resigned yesterday are no great loss. Still, it doesn't make the club look good, and in the end, the Phoenix Club is a business that employs many people." Membership fees were based on a person's economic status—they were not the same for everyone. The wealthier members made it possible for people with less to join, and Lucien didn't ever want that to change. "It can't fail."

"It won't," Ruark vowed. "There are far too many people who will ensure its success. Surely you know how much goodwill you've sown? You help everyone, and I'm confident anyone you ask would help you in return."

"I appreciate you saying that. However, I don't see my aiding people as transactional. I don't expect anything in return."

"Don't be obtuse," Ruark said drolly. "People will do it for the same reason you do—because they want to."

"I suppose." Lucien stood. He needed to speak with Con next. After he went to the club and assessed today's membership damage. "I'll see you at the club tonight, then?"

Ruark also rose, rolling his shoulders back as he straightened. "Yes, but tomorrow, we're taking Kat to a soirée. Can you believe she wants a Season?"

"No. She hates Society events." Lucien had heard her say so plenty of times. The mention of Kat made him want to lick his lip. She'd been staring at his mouth and had licked her lower lip. It had been quite seductive—something he never would have expected from his friend's sister. It was as if Lucien had seen her as a woman for the first time. And a very attractive one at that.

"She's considering taking a husband." Ruark sounded dubious. "I can't believe *that*. But why else would she want a Season?"

Lucien shrugged. He was too consumed with his own problems to give that much thought. "It may be the truth. And now I get to watch you squirm as some jackanapes romances your sister." He laughed tauntingly.

Ruark frowned. "I am not a jackanapes."

"I thought so when you were running around stealing kisses and whatever else—oh, never mind, let's not speak of it—with Cass last Season."

"You expelled me from the club over it," Ruark grumbled.

"You deserved it," Lucien said. "Anyway, it wasn't permanent."

"Just long enough for you to recover from your fit." Ruark smirked, and Lucien turned to go.

"I look forward to watching *your* fits." Lucien put his hand on the door and looked back to Ruark. "Bring Kat to the assemblies. It was *the* place to be seen on the Marriage Mart last Season." And Lucien needed it to be the same this year.

"That won't be a problem. I believe the Phoenix Club is the one place she feels relatively comfortable. Pity she can't be a member."

If Lucien managed to gain full control of the club, perhaps she could. Allowing young unmarried ladies to be members would cause a cataclysmic stir, but Lucien felt certain they could set parameters, such as their sponsors or parents being members, that would be acceptable.

"You should come to the soirée tomorrow night," Ruark said. "It might do you good to be seen out and about. Then you can also hear firsthand what people are saying. You say Cass is popular, but you are one of the most sought-after guests in London."

"Only because I attend fewer events since opening the club." Lucien let out a short laugh. "My infrequency of attendance has made me desirable."

"It's also a good opportunity to talk about Evie's marriage to Lord Gregory. The sooner that's spread about, the better, I should think."

"Excellent point," Lucien said, wondering why he hadn't thought of that. "In fact, I should put a notice in the papers announcing their betrothal."

Ruark moved toward him. "They won't mind?"

"I can't imagine they would, particularly when it will help Evie." Would it, though? Lucien thought of Evie's older sister, who'd also been a courtesan. She'd married her last protector, and they'd been shunned. It didn't help that he came from a family whose fortune was made in trade. "It won't hurt," Lucien said firmly. "I'll see you later. And thank you. You're a good friend."

Ruark clapped him on the shoulder. "I'm more than that, in case you've forgotten. I'm family." He grinned at Lucien and walked him downstairs.

On his way out of the house, Lucien thought about that word: family. To him, that meant the people who supported him and with whom he enjoyed close, mutual bonds. It had nothing to do with blood. If it did, he'd think of his father as family instead of the man who'd just happened to sire him. For as long as Lucien could remember, he was never quite good enough in his father's eyes, always falling short in some way, disappointing or irritating him. Before Lucien's mother had died when he was fourteen, she'd often soothed Lucien's hurt, telling him that his father's words were harsher than his sentiment. And it wasn't as if Lucien didn't know he was demanding, even with Con and Cass.

But with Lucien, it was different. There was no discernible softness as he had for Cass, or pride as he showed for Con. For Lucien, he showed nothing but expectation and disdain, especially for the way in which Lucien cared for and helped others. Why, then, had his father gone to such lengths to help reunite Evie, a former courtesan he looked down upon, with her missing father?

Lucien hadn't asked him when he'd gone to see him, not after the duke had shocked him with his knowledge of the Foreign Office's role with the club. And certainly not after he'd once again shown his utter contempt for the Phoenix Club, basically telling Lucien, and not for the first time, that the place could burn to the ground before he'd offer help.

Lucien's lip curled as fury raced through him. He'd never hated his father more.

CHAPTER 2

*A*fter a second interminable set of dancing, Kat vowed she was finished for the evening. She only wished it could be forever.

Her partner, whose name she couldn't even remember, bowed after he guided her back to where Cass stood with her friend Fiona, Lady Overton. A few inches taller than Cass, Fiona was also white, with red hair and ivory skin. She'd come to London last year as the ward of her now husband. Their marriage had raised eyebrows, but the earl's grandmother was a formidable and highly regarded lady, and her approval had quieted the gossip.

"How was your dance?" Cass asked after Mr. or Lord Whatever-his-name departed.

"Fine." Kat refrained from further commentary, but in her mind wondered how young ladies who didn't like or weren't good at dancing but actually wanted to marry managed. That was actually an excellent question pertinent to her research as far as finding a mate was concerned. She stored it away for potential future study. "I need to visit the retiring room."

"We'll escort you," Fiona offered. "I need to go there as well." She grazed her hand over the curve of her belly. Like Cass, she was also increasing, but her child was due much sooner.

They left the drawing room and made their way upstairs to where the retiring room was located. Fiona moved slowly and paused halfway up the staircase. "Go on ahead," she said with a wave. "I can't go faster than a waddle these days. I think this may be my last event."

Cass went back down two stairs to offer Fiona her arm. "We won't abandon you."

"Thank you."

"Since Cass is helping you, I'll just keep going," Kat said. Once in the retiring room, she fetched a glass of lemonade to cool herself.

A moment later, Cass and Fiona entered. Cass sent Kat a slight frown and a questioning glance. Kat lifted a shoulder. She had no idea why her sister-in-law was looking at her like that.

Cass went into the adjoining room with Fiona, presumably to help her relieve herself. It couldn't be easy with a belly that round and so many garments. Kat doubted she'd leave her house if she were that large and ungainly. That assumed she'd ever have children, which seemed most unlikely.

Kat moved to a corner to sip her lemonade while she waited. Reflecting upon Cass's pointed look upon entering with Fiona, Kat realized she ought to have waited for them instead of continuing on. Sometimes, she didn't consider those around her—a trait her mother commented upon. Ah well, it wasn't as if Kat had left Fiona alone to fend for herself on the stairs.

Two ladies entered the room and went directly to a pair

of chairs near where Kat stood. They bent their heads together and spoke in low tones, but Kat was close enough to hear. Ever the observer, she listened intently.

Both women were probably in their forties, and Kat couldn't have recalled their names under threat of being sent back to Gloucestershire. She couldn't even be sure they'd been introduced. One had blonde hair and a sharp nose, and the other had dark hair with a few gray strands. The latter wore a ridiculously tall trio of peacock feathers at her crown.

"So, she's to be a *lady* now?" Peacock asked, sounding scandalized.

"Apparently, if what I heard tonight is true," Nose responded, pursing her lips.

Peacock wrinkled her nose. "How gauche of Lord Gregory. He always seemed so charming and affable. Clearly, he's been seduced by a siren. A woman like that will never be faithful. Mark me, he'll regret marrying her."

Lord Gregory... They had to be speaking of Mrs. Renshaw and her engagement to him. Cass and Fiona had discussed it earlier this evening. Indeed, they'd been sharing the news with just about everyone they encountered. Did they not realize people would gossip?

"Most definitely," Nose agreed. "What was Lord Lucien thinking employing her and making her a *patroness* of the Phoenix Club?"

"I'll wager he wasn't thinking with his brain." Peacock sniggered. "Perhaps he's been carrying on with her all this time. Yes, Lord Gregory will likely end up a cuckold."

Nose clucked her tongue. "Does Lord Lucien deserve any less? His reputation in the past was that of a devil. Many thought the war changed him, but perhaps he's as dissolute as ever."

Kat had heard more than enough. She took a step closer

to where they sat. "Pardon me, but you seem in need of some education. Lord Lucien is no more dissolute than either of you are pleasant."

Nose gasped, while Peacock's dark eyes narrowed. "How would you know what Lord Lucien is?" Peacock asked.

"He is a dear friend of my brother's, as well as being his brother-in-law. You shouldn't speculate about people. It isn't nice."

Both women stared at Kat, their lips parted.

"And Mrs. Renshaw is a lovely person. She'll make an excellent lady. Who are you to judge her or Lord Gregory?" It wasn't a rhetorical question. Kat wanted to know what they had to say.

"She was a *courtesan*." Nose spoke the word as if Mrs. Renshaw was some sort of terrible villain.

Kat stared at them, nonplussed. "Why does that matter? Does she not deserve happiness like anyone else?"

Both women sputtered.

"Kat, what's going on?" Cass strode toward her, her gaze flicking toward Nose and Peacock.

The women rose quickly from their chairs. Nose murmured, "Good evening, Lady Wexford."

"Good evening, Lady Wenlock," Cass responded to Nose before looking toward Peacock. "Mrs. Hanbury. Do you know my sister-in-law, Miss Shaughnessy?"

Peacock smiled, but it was the kind that made Kat uncomfortable. "I don't believe so."

Kat looked to Cass. "They were discussing Mrs. Renshaw and Lord Gregory. They expect her to make a cuckold of him. And they theorized that Lord Lucien may be a devil. I told them they weren't being nice."

Cass's brows arched briefly then her gaze cooled as she regarded the two women. "That doesn't sound nice at all."

"Pardon us," Nose said, her cheeks flushing dark pink. She and Peacock made a hasty retreat from the retiring room.

"Well, now we shall be part of their gossip," Cass said with a sigh.

"Why? To tell anyone, they'll have to explain how they were caught being rude."

Cass turned to Kat. "That's true. Perhaps they won't say anything about this encounter. What did you say to them?"

Kat shrugged. "That Mrs. Renshaw is lovely. I asked why they thought they could judge her."

Laughing, Cass asked, "Did they answer?"

"Not really. I don't think they appreciated my interrupting them."

Fiona joined them. "Who didn't appreciate your interruption?"

Cass took Fiona's arm. "Kat has taken on the role of defender." She began to relate the tale as they departed the retiring room.

By the time they reached the drawing room once more, Kat was thinking it might be time to leave. Except they immediately encountered her brother Ruark, Fiona's husband, Overton, and Lord Lucien, who must have just arrived.

"Good evening," Lord Lucien said. After asking after Fiona, he turned to Kat. "I thought perhaps you might care to dance with me."

"Are you asking me?" Because he hadn't offered a question.

"I thought I was."

"It sounded like a presumption." Kat didn't think she could suffer one more turn around the dance floor.

Lord Lucien inclined his head. "That was not my intent."

"He meant no offense," Cass murmured beside her.

"I didn't think he did," Kat said. "It was just an odd way of inviting someone to dance."

Cass exhaled. "Just dance with him."

"I don't want to dance."

Cass turned more fully toward her and gently pulled on Kat's arm, so she faced Cass. "We've discussed this. It's rude to refuse a dance invitation." She spoke so softly that Kat had to lean forward slightly to hear her.

"And I've told you that's silly. What if I'm not feeling well? Perhaps I turned my ankle."

"Can't you whisper?" Cass waved her hand. "Never mind. If those things were the case, you wouldn't be standing here near the dance floor."

"I'm only here because we ran into the gentlemen. I was going to say I am just about ready to leave, but I would be delighted to promenade." As it happened, she wanted to speak with Lord Lucien.

"I don't want to keep you from retiring," he said.

She moved to take his arm. "I'll go after we promenade."

He quickly raised his elbow toward her. She put her hand on his sleeve, and they began a circuit of the drawing room.

"This will be rather short," she mused with a faint smile. "This drawing room isn't nearly as big as a ballroom and definitely not the size of the one at the Phoenix Club."

"We can walk downstairs where there are refreshments in the dining room, if you'd like."

"That would be acceptable." Though she didn't really care to take refreshment. She considered how to ask him about his "dissolute" past, but before she could conceive of a question, he spoke.

"Ruark says you are considering the Marriage Mart. That's a departure from last year. Has anyone caught your eye tonight? Ruark said you danced with a couple of gentlemen."

Was he just making conversation, or did he have a deeper, more...meddlesome purpose? She narrowed her eyes at him, pausing in their circuit. "Do not think to play matchmaker with me, Lord Lucien. I've heard about your manipulative ways."

"Have you now?" He laughed softly. "Don't you think it's time you called me Lucien? We are practically related with our siblings wed to each other."

"I suppose so. Then you may call me Kat. Do I have your word that you won't try to match me with anyone?"

He put his free hand over his heart. "My solemn vow."

She pivoted and began walking again, tugging him along with her. "Good. The last thing I want is a husband."

He laughed again. "Then what are you doing exactly? I thought you told Cass and Ruark that you were considering marriage."

Damn, she hadn't meant to say that out loud. "I meant to say the last thing I want is a husband someone else chooses."

"I see. So, you aren't opposed to finding a husband on your own?"

"No." She doubted that would happen, however. Most gentlemen couldn't wait to get away from her. Not that she blamed them. Aside from her abysmal dancing, she wasn't the most engaging conversationalist because she didn't like to talk about mundane things. No one wanted to discuss animals or horticulture or anything *she* found interesting. "I'm also not in any hurry."

She looked toward the dance floor, where people twirled and laughed. A shudder rippled through her frame.

"What's wrong?" Lucien asked.

"What do you mean?"

"You seemed to have a chill there. Would you like a shawl? It's cold tonight."

"It isn't in here. I got rather overheated dancing, but the lemonade took care of that. I was just recalling my dance with...I can't remember his name. It was rather terrible."

"Since you can't recall your partner's name, I shall lay the blame at his feet for an entirely forgettable occurrence."

Kat smiled. "The blame is mine, unfortunately. I am not very good at dancing. My mother hired a dance master for me and my sisters, and he declared no amount of practice would improve my skills."

"He sounds shortsighted and obnoxious. Probably also bad at his job." He met her gaze. "Do you like dancing?"

"Yes, actually. But I don't *enjoy* it." Because things inevitably became awkward when she missed a step or couldn't quite determine how to move *with* the music.

"Dancing *can* be enjoyable. With the right person. Trust me."

"All right." She found that easy to say and do. There was something about him that encouraged openness and confidence. Perhaps that was why so many people sought his help. "Would you like to know the real reason I asked for a Season?"

They'd almost completed their circuit and were near the door that led to the landing. He escorted her out toward the stairs. "Not to consider marriage, I take it?"

"You must promise not to reveal it to anyone."

"Primarily your brother and Cass."

"I didn't think Ruark would support my endeavors, so I told them that nonsense about marriage."

Lucien laughed again. "You have my solemn vow—again —that I will not repeat the real reason for your Season. I hope you will take comfort in the knowledge that I keep a great many secrets. Yours will be completely safe with me."

Kat was intrigued by this. For whom did he hold secrets? "You are an interesting gentleman. Successful club owner, magnanimous helper, prolific matchmaker, and now secret keeper. Is there anything you can't do?"

A smirk twisted his mouth as they descended the stairs. "Certainly, but let's not dwell on that, shall we?"

His voice had taken on a tightness that also intrigued her, but she wouldn't press him. Instead, she returned to her revelation. "I think you know I conduct observations of wildlife?"

"Yes, I've seen some of your sketches. They are quite good. I like paintings of animals and have several in my study."

"Indeed? Why do you like them?"

He shrugged. "They're beautiful and interesting. I haven't thought too closely about it."

"Perhaps you should. I love thinking." They'd reached the ground floor, and he guided her toward the dining room.

"I'll keep that in mind. Are you ever going to tell me your secret?"

She shook the interrupting thoughts from her head. "Yes. Specifically, I've long been interested in mating rituals. I've expanded my observations to people."

"Ah, yes. I recall this was the reason you got yourself into trouble back in Gloucestershire."

"It concluded in an unfortunate manner, but yes, it was for the sake of research." She frowned as she recollected the experience. "Actually, the entire thing was unfortunate. But I digress again. I wish to broaden my observations of mating rituals among people, and the Marriage Mart seemed the best place to do so."

"I can hardly find fault with that. Why do you need to keep this secret?"

"Because I plan to include myself in those observations. It

isn't enough to just watch. I want to know what these things feel like. That's why I plotted to kiss Hickinbottom."

"Plotted? Good God, you sound Machiavellian."

"That's an extreme characterization. Anyway, I learned from that mistake and will be far more careful this time." They'd entered the dining room, but it was too crowded, and she was instantly uncomfortable. "Can we go somewhere else?"

"Certainly." He didn't question her request, just escorted her to another room where only a few people mingled. It was the library, and the hosts had put out interesting objects for people to peruse.

They paused near a vase from China, or so the little card at the base indicated. Kat pivoted toward Lucien. "I want to find someone who will help me with my studies and also keep our...involvement secret. Given the number of rakes in London, I think I should be able to find someone willing to satisfy my scientific questions."

Lucien gaped at her. "You can't be serious. You want a... lover?" The last word was a hushed whisper.

"Not that." Kat hadn't considered that, actually. But if she was looking to experience complete sexual satisfaction—if she could—wouldn't that be something a lover would do? "Fine, perhaps that." A brilliant idea struck her. "If you could match me with someone like *that*, I'd find that most helpful."

Snapping his mouth closed, Lucien pulled her to the side of the room. "You can't seriously think I'd find you a..."

As he struggled to find the right word, she said, "Rake? Surely you know someone appropriate?"

"I absolutely cannot do that."

She took her hand from his arm. "Why not? You help everyone. At least that's what Ruark and Cass say. Why won't you help me?"

His stare was dark and incredulous. "Because it's beyond

the pale!" He kept his voice low, but if there was a way to whisper and yell at the same time, he was doing a fair job of it.

"Barely a quarter hour ago, I heard you called a devil, that you were once dissolute. Why should you judge me in this?"

Lucien wiped a hand over his face. "I thought you hated gossip."

"How do you know that?"

"I'm sure it was mentioned."

"You notice and recall the most interesting things," she mused, cocking her head. "You may be nearly as good as I am at observation."

"I try," he said wryly. "Stick to that—observation. Forget this plan of making yourself part of the...study."

"It's not thorough enough. I've done extensive research already. I've spoken to people about how they mate, and it's more than just mechanics. I suspected that with animals too, at least some of them, but I can't speak to them about the nonphysical aspects. I also have a book, and it is woefully inadequate regarding specific details—"

He held up his hand. "Stop. I'm terrified to think what 'extensive research' means. It's best if I don't know what you've already done. If your brother or your parents knew that you aren't chaste—"

"I *am*," she hastened to assure him. "I've done nothing beyond that one wholly disappointing kiss. It was nothing like what other people have told me about how it should feel to kiss someone. There was no anticipation and certainly no thrill."

He continued to stare at her as if she had five eyes. "What people have you discussed this with?"

"Mostly people at Warefield." A few tenants she knew, and a pair of maids in the house. "All female, I should clarify.

Which is why it's particularly important that I conduct further research with a male."

Lucien shook his head. "This isn't an appropriate area of research."

"I'm sorry you think that. I find it fascinating, in part because I just don't understand it. I feel none of the nonphysical aspects others have told me about."

"What *aspects* are these?"

She recalled her conversations and notes. "In sum, lust, desire, satisfaction, completion. Whatever that means. I feel quite complete. What more would I need?"

"I can't properly answer that." He sounded as if he were choking, and his face had gone a bit pink.

"Can't or won't?" She regretted sharing this with him. "You aren't going to tell my brother about this, are you?"

"God, no!" Again with the whisper-yelling. Then a low near growl.

"Well, thank you for that. Clearly, I should not have confided in you. I didn't mean to cause you such distress." She glanced toward the room, feeling frustrated, before looking back at him. "Really, Lucien, I never would have taken you for prudish."

"I am not." Now he sounded rather outraged.

Kat couldn't help but smile. "Then prove it and help me. Would you at least tell me about these nonphysical aspects from the male point of view?"

The sound he made next was more groan than growl, but it was close. "You can't ask me to do that."

"Too late. But I'll take that as a no. I suppose I shall just have to continue looking for an appropriate male specimen."

Lucien snagged her elbow and gave her a squeeze, but his grip wasn't painful. "You absolutely *cannot* do that." He seemed to realize he'd overstepped because he released her immediately and murmured an apology.

"Then how am I to solve this mystery? For myself if for no other reason?"

"Get married. That will solve it for you."

"How?"

"Your husband will explain. And show you."

"But what if he's like Hickinbottom, or any other man I've met? I feel none of the...stirrings one ought to feel."

He was quiet a long moment, his gaze drifting out over the room. It seemed as though he was thinking. At last, he said, "Do you perhaps feel these...stirrings for any women you've met?"

She hadn't considered that. "No. Should I?"

"Some people only feel passion, or however you want to define arousal, for those of the same sex. Some feel it for both."

"Is it possible some don't feel it at all?" she asked, energized by this discussion. She could hardly wait to get home to document what she'd learned as well as her thoughts.

He blinked at her, looking thoroughly nonplussed. "I don't know."

"Then you must see that my research is important. What if I am an anomaly? More importantly—to me anyway—what if I am not?" Now, she was truly excited. There was no way she would stop her research.

There was a long moment of silence during which his features relaxed and his frame lost its rigidity. Finally, he said, "You have never felt sexually aroused and wish to know if you even can. Do I have that right?"

"Yes. But that's just one piece of my resear—"

"Can we agree that this piece—about *you*—is your priority? Or am I misinterpreting things?"

She hadn't thought that was uppermost in her reasoning, but now that he laid it out like that, she couldn't ignore that this question drove many of her thoughts on the topic.

"Actually, I think you have it right." Strangely, she felt warmth rise up her neck.

"If I can help you determine that once and for all, will you promise to confine your studies to observation?"

She wasn't going to swear to anything. "I'll consider it. You'll actually help me find someone?"

"No, I still refuse to do that. However, I feel confident *I* can help you."

He was going to help her? Personally? She hadn't expected *that*. "How? Are we going to kiss?" Now, she actually lowered her voice. She had to because she suddenly felt as though there were cobwebs in her throat. And that heat in her neck migrated lower to other places.

"Absolutely not." He sounded prudish again, but she decided not to point that out. "What happened when you kissed that scoundrel in Gloucestershire?"

"We were discovered, and my mother was furious."

"No, not that part. What happened to *you*? To your body? You said you didn't feel a stirring. What did you feel?" He was again whispering, but in a very different way from before. There was a huskiness to his words that provoked odd sensations.

Kat shook her head, trying to dispel the strange, provocative heaviness that had suddenly swept over her. "I was… disgusted. His lips were slimy, and he thrust his tongue into my mouth." She'd nearly gagged. "It was thick and wet."

"I think I grasp what you're trying to convey," Lucien said. "Some men—and women, I suppose—lack the talent for kissing. Or they haven't learned it, probably. I find that the best lovers, and kissers, are those who strive to hone their skill in order to give the most pleasure."

She looked up at him, into his velvety brown eyes. Velvety? They made her feel soft and warm. "Is that what you do?"

He hesitated briefly. "Yes."

"I think perhaps you should kiss me. Just to demonstrate the difference. Perhaps then I would understand what it means to be aroused."

He shook his head, disappointing her. "What about this book you mentioned? What does it contain?"

"It's a treatise on a lady's marital duties. It includes a chapter on 'wifely duties.' There are a few drawings of people doing intimate things. There are also descriptions, but everything is vague."

"Looking at those pictures doesn't arouse you?" he asked.

"No. Should it?"

"What about reading the descriptions?" When Kat shook her head, he nodded slightly. "Probably because they are vague," he murmured. "I think we've had enough discussion for one evening. More importantly, we ought not be whispering at the edge of a room together. I'm sure your brother must be wondering where you are. I'll take you back upstairs." He offered her his arm.

"That's it? What about helping me determine if I can be aroused, or if I'm simply not capable?"

"We'll discuss that when I see you next."

She put her hand on his sleeve and felt a slight but definite jolt shoot through her fingertips and up her arm. This was all too peculiar, and she was eager to write it down. "When will that be?"

"I don't know, and if you pester me about it, the answer will be never."

"You needn't speak to me as if I'm a child." Kat nearly pouted, but that wouldn't exactly bolster her admonition, so she pressed her lips together instead.

"Be patient, Kat, and promise me you won't go looking for answers with some other gentleman."

"I won't." For whatever reason, she was now fixated on

Lucien. He must be the one to help her. She was sure of it. He'd ignited something inside her, an...eagerness to know more. Wait, was that arousal? It couldn't be.

Time with him would provide the answers. Kat could hardly wait to find out.

CHAPTER 3

Stalking toward Curzon Street, Lucien was tightly wound, and not entirely because he was about to visit his brother to discuss their despicable father. No, he was rather focused on last night and the conversation he'd had with Kat. He was a man of experience. He'd caroused, had lovers, been to war, spied for the bloody Foreign Office, but never in his life could he have imagined the things Kat had told him. The plans she had. Plans he'd hopefully stopped from happening.

But what if he hadn't?

He couldn't think about that. He had to believe he'd convinced her not to do so, that it would do more harm than good. And yet, he couldn't stop thinking about the impetus for her research. Her lack of…arousal.

Damn if that hadn't been…arousing. Listening to her talk about the efforts she'd gone to in order to study mating rituals. Ah hell, it was easier to just call it what it was: the study of sex. And arousal. And what had she said? Completion.

She'd said a great many things, all of them making his pulse race and his blood heat. He needed to make sure he avoided her completely. Except he'd agreed to help her. How in the hell was he going to do that? The irony of him having such a scandalous conversation with his friend's sister—the very friend who'd behaved scandalously with Lucien's sister—was not lost on him.

Trying once more to push Kat from his mind, he approached his brother's house on Curzon Street. Just in time too, because the gray February sky decided it was too heavy and a drizzle began to fall.

Lucien leapt up the steps to the door and rapped swiftly. Haddock, Con's very proper butler, opened the door. "After-noon, Lord Lucien." In his forties and far better looking than Lucien's own butler, Haddock was married to the house-keeper. They were without question an extension of Con's growing family, and Lucien liked them immensely.

"How are you, Haddock?"

"Very well, thank you. And you?"

"Good enough. Mrs. Haddock and your dear Gray?" Gray was their cat, who had become a treasured member of the household. If anyone had bet Lucien a year ago that Con's butler, housekeeper, and their cat would become so dear, he would have taken that wager and lost.

"Also very well. That's kind of you to ask." Haddock took Lucien's damp hat and gloves. "His lordship is up in the drawing room with her ladyship and young Robert."

"Excellent, I was hoping to see my nephew." Lucien was incredibly grateful for the distraction. There were too many things tugging at his mind, and not in good ways. He left the entrance hall and made his way to the staircase hall. Taking the stairs two at a time, he was shortly at the threshold to the drawing room.

Lucien paused, taking in the scene of his formerly stiff older brother seated with his formerly estranged wife, his infant son cradled on his lap. Con supported the lad's head just above his knees while the babe lay nestled in the crook of his thighs. Watching them made Lucien's throat tighten. They were the very essence of a perfect, loving family.

"Who's the sweetest boy?" Con cooed. "You are."

If it wasn't so adorable, Lucien might have rolled his eyes. "I will never get used to this," he said, announcing his presence as he strolled into the drawing room.

Both Sabrina and Con looked up from their son. "Lucien, I didn't know you were coming today," Con said.

"You said I could stop by any time, and I took that to heart."

Con gave Robert to his mother. "I'm glad."

"I don't wish to interrupt," Lucien said, feeling bad that he'd ruined such a charming interlude.

"You aren't," Sabrina said with a warm smile. "It's almost time for Robert to eat, and then he will take a nice, long nap, won't you, sweetheart?" She cradled him to her chest and rose from the settee. Moving toward Lucien, she asked, "Unless you want to hold him first?"

Lucien loved his nephew and looked forward to when they would hunt for frogs, climb trees, and ride horses. For now, he was always afraid he'd hurt the baby or, God forbid, drop him. Not that he had, and he'd held him an entire *two* times.

"You aren't going to damage him, Lucien," Con said with a faint smile from the settee.

"Didn't you say he was hungry?" Lucien looked at the boy's blue eyes and felt a surge of protection. He could only imagine how strong that instinct was for his brother when he gazed at his son. Had their father regarded either of them that way? Perhaps Con. Lucien imagined the duke's heart swelling with love and pride when he cradled his infant heir. Had he even bothered to hold Lucien?

Suddenly, Lucien held out his arms. "Yes, let me hold him, just for a moment."

Sabrina placed Robert carefully into Lucien's care. "Support his head, yes, like that." She laughed softly. "I don't need to tell you."

"Reminders are always welcome," Lucien said, gently swaying for some reason. "He is the most precious cargo."

"Careful, or you'll find yourself leg shackled with a brood of children," Sabrina said.

Con snorted from the settee. "I doubt that. There is no more confirmed a bachelor than Lucien."

Sabrina gave him a prim look. "Everyone changes. One need only compare present you to past you." Her lips curled into an overly sweet smile.

Lucien laughed, and Robert made a series of noises. Then he twitched. "Did I upset him?"

"No, I think he's just hungry. Here, I'll take him." Sabrina eased her hands beneath the infant and drew him to her. "See you next time, Uncle Lucien," she said, smiling at Robert. Then she flicked Lucien a glance before departing the drawing room.

"What brings you by, Lu? How's the club?" Con stood from the settee and went to the sideboard. "Brandy? Port?"

"Whatever you're drinking is fine." Lucien moved to a pair of chairs near the windows that overlooked Curzon Street below. He sprawled in one of them, feeling weary, likely because he hadn't been sleeping much.

Con joined him a moment later, handing him a glass of brandy. He dropped into the other chair and sipped his drink before settling his expectant gaze on Lucien.

"The club is…I'll get to that in a minute." Lucien took a long sip of the brandy. Con's stock was excellent, and it soothed his agitation about what he was going to tell Con. "I came to tell you about something the duke has done."

Sitting up straighter, Con frowned. "When you call him 'the duke' instead of our father, I know you are particularly angry with him."

"It isn't anger," Lucien said. "All right, it's anger. But it's also a general dislike. We do not share any kind of cordial relationship. Not like the two of you do."

"Come now, you're occasionally…pleasant."

Lucien stared at him from beneath hooded lids.

"Perhaps pleasant is too generous a description."

"You are aware of my club manager, Mrs. Renshaw." At Con's nod, Lucien continued, "And that she was my paramour before that. She broke things off with me to retire from that profession—she's quite good with money, which is only one of the many reasons I offered her the position of managing the Phoenix Club. I knew she couldn't do that as the courtesan known as Mirabelle Renault, so I suggested she leave town for several months then return with a different look and a new name and background."

"Mrs. Renshaw, the widow," Con said. "I can't think why you thought that would work."

"It did work. For two years." Lucien took another drink and leaned back against the chair. "I suppose you're right. It wasn't bound to last. I really wanted it to. She deserves to live a life she chooses instead of one circumstance dealt her."

"Don't we all have to do that? My marriage to Sabrina was entirely circumstance. Certainly beyond my control." Their father and her father had arranged it without thought to Con's or Sabrina's wishes. "But it turned out quite well."

"Thanks to me," Lucien muttered. He and Evie had worked to bring the two of them together. "Now you are living the life you would choose, are you not? And when you had to marry someone you didn't choose, how did you feel about that?"

Con held up his hand. "You've made your point. I don't

begrudge Mrs. Renshaw her happiness or her position at the club."

"Or as Lady Evie once she marries Lord Gregory?"

"Indeed?" Con's brows arched. "I hadn't heard."

Of course he hadn't. He didn't go out much because Sabrina limited her social engagements. She wasn't comfortable in the frenzy of the London Season. Plus, Lucien imagined they would go out even less now that Robert had come along. "So, I can count on you to treat her kindly and with respect?" Once upon a time, Lucien would have expected Con to look down his nose at Evie, to find her unworthy of his notice.

"I've always found her charming, witty, and an excellent conversationalist. I will treat her the same as I always have since making her acquaintance last year at the club. And, because I'm certain you will ask, I will do my best to convince others to accept her in the same manner."

Some of the tension left Lucien's shoulders. "Thank you. That isn't the primary reason I mentioned her, however. She is originally from France. She was born during the Terror and fled with her family as a baby, except for her father, who stayed behind and was imprisoned. They thought him dead all these years."

Con looked at him intently. "But he wasn't?"

"No. He was finally released and made his way to England, where a group of gentlemen help men like him find their families who came here. He and Evie were reunited two days ago."

"That's extraordinary." Con shook his head gently. "I can't imagine losing Robert and not seeing him for…how long?"

"At least two decades," Lucien said. "The part that is truly astonishing, however, is who orchestrated their reunion." Lucien paused. "It was the duke."

Con's hazel eyes widened. "Father?"

Lucien nodded, then took another drink.

"How do you know?"

"Evie met her father at Evesham House. Then she and Gregory came to tell me. I rather wish they hadn't. It makes no sense to me. No, it's worse than that. It angers me. Why is he so kind to others and not to me?" Hell. Lucien hadn't meant to say that out loud. He hastened to add, "Apparently, his association is only temporary. Gregory's father was a member of the group, and the duke stepped in after his death. He doesn't plan to continue. I can't understand why he'd do it at all. The man helps no one, not even his own children."

Con opened his mouth, but Lucien went on, "You'll say that he helped you, but he did so in his self-interest. You're his heir. He needs to make sure you will carry on his legacy in a way that he sees fit."

"It's amazing to me that you're this cynical about *him* and absolutely nothing else." Con sipped his brandy.

Lucien ignored his brother's criticism. "You've nothing to say about this behavior? You have to concede that it's shocking."

"I do, but he does possess a softer side, which he'd deny."

"I'd also deny it. What proof do you have?"

Con looked down at his glass as he swirled the brandy in the bowl. "I haven't ever told you this, but that day at Evesham House last year after that disastrous party Sabrina and I hosted, Father revealed that he blames himself for Mother's death and that losing her was beyond devastating."

Lucien wasn't surprised to hear this. It certainly accounted for the duke's nearly ever-present surliness. Still, it was shocking that he'd exposed any kind of vulnerability. "Why did he tell you this?"

"Because he was explaining to me why he'd chosen Sabrina as my wife. He didn't think there was any chance I'd fall in love with her, ergo, if I lost her as Father lost Mother, I would not suffer the same devastation that he had. He hoped for that for all of us, actually."

"What horseshit." Lucien snorted. "That isn't a softer side, that's horrific manipulation. *You* should decide what you will and won't risk."

"Try to see his perspective, Lucien. I don't think it had to make sense in his mind. It's just what he felt he had to do to protect me."

Is that why he basically didn't show them love at all? Oh, he was proud of Con and fond of Cass. And he tolerated Lucien. What a frigid son of a bitch. "What kind of father hopes to keep their children from falling in love? Would you wish that for Robert?"

Con adjusted his weight in the chair. Or perhaps he squirmed. "No. But I haven't been through what Father has."

"You can't be that understanding. He forced you and Sabrina together—against both of your wills."

"Yes, and I was angry. It was terrible of him to manipulate us in that way." Con exhaled. "But I don't see the point in holding on to that. Perhaps if you ever have a son of your own, you'll understand how emotions change, how things that seem vital really aren't. Such as grudges and right-eousness."

Lucien wasn't holding a grudge. His relationship with the duke was irreparably broken. "I suppose I'm glad you've made your peace with him, but you can't expect me to do the same." The duke hadn't ever given Lucien any sort of explanation for his treatment of him, and Lucien didn't think he ever would.

Con gave him a single nod. "I don't suppose you asked him about the business with Evie's father?"

Lucien scoffed. "Hardly. I did go to see him, and I'd

planned to, but our conversation went poorly so I never got to it."

"What *did* you discuss?"

"The club." Lucien wouldn't tell him that he'd gone asking for money. It was too painful to expose his rejection to the favored son. "On that note, since you mentioned it earlier, I wonder if I might impose upon you to spend a little more time there over the next month or so? While this scandal dies down. I know it's difficult with Robert now."

"Because there's nowhere I would rather be than here with my wife and son, yes." Con grinned, and Lucien felt a surge of warmth. His brother had rarely done that before he and Sabrina had fallen in love last year. "But I also want to help you as much as I can. I wasn't very supportive of you when you opened the club."

"I didn't really encourage that. It wasn't as if I made sure you were invited to join."

"That's true," Con said with a wry glance. "I'm glad we are closer now. It means the world to me that you care for Robert too. I'll do my best to come a few times a week. I'm sure Sabrina will join me, especially on Tuesdays. The Phoenix Club is one of the few places she feels comfortable."

The Phoenix Club was unique in many ways, not the least of which was the divided nature of the club, with a men's side and a ladies' side. They each kept to their own spaces, with the exception of Tuesday nights when the men's side was open to the ladies. The ladies' side was never open to the men—just their half of the ballroom during the Friday assemblies during the Season.

"I'll also try to have meetings there," Con said. "Are there other gentlemen from the Lords whom you can invite to join?"

The House of Lords was not their primary recruiting ground. Indeed, it was probably the last place they looked since those gentlemen were typically engaged at White's or Brooks's. Still, there were several peers who were members, and even more younger sons who were seeking to make their way in the world since they weren't heirs to a title. Men like Lucien.

"Probably. I'll have to think on it. Though, don't you think Hargrove and his cronies will keep others from accepting invitations?"

Con made a face, his nose wrinkling. "Hargrove is a dolt. Ignore him. He doesn't have as much influence as he'd like to think. And no one cares for his wife. As you said, the scandal will fade. In the meantime, behave as if nothing is different."

Except it was. "A few dozen people have already resigned," Lucien said quietly. "Attendance has been lackluster."

"It's only been a few days," Con reassured him. "Give it time. Do not write the club's death notice. Where is my brother the optimist who fixes everything?"

"Why does everyone think I can fix everything?" Lucien tossed back the rest of his brandy.

"Because you usually do." Con shrugged and finished his brandy as well.

They stood, and Con said he'd come to the club tomorrow night. Lucien thanked him and departed the drawing room.

Downstairs, Haddock handed him his hat and gloves. "Mrs. Haddock made sure your things were dry."

Lucien pulled the gloves onto his hands and sighed. "And warm. Hug her for me, please."

Setting his toasty hat on his head, he ventured into the cold afternoon, where the drizzle had faded to a fine mist. He decided to hail a hack to his house on King Street.

The door opened before he even reached the threshold.

Lucien immediately removed his hat. "Reynolds, you've an uncanny sense for when I shall arrive."

"There is a window, my lord."

Lucien glanced toward the room to his left. "In the dining room."

"Yes." Reynolds took Lucien's hat and gloves. A white man with receding dark hair and gray eyes, the butler was excessively tall with broad shoulders. "The post was delivered from the club. I put it in your study."

Someone had delivered something on Sunday? "More resignations, probably."

Lucien shared almost everything with his butler. The man had accompanied him home from Spain. Like Lucien, he'd been wounded. Unlike Lucien's minor scars to his arm and back, Reynolds sported a rather vicious mark on his cheek. The red had faded to dark pink, but it made him look most fierce. That and the fact that he rarely smiled, which wasn't to say he didn't feel humor. He possessed perhaps the driest wit of anyone Lucien knew and was indeed quite affable. Because of his size, it was easy to believe he'd been a soldier and made him look slightly out of place as a butler.

He was, however, an excellent manager of Lucien's household, not that it was large. There was just him, a maid, the cook, and a boy who worked in the scullery.

"Actually, there was only one letter," Reynolds said.

"Well, that's relieving."

Reynolds looked him in the eye. "The club will be fine. I've no doubt of it."

Lucien appreciated the man's faith, even if it was likely misplaced. "How can you possibly know that?"

"Because you're at the helm." He inclined his head then departed the entrance hall with Lucien's accessories.

Stalking straight to the back of the small terrace house where his study was located, Lucien removed his coat and draped it on the back of the chair at the desk in the corner. His gaze caught the painting hanging above it—a pair of hounds in the middle of a fall landscape, a riot of colorful trees casting leaves about them. In his mind, the hounds were a couple who'd already created several litters of pups together. They were comfortable with one another, their bond strong and enduring.

Why he'd paired them romantically was a mystery to Lucien, but that was who they were. Looking at the painting made him think of Kat and when she'd asked him why he had them. He realized every animal on the walls in this room had a story he'd concocted for them.

But why animals and not people? Because people could tell their stories, and Lucien could be wrong about them. This way, he could imagine what he liked, and he'd never know if it wasn't true. It was silly now that he actually thought about it.

The letter Reynolds mentioned sat atop the desk. Lucien recognized the handwriting immediately. It was from Oliver Kent, his superior at the Foreign Office and one of the two anonymous members of the Phoenix Club membership committee. Kent, along with the other anonymous member, dictated who was invited and who was not. He was also responsible for instructing Lucien to expel Evie from her employment, as a patroness, and as a member.

Lucien had yet to tell him that he wasn't going to do it, that when she returned from wedding Lord Gregory, things would continue as they had. She would be a member, a patroness, and manager of the club—if she still wanted to be.

Tensing, Lucien opened the missive. It was short and to the point, which was expected. Kent wanted to meet as soon as possible.

It was necessary of course, and it wasn't as if Lucien could refuse. This situation was untenable. When Kent had sold him the idea of opening the Phoenix Club—secretly with the Foreign Office—as a place to act as a location for clandestine meetings, Lucien was to be the primary operator. For the most part, he was, but recent occurrences had made it clear he was not.

And yet, how would Kent go about replacing Lucien if they didn't like what he was doing? It wasn't as if they had another person who could take over. Furthermore, how would that look? All of London saw the Phoenix Club as Lucien's. If he suddenly walked away, it simply wouldn't make sense.

That gave Lucien bargaining power. He intended to use it.

CHAPTER 4

*K*at had reread the notes she'd made after the soirée the night before last at least a dozen times. She'd recorded several questions to ask Lucien the next time they met, the latest being: *What do breasts have to do with mating?*

She'd been reviewing the book with the drawings, and in the one where the man was lying on top of the woman, he had his hand on her breast.

"Kat?" Cass called from the doorway as she pushed into Kat's chamber.

Startled, Kat turned the notes over on the desk. She was glad she'd already put the book away.

"Was my door open?" Kat asked. It was unlike Cass to walk in uninvited, but Kat hadn't realized the door wasn't closed.

"Yes. Am I disturbing you?"

The maid must have left it ajar. "No," Kat said, rising from her chair.

"Oh, good." Cass smiled. "I, ah, wanted to speak with you about what happened in the retiring room the other night."

Kat moved to the small seating area in front of the hearth, where there were two small, but cozy chairs. She sat down on the edge of one of the chairs. "Is this about me not waiting for you and Fiona? I should have done, and I apologize."

Cass joined her, perching on the other chair. "Well, yes, you should have, but no, that's not what I wish to discuss."

"Did I do something else wrong?" Kat asked. That was typically what prompted this sort of conversation. Kat wasn't always good at social interactions. She didn't mean to offend anyone, but she had never mastered the art of prevarication and frankly didn't feel the need to.

"Not wrong, no," Cass said kindly. "However, your behavior might provoke Lady Wenlock and Mrs. Hanbury to share what happened, misrepresenting their conversation, of course, which could reflect poorly on you."

"On *me*? I wasn't the one gossiping and saying horrid things about others." Kat scowled toward the hearth with its glowing coals. "I will never understand Society," she grumbled.

"I know, and I agree that it doesn't make sense."

"You can't tell me you care about this. Anyone who gossips about what I said to them is guilty of the same transgression I chided them for."

"That's true. However, we are doing our best to keep, ah, gossip to a minimum because of the situation at the Phoenix Club."

"What does that have to do with me?"

"Nothing directly, but you are my sister-in-law, and Lucien is my brother. We want to make sure there is nothing else for people to talk about with regard to him."

Kat thought this was stretching credulity, but she didn't want to cause Lucien problems, especially when he'd agreed to help her. "I understand. I'll try to keep quiet. It's dreadfully hard sometimes."

"I know, and I love what you said on Evie's behalf. I was quite proud, actually. If it weren't for the timing, I would encourage you to continue. However, it won't help you in the long term, particularly if you truly wish to wed. Sometimes—almost always, in fact—it's better to ignore people."

Kat could acknowledge that was true while also finding great fault with it. "I disagree with that, and I'll never keep quiet for the sake of others' comfort or to make myself more acceptable. I don't give a fig about my reputation. If that means I never find a husband, then so be it." She fully expected that to be the case anyway and was absolutely fine with spinsterhood. "But I'll do this now for you—and for Lucien."

"Thank you," Cass said, glancing toward the desk. "Are you hard at work on something? We barely saw you yesterday, and you didn't come to church."

Kat rarely went to church and only when her mother made her. There were so few clergymen who could orate well. "Just working on some research. You know I've long been interested in mating rituals." Kat wouldn't tell her exactly what she was doing, but perhaps Cass could be helpful...

"What animal are you studying now?"

"I've actually been thinking about people. At the soirée, I observed people as they danced and conversed. It's interesting to watch flirtation—and avoidance."

"It is indeed. I sometimes think wallflowers have the best position in Society. They see and hear so much."

"How would you know?" Kat asked sarcastically but with a smile to soften the question.

Cass laughed. "That is a valid question. I have never been a wallflower, but then I was only out for a short period before I married your brother."

"Yet you were already two and twenty." A year older than Kat was now. "That's rather old for a first Season, isn't it?"

"Yes, but I kept putting it off." Cass turned her head toward the fire, her features tightening. "I was sad that my mother wasn't here to sponsor me. My friends would go shopping with their mothers, and plan endlessly. I just...I didn't want to do it without her." She looked back at Kat with a frail smile.

"I'm so sorry. I didn't realize. How old were you when she died?"

"Seven. I know it seems silly to have not got over it, but I'm not sure I ever will."

"And why should you? I've never understood that about grief. When we lose someone, especially if they were very close to us, how is it not as if a piece of your heart has gone missing?"

Cass pressed a finger to the corner of her eye. "Yes, that's it exactly."

Kat hadn't ever lost anyone like that. She had her parents and her sisters, and Ruark. He'd lost his father when he was young. He never talked about it and mentioned his father only rarely. Sometimes Kat wondered if it bothered him that his mother remarried so quickly, and that she'd wed the estate's steward. Their mother had caused quite a scandal in Ireland, so she and her new husband had moved to Ruark's estate in Gloucestershire to escape it. Which made Kat's mother's outrage at Kat's "scandalous" behavior all the more ridiculous.

"Did the fact that you and Ruark both lost a parent draw you together?" Kat had been more interested in what drew people together physically, but she had to think that for humans, there was more to mating than just primal urge. Or was there? Did there need to be some sort of emotional, intellectual, or some other connection? She would make a note to ask Lucien.

"I think so, yes, but honestly, it was more…visceral than that. At least at first." Cass pressed her hand to her cheek. "Goodness, I shouldn't have told you *that*."

"Why? Because I'm unmarried? How am I to learn things? I find it vexing that young ladies are supposed to go the Marriage Mart lacking important information."

Cass tipped her head to the side. "Such as?"

"What to look for in a husband. How to tell if someone is a good match. How did you know Ruark was the man you wanted to marry?"

"It's so hard to think of the precise moment, but the more time I spent with him, the less I wanted to be away from him. I looked for every opportunity to be in his presence. The air is just sweeter when you are in the company of the one you love."

Kat wanted to memorize that line to write it down, as well as the look of utter rapture on Cass's face. "Did you fall in love with him right away?"

"Not *right* away, but then I'd known him as Lucien's friend for a long time before I considered him romantically."

"And what made you decide to do that?"

Cass froze for a moment. "Er, it was a…unique circumstance. We found ourselves…together in a close situation and things just…developed."

Given the pink hue of Cass's cheeks and the halting way in which she answered, Kat surmised she was not revealing everything. "Was there flirting? Perhaps a stolen kiss or two? Is that how you knew you loved him?"

"I really shouldn't talk to you about this." Cass stood abruptly.

"I won't tell anyone. Please? I'm not asking for details." Though those would be helpful. But perhaps not from her sister-in-law. That seemed...strange. "I'm just wondering if I ought to practice flirting. Or kissing."

"Flirting is fairly typical for courtship," Cass said, her fingers fidgeting with her skirt. "Kissing is not."

"So, you and Ruark didn't do that? How could you know if you wanted to wed him without kissing?"

Exhaling, Cass sat back down. "All right. I'm going to share some...things with you, but if I find out you've told anyone, I'll be very disappointed. Do you promise to keep this secret?"

Anticipation raced through Kat. She leaned forward slightly. Sometimes, perhaps often, she struggled to keep secrets, but when someone was explicit and the secret was clearly important to them, Kat did her absolute best to protect it. "I promise."

"It started with a kiss between us. It was precisely the connection of that kiss that prompted everything else. I couldn't forget it, and neither could he. But our attraction eventually got us in trouble."

"Why?"

"Because we were discovered, and at the time, Ruark refused to wed. He had made a vow to his father that he wouldn't marry until he was thirty. He wanted to make sure he was making the right decision. You remind me of him with your questions. Are you worried you'll regret the choice you make?"

"Perhaps," Kat fibbed. She didn't think she'd regret her decision not to marry. "Ruark came around, though."

"Yes, he realized he was desperately in love with me, that I was the absolutely right choice." Cass grinned.

Kat sat back in the chair and thought for a moment. "What a leap of faith marriage is. I gather my mother and Ruark's father weren't happy, and yet she and my father are." It occurred to Kat that she ought to ask her mother to explain the difference in her feelings toward the two men, but she wasn't sure her mother would tell her. They didn't have a close relationship, not like Kat did with her younger sisters, Iona and the twins.

"It is indeed," Cass said. "And many marriages are not happy. That was the case for Con and Sabrina at first. But then their union was arranged. I do not recommend that."

"I don't think I have to worry about that. My mother might want to try to match me, but my father won't allow it."

"I daresay Ruark wouldn't either," Cass said with a laugh, her sherry-colored eyes gleaming. "He loves you very much and would never support something you didn't want."

"I know, and I'm grateful you both allow me to live here with you. I appreciate you answering my questions. I won't repeat a word."

Cass looked at her intently. "The most useful advice I can give you is to listen to your instincts and trust your heart. Also, don't get caught kissing." She winked at Kat and stood again.

The moment she departed, Kat leapt up and closed the door firmly. Then she returned to her desk, where she immediately recorded everything they'd discussed along with a series of new questions.

Pausing, she stared toward the window to her left, but she didn't really see anything. Her mind was going over everything Cass had told her. Clearly, that first kiss she'd shared with Ruark had sparked the very thing that Kat was missing. Dammit, she should have asked if Cass had felt that way toward anyone else—even without kissing them.

She knew people felt attraction, or at least admiration, based on physical traits of others. Her younger sisters often commented on which gentlemen in the district were attractive, and their mother joined in those conversations. Kat invariably got into debates with them about what constituted attractiveness. Was it that they were objectively handsome? Could anyone be objectively attractive to everyone? She didn't think so. But her sisters had argued that Mr. Shiveley, a gentleman who lived in the next town over, was indisputably and perfectly handsome.

Kat thought Mr. Shiveley's nose was too small. She supposed he was fine to look at, but certainly not to discuss at length or potentially *swoon* over. Swooning itself seemed completely absurd. How could anyone be so affected by another person that they fainted? Kat would never.

Closing her eyes, she tried to think of the best-looking gentleman she'd met. Lucien immediately came to mind, but she reasoned that was because she'd been thinking of him a great deal since their conversation the other night. Still, she felt she could argue convincingly that he was objectively handsome with his sable hair, dark, intelligent eyes, athletic frame, and dazzling smile. He really did have a disarming grin. And those were just a few of his physical attributes. He possessed many other admirable qualities such as generosity and kindness. It was no mystery that he was well liked, and people sought his assistance and counsel on a great many things. Not that Kat knew what any of those were.

Kat blinked her eyes open. She kept coming back to the same issue: she needed to kiss someone else. Or several someones. Without getting caught.

～

The private meeting room on the uppermost floor of the men's side of the Phoenix Club was windowless and cramped, but that was because it was supposed to be a storage room. And that was what almost everyone else thought it to be, including Evie and other employees of the club.

This was where Lucien occasionally met with Oliver Kent and where other meetings—many of which Lucien didn't know the particulars of—happened. Kent was due to arrive any moment.

While he waited, Lucien sat in one of the four simple wooden chairs tucked into the small space and sipped a glass of Irish whisky. He generally preferred the Scottish variety, but the club was currently low on supply.

Kent arrived on time, slipping into the small room that he liked to call the "meeting cupboard" and closing the door with a soft snick. Tall and thin, Kent was a white man who had reached the age of sixty last spring, though one might have estimated he was younger given the thickness of his dark gray hair and the clear, piercing quality of his blue eyes. He swept off his hat and tugged away his gloves, then set them on one of the empty chairs. "Evening, Lucien." There was a formal quality to his tone that wasn't normally present. Perhaps he was as tense as Lucien, then.

"Evening, Kent."

Moving to the small cabinet in the corner, Kent poured a glass of port. He sat opposite Lucien and sipped his wine, closing his eyes for a brief moment as a smile danced over his lips. "My very favorite port."

Lucien knew that, of course. Evie always made sure they kept it on hand, and that was before she'd rightly guessed that Kent was one of the unknown people on the membership committee.

"I suppose we should get right to it," Kent said before taking another drink. "How many resignations?"

"Thirty-eight."

Deep lines burrowed into Kent's brow. "Who?"

Lucien rattled off the names. He got through perhaps half before he had to take the list from his pocket.

"Too many," Kent said darkly when Lucien finished.

"It's not even a tenth of the current membership."

"It's only been five days. You can't think the exodus is over?"

Taking a breath, Lucien focused on retaining his calm exterior. "What I *think* is that this will not affect the operation. Why would it?"

"Because the club is losing popularity. Its reputation is failing. It will lose its effectiveness. Furthermore, some of the people who resigned are members the Foreign Office wanted here."

To a certain extent, Lucien had known that. He didn't necessarily know which people had been invited specifically for that purpose, but he could guess at several.

Kent shifted in his chair. He frowned—but at his glass, not Lucien. "My superiors are not happy with this current course of events." Now he looked up.

Lucien gave him a wry half smile. "Perhaps now is not the best time to inform you that Evie isn't leaving the club." He took a sip of whisky, grateful for the heat coating his throat and easing some of his agitation.

"She *must*." Kent's nostrils flared and his eyes widened. "Her departure wasn't a choice." He gripped his wineglass with more force than Lucien had seen before.

Though Lucien had expected him to be displeased, Kent's reaction seemed a trifle severe. "I know what you and Lady Pickering said." Lucien referenced the other secret member who directed the membership. Her association with the Foreign Office was less clear than Kent's. Lucien only knew that she helped them with certain operations. She was one of the most respected members of the ton, and she was not a member of the Phoenix Club. She'd ignored the invitation Lucien had issued two years ago, probably because it helped keep her identity on the membership committee from being discovered. Surely no one would think someone who wasn't a member of the club would be on it. "However, this is my club, and it won't run as efficiently without Evie," Lucien continued.

"I vehemently disagree. Lady Warfield seems perfectly capable." He meant Ada, the bookkeeper. Evie had brought her back to London when she'd returned from her transformation from Mirabelle Renault to Evangeline Renshaw. She had an excellent head for numbers and organization and was perhaps the sunniest, most delightful person Lucien had ever met. That she'd married the surliest, most damaged man of Lucien's acquaintance—his friend and former comrade in arms, Maximillian Hunt, the Viscount Warfield—was one of life's great ironies.

"Ada is more than capable, but she's also dividing her time between the club and being a viscountess." Max's family estate was a day's ride from London, and they spent a great deal of time there, in part because Max had allowed it to fall into disrepair after returning from the war in Spain. Max also disliked London and having to serve in the Lords, but Lucien had begun to wonder if Ada's charm and equanimity were wearing off on him. He was far less grumpy than he had been six months ago, whereas Lucien had become more agitated of late with everything going on. "Evie is staying," Lucien reiterated.

Again, Kent looked at his glass rather than Lucien. "You seem to be suffering from a delusion that you are in control here. I must remind you that you are not." He took another sip of port, and Lucien would have sworn his hand shook slightly. Was he that angry?

"That's debatable, I think," Lucien said evenly. "If the Foreign Office is so disappointed in the club's path, then perhaps they should let it go."

Kent slammed his glass down, sloshing port nearly over the rim. "Dammit, Lucien, they've made too much of an investment to walk away. That you think such a thing could happen is beyond reason. I thought you wanted to serve the crown."

"I do. But *I've* also made an investment in this club—a personal one. I will not turn my back on one of my dearest friends. When Evie returns to London in a month or so, the gossip will be ancient history, replaced by any number of scandals. She will also be the wife of the brother of a marquess. Surely that will help matters."

"What would help matters is if that marquess—Witney— were to be invited to join the club."

Lucien clenched his jaw. "Absolutely not."

"My superiors want him here." Kent swirled his wine and watched it coat the interior of the glass. "It's not up for debate."

"Witney tried to blackmail his way into the club. I don't want that sort of member here. It's antithetical to the mission of the club. If you'll recall, the whole point was to not have a club like White's or Brooks's. How can the sort of people who need to meet here attend if there is nothing but arrogant, shallow peers running about?"

"Because they are in the minority, by our design." Kent frowned deeply. "You are being stubborn."

"Why do you want Witney of all people? He's a weasel."

"We have our reasons."

"That I shall not be privy to," Lucien muttered. He imagined Witney was either someone the Foreign Office wanted to observe or, and this stretched Lucien's belief, he was also working for them. It had to be the former. Well, they could do that somewhere else. "No. I refuse to invite him."

Kent narrowed his eyes and gripped his glass tightly again so that his fingertips turned white. "You can't."

Lucien decided it was time to play his hand. He leaned forward, maintaining his composure. "What will happen?

The Foreign Office will force me out? How will that improve the club's reputation? I am synonymous with the Phoenix Club. If I walk away, so will everyone else, and then it *will* fail."

A low, guttural sound came from Kent's throat as he squashed his lips together in frustration. The flesh around his mouth went white, and his thick, gray brows pitched low over his eyes. "Do you really want to defy your superiors?" he asked softly.

What Lucien wanted was true freedom. He wanted to own the club outright. He'd find a way to come up with the money. Still, the Foreign Office would need to sell to him, and according to his father, they wouldn't. He wanted to ask Kent how the duke knew about this arrangement, but what if Kent didn't know? What if the duke had been informed by someone else?

"I want us to find a compromise," Lucien said. "I can't operate the club as we agreed without Evie or by inviting people who don't match the club's mission. Already, people wonder how Lady Hargrove was ever invited, let alone made a patroness, when she so clearly didn't belong here." That those people wondering were Lucien's close friends and family didn't signify.

Kent made a face that looked as if he'd smelled something very bad. Turning his head, he stared at the door for a moment before returning his attention to Lucien. "We'll have to find an accord, then. Can you at least get back the members who resigned?"

Lucien blew out a breath. Some would be achievable while other might prove impossible. "Does that include the Hargroves?"

"Honestly, it would be best if they came back, but you won't get them to, not without making the changes you've refused to make." Kent drank the rest of his port.

Lucien knew they were about finished. They usually kept these meetings brief. And this one was begging for conclusion. "I'll do my best to get the others back."

"I will convey that to the Foreign Office." Kent rose and set his empty glass on the cabinet. Fetching his hat and gloves, he set the former on his head then drew on the latter. "Don't push them too hard." His gaze met Lucien's. It held understanding along with weariness. "You must know that they won't allow you to be in control of their project. They'll do whatever it takes to reach their ends—and they won't lose." Setting his mouth into a firm line, he bid Lucien good night, then left.

What kind of threat was that? To what lengths would the Foreign Office go in order to get what they wanted? Lucien didn't suspect anything nefarious, but they'd explore their options. With his refusal to toe the line, he'd forced them to do just that.

He tossed back the rest of his whisky, then fetched Kent's dirty glass. He'd deposit both of them elsewhere in the club, and a footman would pick them up for cleaning.

His mind turned with what he needed to do: regain some of the members who'd left, recruit new members who would please the Foreign Office, and ensure the club maintained its membership as well as its popularity.

There was no way Lucien would leave the Phoenix Club. They'd have to drag him away.

CHAPTER 5

*S*urprisingly, given his meeting with Kent, Lucien had slept better last night than he had in days. Perhaps it was because he felt as though he finally had something active to do in working to woo back the members who had resigned. He'd made lists after the meeting last night. Some people, he'd approach personally. The rest he'd assign to his brother or others on the membership committee. He briefly wondered if he ought to add Con to the committee, but he doubted Con would accept. He was far too busy with his family as well as his duties in the Lords.

The February afternoon was mild and far drier than yesterday. The sun was even peeking through the clouds as Lucien strode into Hyde Park. He walked toward the Ring, keeping an eye out for Ruark and Cass, whom he was meeting. Ruark had extended the invitation—weather permitting—but Lucien had planned to call on him today. He had a list of members who had resigned, and he needed Ruark and Cass to coax them to return.

This was better than Lucien calling at their house because he could avoid seeing Kat. He'd actually dreamed of her last night. They'd had another conversation about *completion* and whether she could find it. He'd thankfully awakened before that image could reach...completion.

As Lucien neared the Ring, he caught sight of Ruark, who seemed to see Lucien at almost precisely the same moment. But Ruark was alone. Lucien glanced about for Cass and saw her standing near a tree just off the track near the Ring. She *wasn't* alone. Kat stood beside her.

"Afternoon, Lucien," Ruark said. "Let's take a stroll to the walnut trees and back, then we can join the ladies."

"You invited me for a specific purpose today," Lucien said with a slight smile. "As it happens, I have a purpose for seeing you as well."

Ruark grinned. "Brilliant. We'll just take care of business, then."

"My business also pertains to Cass, but you can inform her of the details later."

"I'll do that," Ruark said as they made their way along the track. "Do you want to go first?"

Lucien glanced toward his sister and Ruark's sister. Kat was watching him. She didn't even try to avert her attention when he looked her way, so their eyes met. Though the distance between them was great, he felt a short but potent jolt of awareness. It settled in his shoulder blades so that when the ladies were behind him, he swore he still felt Kat's gaze.

"No, you go." Lucien needed a moment to push his friend's sister from his thoughts.

"The reason we're here and Cass and Kat are over there is because I need to speak with you about Kat. She thinks I'm talking to you about club business."

"Well, that will be true shortly," Lucien said.

"I thought as much. I've a favor to ask." Ruark sent him a glance tinged with concern. "I wonder if you might help smooth Kat's reputation." He tipped his head from side to side. "Not just that, but how she's received now that she'll be spending more time out in town."

"I wasn't aware that her reputation was suffering. I rather thought all London was focused on the Phoenix Club, Evie, and me."

"Primarily, yes." Now Ruark looked at him with sympathy.

Lucien waved his hand. "We'll survive. Has the incident from Gloucestershire last year reached London at last?"

"Not that I'm aware of, but my mother wrote to tell me that Hickinbottom's parents are coming to town to give his younger sister a Season."

That could be problematic if they ran into Kat. "Are you concerned what will happen if Kat encounters them in Society?"

"Definitely. However, I don't know how to avoid it."

"They may not run in the same circles as you," Lucien said.

"That's certainly possible. Just don't go inviting any of them to join the Phoenix Club, please." He laughed.

"You can count on that. I'll keep an eye out for them and listen for anything being said either by or about them."

"Thank you. There is more," Ruark said. "Kat doesn't always think through what she says before it leaves her mouth."

Lucien had seen that firsthand. "I may have noticed that."

"Of course you have. The other night at the soirée, she rebuked a couple of gossiping ladies in the retiring room."

Smiling, Lucien wanted to hear this story. "This sounds delightful. I'm always in favor of stanching the flow of nonsense."

"You will be especially in this case because it involved Evie."

"Not surprising. What did Kat say?"

"That they shouldn't judge others and that Evie is a good person."

"How lovely of her," Lucien murmured. He didn't think Kat knew Evie very well and found her defense of someone she'd only met a few times both charming and generous.

"It was Lady Wenlock and Mrs. Hanbury." Ruark sent Lucien knowing look. They were relentless with spreading gossip. If Lucien wanted something known, he'd tell them.

"I don't suppose Kat told them Evie is marrying Lord Gregory."

"They were already discussing it, but she said she thought Evie would make him a wonderful wife."

Lucien would thank her later.

Ruark continued. "In any case, between Kat's penchant for giving her tongue free rein and the potential for the Gloucestershire scandal to spread here, I worry she is in danger of ruin at any moment."

Lucien nearly tripped, for Ruark didn't even know the half of it. If he was aware that his sister was hoping to research kissing and other mating rituals by participating in them, he would likely send her to a convent in Ireland.

Ruark cast him a sidelong glance. "If you could also keep an eye on Kat if you happen to be in the same place as her, particularly at the Phoenix Club assemblies, I'd be grateful. It probably goes without saying, but whatever you can do to recommend her would be splendid."

Keep an eye on Kat... They'd reached the walnut trees and were now turning around to return to where she and Cass stood near the Ring. Lucien picked out Kat's light blue skirts and couldn't help but think that if Ruark were aware of what Kat had asked of him, he'd tell Lucien to stay far away.

"I'm not certain I'm the best person to help her reputation. Mine isn't exactly in its finest shape."

"It's still better than your younger rakehell years."

"I think you mean *our* younger rakehell years."

Ruark chuckled. "Yes. Your reputation is fine. Have your invitations dwindled?"

Lucien couldn't say. It had been less than a week since the news about him and Evie had been published, and he'd been too busy to pay attention to invitations. "Time will be the judge. However, when I promenaded with Kat the other night, she mentioned hearing someone call me a devil." Now he wondered if that had been Lady Wenlock and Mrs. Hanbury.

Rolling his eyes, Ruark grunted. "You're the person everyone turns to in their hour of need. Anyone denigrating you is jealous or doesn't like you. And since the number of people who fall into the latter category isn't very large, I'd wager that was Lady Hargrove."

Lucien would believe that too. He'd expelled her from the club last week after she'd caused a scene. He'd pulled her into his office to allow her to explain herself, but she'd dug her feet in, sharing her ire at having her membership and patroness recommendations ignored. When Lucien had informed her that she wasn't going to get her way and suggested she might be happier away from the Phoenix Club, she'd threatened to expose Evie's past.

"For whatever it's worth, I'll do my best to ensure Kat is held in high esteem. Has it occurred to you that she'll tire of the Season?"

Ruark exhaled. "I expect that, actually. I don't for a moment believe she's considering marriage. She's never shown the slightest interest, not like my other sisters."

"What does that look like? Not showing interest, I mean?" Lucien asked. He wanted to understand Kat given what she'd told him about herself. If she'd never felt attracted to anyone, didn't it make sense that marriage seemed undesirable?

"She's never been interested in attending assemblies or discussing courtships happening in the district. She certainly doesn't care about shopping for the latest fashions or styling her hair to attract attention."

"And she's invested in those things now?"

"I can't say she is, no." Ruark shook his head. "I don't know what she's up to, but I'd wager it isn't finding a husband."

Lucien contemplated whether he should tell Kat that her brother wasn't falling for her ruse. He certainly wasn't going to reveal her intent to Ruark, unless it became necessary. "About the club..."

"Yes, your turn," Ruark said. "How can I help?"

"I need you to try to get Lord and Lady Coggeshall and the Dunhills to come back to the club."

Ruark paused, turning toward Lucien. "Truly?"

"Yes. They likely didn't want to leave but were coerced into doing so." Lucien was fairly certain that was the case with the Dunhills. Joseph Dunhill was an ambitious barrister with a bright future.

"Mrs. Dunhill is Irish. Is that why you asked me to speak to them?"

Lucien smiled. "It doesn't hurt. And I know you can charm Lady Coggeshall."

Ruark groaned. "I suppose I can dance with her. There's a ball later this week, I believe."

"That will go a long way in convincing them to return. Coggeshall will do anything she says." Lucien then listed several more names that he specifically wanted Cass to speak with.

"I'll tell her," Ruark said. "She'll be thrilled you want her assistance with the club."

They started walking toward the Ring once more.

"Happy to help." Ruark clapped Lucien on the shoulder. "It's nice to be the one helping you for once."

"It isn't just me—it's the club as a whole. I know you care about it too."

"I do. It's all going to work out," Ruark said.

As they neared Cass and Kat, Lucien wondered if he ought to excuse himself. He'd conducted the business he needed to, as had Ruark. There was no reason for him to stay.

"Afternoon, Lucien," Cass said, presenting her cheek for him to buss. "You can escort Kat while we walk around the Ring."

So much for leaving.

"I should be delighted," Lucien said. He couldn't help but notice Kat was watching him with an unparalleled intensity. Indeed, he'd never felt more like prey, not even when he was a young buck being eyed by marriage-minded mothers hoping to match him with their daughters. Except in this instance, his reaction was wholly different. He *liked* the way she was looking at him. It was singularly intoxicating.

Kat took his arm, and they started their circuit of the Ring. "I was hoping to speak with you privately," she whispered, indicating she could, in fact, lower her voice, which she'd mostly failed to do when they'd spoken at the soirée the other night.

"It doesn't look as though that will be possible," he said softly.

"Pfft." Her tongue peeked between her lips as she made the rather unladylike sound.

Lucien would have laughed if he hadn't been distracted by the vision of her pink tongue against her pink lips. Dammit.

"What did you and Ruark discuss?" she asked.

"Phoenix Club business."

"I realize that." She sounded beleaguered. "What specifi- cally did you talk about? Or is it boring?"

"I'm sure it's boring to some. I need your brother to convince some people who recently resigned to come back." Why was he telling her this?

"He's a good choice to do that. Ruark could charm the petticoats from a nun."

Lucien laughed loudly, which drew Cass to look over at them. Then her gaze moved past Lucien, and she paused.

Stopping, Lucien wondered what—or who—she saw.

"Pardon us," Cass said. "I see Lady Sansberry." She cast Lucien a determined look, and he knew the woman didn't stand a chance against Cass. The dowager would be back on the membership roll by nightfall.

"What good fortune!" Kat grinned as she watched her brother and Cass depart. She squeezed Lucien's arm as she looked up at him. "Now I can ask you the questions I've accumulated. As many as I can in the time we have. I shall have to speak quickly."

Lucien braced himself. "I think you should know that your brother doesn't believe you are looking for a husband."

She lifted a shoulder. "Can't say I'm surprised."

"Or concerned, apparently," Lucien said with a laugh.

"Not particularly. I should probably explain." She exhaled. "He'll caution me, but he'll understand."

"You can't think to tell him what you told me? What you're hoping to learn and how you'd planned to do so?"

"Heavens no! Now be quiet so I can ask my questions."

Lucien paused to stare at her before breaking into laughter once more. "You are a singular woman."

"Thank you. Actually, before I ask my questions, I've decided I absolutely must try kissing again."

The image of her tongue against her lips filled his mind once more, and now he was thinking of kissing her himself.

Hellfire. He glanced at where Ruark stood with Cass and Lady Sansberry. "No, you must not."

Kat waved her hand as she started walking again. Lucien had no choice but to go along with her. "I'm not asking you to find me a rake. I'm confident a kissing opportunity will present itself."

Again, Lucien had to check himself before he tripped over his own damned feet. "What in God's name is a 'kissing opportunity'?"

"I'm not entirely sure, but I suppose it involves being close with a gentleman in a secluded area. I'll know it when it happens."

"Not if you don't get close to gentlemen in secluded areas." He threw her a weighty glare. "Dammit, Kat, that is how you get compromised. That is how you are *ruined*. Did you learn nothing in Gloucestershire?"

"I told you I did—not to get caught. You sound like my brother with that tone. Please stop." She frowned at him. "I think you must consider that you really are prudish after all."

"I am not." Why was he feeling defensive about that? "Why are you convinced you need to kiss someone?"

"I was speaking with someone recently, and in their experience, a kiss changed a platonic relationship to a romantic one."

Recently had to be since their conversation three days ago. To whom would she have spoken? It didn't matter. She shouldn't be talking to *him*. Except, he said he'd help her. How could he do that without kissing her himself?

"There are other ways to feel attraction for someone without kissing. Perhaps you just haven't met the right person."

"Lucien, how many lovers have you had?"

He finally tripped then. His foot caught on air as he struggled to parse what she'd said. She clutched at his arm, not that he was in danger of actually falling.

Righting himself, he took a breath and shook his shoulders out.

"I startled you with that question," she said.

"I'm not answering it. If all your questions are of that nature, we may as well move on to another topic."

"No, in fact, I hadn't even planned to ask you that. How do you know when you want to physically engage with someone? What about Mrs. Renshaw? She was your paramour. How did you choose her?"

Every curse word Lucien knew flitted through his brain. "Not answering anything to do with Mrs. Renshaw or anyone else I've...engaged with." He'd almost said shagged. Bloody hell, he was starting to perspire, and it wasn't remotely warm enough for that.

Her dark brows drew together over her sapphire eyes. "You are incredibly frustrating today."

"You are insatiably inquisitive." He would try to mollify her. "If I tell you how I decide to take a lover, will you cease asking me personal questions?"

"For now."

"Fine." Lucien chose his words as carefully as possible. How did one describe the feeling of wanting to caress someone, the desire to give them pleasure, and lose yourself in them in the pursuit of your own ecstasy? "Keep in mind, this is different from choosing a spouse. I can't speak to that at all. I am attracted to women who are intelligent and confident. I like a woman who is comfortable with herself and isn't too serious."

"That excludes me, then, because everyone tells me I'm too serious. And too focused."

Lucien would certainly agree with the latter. Hell, was she hoping he'd find her attractive? He realized he did. Find her attractive. She was everything he'd just described. Contrary to what she thought, he didn't see her as too serious, at least not about things that didn't matter. "Allow me to clarify," he said. "I mean too serious about themselves. They need to be able to *laugh*. I've seen you laugh."

"That's true. So, you aren't attracted to women based on their physical attributes at all? I find that fascinating. My sisters are always going on about a gentleman's appearance."

"I'd be lying if I said it didn't matter, but I find I'm attracted to the sum of all the lady's parts. Appearance alone isn't enough to entice me."

"That is also fascinating," she murmured. "I wish I'd brought my notebook."

"Don't you think it would look odd if we stepped off the path intermittently so you could write things down?"

"I don't give a fig how anything *looks*." No, she clearly did not. And dammit if he didn't find that *incredibly* attractive. "You've told me what sort of woman you find attractive, but how do you go about making them your lover?"

"It depends. Usually, they are also looking for a lover… or a protector." Was he really going to talk to her about paying for a mistress? He hadn't done that since Evie, actually. He'd been too focused on the club. That didn't mean he'd been a monk, however. "It tends to be a mutual agreement."

"Sounds very organized. What about the passion? The animal instinct? You've never been carried away with someone and simply succumbed to desire?" She asked these questions with an even, businesslike tone. Despite that, Lucien found himself growing aroused, and that would simply not do.

He looked toward Ruark, hoping they'd finish with Lady Sansberry quickly so he could be rescued from this torture by temptation.

Was it really torture? Yes, because he couldn't do a damn thing about it.

"You said you would stop asking me questions. For now," he added.

"I suppose I did." She sounded disappointed.

They walked in silence for a few minutes, during which Lucien worked to slow his racing pulse and stop thinking of Kat's prurient questions. He began to think there would be no satisfying her curiosity until she kissed someone. And he wasn't about to arrange that for her.

Which left him. Kissing her.

Shit.

"Look at that couple, there," she said, inclining her head to a young lady and gentleman standing just off the track. An older woman stood nearby, probably the girl's mother. "They appear to be flirting. Do you agree?"

Their heads were bent toward each other, and the woman's hand was around the man's elbow. "In my experience, the higher the woman's hand on a man's arm, the more interested she is in him. And the closer the man holds his arm to his side, the more it indicates he is also interested."

"What a helpful observation. What makes you say that?"

"Both indicate intimacy—or a desire for it. By holding his arm close to his side, he's pressing her hand against him. She doesn't appear to mind, plus her grip higher on his arm puts her hand in that position to be close to him."

"Is this something everyone knows?"

"I've never discussed it with anyone." He gave her a faint smile. "You are the first person I've met who's taken a scientific approach to these matters."

"I really need to carry a notebook," she murmured.

At last, Ruark and Cass were walking away from Lady Sansberry. Lucien wasted no time altering their direction to meet them.

"Where are we going?" Kat asked. "Ah, I see Ruark and Cass are free. I suppose you must be on your way?" Again, she sounded disappointed.

"Yes. I'm sure I'll see you again soon." He hoped not, though since he'd agreed to help her stay out of trouble—not that Ruark had used that description, but it was bloody accurate—he supposed he must.

"There's a ball on Saturday, I think. Perhaps I'll see you there. I'll save you a dance." Her nose wrinkled slightly.

Lucien laughed. "How can I refuse your avid excitement?"

She turned her head toward him and smiled broadly. She was dazzling. "Hopefully you can't." She took her hand from his arm, but not before she briefly slid it up nearly to his elbow.

Had she done that on purpose?

"Thank you, Lucien. Today has been most enlightening." The mischief in her blue gaze said yes, she'd done that wholly on purpose.

And he'd thought she was the one who needed protection from trouble. He was already there.

CHAPTER 6

The small notebook just fit into Kat's reticule, which she secured around her wrist before climbing down from the coach in front of Viscount Fallin's house. Rather, Lady Fallin's new home. Jessamine had become a dear friend of Kat's after they'd spent a few weeks together staying with Lady Pickering last summer. Neither had wanted to leave London with their families, so the baroness had taken them in. Jessamine had even traveled with Lady Pickering to her home in Hampshire. Kat hadn't wanted to go there either, plus Ruark and Cass had returned to London while they were gone.

During their time together, Kat and Jess had come to know each other well. Jess was exceptionally good at solving puzzles and riddles. And she liked to read as much as Kat did.

Kat had looked forward to spending more time with her when she'd returned to town, but then Jess had gone and married Lord Fallin. Since then, they'd been in Scotland at his father's estate. Kat hadn't been sure when they'd be back in London and had been delighted to receive Jess's note yesterday, which had included an invitation to call today.

The butler admitted Kat to the house and immediately showed her upstairs to the drawing room. Jess rose from the settee. She was white like Kat, but close to five years older. Her eyes were a cobalt blue instead of Kat's darker color, and her light brown hair was arranged in a neat but unfussy style. She hurried forward, smiling. "Kat!"

They embraced, and Kat immediately noticed Jess felt a bit different. Taking a step back, she glanced down at Jess's abdomen. "Are you increasing?"

Jess blinked, then laughed softly. "You are still the most observant person I've ever met."

"About some things," Kat said. Her mother would be the first to say that Kat could be quite obtuse. That typically happened when she was focused on something. Which, admittedly, was much of the time. "I'm right, then?"

"Yes, but I didn't think it would be noticeable."

"I could feel you're thicker, but I don't think anyone could tell by looking. Are you trying to keep it secret?"

"Perhaps for a while longer." Jess waved her hand. "It probably doesn't matter. I'm nearly to the halfway point, I think."

They moved to sit at a small round table near the window as a maid entered with a tray bearing tea and cakes. She poured, then took her leave.

"I'm so pleased you're back in London," Kat said, stirring cream and sugar into her tea after setting her reticule on the table. "Are you staying for the Season?"

"Yes. Dougal has business here, and it looks as though he may take a government position. Nothing is finalized, but he's glad to be back. As much as we love Scotland—it's unbelievably beautiful—we both adore London."

"I don't think I'd want to live anywhere else." Kat hadn't considered that before, but she realized it was true.

"What have you been doing while I was gone? Any new research?"

"Actually, yes. I'm continuing to study mating rituals but am now focusing on people."

Jess's eyes widened briefly. "How is that going? I mean, really, how do you do that? It's not as if you can take a notebook into a ballroom to draw or record observations."

"That is true." Kat opened her reticule and withdrew her notebook and a pencil. "But I have decided to take it as many places as I can."

Laughing, Jess plucked a cake from the tray. "What can you possibly hope to learn here today with me?"

"I'm hoping a great many things." Kat sipped her tea. She set her cup down and plucked up her pencil. "I've told Ruark and Cass that I want to participate in the Season. There is no better place than the Marriage Mart to observe humans mating. Or attempting to."

"That's quite brilliant, really. Do they know that's what you're doing?"

"I said I was considering marriage. However, Lucien has informed me that Ruark didn't believe that. I should have realized. I would have told him the truth, but I thought he'd try to dissuade me."

"You're probably right," Jess agreed. "Lucien informed you? Have you and he become friends while I was away?" She took a bite of the cake she'd taken.

"I suppose we have. We are somewhat related, after all."

Jess finished swallowing. "Is he your brother-in-law or something else? Brother-in-law once removed, perhaps?"

"I don't know if there's an official name for the connection. I refer to him as my sister-in-law's brother. Anyway, I asked for his help since that is what he does."

"With your research?" She sent Kat a rather shrewd stare. "You didn't ask him to show you mating rituals, did you?"

"I did not. I asked if he could find a rakish sort of fellow with whom I could conduct experiments, but he—"

"Said no, I hope!" Jess laughed. "Only you would think that was possible."

Kat frowned. "Well, it *is* possible."

"In theory, yes, but in practice, there is no way a gentleman such as Lucien would help you in that manner."

"He said as much. So, I convinced him to help me."

"With experimentation?" Jess popped the rest of the cake into her mouth.

"No, but I confess I wouldn't be opposed to kissing him. I am most eager to try that again." She'd told Jess all about kissing Hickinbottom last year.

"I can't say I blame you given the experience you had."

Kat recalled that Jess had also shared her kissing experience. It had been years ago with an American she'd hoped to wed, but her parents had sent him away. "Yours was much better. If you don't mind my asking, how does it compare to Fallin?"

"There is no comparing them. Indeed, after kissing Dougal, I quite forgot that I'd even kissed anyone else ever."

"But I remember you saying you'd enjoyed kissing the American. You specifically said so after I described my kiss—if you can call it that, apparently—with Hickinbottom."

"I did say that, and I suppose I can recall that it was fine." Jess shrugged. "I presume that's the comparison. That kiss *was* fine. Perhaps even pleasant. But kissing Dougal is like seeing the sun after weeks of cold, dark damp. Or smelling your favorite food and realizing the hunger you hadn't even noticed was going to be wholly and wonderfully satisfied."

Kat wrote down what she said. "What a lovely description. Did you feel that way about his kisses immediately?"

"Yes. From the start, I couldn't get enough."

"How did that happen? Your first kiss, I mean?" Kat

tapped her pencil against the table a few times. "I am trying to determine how to kiss someone without being caught this time."

"Er, it's a rather convoluted story, but he was in Hampshire when I was there with Lady Pickering, and we had occasion to be alone together." Jess reached for another cake. "It was slightly scandalous."

"But you didn't get caught!" Kat marveled. "How did you manage that?"

"Pure luck."

"Damn, I was hoping you would tell me something useful." Kat smiled. "You give me hope that I will enjoy a kiss with someone who isn't Hickinbottom."

Jess's brows drew together. "Are you concerned you won't? I don't recall you mentioning that before." She nibbled the cake.

"I've been thinking about it more and more." Particularly since her conversation with Lucien at the soirée. Perhaps even more so after walking with him in the park the other day. She was all but certain she'd caught him staring at her mouth more than once. "The reason I am concerned about it is the fact that I've never been moved to want to kiss someone. Hickinbottom was entirely about research. You *wanted* to kiss the American and, presumably, Fallin."

"I did want to kiss Dougal. Very much. We'd spent some time together, and I was attracted to him from nearly our first meeting."

"Can you describe that attraction? I asked Lucien a similar question, and he listed attributes he finds attractive, none of which were physical."

"Really? Well, I don't mind saying that I found Dougal incredibly handsome. Just looking at him made my heart beat faster." Jess's lips curved up, and her gaze took on a warm sheen.

Kat recorded everything Jess said in the notebook. "I don't think I've ever experienced that." When she'd seen Lucien at the park the other day, something in her chest had pinched, but she'd attributed it to too many kippers at breakfast. "What if I'm just not capable of feeling arousal?"

"That can't be possible." One of her brows arched. "Can it?"

"I mean to find out. But it's deuced hard if I can't kiss someone. Or, ideally, multiple someones."

"Are you hoping to identify someone you'd like to kiss when you're out in Society?"

Kat loved how Jess didn't question what she was doing. She was asking questions, but they came from a place of interest and support, unlike Lucien's outrage. Perhaps he wasn't the friend she thought him to be. "I suppose I am. There's a ball tomorrow night."

"You might have better luck, especially with respect to not getting caught, at places like the park or Vauxhall. Of course, it's far too early in the Season for pleasure gardens."

It was, and if Kat had to wait until the weather warmed to conduct that aspect of her research, she'd scream with frustration. "I'll keep that in mind. Not getting caught is a chief concern, obviously."

"What about the Phoenix Club?" Jess mused. "There are semiprivate alcoves and retiring areas. Will you be attending the assemblies?"

"Yes, the first one is next Friday. I suppose you're a member now?"

"I am." Jess grinned. "I can hardly wait to visit the ladies' library."

"I'm incredibly jealous. That is the primary reason— really, the only one—I want to be invited."

"I am also looking forward to going to the men's side on Tuesdays. I was sorry the weather delayed our journey so that we missed it this week." Jess finished her second cake, then glanced at the tray. "I could eat the entire plate. Well, all the cakes on the plate, I mean."

"Don't let me stand in your way. I'm too focused on recording my notes to eat."

"If you insist." Jess flashed her a grin before taking a third confection. "The babe drives me to eat cakes and biscuits. I will likely be as large as a coach soon."

Kat considered Jess's advice. "Do you have any suggestions for how to determine whom I might want to kiss?"

Want? When had that become important? She hadn't wanted to kiss Hickinbottom. She'd selected him as a target because of his unavailability. He wouldn't think she expected marriage because she absolutely did not. She'd have to make that clear to anyone she kissed before doing so.

"You say you don't feel attracted to anyone—do I have that right?" At Kat's nod, she continued. "In that case, you may want to observe a variety of gentlemen on several different occasions to cultivate a list of perhaps five to ten who might suit."

"That's brilliant." Kat scrawled several ideas. She'd look for men who flirted. Excessively. No one married or betrothed—she'd learned that lesson. "I suppose I should hone my flirting skills, which are nonexistent, by the way, so that I can use them to ascertain a gentleman's interest."

"I daresay if you make it known that you're amenable to kissing, you won't have trouble finding multiple interested parties," Jess said with a sardonic laugh. "But you must be careful. Some gentlemen won't want to stop at just a kiss." She frowned. "In fact, I'm not sure this is safe."

"Why not? You kissed Fallin before you were wed."

"He was a complete gentleman about it too. I felt entirely safe."

Without looking down, Kate wrote the word "safe." "In what way?"

"He asked me first, for one. And he continued to make sure I was comfortable with our…intimacy."

Kat leaned forward slightly, her pencil poised above the notebook. "Did you do more than kiss?"

"Er, yes." Color splashed onto her cheeks just before her gaze shifted to the doorway. "Dougal, darling."

Kat shifted in her chair so she could see the door. Fallin, a tall Black man with almond-colored skin and an easy, disarming smile, strode in. Behind him came Lucien. That strange pinch squeezed in Kat's chest again. And damn if her pulse didn't pick up.

Wait. Was she attracted to Lucien?

If it was true, this was wonderful. But how could she be sure?

They came toward the table, and Fallin went to Jess's chair. He touched her shoulder. "Enjoying more cakes, I see."

"Don't begrudge me—or the babe—what we crave."

"The babe?" Lucien asked.

"We are to be parents this summer," Fallin said with a face-splitting grin.

"That is spectacular." Lucien slapped Fallin's upper arm. "Congratulations." He bowed to Jess. "I'm delighted for you."

"Thank you," Jess said. "I didn't realize you were coming, Lord Lucien. Should I ring for more refreshments?"

"Just Lucien, please. Your husband is one of my oldest and dearest friends."

Jess smiled up at him. "Then you must stay for tea—and cakes—Lucien."

"We've Phoenix Club business to discuss."

Kat shook her head. "Really, Lucien why is the membership committee such a secret when it's plainly obvious that it's you, Mrs. Renshaw, my brother, Lord Overton, and Fallin here."

"I refuse to confirm anything." He narrowed his eyes at her and leaned slightly toward her chair. "You're far too observant for your own good. Definitely for mine," he murmured.

A shiver stole up her spine and settled on her nape, making her flesh tingle. Was that attraction too? Her fingers itched to record the sensation. She suddenly wanted them to leave so she could ask Jess about it.

"Don't let us keep you," Kat said sweetly.

Lucien's eyes darkened briefly, and a slight frown tugged at his lips. But he looked away from her, and the expression vanished. "We just wanted to come in so I could welcome you back to London, Lady Fallin," Lucien said.

"You can't expect me to call you Lucien and then address me so formally. I am Jessamine. Jess to my friends, of which you are one. I hope."

"Most definitely."

"We'll be in my study," Fallin said, dropping a light kiss on Jess's forehead.

As they left, Kat watched Lucien walk, taking note of the way his coat moved across his broad shoulders and the manner in which his legs moved the tails. He had long legs. She suddenly wondered what they looked like beneath his clothing.

"Kat?"

Realizing she was staring at an empty doorway, she turned back to face Jess. "Just a moment." Kat wrote down the sensations she'd felt seeing Lucien, finishing with *attraction?* She circled the word.

"Attraction?"

Kat looked up to see Jess had lifted from her chair so she could see across the table to read what Kat had written.

Closing the notebook as a rush of heat overtook her face, Kat pursed her lips. "Well, we were discussing that."

"Yes, and then you eagerly jotted notes after Lucien came in. Are you attracted to *him*?"

"That seems to be the question." Now Kat wondered why she'd reacted in that way—closing the notebook and feeling embarrassment. "I'd intended to ask you. I don't know why I was trying to hide my reaction just then."

"Because you don't know what to make of the feeling of attraction." Jess smiled at her with encouragement. "What did you feel upon seeing Lucien? Did your pulse speed up?"

"It did, actually. And I felt this odd squeeze in my chest. That happened the other day at the park too. I thought it was something I ate."

Jess laughed. "I daresay it wasn't that. Your eyes lit when Lucien came in—that was my first clue."

"Did they? I notice that happens with Cass and Ruark when they see one another, particularly if they've been parted for a while, all day for instance. That's attraction?"

"It could be a great many things, and I would wager it's also love between your brother and sister-in-law. But since I doubt you're in love with Lucien, it's attraction in your case."

Kat was all but certain she was attracted to Lucien. He was physically appealing, as evidenced by her thoughts regarding his legs. "I wish I could get him to kiss me. But he refused to participate in my study."

"I can't imagine he's the sort to want to be part of an experiment. Perhaps you should try a different course of action."

"What do you recommend?"

"Do you think he shares your attraction?"

"I have no idea, but he did stare at my mouth several times the other day."

Jess smiled coyly. "I'd say yes, he shares your attraction."

Jess took another cake and slowly nibbled it as she looked toward the window. After she'd finished the cake, she fixed Kat with a determined stare. "You're both here in the same house. I'm sure we can contrive to ensure the two of you are alone. Leave it to me—to get you alone together, that is. The rest, my dear, is up to you. I'd say you need to hone your flirtation skills very quickly."

"Now? Today?" Heat flushed her body, and she knew at least part of it was a sudden anxiety. She typically only felt that when she was overwhelmed in a crowd of people, when the noise and heat became too much.

"It's the perfect opportunity. You're both here, and you have an accomplice." Her eyes glowed with anticipation.

"You are the best of friends," Kat said softly before straightening and looking intently toward Jess. "Now teach me how to flirt."

CHAPTER 7

"Something to drink?" Dougal asked as he closed the door to his study behind Lucien.

"Since I'm sure you brought whisky back with you, definitely." Lucien sat in one of the chairs near the hearth.

"It's an excellent batch, if I do say so. I also brought ale from my cousin. His brewing skills are unparalleled."

"Why isn't he supplying the Phoenix Club?"

Dougal laughed. "He can barely keep up with his orders in Edinburgh. I get special family treatment." He winked at Lucien as he came toward him carrying two glasses of whisky. After handing one to Lucien, he sat down.

Lucien raised his glass. "To fatherhood."

"Yes." Dougal flashed a grin before taking a sip.

"Mmm, this is very good," Lucien remarked after taking a drink. He rested his elbow on the arm of the chair and set the glass at the end, keeping his hand around it. "You look completely, besottedly happy."

"I am. It's so unexpected and somewhat overwhelming, if I'm to be honest."

"I can only imagine. It hasn't even been a year since your brother passed."

Everything had changed for Dougal last summer when his brother had died suddenly. Dougal had become the heir and learned his father was suffering from a weakened heart. He'd had to terminate his career with the Foreign Office in order to learn how to be the next Earl of Stirling, something he'd never anticipated. His final mission for the Foreign Office was to pose as the husband of his now-wife, Jessamine, who'd been recruited for her puzzle-solving skills. They'd investigated a pair of purported French spies. Jess had also been tasked with investigating Dougal to make sure he wasn't working against the Foreign Office.

Lucien went on, "I imagine your father is delighted that you and Jess are expecting."

"He is, indeed. It was tough to leave him, but he's planning to come to London in the spring for a couple of months."

"He's doing well, then?"

"Wonderfully, actually. The doctor now says it could be several years before his heart decides to quit."

Grinning, Lucien leaned over and lightly tapped Dougal's knee. "That's fantastic news." They each sipped their whisky. "Does this mean you'll return to the Foreign Office?"

"I'll provide assistance from time to time if they need it, but no, I'm giving my full focus to Jess, my father, Stagfield, and, of course, the babe when it comes. How is your brother enjoying fatherhood?"

"More than should have been possible," Lucien said with a laugh. "Not that I blame him. Robert is an angel—he's taken completely after his mother. Just as you aren't interested in rejoining the Foreign Office in favor of spending more time with your family, Con has been spending less time in meetings. I think he may have given up a committee too. He says he doesn't miss it, but it hasn't been very long."

"I don't miss my work either, but as you say, it hasn't been that long, just a few months, really."

Lucien swirled the whisky in his glass and considered how to phrase his next words. "You know the Foreign Office is somewhat entangled in the Phoenix Club." Dougal was aware of the meetings held there and that people working with the Foreign Office lodged there from time to time. He did *not* know that it actually owned the club, because Lucien was supposed to keep that secret. However, Lucien needed to confide in someone. More than that, he needed help, and no one was better suited than Dougal, who had worked for the Foreign Office. "But I haven't been entirely honest with you as to the extent of their involvement."

Dougal paused in lifting his glass to his mouth, his dark eyes fixing on Lucien. "This sounds serious."

Pressing his lips together, Lucien tamped down the frustration that was nearly ever present when it came to the Foreign Office's control of the club. "I don't own the club outright. I invested money, but the majority came from the Foreign Office in exchange for using the club as they need."

Dougal frowned after swallowing his sip of whisky. "I didn't realize they had a financial interest."

"It's more than that. The two anonymous members? Oliver Kent and Lady Pickering."

"I'd suspected Kent," Dougal said. "But Lady Pickering is a surprise. I confess I'm bothered that I wasn't informed of this. I worked more directly for the Foreign Office than you did. Or so I thought." Dougal had been tasked with conducting investigations on English soil on behalf of the Foreign Office. His primary focus was rooting out spies and cultivating informants.

"You know how they are," Lucien said. "Nobody knows everything about everything."

"That's how they like it."

Lucien scowled. "I keep wondering what it is that I don't know."

"I'm wondering that too," Dougal said with a slow nod. "Beyond this business with the club."

"I met with Kent the other night and it was…odd. No, *he* was odd."

Dougal's brow furrowed. "In what way?"

Shrugging, Lucien lifted his glass toward his mouth. "He was very angry. And he kept averting his eyes from me while we were speaking." He sipped the alcohol, letting it coat his tongue and linger in his mouth before he swallowed.

"That doesn't sound like him," Dougal noted.

"I didn't think so. He's been at this a long time and is typically unruffled. I can't recall that I've seen him truly angry before."

"He was tense after Giraud was killed, likely because he suspected I might be involved since I was the one who found him." Dougal referred to a Frenchman who worked as a courier for the Foreign Office. Dougal went to meet him and discovered his body with his throat slit. Shaken by this and another mission that had gone badly, Dougal had launched his own secret investigation. Ultimately, Kent had found evidence—a coded letter—that Giraud had been working against the Foreign Office for France. It was assumed that someone from the Foreign Office had assassinated him, but they didn't know the assassin's identity.

"But the investigation into his murder was closed before you went to Scotland," Lucien said. "It's been months. I don't think this is due to that."

"You may be right." Dougal shifted in his chair. "Something about that entire situation doesn't sit well with me. It never made sense that Giraud had turned and gone back to France. He despised his homeland and Napoleon in particular. Either I am terrible at gauging people or Giraud was set up to take the blame and murdered by whoever was actually stealing secrets and giving them to the French."

"It never sat well with me that Kent suspected *you*," Lucien said darkly. "Or that he engaged Jess to spy on you."

"That will probably always trouble me." Dougal's expression was grim. "I confess my relationship with Kent will never be what it once was."

"Perhaps that entire situation is what's bothering Kent." But it couldn't be everything. "Or at least part of it. He's still agitated about the club. They insisted I expel Evie entirely, but I refused. Hell, you don't know what happened, do you?"

"I do. Jess and I caught up on the London news on our journey south. I am so sorry Evie's past was exposed." Dougal had known that she was Lucien's paramour. "How is she doing?"

"She's getting married in a few weeks to Lord Gregory Blakemore."

"Is she?" Dougal smiled, his eyes glowing with joy. "I'm so happy for her. And I'm very pleased you refused their edict. What was their reasoning behind the demand?"

"That it would drive members away and affect the club's popularity. That, in turn, would cause problems for the Foreign Office. They need a club that is busy so that people can blend in. They also want certain people on the membership roll. I agreed to try to persuade several who have resigned over the past week to return. If you don't mind, I've a list I'd like to give you to help with that endeavor."

"Happy to do that," Dougal replied. "As much as I can."

As a Black man raised by white parents—Dougal's mother had engaged in an affair with a Black ship's captain, and Dougal's father had eagerly raised Dougal as his own—and the second son of a Scottish earl, Dougal wasn't entirely embraced by the ton. But that was what made him perfectly suited for the Phoenix Club. He was precisely the sort of member Lucien wanted in his club. "You're the heir now. I'm confident you will be welcomed by everyone."

"Somehow I doubt that," Dougal said wryly. "I'm glad Evie won't be leaving."

"It's not going to be easy, but things will calm. Back to Kent and this Giraud business," Lucien said. "Should we continue investigating his death?" He'd helped Dougal look into the matter—or tried to anyway. He'd attempted to gain access to reports or documents having to do with Giraud and stolen secrets, but there hadn't been anything to find. Or, perhaps more accurately, those things weren't available to him.

"As far as Kent was concerned, the matter was solved. He had Jess decipher a coded message in which Giraud admitted to creating false messages and destroying what had really been delivered from France." Dougal turned his gaze toward the hearth, his eyes narrowing. He was quiet a long moment, clearly thinking, and Lucien didn't want to interrupt him. Finally, he shifted his focus back to Lucien. "What if the coded message was fake?"

Lucien's pulse gathered speed. "Created by the real turn-coat within the Foreign Office?"

"It's possible, isn't it?"

"We need to find out who murdered Giraud."

"Yes, I think we must." Dougal tapped his finger against his whisky glass. "I wonder if that's why Kent is upset. Perhaps he's determined the message was fake."

"That's also possible. Should we just ask him?"

Dougal stared at him in mock outrage. "You can't mean to use explicit communication with someone in the Foreign Office?"

Lucien chuckled. "I think it's time we do. But perhaps I shouldn't involve you in this."

"Oh, I'm already involved. If I can prove Giraud's innocence, which I'm growing more and more inclined to believe, it's the least I can do for the poor man. He served England well. And he was a friend," Dougal added softly. He lifted his glass and took a swig.

Joining in the silent toast, Lucien sipped his whisky. There was still more to reveal. "I've something else to share: my father is aware of the Foreign Office's involvement in the club." He saw the flicker of unease in Dougal's eyes and knew immediately that his friend had known. "*This* is what I didn't know, what was kept from me by the Foreign Office. Hell. And of course you weren't permitted to tell me."

Dougal's gaze was apologetic. "The duke has been involved there for years, but he took a step back after you were sent home from Spain."

"Why?" Lucien thought of his father's disappointment when he'd returned to England after suffering a wound. Honestly, the injury hadn't been serious enough to warrant Lucien's discharge, and perhaps that alone had been the reason for his father's disdain.

But now that Lucien knew his father had ties to the Foreign Office, he had to wonder what he knew. Lucien's wound had resulted from helping his friend Max, who'd attacked a small group of French soldiers. Max had wanted revenge because they'd killed the woman he'd planned to marry—and she'd also been carrying his child. He'd gone mad with rage and pain, and Lucien had pursued him, ultimately saving Max's life. Then he'd lied to protect Max, saying they'd suspected the soldiers had stolen intelligence. He'd planted a letter on one of the dead, which had confirmed Lucien's "suspicions."

Max and Lucien had both been wounded and were seen

as heroes. They were sent home to England, where Lucien had continued to work for the Foreign Office reviewing reports and coordinating investigations, such as the ones Dougal conducted. Later, Kent had approached him about finding a place in London that could be used for clandestine activities. Lucien had conceived of the club—something he'd also wanted to do as an option for those who wouldn't or couldn't join one of the established membership clubs—and suggested it to Kent. That was how the Phoenix Club had been born.

Was Lucien's father somehow aware of the truth behind what had happened with Max in Spain? Was that why he loathed his middle child?

It couldn't be that, for the duke had found fault with Lucien for as long as he could remember.

"I don't know why he retreated from active service," Dougal answered. "If I did, I'd tell you."

"Like you told me about his involvement?" Lucien waved his hand. He wasn't angry. "I know why you didn't. It's why I didn't tell you everything to do with the club." He looked directly into Dougal's eyes. "But I am now. So, if there's anything else you'd like to share, I'd ask you to do it now."

"I've told you everything I know, and I'll keep you apprised of everything I learn. We are in this together." He gave Lucien an earnest stare.

Lucien nodded. "I'll do the same. I'm not going to blindly follow their directives anymore. I was happy to use the club to help them, and the truth was that I couldn't have financed the endeavor at its current level without their support."

"Have you considered buying them out?" Dougal asked.

"Yes, but how would I do that? I don't have the funds." He flinched. "In the interest of full disclosure, I'll tell you—and only you—that I went to my father to ask for the money. I didn't even get the request out before he refused. He said I wouldn't be allowed to buy them out, even if I had the money."

Dougal grimaced. "I should have realized that, of course. But you'd still allow them to use it as they have been, so why should it matter if you own it outright?"

"Because then they can't direct anything, such as whom we invite. The irony is that everyone thinks I've the final say about members, but I absolutely do not." When it truly mattered, anyway. He'd never been denied a potential member, but he'd also been instructed to invite a good number of people, some of whom he would not have chosen as they didn't align with the mission of the club.

"I can see why you'd want that freedom. But perhaps you can come to a new agreement with the Foreign Office."

"Not so long as Kent is my superior in this. He wanted to force me to remove Evie, but I explained that they'd have to remove me too and my departure would ruin the club faster than anything."

Dougal blew out a breath into a near whistle. "I can't imagine he liked hearing that."

"He did not. He told me not to push too hard, then I agreed to try to convince some of the resignations to return."

"Does that include the Hargroves?" Dougal asked. "I confess I was quite glad to hear Lady Hargrove would no longer be a patroness."

"We agreed that their return would cause more harm than good, so they are thankfully gone forever."

"Excellent." Dougal finished his whisky and sat forward, setting his elbows on his knees. "This is all troubling, however. There seems to be something going on at the Foreign Office."

"I agree, which is why I think investigating Giraud's murder is the best place to start. That's when you noticed things began to get...strange?"

"Yes."

"I wonder if my father knows anything?" Lucien snorted.

Dougal arched a brow. "Perhaps you should ask him."

They looked at each other a moment, then burst into laughter. A knock on the door interrupted their amusement. Dougal called out, "Yes?"

The butler opened the door enough to peer around it. "Your presence is requested in the drawing room, Lord Fallin."

Dougal stood. "Is everything all right?"

"I didn't notice any trouble, my lord. Lady Fallin simply asked you attend her."

Setting his whisky glass down on his desk, Dougal glanced toward Lucien. "Do you mind waiting?"

"Not at all. There's more whisky, I presume?"

Dougal flashed him a grin, then departed the study, leaving the door ajar. Lucien tossed back the rest of his drink, then rose to pour more.

The soft click of the door latching drew him to turn. "You can't be back so quick—" The rest of the word fell out of his mouth as he took in the person who'd entered. Not Dougal. *Kat.*

"What are you doing here?" Lucien asked, darting a look at the closed door.

"Jess needed to speak with Fallin about something, so I decided to take advantage of you being alone. There are things we need to discuss." She sauntered toward him, her hips twitching in an odd way. She blinked at him several times. What was she doing?

"Are there?" Lucien asked. "I thought we'd covered everything at the park."

She kept moving in his direction until she was close enough that he caught her lavender scent. "Not at all. I continue to make observations and learn things, which necessitates I query you—since you are my only male informant. How else am I to complete my research? Unless you've thought of a rake who might help me instead. I've decided it's simply imperative that I kiss someone." She parted her lips and did the blinking thing again.

He realized she was trying to appear seductive. She wasn't very good at it. Not that it mattered, because her mere proximity was playing merry hell with his resolve not to touch her. Christ, they were alone in a room with the door closed. This couldn't be borne.

"This is inappropriate," he said, his voice higher than it usually sounded, at least to his ears.

"In speaking with Jess today, I've learned there are different kinds of kisses. It may be that Hickinbottom was just very bad at it."

"I believe I indicated that as well."

"You did." She took a step closer so that she was directly in front of him. He could reach out and pull her against him, eliminating the few inches that separated them. "I'd like to kiss someone who is not. Bad at it, I mean."

Lucien swallowed. Dammit, his heart was pounding, and his cock was actually beginning to harden. This was very, very dangerous.

Kat put her hand on his arm—above his elbow, he noted. "I've also learned that I may actually feel attracted to you. But I can't be sure unless you kiss me. We have just a few minutes alone here, and I'm hoping you could—"

"Absolutely not." He shook his head rather violently, hoping he could toss the lust out of his brain.

She pouted, putting her lush pink lips on full, kissable display. "I'm not asking you to seduce me. Just a simple kiss. You don't even have to use your tongue."

A low groan vibrated in Lucien's throat.

"I just need to do this small bit of research," she continued. She glanced toward the door. "But we're running out of time. I need to leave before Fallin returns."

Some small part of Lucien's brain registered that Jess had to be in on this little scheme, but the rest of him didn't care about anything but providing what Kat needed.

And what they both wanted.

"You think you're attracted to me?" Again, his voice was too high. Too agitated. Too desperate. "Why?"

"Because when I look at you, my chest pinches and my heart beats faster. I feel rather...breathless. Jess says that sounds like attraction. My hope is that if you kiss me, I'll be able to confirm it. Or, perhaps you'll kiss me and I'll be as thoroughly disgusted as I was with Hickinbottom, which will confirm that I am some sort of aberration. It's not as if people haven't thought that—"

"*Stop.*" Lucien did what he'd imagined a moment earlier and grasped her waist, pulling her toward him. Her chest collided with his. "Just stop," he whispered in the second before his lips touched hers.

CHAPTER 8

*E*verything happened so quickly, but Kat tried to separate each moment, to process what was happening for maximum information gathering. But it was too much. Too fast. Too devastating. She simply couldn't think as she ought.

The second his hand touched her waist, her breath rushed from her lungs and shivers spread up her spine and down the backs of her legs. Then her chest met his, and there were more sensations spreading over her, making her...*tingle* in the oddest places. Well, not odd if she thought about it, which she absolutely could *not* right now.

When his mouth met hers, she knew instantly it was not going to be like Hickinbottom. It was as if lightning had struck, but not the kind that would electrify her in a painful and possibly lethal way. This lightning was bright and wondrous, and it gave her a soaring sensation she'd never experienced, as if she could touch the sky.

Or heaven, if she believed such a place existed.

Oh, it existed, and it was right here in Lucien's arms. His lips moved over hers, coaxing her to do the same to him. She didn't stand motionless—that hadn't ever been her intent. She was a willing participant in this study.

Lucien slid his mouth from hers and kissed along her cheek and jaw until he reached her ear. "You're thinking about this too much. I can hear your mind churning."

He was right. "It's hard not to."

"Don't think. Just feel." He suckled—suckled!—her earlobe before turning to her mouth to kiss her again. He kept one hand on her lower back, holding her to him, while his other hand cupped her nape.

Kat wondered if she ought to do something with her hands. The one was still on his upper arm while the other hung pointlessly at her side.

Don't think. Just feel.

Banishing her thoughts, Kat allowed herself to sink into him. She closed her eyes as his lips molded to hers, and she relaxed her body. The moment she did that, he slipped his tongue into her mouth. Lightning struck a second time, sending a cascade of heat and longing through her. This was arousal, she was sure of it.

Don't think. Just feel.

She gripped his arm and slid her other hand beneath his coat to clutch at his side. He was warm and solid, muscular. She became aware of everywhere they touched, including the way his hips pressed against hers.

Don't think. Just feel.

He smelled of sandalwood and spice. His tongue glided along hers, teaching her how to take and give pleasure. It was all so simple, and yet the sensations were anything but. Her body thrummed with…desire.

His fingers pressed gently into her, both crushing and cradling her at the same time. She felt revered and cherished. Then his tongue took on a more conquering stroke, driving into her mouth, and she suddenly felt ravished and desperate. Her entire body was aflame.

He dragged his thumb behind her ear and swept it up to her jaw, gliding the pad along her flesh. She couldn't breathe, and she didn't care. She'd never felt such wonder, such bliss. Her legs were weak, and she tightened her hold on him.

The kiss softened, his tongue gentling as he pulled back. His lips left hers briefly only to return as he shifted his head slightly. A sound from outside the study permeated her trance.

Lucien stepped back, and Kat finally understood how it was possible to swoon. Her legs were indeed weak from passion, and she started to crumple to the floor. His arms came around her once more, and he brought her back up.

"How embarrassing," she murmured.

"Shh." Lucien turned his head toward the door and stood stock-still. All was quiet save the sounds of their rapid breathing. Kat felt as though she'd run from the stables at Warefield to the house and back again.

Belatedly, she realized they might be in danger of being caught. She glanced at the door, but it remained closed.

Lucien looked down at her. "Are you all right?"

"Did I swoon?" She clutched at his biceps, which was where she'd grabbed hold of him after he'd kept her from hitting the floor. "Do men ever swoon? I should study that too. It's the strangest sensation to have your lower half feel as though it isn't even attached to you. I thought I might be flying, but that's silly—"

Lucien's lips were on hers again, and the spark within her was instantaneous—if it had ever diminished in the short time between kisses. This time, she put her tongue in *his* mouth.

He groaned softly as he hauled her against him again, holding her to him with a savage intensity that burned straight through her. Kisses could be many things, she realized. This one was dark and forbidden. Utterly delicious.

She moved her hands up to his shoulders and pressed her body into his, eager for whatever contact she could find. There was an urgency within her, a desperation to feel more. To feel until she reached some...end. What was that word? Completion. Yes, she wanted completion. With him.

His mouth left hers. "Can you stand?" he asked, sounding hoarse.

"Are you asking whether I'm going to swoon again? I don't think so. But why did you stop kissing me?"

He shifted his gaze down to hers. She'd never seen his eyes darker or more intense. They seemed to reflect the pure passion she felt in her bones.

"Because this is madness. You need to go. I shouldn't have kissed you again after that noise outside the door." He let her go, keeping his hands near her arms, clearly waiting to see if she would topple over. "Hell, I shouldn't have kissed you the first time."

"I'm fine," she said in reference to his positioning. "I can't go yet. I have more questions now."

He gaped at her. "You can't think *this* is the time?"

"Fine. I'll go upstairs and write them down in my notebook so I can ask you another time."

"You brought your notebook here?" He wiped his hand down the side of his face. His eyes narrowed briefly. "Does Jess know about this?" He shook his head. "Never mind. You need to go. *Now.*"

Lucien moved to the door and started to open it, giving her no choice but to leave.

She took a deep breath, but her pulse was still faster than normal. "I'm going. But we aren't finished."

"We need to be." He spoke through gritted teeth.

Kat stared at his mouth. His lips were darker, likely from

their kissing. She felt a new swell of arousal. Then she smiled because it was so wonderful to know what that felt like. And to acknowledge that she wasn't an aberration after all. At least not about that.

"But I'm not satisfied," she said, walking toward him.

"No, I can't imagine you are." He inclined his head rather forcefully toward the door.

Exhaling, Kat left the study. Before she walked away, she heard him say, his voice low and sensual. "Neither am I."

Kat carefully returned the way she'd come, using a route that Jess had said would keep her from encountering Fallin. Jess would want to hear if their endeavor was successful, and Kat would spill every detail. There were questions Jess could likely answer, such as what the persistent throbbing between her legs was all about. She knew it had to do with her sex, of course, but what would ease that sensation? Or would it eventually go away on its own? She had to think it had something to do with the completion part of the event.

One thing was certain: more research was required. And it had to be conducted with Lucien. Introducing another subject at this point would ruin the experiment. Furthermore, what if Kat only felt arousal for *him*? Well, that was another question to pose and potentially answer at a later date. First, she was intent on finishing *this*. With him.

She reasoned that they both needed satisfaction. Surely Lucien couldn't argue with that?

~

*L*ight and laughter greeted Lucien as he walked into Edgemont House in the heart of Mayfair. Lord and Lady Edgemont typically held one of the first balls of the Season. This year, they'd expanded their guest list, but

Lucien noted that they'd invited members of the Phoenix Club who weren't regularly included in balls thrown by Society's finest, which the Edgemonts were. Perhaps Lady Edgemont felt inclined to do so now that she was a patroness of the club. Whatever the reason, Lucien was glad to be at a gathering where he felt nearly as comfortable as at the Phoenix Club. Still, he'd be glad to be on his way back there after making his appearance.

He was on edge, and he wanted to say it was because of the club and the Foreign Office, but he knew that wasn't the entire problem. It had been two days since he'd lost his senses completely and kissed his best friend's sister.

Two days during which he'd relived every caress, every breath, every beat of desire. Two days during which he'd chastised himself for his exceedingly poor judgment and utter recklessness. Two days during which he'd endlessly wondered whether he would have the opportunity to do it again. And if so, *when*.

It seemed his senses had still not entirely returned.

After greeting his hosts, Lucien made his way to the gaming room, though he wasn't interested in playing. He was avoiding the ballroom, where he'd almost certainly run into Kat. But why was he even here if he had no intention of going to the ballroom?

Because he was showing support for one of his new patronesses. He also knew it was better if he appeared in Society as usual. People would theoretically be less inclined to talk about him or the club when he was standing right in front of them.

He needed—no, he wanted—to act as though nothing was wrong, that the Phoenix Club was as spectacular as ever. And dammit, it was.

And *that* was where his focus needed to be—on the club and dealing with the Foreign Office, including the investigation into Giraud's death. Not on a certain dark-haired, blue-eyed siren intent on his complete surrender.

"Lord Lucien, may I have a word?" Lord Edgemont approached, the center of his forehead pleated with concern. A white man with receding dark hair flecked with gray, Edgemont's face was round and cheerful. He could typically be counted on to laugh and spread good humor.

"Certainly." Lucien followed him to a corner of the room where it was quieter.

"I do appreciate you coming tonight," Edgemont said. "Lady Edgemont is so glad to be a patroness of the Phoenix Club."

Lucien smiled. "And we are glad to have her."

The pleats in Edgemont's forehead deepened. "I confess I am concerned about the scandal surrounding Mrs. Renshaw. Lady Edgemont likes her very much, of course, but it's still a scandal, and I don't particularly care to have my wife associated with it. I'm sorry to have to say that." He actually looked as if he felt a bit ashamed, his face turning pink and his eyes shifting with discomfort.

"I can understand your worry," Lucien said evenly. "I think you know the rest of the story about Mrs. Renshaw—that her father was a French chevalier, and she is to wed Lord Gregory Blakemore next month."

Edgemont blinked at Lucien. "I didn't know that about her father, actually."

Damn, Lucien realized that was another aspect they should be publicizing. It was ridiculous that her pedigree should potentially save her reputation, but that was the framework upon which Society was built. Who you were and where you came from were of vital importance. "As it happens, her father is now here in England. I'm confident you'll meet him at some point."

"How extraordinary. But how tragic that he abandoned his family. Where has he been all this time?"

Lucien gritted his teeth. "In a French prison since the Terror."

Edgemont's blue eyes rounded. "Good heavens! That is indeed tragic. I'm so pleased he was able to be reunited with his daughter."

"As you can see, Mrs. Renshaw has had to make some... difficult choices due to her unfortunate, and yes tragic, circumstances. She's been a wonderful patroness and manager of the Phoenix Club, and I should hate for her life to be upended a second time. I'm sure you can imagine how awful it was for her family to be separated when they fled from France."

"Yes, yes, of course. More people should know about this. I think they would be much more amenable to her presence."

It grated on Lucien's nerves that Evie should have to explain herself, but perhaps her story should be shared widely. Lucien would discuss it with Ada, who knew Evie well. Plus, he'd need to write to Evie. He wouldn't publicize the details of her life without her permission.

"I'll keep that in mind," Lucien said with a mild smile. He was eager to move away from this conversation. "I think I should go to the ballroom now. I told my sister that I'd look for her."

"Of course. I do appreciate your time," Edgemont said.

Lucien took his leave from the gaming room but didn't go directly to the ballroom. Instead, he stopped by a men's retiring room, which was really just an excuse for male guests to obtain a variety of liquor instead of the ratafia in the ballroom.

However, before Lucien could acquire a glass of whatever was on offer, a man called Pawley strode toward him. Short, with dark blond hair and small brown eyes, the man wore an expression of extreme distaste. Lucien braced himself because Pawley was a friend of Lord Hargrove's.

"You've a nerve to show up here," Pawley said with a sneer.

"I was invited," Lucien said calmly despite the riot of emotion inside him. He needed to keep control of his anger. Pawley was one of the members who'd resigned whom the Foreign Office wanted Lucien to convince to return. "And good evening to you."

"Save your niceties for someone who cares about your... nonsense. You are an embarrassment and should not be included in Polite Society. I don't care if your father is the Duke of Evesham."

Lucien had to stop himself from saying, *"And he doesn't care that I'm his son."*

Pawley continued, "You've ruined the Phoenix Club completely. What were you thinking involving your former paramour in anything to do with it? You—and she—are a disgrace. And to send Aldington to persuade me to return?" He let out a caustic laugh. "I wouldn't go back to the Phoenix Club if it were the last membership club in London. Furthermore, I'll do everything I can to ensure the club is seen for what it is: a den of scandal and impropriety!"

Lucien flexed his hands in an effort to ease the tension teeming through him. But he didn't need to come up with a response, because Pawley stalked from the room.

Ignoring the shocked stares of the other gentlemen, Lucien went to a footman and asked for a brandy. He downed it quickly, then returned the empty glass. No one spoke to him as he made his way from the room.

Instead of going to the ballroom, Lucien found a door to the garden and went outside. The late February night was on the warm side, with just the barest hint of spring in the air. He took a deep breath to try to calm his ire. After several

minutes, he felt marginally better and decided that was as
good as things were going to get. Turning, he started back
toward the house, but stopped short when he saw a white
lady standing just outside the door.

Lady Pickering sauntered toward him. A fashionable
turban with a red feather covered her dark hair. As she
moved closer, a lantern brought her face into the light. She
wore light cosmetics on her ivory skin, and her green-blue
eyes sparkled like gemstones. "Lucien, it isn't like you to
skulk."

"Is that what you think I'm doing?"

"Yes. And you need to be in the ballroom, holding your
head high and showing everyone that you—and the Phoenix
Club—will outlast this...unpleasantness."

It seemed she knew what had just happened. "You've
already heard about Pawley's outburst?"

"Pawley is crowing about it to anyone who will listen.
He's telling everyone how he put you in your place, and since
you have yet to be seen in the ballroom, he's adding that you
likely ran back to your failing club with your tail between
your legs."

Normally, this sort of behavior would provoke Lucien to
laugh. But the idea that the Phoenix Club could fail was all
too real.

Lady Pickering frowned. "Your silence is concerning.
Where is your usual witty rejoinder? You can't think to allow
Pawley to continue as he is. Be strong, this will pass."

"Will it? Or have I committed an unforgiveable sin in
hiring my former paramour?"

"To some, yes, you have. But you don't care about those
people, nor do you want them at the club. Or am I wrong
about that?" She was speaking as if she weren't part of the
very entity dictating whom he had to include.

"Does it matter what I want? The Foreign Office—and you—have made it clear that I need to play by your rules."

"Except you aren't. You are keeping Mrs. Renshaw, and we must deal with the repercussions. I'm here to tell you that skulking in gardens is not how you deal with this. Honestly Lucien, you are not yourself."

No, he wasn't. Between the club and the Foreign Office, his father, and whatever was happening with Kat, he was decidedly out of sorts. "How should I deal with it, then?"

"Go to the ballroom and laugh. Dance with someone. Show everyone that you are completely unbothered by Pawley."

"He said he won't come back to the club and will do his best to ensure others stay away." Those weren't his precise words, but that was most definitely his intent. "Doesn't that upset you? I was instructed to bring him back to the club."

Lady Pickering exhaled. "Clearly, that isn't happening. So, you must do your best to mitigate whatever damage he's trying to cause. And don't forget that people like you far more than they do him. Why don't you try to identify some new people to invite?"

"How about you? Your invitation is two years old now. I don't understand why you don't accept it. No one is ever going to know your association with the entity behind the club because no one knows there *is* an entity behind the club."

"I like being an observer in this case. Besides, it supports my role as a discerning member of the ton that I haven't accepted an invitation."

He countered. "But it would help the club if you did."

She shrugged. "I will do so if and when it becomes necessary. I've a reputation to uphold, Lucien, even if it isn't entirely reflective of who I am." She lowered her voice to a gravelly whisper. "You know I'd love to be there on Tuesday nights. Now, go to the ballroom."

As she pivoted, her persimmon skirts caught the light before she made her way back to the house. Lucien watched her go and wondered what it was that she knew and he didn't, or what he knew and she didn't. Or was she high enough in the Foreign Office that she knew everything? Was anyone that high save Castlereagh? Certainly not Lady Pickering. Her involvement had always seemed nominal to Lucien.

He couldn't help but think he was viewing the Foreign Office in a new light since learning his father was aware of his arrangement with the Phoenix Club. He would actually have liked to separate himself from the Foreign Office entirely, but doing so would mean walking away from the Phoenix Club too.

There had to be a solution. Lucien couldn't continue to run the club looking over his shoulder. Groaning in frustration, he cut through the garden toward the doors to the ballroom.

And ran straight into another woman. Only this one was far more dangerous.

Kat cocked her head. "I thought that was you."

Suddenly, all he could think of was dragging her into a shadowy corner where he would kiss her until they both forgot how to breathe. His mood, already in danger of absolute blackness, plummeted even further.

"Kat, I don't have time for you right now."

She blinked at him, then arched a brow. "You seem rather upset. I can think of one thing that might relax you."

"If you think I'm going to kiss you in the middle of a ball, you are sorely mistaken. No matter how badly we both want to."

Why the hell had he said that? Because whenever he was

in her presence, he increasingly lost the ability to maintain his wits. His body took over and would force his complete surrender.

"We aren't in the middle of a ball. We're in the garden, and no one knows we're out here together. Seems to me that it's the perfect time and place to kiss, particularly given—how did you say it?—how badly we both want to."

He almost did it. The urge to pull her into the darkness and ease himself was almost overpowering. But he wouldn't do that to her. She wasn't ready for total sensual consumption, nor should he be the one introducing her to such things.

"Kat, for your own good, I'm going to decline. Now, if you'll excuse me." He started to walk past her, but she snagged his arm, her hand above his elbow and her fingers digging through the layers of his clothing.

He knew in that moment he was lost.

CHAPTER 9

"*F*or my own good?" Kat asked. "What good is that exactly? You're helping me with my research. Plus, it's quite pleasurable. You refusing me is the opposite of my own good."

"Until we're caught together, and your already-teetering reputation falls entirely off a cliff."

Kat took her hand from his arm. "My reputation is fine."

"You seem to forget what happened in Gloucestershire. Are you aware that Hickinbottom's parents will be here this Season for his younger sister to attend the Marriage Mart?" Lucien made a sound in his throat. "Never mind. It's not my place to discuss it with you."

"Ruark told me they are coming, but he also said we'll avoid them. I'm not concerned. Why are you? In fact, why are you even aware of that?" Kat suddenly knew. "Ruark asked you to watch out for me." Then she laughed.

Lucien narrowed his eyes at her. "What is so amusing?"

"That my brother would ask you to keep an eye on me. It's rather like putting the fox on guard over the hen house, don't you think?"

His features darkened, and she could see that he was not in a good mood at all. "Perhaps." The word cut from his lips in a sharp clip.

"What's wrong?" she asked. "You're clearly upset."

"As I said, I don't have time to get into it. I need to go into the ballroom. In fact, you can aid me by dancing with me."

She made a face. "I've already danced two sets. That's my limit, I'm afraid."

"Well, thank you for your assistance."

"All right, I'll dance with you." She'd never seen him so out of sorts. "I suppose it's the least I can do after the help you've given me. On that note, I still have questions prompted by our kissing the other day."

"Don't you understand that I can't help you anymore? You shouldn't even be doing this *research*."

Now she was angry. "Fine, I'll find someone else to help me." She spun on her heel, but he grabbed her elbow.

"You can't do that."

She looked back at him and pulled her arm free. "You can't stop me."

"I'll tell Ruark what you're doing." He'd hesitated before he said it, which made her think he wouldn't really.

"Then you'll have to admit that you kissed me." She pivoted to face him, crossing her arms over her chest. "And if you don't, I'll tell him. What do you think will happen then?"

He growled at her. Like an animal. It was actually somewhat arousing. She could now identify that sensation with ease. Indeed, now that she'd kissed Lucien, she felt a deeper, more visceral desire for him. She thought about him almost constantly. It was almost annoying at times because she had things to do.

"I think he'll suggest we marry, which neither of us wants."

He was right about that. Kat had never wished she were

an older spinster more than in that moment. Then she could simply propose a discreet but torrid affair that wouldn't get either of them in trouble.

Couldn't they still do that if they kept the focus on *discreet*?

"Go on back to the ballroom," Lucien said, sounding suddenly weary. "I've too much occupying my mind, and I don't need you adding to my worries."

That's what she was to him?

Flinching, she uncrossed her arms and spun about, stalking toward the doors to the ballroom. The moment she stepped inside, she felt unsettled. There were so many candles, and it was far warmer than it had been outside. Plus, there was the music and the conversation. It was an absolute crush. Kat had always wondered where that word had come from. It perfectly described how an event like this felt to her. It was as if she were being crushed by the noise and crowd. If people touched her, she'd want to scream. There would definitely be no dancing now.

Hopefully, she could regain her equilibrium. She looked about for Cass, but saw Jess instead. And she was with Lady Pickering.

Jess caught Kat's eye and smiled. There would be no avoiding them now. Was that what Kat hoped to do? Wouldn't it be nice to speak with them? They could reminisce about the time they'd spent with Lady Pickering last summer.

Kat forced a smile and made her way to them. At least they were on the periphery of the ballroom so she could be on the edge of the cacophony.

"Kathleen, you look lovely," Lady Pickering said. She took Kat's hand and bussed her cheek.

Working hard not to pull back from the contact she

didn't want in this moment, Kat clenched her jaw. Thankfully, Lady Pickering didn't keep hold of her hand.

"It's good to see you, Lady Pickering."

"I'm just back from Hampshire this week," the older woman said. "I picked this turban up yesterday. What do you think? It's my first one." She turned her head from side to side.

"It's most elegant," Jess answered. "And that red feather complements your gown perfectly."

Kat wasn't interested in discussing fashion. But then she was struggling to deal with the noise and heat, which made everything more agitating. A group of young ladies walked by them, and their chatter strained Kat's nerves.

"I may as well share my news," Jess said, distracting Kat, for which she was grateful. "Fallin and I are to be parents in the summer."

Lady Pickering's eyes sparked with delight. "How marvelous. I imagine Stirling is thrilled." She referred to Jess's father-in-law. "As I'm sure your parents are as well."

"Yes. My mother is particularly enthusiastic about being grandmother to a future earl."

"With you happily wed, I daresay we must turn our attention to Kathleen." Lady Pickering pivoted toward Kat with an expectant look. "Since you are here tonight, may I assume you are in the market for a husband?"

Kat now wished she'd ignored Jess and walked straight through the ballroom. She'd find a footman and ask him to locate Ruark or Cass—this was the standing plan if Kat needed to leave an event. Then one or both of them would meet her in the entrance hall, and Kat could make her escape. Alas, she'd thought she could recover before she became too agitated. Perhaps Lucien's mood had rubbed off on her.

"Not necessarily," Kat said. "I'm enjoying just observing people."

"Still not sure if Society is for you?" Lady Pickering asked. Kat had said something like that to her last summer in response to why she'd been all but absent from last Season's events. "Plenty of people don't find their spouse in Society. Just look at Jess."

Kat wondered if Lady Pickering could invite her to Hampshire where Kat could happen to encounter Lucien so they could conduct an illicit but *private* affair. Not that Jess and Fallin had conducted a liaison. What *had* happened, exactly? Jess had been vague, and now Kat wanted to know the specifics.

But why? It wasn't as if Lucien would be interested in engaging in any of that sort of behavior with her. He clearly regretted kissing her and didn't want to repeat the occurrence.

Was there something wrong with her? She'd been sure he'd enjoyed it, especially after what he'd said about not being satisfied. Then when she'd met him in the garden tonight, he'd said he'd wanted to kiss her badly. It seemed he was doing everything possible to avoid her and whatever he felt for her.

Hadn't he made his reasons for that clear? If they were caught, it would be a disaster. Well then, they wouldn't get caught. There had to be a way to conduct an affair. Which was precisely what Kat wanted. How else could she fully conduct her research?

Kat realized that Lady Pickering had continued to talk about how and where Kat might find a husband.

"But what if I don't really want one?" Kat said quickly. "What if I'd prefer to be a spinster?"

"That's all right too," Jess said softly, which made Kat think she'd said something wrong. It was time to leave before she completely lost control of herself.

"Will you excuse me?" Kat said. "I need to find the retiring room."

She didn't wait for their responses before threading her way through the ballroom. Someone grazed her arm as she walked, and she nearly elbowed them. Instead, she made a sound that she realized sounded much like Lucien's earlier growl. Did he get overwhelmed like she did? No, of course not. No one did.

Just before she reached the doorway that would take her away from the discord, she encountered a footman. She asked him to please find Lord or Lady Wexford and have them meet her in the entrance hall, and she directed him to move with alacrity.

The footman departed, and Kat walked quickly toward the entrance hall. As she entered the staircase hall, she ran into the one person who was guaranteed to increase her current agitation.

Lucien's eyes widened as he saw her. "Kat, is something wrong?"

How could he tell? She couldn't bother with him now. She needed peace and to be by herself. "Go away, Lucien."

"Please permit me to apologize for earlier." His words were delivered with a sympathetic tone she didn't want to hear in that moment. She didn't want his concern or his company. Keeping her gaze averted from him, she told him to leave her alone. Then she hastened into the entrance hall.

Worried that he might follow her, she began to clench and unclench her muscles, hugging her arms around herself and squeezing for a moment. She did that twice, which was all she could allow without drawing notice from the people filtering through the space. She'd done this to soothe herself for years, but her mother had forbidden her from doing it in front of others. She said it was confusing and strange, that people would think her an aberration.

But then, she was exactly that.

Cass and Ruark came into the entrance hall, their expressions drawn with concern. How Kat hated that. She didn't need their pity or worry. This was a normal occurrence for her, and one that was rectified by removing herself from the environment.

"I'll fetch the coach," Ruark said, leaving Cass with Kat.

"All right?" Cass asked.

"I'm fine," Kat bit out. "This isn't a problem."

"I didn't say it was," Cass said calmly. "I suppose I'm trying to gauge how you're feeling."

Kat understood that her sister-in-law was only trying to help, that she wanted to know whether Kat's situation had reached catastrophic levels. It had not. "I'll be fine, truly. If you and Ruark want to stay, you should. I'll send the coach back for you. I just need quiet."

"Of course." Cass gave her a warm smile. She really was the most wonderful person Ruark could have married. She worked hard to understand Kat and be supportive, in ways Kat's own mother and sisters hadn't.

Ruark returned. "It will be a few minutes unless you want to walk down the street to meet the coach."

"Why don't you do that?" Cass suggested before Kat could respond. She looked to Ruark. "You walk with her and put her in the coach. She doesn't need us to come with her."

Kat wasn't paying close attention to them, at least not visually. But she could hear the unspoken communication. They were very good at that with each other.

"Fine by me," Ruark said. He offered his arm to Kat. "Shall we?"

"Thank you," she murmured. She reached out and briefly touched Cass's arm, then turned and left the house with Ruark.

They were away from the house walking along the line of

coaches parked on the street, when he spoke next. "I hope nothing bad happened. You know you can always talk to me, whether it's now, tomorrow, or in a month."

"I know. And I love you for it."

"I love you too." He fell silent until they reached the coach, and she was never more grateful that he was her brother. He never pushed, and he never expected more than she could give.

He opened the door to the coach and helped her inside, then went to speak with the coachman. When he came back, he looked inside and simply smiled at her.

Then he closed the door, and the coach started forward. She saw that he remained on the pavement until she'd moved out of sight.

CHAPTER 10

"**G**ood afternoon, Lu," Cass said as Lucien made his way into her drawing room. "If you came to see Ruark, he's not here."

"So your butler informed me. As it happens, I came to see you—and Ruark, of course, if he was here."

"This is just a normal social call?" Cass blinked at him. "Without an agenda?"

Lucien laughed as he made his way to the table where she was taking tea. "You make it sound like I never come without a specific purpose."

"It seems that way of late," Cass said. "Which I absolutely understand."

The butler came in with a small tray bearing a teacup for Lucien. He set the cup on the table and poured for Lucien, adding milk and sugar just as Lucien preferred.

"Thank you, Bartholomew."

The butler inclined his head, then departed.

Cass picked up her tea. "You seem in better spirits today."

After sipping his tea, Lucien set his cup down. "Have I

been in a poor mood?" What a bloody disingenuous question to ask his own sister.

"Haven't you? You've seemed tense, which is perfectly reasonable. I'm just glad to see you perhaps relaxing."

"You're not wrong. I have been...tense." And things had reached a climax last night. He'd been in a terrible state of mind and had been rude to Kat. Then he'd encountered her, seen she was in distress, and that had shaken him from his gloom. "Lady Pickering gave me some advice last night, and I took it to heart. I'll have better luck keeping members at the club if I'm not so bloody morose."

Cass laughed. "I would agree. I'm glad she told you that. *I* should have said so."

"Where is Kat?" She was, in fact, the real reason he was calling. He wanted to make sure she was all right. "She seemed out of sorts last night. I hope all is well."

"You saw her at the ball?" Cass's brows lifted briefly. At Lucien's answering nod, she continued, "She wasn't feeling well and left early. Today, she is having an alone day."

"What does that mean?" Lucien helped himself to a biscuit and popped it into his mouth.

"Exactly what it sounds like—she spends the day alone. Primarily. It gives her a chance to recover her...I don't know what to call it." Cass shrugged. "Anyway, she does this from time to time, particularly after she has an...episode like last night."

An *episode*. "What does that mean?"

"She gets overwhelmed. It's akin to how Sabrina feels when she's around people she doesn't know."

"Anxious?" Lucien asked. Sabrina had worked hard to try to feel more comfortable when out in Society. Her anxiety in social situations made her seem aloof at first, but that wasn't the case. Con hadn't realized that about her when they'd first wed because they hadn't been given the chance to get to know one another. Now, they all made a point of ensuring she was comfortable when they were out together. Lucien paid particular mind when she was at the Phoenix Club, though at this point she'd been there enough that she knew precisely where to escape if she needed peace or solitude.

"Yes, but it's more than that. It's the noise and the closeness. It affects her physically and emotionally, which I know sounds strange. Apparently, it was worse when she was younger and could be provoked by a variety of things such as clothing that she didn't like or when she had to stop doing something she enjoyed."

This was all new information for Lucien, but then he didn't know Kat as well as his sister since they lived in the same household. "That must have been difficult for her as a child."

"It was, and for the entire family, or so Ruark says. He wasn't there much, but his mother often gave him an earful. However, things improved as she grew older. I do think their mother was grateful when Kat came to live with us. Particularly since Kat had made it clear she wasn't ready to be married off."

"Mrs. Shaughnessy wanted Kat off her hands," Lucien concluded, feeling a sudden irritation toward Ruark's and Kat's mother.

"It seems that way to me," Cass said quietly. She picked up a biscuit and took a small bite. Then she regarded Lucien with slightly narrowed eyes.

"What?" he could hear her mind turning.

"Why are you interested in Kat?"

Damn. He hadn't meant to draw attention to...whatever was between them. "She's family."

Cass didn't look entirely convinced, but she responded with "Yes, she is," then finished her biscuit.

Why *was* he so interested? He found he wanted to talk to

her about what Cass had told him. He wanted to understand how she'd felt last night and what had driven her to need an entire day of solitude. "Does she truly spend the entire day alone?"

This was almost unimaginable to Lucien, who craved interaction. Running a membership club where he could talk with a variety of people on any given day was bloody paradise.

"Pretty much. She'll see her maid, of course, but sometimes that's all. Occasionally, I'll visit with her. That happens more and more as we've grown closer."

"Have you? Grown close, I mean."

"I think so. It's nice to have a sister. Certainly better than two annoying older brothers."

Lucien grinned. "That's fair." He drank more tea and ate another biscuit and realized he was disappointed that he wasn't going to get to see Kat today. He'd wanted to apologize for his prickliness at the ball.

Yes, he'd been in a horrid mood after Pawley's tirade in the gaming room, and running into Kat had amplified his frustration. Because she provoked him with her bloody research and her tempting mouth. He could ease his frustration with her—he was certain of that. And that made him even *more* agitated.

It was a goddamned problem.

Unless he simply avoided her. *Simply.* He had to keep himself from laughing. He'd been trying to do that and failing rather miserably. How was he to keep from seeing her when she was a member of his sister's household? That was nonsensical as well as impossible. He just had to find a way to stop thinking of kissing her, of helping her conduct her infernal research, of fulfilling both of their deepest carnal desires.

And now he was starting to grow aroused while drinking

tea with his bloody sister. Enough! He was better than this. Wasn't he?

"Papa was asking about you," Cass said.

Lucien was grateful she hadn't noticed his woolgathering. Or if she had, that she hadn't called attention to it. "One would think I would have long grown used to you calling him Papa."

"You never called him that?"

"Not that I can recall. Con doesn't call him that either."

"You're avoiding my question," she said sternly.

"I think you have your mother voice ready," he said with a smirk. "You didn't ask me a question, actually."

She pursed her lips. "You know what I mean. You have no response to Papa asking about you?"

"No."

"Well, he's hoping you'll call on him soon."

Despite their tumultuous relationship, Lucien still paid regular calls on his father. It was just what he'd always done. Not anymore. He could no longer ignore his father's treatment. Why should he subject himself to the man's disdain?

"Tell him that's hopeless. I've nothing to discuss with him." Lucien snagged another biscuit and chewed it rather more vigorously than was necessary.

Cass frowned. "You seem more cheerful today, but I think it's not entirely true. Where is my optimistic, charming brother? Is the situation with the club that dire? I thought you and the others were able to convince some people to return?"

So far, they'd coaxed back ten people. It was better than zero, but would it satisfy the Foreign Office? Dammit, but he was tired of worrying about them. "Some, yes. However, attendance is down." He was worried about the first assembly that was scheduled for Friday. That would undoubtedly set the tone for the Season. Last year, they had been the most popular events in London.

"It's still early in the Season," Cass said. "I'm sure the assembly on Friday will be a crush. Who can resist a Leap Year theme where the women will be asking the men to dance?"

Lucien hoped she was right. He was suddenly in a far worse mood than when he'd arrived. Was it because Cass had brought up the club, or was it because he wasn't able to see Kat?

Whatever the reason, he felt as though a dark cloud had parked directly over his head and would soon send thunder and rain all over him. He quickly finished his tea.

"I must be off." He did, in fact, need to meet Dougal, who'd requested a brief meeting in Grosvenor Square. Lucien leaned over and kissed his sister's cheek.

"Thank you for the visit. It's nice to see you alone once in a while. Think how nice it would be if you and Con and I got together. Just the three of us."

"Good luck prying him from Robert," Lucien said with a chuckle. Then he glanced toward her midsection. "That will be you soon enough."

"But never you?" Cass asked, her eyes glinting with hope.

"That is not my plan." Without a good paternal example, Lucien doubted he could take on the role. He was honestly terrified he'd make a hash of it. "Give my best to Ruark. And to Kat," he added. Hopefully, Cass wouldn't read too much into that either.

Probably she would.

Lucien departed the house and couldn't help glancing up at the façade as he moved along the pavement. He knew precisely where Kat's room was located, and his gaze went directly to her window on the second floor. What was she doing? Was she aware he'd been in the house? That he was looking up at her now?

Shaking out his shoulders, Lucien strode to Grosvenor Square. He was a few minutes early, but kept to the farthest possible point from his father's house situated on the other side of the square near South Audley Street.

Dougal approached him from Grosvenor Street, where he lived. "Are you glowering at Evesham House?" he asked, following Lucien's gaze.

"Not on purpose. I'm afraid it's my natural state when it comes to my father." Not at the house, though. He had many fond memories growing up there with Con and Cass. He turned to Dougal, eager to banish his father from his thoughts. "What news?"

"Not much, I'm afraid, but I did learn some things about, ironically, your father."

"Is that why you wanted to meet here?"

Dougal lifted a shoulder and again glanced toward Evesham House. "I thought you might want to speak with him."

"Doubtful. What did you learn?" Lucien was surprised to find he was almost desperate to know. No, not surprised. Disappointed. He didn't want to care about anything to do with the duke.

"He's no longer associated with the Foreign Office at all, but he was once rather high up. I couldn't discover what he did officially, but he was a trusted officer, from what I can glean. He still has friends there."

"Is that how he knew about the club? Or was his departure recent enough that he was aware?"

"He left several years ago. Right about when you returned from Spain, actually."

That was curious. "I don't suppose you know why?"

"Not specifically, but I had the sense he was either ready to move on or he was leaving to make room for you."

"What does that mean? He gave up his position so I could have one? That doesn't make sense."

"And this is why I thought you might want to speak with him. You could just ask him."

Lucien snorted. "As if he'd answer. I should have realized long ago that he worked for the Foreign Office. He certainly possesses the evasiveness that's required. The arrogance too."

"Well, one might argue you and I are that way too." Dougal grinned.

"One might. But we are not even in the same vicinity as my father when it comes to those traits." Lucien looked back at Evesham House. His father would be home. He liked to spend Sunday afternoons reading. And Cass had said that he wanted to see Lucien…

"I've never seen you this angry with him before," Dougal noted. "Just go. You don't have to stay."

Lucien frowned down at his chest. "But I'm wearing a white cravat." He always wore a garishly colored neckcloth to annoy his father. Except the last time he'd visited, when he'd been hoping for a loan of funds to buy the Phoenix Club from the Foreign Office. That time, he'd worn white as a sort of sign of surrender. It had been utterly futile.

Dougal pulled a puce-colored cravat from his pocket. "I thought of that."

"You can't expect me to change clothes right here?"

"If you and I can't be surreptitious about something like that, we've no business working for the Foreign Office at all."

"Well, you don't anymore," Lucien said tauntingly.

"Stop being an ass, and just slip behind a tree over there and swap out the cravat."

"I'm shit at tying them." It wasn't a lie.

Dougal put his hand to his cheek and rounded his mouth

in faux shock. "You can't possibly visit the duke in a puce-colored cravat that looks as if it was tied by a toddler. What would he think?"

"Oh, give me that!" Lucien snatched the silk from a smirking Dougal. "You're hilarious."

"I think so."

Lucien exhaled, then frowned at Evesham House. "Fine. I'll see what I can find out."

"Here, let's move over to that tree, and I'll just block you from view," Dougal offered.

"How gallant of you. It's the least you can do," Lucien muttered.

With Dougal in position, Lucien turned toward the tree and quickly pulled off his white cravat. He thrust it behind him, expecting Dougal to catch it. Then he did his best to tame the puce silk into some semblance of order.

He turned back to Dougal, who was stuffing the white one into his coat pocket. "Will this suffice?"

Dougal cocked his head to the side, then tugged at the knot Lucien had made. "Good enough. And it will annoy him, so that should please you."

"Immensely." Lucien began to pivot.

"Aren't you going to thank me?" Dougal asked.

Lucien glared at him from the side of his eye. "Not today."

"Fair enough. Good luck!" he called jovially as Lucien stalked toward Evesham House.

He'd make this quick. He'd ask the duke his questions, which the arse wouldn't answer, then he'd leave. His pace slowed as he approached the house. Why was he bothering?

Because his curiosity had the better of him.

Barely knocking before Bender opened the door, Lucien smiled at the butler. "Afternoon, Bender."

"His Grace is in his study."

"Do you want to announce me?" Lucien asked.

Bender gave him a peculiar look, as if Lucien had asked a question that he should know the answer to. "Unless he instructs me otherwise, you and your brother and sister are always welcome."

"I wasn't sure that was still the case." Lucien gave his hat and gloves to the butler, then made his way to the duke's study.

The door was half-open, which indicated he was busy but could be interrupted. Lucien sometimes forgot how much of Evesham House was run on a series of rules and routines—all centered around the duke.

He sat in his favorite chair near the hearth where a blazing fire crackled, a book in his hand. He didn't look in Lucien's direction.

"Lucien," he said.

"Father. Cass said you were asking about me."

"Did she?" Of course he wouldn't admit it.

"Yes, but you can pretend you didn't. Will you also pretend our last conversation didn't happen, or may we discuss it?" Lucien moved to stand behind another chair that faced his father's. He wouldn't sit.

Now the duke looked up from his book as he lowered it to his lap, closing it around his finger, which held his place. "Sit."

"I'd rather stand, thank you. Sitting is so...sedentary."

His father's gaze locked on the puce cravat, and Lucien decided he would do more than thank Dougal, he would send the man a bloody room full of flowers. "I preferred the white."

"Really? I think this one makes me look robust."

"If you came to be snide, you may go on your merry way."

"I came because you asked about me and because I want to know how you knew about the Foreign Office's involvement in the Phoenix Club. It's my understanding that you left around the time I returned from Spain. Which tells me you knew precisely why I came home and that I hadn't actually 'squandered' my military career—I believe that's the word you like to use—but had taken on a different role working for the Foreign Office. Did you know I was spying for them in Spain?"

"Who do you think arranged that?"

Lucien should have sat down. Instead, he gripped the back of the chair, his fingertips digging into the fabric. "I'm not sure I can believe anything you say." Nor did he want to. How could he reconcile a father who'd seen him promoted to spy with the father who routinely said he was a wastrel and a disappointment?

The duke shrugged. "Then don't."

"Why did you leave the Foreign Office?"

"Because I'd passed on the mantle to you."

Lucien stared at him as myriad emotions rioted inside him. "You make it sound as if you groomed me for a role, then happily handed it down. I am not Constantine."

"No, you are not. And you've disappointed me yet again with this Phoenix Club nonsense. You should never have hired your former paramour, and you most certainly should not have allowed her to stay."

The emotions hardened into one—fury. Lucien worked to keep it in check. Losing his temper in front of the duke was a sure way to increase the man's disapproval. "We will never agree on that point. Evie is as dear to me as family. Dearer than some, in fact." Lucien took satisfaction in the very faint shadow that passed over the duke's features.

"You'd choose her over your country."

"Not at all. I can still conduct the Foreign Office's business in the same manner at the club. I really don't understand the fuss over this."

"You've lost members, and attendance is down. The

arrangement you have requires a certain membership and a bustling environment. Without those, the entire scheme is a failure."

"Not everything is as black and white as you seem to always make it." Lucien flexed his hand against the chair. "We've regained some members and will continue to do so. By the time Lady Evangeline returns, people will have all but forgotten, especially if I make it known that she had recently been reunited with her father—a French chevalier. Really, Father, I'm surprised you had anything to do with that when you could have let her languish in scandal. This will only help her cause."

"I'm not heartless, regardless of what you think," the duke said coldly, in utter contradiction to what he said. "And I don't believe it will help her as much as you think it will, but good luck to all of you."

Lucien was surprised at how forthcoming the duke was being. Where was his typical obliqueness? "Why did you bring them together? I simply can't make my brain understand your involvement in such a heartwarming and generous endeavor."

Frowning, the duke glowered at Lucien from beneath his thick dark brows. "I was doing a favor for a friend when I stepped in for Witney after he died suddenly."

"Since when do you do favors?"

"When they are owed."

Hell, now Lucien wanted to know why he'd owed Witney a favor, but he suspected he'd exhausted his father's capacity for sharing. "I'd ask what you did to owe Witney a favor, but I suspect that's something you prefer to keep to yourself."

"He wanted to court your mother, but I asked him not to. If she'd had a choice between me and him, she would certainly have chosen the Marchioness of Witney."

Lucien had to work to keep his mouth from falling open.

This was perhaps the most personal thing his father had ever shared with him. He didn't know how to respond.

"Lucien, do what the Foreign Office wants. If they ask you again to expel the Frenchwoman, do it. Or compromise. Allow her to retain her membership, but give up her duties."

He would never do that, but he wasn't going to argue with his father about it anymore. He was too thrown by all he'd learned today. "I'll let you get back to your book." Lucien started to turn, but hesitated. "I wish you would trust me."

"*I* wish you would make better choices."

"Just because they aren't what you would do doesn't make them bad," Lucien said softly. He walked to the door.

"Have you ever considered that's how I know they're bad?" the duke muttered.

Lucien turned his head, not entirely sure what his father had meant. Was he trying to say that he was speaking from experience? That he'd made choices he thought were poor?

The duke was reading his book once more, which meant the interview was over. Good, because Lucien didn't think he could handle any more from him today.

As it was, he was going to need a good stiff drink.

Or ten.

CHAPTER 11

$\mathcal{K}$at went downstairs to the breakfast room on Monday morning feeling refreshed after a long, excellent night of sleep. Spending the previous day in her room reading and relaxing had been just what she needed to restore herself.

Cass was seated at the breakfast table perusing a newspaper while she nibbled on a piece of toast. She looked up as Kat entered. "Good morning! You look well."

"Thank you. I am feeling much better." Kat went to the sideboard and loaded her plate with her favorite foods, then sat down at the table with Cass. "I appreciate you and Ruark leaving me be when I need to be alone." That had often been a problem with her family back home at Warefield. Her mother expected her to feel just splendid after becoming overwhelmed, even if she'd had an extraordinary external outburst, which hadn't happened this time. Actually, her mother expected her to stop permitting herself to become overwhelmed. Unfortunately, it wasn't that easy. But Kat *had* learned to manage her reactions better as well as how to best recover.

"We want you to always feel comfortable here." Cass gave her a warm smile. "You needn't live up to any standards but your own."

Kat slathered fig jam on her toast and took a large bite. Too large a bite, her mother would say. After swallowing, she asked, "Is Ruark riding this morning?"

Cass nodded.

Kat typically rode with Ruark a couple of times each week, usually on Tuesdays and Fridays, weather permitting. In the country, they rode together nearly every day. Riding never failed to make Kat feel restored.

Since Kat hadn't seen Cass or Ruark since the ball on Saturday night, she hadn't asked them about what Lucien had said, that he'd been asked to keep an eye on her. "Did Lucien call yesterday?" She'd seen him out her window. He'd been looking up at her room, as if he'd known precisely where she was.

"Yes. We had a nice visit."

"Did you and Ruark ask him to watch over me?"

Cass paused in lifting her teacup. Her gaze met Kat's and her cheeks flushed a faint pink. "We may have mentioned something to him. Only because he's family and well connected—if there were any rumors about you, he'd be likely to hear them." She sipped her tea.

"Why are you worried about rumors?"

"Because the Hickinbottoms are coming to town. There's no knowing if they'll tell people about what happened with you and their son. Hopefully not, since all ended well." Cass set her cup down.

While Kat typically appreciated their support, she didn't like feeling as though she were being managed. "I'd rather you not assign people to supervise me without my awareness or consent. It makes me feel like a child."

"That was not our intent," Cass said. "I apologize."

"How would you feel if your brother had done that to you?"

Cass grimaced. "I would have reacted in the same way. Actually, I would likely have demonstrated more pique. You are to be commended."

Kat waved her hand. "I understand your concern. I did solicit a gentleman who was betrothed to kiss me. Rest assured, I will not do anything further to harm my reputation." She'd learned from that mistake—she'd taken great care to organize the situation when she and Lucien had kissed.

Still, she heard Lucien's voice in her head warning her of the dangers of them getting caught. He'd made it clear he wouldn't risk it, which meant it was time for her to find another subject.

As she cut into her ham, she felt a pang of disappointment. More than a pang, it was a saturation that seemed to weigh down her limbs. She didn't want to move on from Lucien. Not when she'd never been attracted to anyone before. What if she was never attracted to anyone ever again?

She refused to think like that. Defeat had never been an option for her. She needed to get back to her research.

"Cass, where might I find books about mating and human sexual relations?"

To her credit, Cass didn't choke on the tea she'd just drunk. She did, however, set the cup into the saucer with a louder than normal clack. "Er, why?"

"It's for my research. Since I can't actually experience those things for myself, I must rely on others to inform me."

"Well, I do appreciate you not interviewing me about specifics," Cass said with a laugh. "Perhaps surprisingly, I know precisely where you should go to find some excellent…literature."

Kat leaned forward slightly. "Do you?"

"The ladies' library at the Phoenix Club. There are several books that might interest you, including fiction of an…erotic nature." She lowered her voice to a whisper. "Don't tell Ruark. Or any man. We don't want them stealing anything from our library."

The excitement Kat felt was tempered by the fact that she wasn't a member of the club. "But I'm not allowed in the library. Unless I can go during the assembly?"

"You can, actually, but if you want to bring some books home, you won't want to bother with that, then. It's better if you go another time." Before Kat could remind her that she wasn't a member, Cass went on, "I'll have to smuggle you in somehow."

"You will?" Kat's pulse sped at the notion of not just getting her hands on those books, but being allowed into the Phoenix Club outside an assembly.

"I think tomorrow night would be best. On Tuesdays, the ladies' side of the club is completely empty."

"Because everyone prefers to invade the men's side?"

Cass grinned. "Definitely. There might be a handful of ladies on our side, so we'll disguise you." She tipped her head to the side. "A wig and some cosmetics, I think."

Excitement rushed through Kat. "I confess I'm surprised you'd support this, let alone suggest it."

Cass laughed. "You wouldn't be if you knew that I'd stolen into the club dressed as a maid last year. With Fiona. It ended up being a very eventful occasion," she added, her eyes sparkling.

"I'd no idea you were that brash," Kat said. "How did you manage to dress as maids?"

"Prudence was Fiona's companion at the time." Prudence had been Cass's companion after serving as Fiona's. Then, in a bizarre revelation of events, she'd been found to be Cass's cousin—the illegitimate daughter of the Duke of Evesham's younger sister, the Countess of Peterborough and the now-deceased Viscount Warfield, which also made Prudence the half sister of the current viscount, who was married to the Phoenix Club's bookkeeper, Ada. Kat had needed to hear the connections multiple times before they'd stuck in her brain.

Cass continued, "She'd been in the club and was able to tell us what to wear so we'd go unnoticed. We made our way in through the kitchens."

"That is magnificent. Why was it so eventful?"

"Well, we went earlier in the day, when we thought no one would be there. Unfortunately, it just happened to be a day when the patronesses were meeting with the membership committee."

"You saw who was on the mysterious membership committee?" Kat rolled her eyes. Much was made over the secrecy, and she'd never understood why.

"I suppose we might have, but in truth, I hid in a cupboard to avoid being caught. Fiona and I were separated." Cass put her hand to her mouth to stifle a laugh. "As it happened, Fiona was caught by her guardian. Overton tried to smuggle her out through the garden, but they encountered a patroness, and he had to kiss Fiona to keep her from being seen and recognized. Since she was dressed as a maid, the patroness thought Overton was taking advantage of one of the club's employees."

"My mishap in Gloucestershire doesn't sound so bad now," Kat said smugly.

"That's not quite everything." Cass leaned forward over the table, her eyes gleaming with an untold secret about to be spilled. "Your brother found me in the cupboard and thought I was a maid. Then he kissed me, and I had to tell him who I really was."

"You knew him, but he didn't know you?"

"Your brother's Irish accent makes him rather easy to

discern, even in the dark. When he opened the door and light got in, he was able to determine my identity. He was… displeased to learn he'd kissed his best friend's sister." Kat couldn't help laughing—rather loudly—and her amusement was perhaps due even more to the fact that the same best friend had also kissed *Ruark's* sister.

"It all turned out well, however," Kat said. She suddenly glimpsed a future in which she ended up married to Lucien. No, she didn't want that. Not at all. She wasn't getting married. Ever. Neither was he.

She forced herself to take a deep breath.

Cass grinned. "Yes, it all worked out wonderfully. Now, let us plan the specifics for tomorrow night, then I must find you a wig."

"Do you have any?"

"I might. If not, I'll send my maid to fetch some. Oh, this will be most diverting."

Kat would suffer through a wig and cosmetics if it meant gaining access to the ladies' library and these helpful books. Perhaps then she could determine her next move when it came to conducting her research.

Whatever it was, it wouldn't involve Lucien.

~

The ladies' side of the Phoenix Club was indeed silent as a tomb on Tuesday evening. Thankfully, Ruark had wanted to arrive at the club early, so Kat and Cass had taken the coach and been able to enter the club on the ladies' side. The footwoman at the door greeted them, and Cass spoke loudly, cheerfully, and incessantly, which hadn't allowed the poor employee to ascertain Kat's membership. Cass's plan to get them inside had worked beautifully.

"Here is the library," Cass said as they entered the large

room on the first floor. Shelves lined three of the walls, and a wide hearth was centered in the fourth. There were three seating areas in the room, including one with a rectangular table perfect for sitting and conducting research where one might need to record information or make sketches.

Kat gazed longingly at the rows of books and was glad she'd brought a bag in which to carry what she planned to take home. "I could spend a week here. Weeks, really."

"When you are a member, you can spend as much time here as you like."

"That won't be for a very long time. If ever," Kat said wryly.

"You never know. Perhaps you'll find the man you simply can't live without."

The thought of that, of having someone upon whom you depended so greatly, was completely unappealing to Kat. "The only person I can't live without is me."

"Don't be so literal," Cass said with a soft laugh. "What I mean is a man who consumes you body and soul. A man for whom you are willing to forgo any vows you took or promises you made because beside him they all fall to dust."

"That still doesn't encourage me. I don't like to break promises."

"Then you are right. Perhaps marriage is never for you." Cass didn't sound convinced, but she knew when to surrender and for that Kat was grateful "The books you want are over there in the corner on the bottom two shelves." Cass pointed to the opposite side of the room, then turned toward Kat. "Do you need anything else before I go?"

Kat shook her head, then glanced toward the clock on the mantel. "I'll meet you at the coach at half eleven."

"Yes. Ruark won't want to leave that early." Cass gave her a reassuring pat on the arm. "Remember, don't go anywhere.

I doubt anyone would recognize you with that blonde hair and all those cosmetics, but it's best not to chance it."

"If you think I'd want to leave this place at all, you'd be quite wrong." Kat gave her a gleeful smile, then practically skipped to the corner Cass had indicated.

"See you later!" Cass called.

Kat didn't even turn to watch her go. She began to pluck book after book from the shelf, then carried them to the table. After placing most of them in the bag, she sat down to flip through the one that looked the most interesting. It was called *Diary of a Covent Garden Lady*.

Opening the tome, Kat began to read. It was a lively tale of a young woman's life as a prostitute told to someone called A. Leffler, presumably because the woman couldn't write. There were not, however, any descriptions of sexual activities for several pages. Disappointed and eager to find something useful, Kat began to turn the pages more quickly, skimming words as she went. She stopped cold when she found a folded piece of parchment stuck between two pages.

Curious, she plucked it free and opened the paper atop the book. It was a short letter and completely unintelligible. She'd seen things like this before when she'd stayed at Lady Pickering's with Jess. It was some sort of riddle or code, and Jess was exceptionally skilled at solving them.

What could it be? Did it pertain to the book, or had someone stashed it in the book as a hiding place? Why would they hide something like that here? Perhaps it was a forgotten letter, lost to whoever had slid it into the book.

Kat slipped it into her pocket. She'd give it to Jess to decipher, and hopefully, that would solve the mystery of why it was there. Perhaps it was something helpful to Kat's research. That would be the best outcome.

She continued her cursory review of the book, stopping in a few places to read where the woman finally described a sexual act. While she went into detail, the writing lacked a sense of what it was like for her. Had she left that part out or had A. Leffler been a poor documentarian?

Closing the book, Kat rose to return it to the shelf. She briefly considered taking it home so she could replace the letter after Jess deciphered it. However, she didn't want to carry more than she needed to. In the end, she put the book back.

Kat frowned at the bag of books. What if they were all like that one? She'd yet to read anything that rivaled what she'd felt when Lucien had kissed her. She needed to do that again. Preferably with him, but since that was unlikely, she ought to find someone else. And here she was in a disguise. At the Phoenix Club. Where there were men.

Why couldn't she go over to the men's side? She might find someone who was in the mood for kissing, and they need never know her identity. She'd be a widow who hadn't spent much time in London of late.

Cass would be upset with her for leaving the library. But why would she need to know? Surely Kat could avoid her. She knew Cass tended to prefer the men's library. That seemed to be where she and her friends congregated, rather than the members' den.

Anticipation unfurled inside her. Kat picked up the bag—goodness, it was heavy—and carried it to the doorway. She set it on the floor next to the wall, then straightened, smoothing her skirts. Then she marched out of the library.

Now, how did she get to the men's side? She seemed to recall there was access via the mezzanine over the ballroom. It took her a few minutes to find how to reach the mezzanine from this floor, but she stumbled upon it and felt a surge of victory.

She made her way along the mezzanine until she came out on the other side into a small chamber. From there, she walked out onto a landing near the staircase. Conversation and laughter greeted her. She was on the men's side.

It was probably best if she went down to the ground floor. She'd be sure to avoid Cass there. Keeping to the wall, she walked slowly to the top of the staircase. A gentleman stepped onto the landing and met her gaze. He smiled. "Good evening."

"Good evening," Kat managed, her heart racing.

He'd moved on before she could think of something else to say. She was going to have to think and react more quickly if she wanted to find a kissing opportunity.

She started to move toward the wall again, then decided that was futile, particularly on the staircase. Holding her head high, as if she belonged there, she picked her way down the stairs, passing a pair of ladies as she descended. At the bottom, she exhaled as she decided where to go next. There was a dining room, wasn't there? The ladies' side had one.

Kat moved quickly through the reception hall so as not to draw the attention of any of the footmen. What if they immediately realized she wasn't a member? That assumed they'd memorized everyone by their faces, and that seemed nearly impossible. Except, she'd wager Lucien knew every single member upon sight.

Did she hope to see him? Yes, but he'd be furious to find her here. Probably. Best to avoid him too.

Honestly, she ought to go back to the ladies' side. The likelihood of her finding a kissing opportunity tonight seemed exceedingly low.

Feeling defeated, she started to turn and nearly ran into Jess. Thank God!

Kat hadn't realized she was nervous until seeing a friend made her feel grounded again. "Jess!"

Jess blinked at her. "Kat?" She leaned forward, her eyes narrowing as she regarded Kat closely. "I wouldn't have recognized you if you hadn't spoken. What on earth are you doing?" She glanced up at Kat's blonde wig.

"Research."

"Here? How did you get in? A disguise shouldn't be enough—unless you gave them a name that's on the membership rolls." She grinned. "You are even cleverer than I thought."

"Not really. This was Cass's idea. I was to be reading books in the ladies' library. The disguise was just in case I ran into any of the ladies over there. However, I wanted to see the men's side." She decided not to tell Jess of her plan to find a kissing opportunity. It seemed foolhardy upon reflection.

"Now that I have, I think I shall be on my way back," Kat said, "But first, I have something I want to give you." She glanced about. "Is there somewhere more quiet we can go?"

"This way." Jess escorted her from the staircase hall past a thick drape into an antechamber that looked as though it led to the ballroom where the Friday assemblies were held.

"I'm glad I ran into you, because I found an intriguing item in the library." Kat pulled the folded parchment from her pocket. "This was tucked into a book. I immediately recognized it as a code and thought you might want to decipher it."

Jess took the letter and opened it. Her gaze moved across the paper and immediately lit with interest. "You found this in a book?"

"Yes. What do you think it is? It was in a book about a prostitute, but nothing in the publication itself was coded that I noticed."

"I don't suppose you have that book with you?" Jess asked.

Kat shook her head. "I put it back on the shelf."

Jess looked back down at the letter. "I may need it to work out the code. Sometimes texts are used to create codes, and thus to decipher them as well."

Kat frowned. "I should have thought of that."

Jess laughed softly. "Why? It's no trouble. Just tell me where I can find the book, and I'll fetch it before I leave tonight."

"It's called *Diary of a Covent Garden Lady*, and it's in the far corner on the bottom shelf. You'll find it easily because there is a great deal of empty space on that shelf and the one above it since I borrowed several of the books. For my research," she added. "Do you suppose the letter has something to do with the prostitute's work?"

"It may have nothing at all to do with the book. Indeed, if the book was merely used as a code, the letter could be anything. Perhaps it's a love letter." Jess giggled. "I've actually found a few of those written in code."

"Have you?" Kat was fascinated. "Do love letters add to the courtship?"

"These were letters between a married couple," Jess said. "They liked to flirt in writing. That's the best way I can describe it."

"Were they…titillating?"

"I suppose so. They were certainly explicit." Jess waggled her brows. "Anyway, if this is indeed a love letter you found hidden on the ladies' side, it has to be between two ladies. Doesn't it?"

Kat lifted a shoulder. "That makes the most sense. It would also explain why it's in code. No one would want to advertise their love for another woman."

"Which is unfortunate. I don't understand why it should matter what people do in private or whom they love."

"I agree. I wondered if I might prefer a relationship with a woman," Kat said. "Since I hadn't felt attraction for a man until Lucien."

"I'm surprised you didn't mention that part—about perhaps preferring women—last week when we talked." Jess's lips curled into a sly smile. "Or were you too focused on Lucien?"

Jess knew they'd kissed in Dougal's study. Kat had felt beholden to tell her since she'd helped organize the scheme. Even so, Kat would have told her anyway. She'd needed to discuss it with *someone* despite recording copious observations in her notebook. "Probably that," Kat admitted.

She was *still* too focused on him. As much as she knew she needed to find someone else to help with her studies, she only wanted Lucien.

"I should get back to the ladies' side," Kat said. "Should I just go through the ballroom?"

"I'm not sure you can. It may be closed up. Also, sometimes people go in there, so if you want to avoid running into anyone, I'd say you should find another path. Is that how you came over here?"

"No, I went along the mezzanine."

Jess nodded. "I'll walk upstairs with you, and you can return that way."

As they went up the stairs, Kat almost wished she could stay, at least to see the men's library, but that would be the height of foolishness since she'd almost certainly see Cass or even her brother there. Indeed, at the top of the stairs, Kat saw Cass coming from the left. Alarm surged in her chest.

"You have to intercept Cass," she whispered urgently to Jess.

"I'll take care of her. You go. Quickly." Jess hurried to the left, and Kat heard her loudly greeting Cass.

Kat took off to the right and, in her haste, walked right past where she should have gone to find the mezzanine. Then she saw Ruark, standing just inside a large chamber—the members' den, if she wasn't mistaken—and panicked.

Twirling about, she saw a door and went inside without

hesitation. She should have retraced her steps to the mezzanine.

"Good evening." Lucien regarded her with interest from where he stood behind a desk. This had to be his office. Of all the places to find herself…

Wait, did he not recognize her? Perhaps she could escape without him discovering her identity. She suddenly thought of Cass being trapped with Ruark in a cupboard and how she'd recognized him by his voice. If she disguised her voice, mightn't that help her cause?

"Evening, my lord," she said in her best Irish accent. Honestly, she was terrible at affecting an accent, and Irish was the only one she could marginally approximate thanks to her parents and Ruark.

Lucien's eyes narrowed, and he moved around the desk. Kat could see he was suspicious. She put her hand on the door. "I'm clearly in the wrong place. I beg your pardon."

However, before she could escape, Lucien was beside her, his hand next to hers flat against the wood. "Kat?"

"Who?" she said, avoiding looking at him.

He exhaled. "How did you get in here?"

Kat considered whether she ought to continue pretending ignorance as to who Kat was, but decided it was pointless. "I came across the mezzanine. I'm just here to look at books in the ladies' library."

"Except you are not doing 'just' that," he said.

Kat looked up at him and saw a spark of mirth in his eyes. "You aren't angry?"

"I'm annoyed that you so easily infiltrated the club, but I suppose I'm impressed."

An absurd happiness flipped through Kat's chest. "How did you recognize me? I thought Cass's disguise was awfully good."

"Cass?"

Hell. "Forget I mentioned her."

He laughed. "Not going to happen. But I won't tell her, provided you go directly back to the ladies' side. No one will know who you are, and in a quarter hour, everyone will be wondering who the stunning blonde is."

"You think I'm stunning?"

"Well, yes. And the cosmetics make you look quite... worldly. You'll garner far too much attention, and when no one can identify you, everyone will scramble to discover who you are. Then they'll find out you aren't a member, and that will be another scandal for me to deal with."

Now Kat felt badly for causing him trouble. "That would really be a full-blown scandal?"

"Not full-blown, but it's a worry I don't need. So, let's get you back where you belong. Which isn't in the club at all, actually. You can come back on Friday. Why didn't you just visit the library then?"

"Cass thought it would be better tonight while that side is practically empty. Because I'm looking at certain books."

He arched a brow. "What books?"

"There are books in the ladies' library that are pertinent to my research."

"You couldn't have known that, so Cass must have told you." Realization dawned on his face. "She organized this entire scheme. Perhaps I *will* speak with her."

"No, don't. There's no harm done, truly. I'll just go back now." Kat reached for the latch.

"You really do look different. Like someone else entirely. I can almost imagine you aren't you."

Kat lowered her hand and faced him directly. "Would that be a good thing? I've been wondering if you would have continued to help me with my research if I weren't Ruark's sister."

His nostrils flared, and she thought she glimpsed desire in

his eyes before he blinked it away. "That's not worth contemplating since you *are* Ruark's sister."

"I can see I'll need to find someone else to help me." She realized she was taunting him now, that he would not support her doing that.

"You can't do that."

"Why not? I don't plan to marry, and I will be discreet." Kat rolled her eyes. "Oh, never mind. I'm never going to convince you to mind your own business. I don't know why I keep talking to you at all."

"I'm only trying to protect you."

"That's not your job," she snapped.

"No, it isn't." He frowned at her. "I wanted to apologize about the other night at the ball. I was in a terrible mood, and I wasn't kind to you. Did I cause you to have to leave and spend the next day recovering?"

Kat stared at him. What did he know? She'd seen that he'd called the day after the ball, but what had Cass told him? "You didn't cause anything." Except disappointment.

"I'm still sorry you were troubled. Can I ask what happened?"

"It wasn't anything specific. Sometimes, I become overwhelmed when there is too much noise or too many people." She noted the concern in his gaze. "Are you truly interested?"

He nodded. "I am. What is it like?"

"I, well, sometimes I feel itchy. Or hot. Sometimes I want to scream and rant. And other times I actually do, though I don't do that as much anymore. It's become easier to control my impulses as I've matured." His interest and care seemed genuine, so she decided to tell him the truth. "I think you did upset me. If I'm on edge or feeling stressed for any reason, that can contribute to the pressures going on around me."

"You've always had these…problems?"

"Yes, but I couldn't really recognize or understand them

when I was younger. I would just get upset or retreat some-where alone. It was very frustrating to my mother, and my father would just shrug and say I'd grow out of it. He likes to tell her that he told her so."

"But you haven't grown out of it," Lucien said.

"No, but I've learned to cope. Mostly. It's easier living with Cass and Ruark. They let me be who I am instead of who they'd like me to be."

"The rest of your family expects that?"

"My mother and sisters."

"Does that mean you don't have a close relationship with them?"

Kat shrugged. "More with my sisters than my mother. Do we enjoy the same things? Not really. They are far more interested in needlework, dancing, and, most importantly, finding husbands."

"They are not interested in your study of mating rituals?"

Kat laughed. "Not at all. Not even when I performed a demonstration of a peacock's dance when I was fifteen. They were not impressed, but it is awfully hard to convey when one doesn't have a full array of feathers at one's back. They did, however, covet the peacock feather headband I'd persuaded Mother to buy for me."

Now Lucien laughed. "I should very much like to see this dance."

"Truly?" She narrowed her eyes at him, not quite sure if he was in jest. "So you can laugh at it?"

"Perhaps, if you are particularly enthusiastic about it and shake your rump with vigor. Hopefully, I'd be laughing *with* you."

"It's not meant to be funny. It's supposed to entice the female to mate."

"You're telling me that you found no amusement in pretending to be a peacock strutting about?" Lucien put his hands on his hips and walked away from the door wiggling his behind. "Do I have it right? Tell me this does not amuse you."

Kat stifled a giggle. "Fine. Yes. I have been known to be too literal from time to time."

"And I have been accused of doing the opposite nearly all the time." Grinning, he came back toward her, continuing his avian strut. "How do I look?"

"Ridiculous without any feathers. Which was probably how I looked." She grimaced. "Perhaps I was too harsh regarding my sisters' disinterest."

"On the contrary. It sounds as if they took you—and themselves—too seriously." He sobered. "And I'm sorry for that." When he came to a halt, he stood just in front of her.

With her back to the door, Kat looked up at him. "Thank you. For asking about…me. And for being kind."

"You are one of the most enchanting people I've ever met, Kat, and probably the most authentic."

"What do you mean?"

"You are always unapologetically and entirely *you*. That is an exceptionally admirable quality, I think."

The now-familiar sensations she felt in his presence—the pull in her chest, the warmth spreading through her, the quickening of her pulse—intensified. "I really do wish you could help me finish my studies."

"Finish?" he asked softly. "What would that entail?"

"Finding completion so that I may be fully aware of what occurs between a man and a woman."

His gaze darkened, and he lifted his hand to gently trace his fingertip along her jaw. "That would take a very long time —the fully aware part." The low timbre of his voice echoed in her body, making her yearn for him to touch her more. Everywhere.

"Why?"

"Because there are so many ways to give and find pleasure and discovering that with a partner...*that* is the joy of coupling."

Kat shivered. She felt in danger of swooning again. Thankfully, the door was a solid pressure against her back, keeping her upright. "I would very much like to experience that."

"I'd like nothing more than to help you. But I can't. You understand that, don't you?"

"I understand that you think you can't, but my brother never needs to know. No one ever needs to know. And if I can steal into your club without being noticed—"

"Kat, Kat, Kat," he murmured her name as his eyes hooded, and he lowered his head.

She put her hands on his shoulders and leaned toward him, desperate for his lips against hers.

"Lucien?" Ruark's voice carried through the door along with a knock, working in concert like a thunderclap. Kat jerked forward into Lucien as she clapped her hand over her mouth to keep from gasping.

"Just a moment!" Lucien grabbed Kat's hand and tugged her across the room to a corner with a bookcase. He pulled on a book, and the case swung inward to reveal a passageway. "I'm sorry that it's dark, but feel your way along the right side. There's a short flight of stairs down, then a door that will take you to the mezzanine. You can find your way from there."

Before she could respond, he gently shoved her into the passageway and closed the door, plunging her into darkness.

"Good thing I'm not afraid of the night like Aislinn," Kat muttered, referring to one of her younger sisters.

She put her right hand out and walked slowly, anticipating the stairs with each step. When she finally reached them, she exhaled, realizing she'd been holding her breath. It was a short flight—just five steps—and after a few more steps, she was at the door. Pushing it open, she found herself on the familiar mezzanine and breathed even easier.

After shutting the door, she noted its placement in the wall. If she hadn't known it was there, she never would have recognized it for a door.

She returned to the library and checked the clock. It was just after ten. She had plenty of time to read her books. Or make notes.

Or dream of Lucien's touch.

The latter won out, and she realized there was no hope for her finding a surrogate research partner. No one but Lucien would do.

CHAPTER 12

"It will be fine," Ada Hunt, the Viscountess Warfield, assured Lucien as they stood together surveying the ballroom. Flowers and brightly colored décor with signs reading, "Happy Leap Year," filled the space. They'd gone to some excess for the first assembly of the Season, but it was nothing when compared with the plans they had for next week's Frost Fair theme.

"I still wish Evie were here. And that's not a lack of confidence in your abilities," he told Ada pointedly.

"I know. It's the first time you've done this without her," Ada said softly. A petite white woman in her midtwenties, with dark hair and blue-gray eyes, Ada was a force of positivity and reliability. She'd been the club's bookkeeper since its inception. Like Evie when she'd left town to change her identity, Ada has also been in need of reinvention. That had been the Phoenix Club's gain. Then, when Lucien had sent her to help his friend Max put his failing estate in order, she'd not only turned it around, she'd utterly captivated the beast and was now his beloved wife. While it hadn't been

Lucien's intent to match them together, he didn't mind taking credit for making it possible.

Lucien pivoted to inhale the fragrance of a rose in one of the bouquets situated about the room. "I'm just sorry she's missing it. She should be able to enjoy the fruits of her labors, especially with her betrothed. I should have liked to toast them during the assembly."

"But it's a Leap Year theme, so it's probably best if I or your sister toasted them." Ada winked at him. On Leap Year, it was up to the ladies to take the lead. Tonight, only they would be allowed to ask for dances. The tables would be entirely turned.

"True, but you can't either since they are, regrettably, in Oxfordshire."

"How about we toast them anyway? Surely, they'll feel our good wishes all the way at Threadbury Hall." She referred to Evie's sister and brother-in-law's home.

"Brilliant idea. You are, without question, the sunniest person I've ever met."

"Why, thank you. I would say you are also quite charismatic, though you've been a trifle...preoccupied of late. I understand why, of course. I do hope things will improve."

"Tonight will be a good indicator." Lucien's insides churned with anxiety. "We need this event to be a success."

Ada briefly squeezed his arm and gave him an intense but optimistic stare. "It *will* be. Everything looks beautiful. The refreshments are wonderful. The musicians are even better than last year."

"I mean in numbers. All that will be for naught if we don't have at least as many attendees as last year." Last Season's assemblies had been the talk of the ton, and attendance had soared each week, with people clamoring to find a way to be included if they weren't members. Lucien doubted that would happen given their recent troubles and the fact that there was a competing event this evening. "I suspect a good number of people who came last year will be otherwise occupied tonight."

"It is my opinion that anyone who goes to Lady Hargrove's ball instead of coming here is welcome to stay away." Ada made a face, then a sound with her tongue that was most unladylike. Lucien couldn't help but laugh. "You give her too much credit. She's not as popular as she'd like to think."

While that was true, she'd garnered sympathy after widely sharing her side of her expulsion from the Phoenix Club. She'd described Lucien as an unfeeling cad who'd tossed her out simply because she'd questioned why one of her friends hadn't been offered membership. It hadn't been *one* friend and she hadn't *simply questioned* anything. She'd badgered, harangued, and ultimately made a scene at the club, which had culminated in Lucien asking her to leave. That version of events had also been shared by many, but there were people who would choose to believe the tale that resulted in grievance. Lady Hargrove had mastered the art of convincing others that such treatment could happen to them if they associated with the Phoenix Club.

Lucien smiled at Ada. "I appreciate your optimism. Perhaps it will coax mine out."

"I hope so. We miss the real Lucien."

"We?" Clearly his friends, and perhaps even his siblings, had been discussing him. "I hope you aren't all wasting time worrying about me."

"Not worrying so much as trying to find ways to help. I am confident the attendance will be what you hope. Tuesday was steady, was it not?"

"If you mean the attendance was the same as last week, it was. However, it still wasn't a regular Tuesday."

"Have faith," she said as a maid came toward her carrying another bouquet of flowers.

Lucien would let Ada deal with whatever that situation was and made his way toward the men's side. Tuesday hadn't been disappointing, but that was entirely because of his encounter with Kat. She'd distracted him from his concerns. Hell, she'd somehow dissuaded him from being annoyed that she was even in the club. And she hadn't even tried. She'd just been her usual intriguing self, which was enough to completely ensnare him. He would have kissed her again if not for the untimely arrival of her brother.

After practically shoving her into the secret passageway, Lucien had poured himself a glass of brandy and downed it before opening the door for Ruark. The alcohol had done little to slow the rampant lust cascading through him, but it was better than doing nothing.

Thankfully, Ruark hadn't noticed anything odd about Lucien, and they'd gone about their evening. Still, Lucien had thought of Kat incessantly. Then he'd dreamed about her in the passageway alone in the dark. Of him pursuing and catching her before she'd made it to the other end. The rest of it was erotic and obscene and utterly thrilling. He'd awakened in a sweat and with a fierce need to frig himself.

What spell had she cast on him?

He was coming to realize that his resistance was failing. It might even become completely futile. Would it be terrible if he just surrendered to what they both wanted? Then he could exorcise her from his mind and body, and she'd do the same.

He climbed the stairs toward his office. But was forever with one person even possible? He always tired of his lovers. Except Evie. He'd told her that sometime later, after she'd returned to London. He'd thought he was fine with her dismissal of him, but he'd been hurt. What about her had been different? She'd wondered if it was because they'd become friends—had he done that with anyone else? He hadn't, and he thought that might be the distinction. However, where that had made him think he probably loved her, it had prompted Evie to end their arrangement. Clearly, the feelings of intimacy and friendship hadn't been the same for them.

And now the love he felt for Evie was *purely* friendship—the kind in which the thought of physical intimacy wouldn't be right. It made him wonder if he'd ever actually fallen in love with her or if that was a story he told himself to prove that it was possible, that he *could* love.

"There you are, Lucien."

Torn from his thoughts—and gratefully so—Lucien looked up to see Dougal standing outside his office. His brow was creased, and there was a gleam of anticipation in his dark gaze. "What news?"

Dougal nodded toward Lucien's office and ducked inside. Lucien followed him, closing the door. He noted that Dougal carried a book. "What's that?" Lucien asked.

"The reason I'm here bothering you on the afternoon before the first assembly of the Season. My apologies, but it couldn't wait. There's a story to tell, but perhaps it's best if I just let you read this first."

Lucien frowned. "The book?"

Shaking his head, Dougal opened the tome and removed a piece of folded parchment. "No, this letter."

Upon taking the paper, Lucien realized there were two pieces. The first was clearly a code given the jumble of letters that made no sense. He glanced toward Dougal, who inclined his head toward the paper. "There's a translation."

Lucien moved the second piece of parchment to the top and read:

Problem with Lady Macbeth. May need to do the same as with
G. Meet afternoon sixth March. Meeting Cupboard.

Very short and to the point, and yet the coded part was
much longer. Lucien looked at Dougal. "This small message
came from all that?"

"Yes. It was very complex. Jess has been working on it
since Wednesday morning."

That was going to be Lucien's next question. He couldn't
imagine who else Dougal would have had decipher a code.
Jess had been recruited to the Foreign Office because of her
code-breaking and riddle-solving abilities. "Why are you just
now telling me about this? And where did you get it?"

"Jess only told me about it this afternoon when she'd
finally finished breaking it." Dougal's brow darkened. "She
didn't think it would be anything like this. Miss Shaughnessy
found it in the ladies' library *here*. She gave it to Jess to decipher. They assumed it was a love note or some other
innocuous communication."

Kat had found this? Lucien reread the note several more
times. "The 'meeting cupboard.'" He frowned at Dougal.
"That's what Kent calls the meeting room upstairs."

"I know. Does anyone else from the Foreign Office call it
that?"

"I don't know, but it's possible. We can't assume this note
was written by or intended for Kent."

"No, but I think it's incredibly likely, don't you?"

"I don't want to believe that, but yes." Lucien regarded
Kent as a mentor. To think he was involved with Giraud's
murder, assuming the G referred to the deceased courier—
and potentially killing someone else as this note seemed to
indicate—was more than disappointing. It was nearly devastating. "Who is Lady Macbeth?"

Dougal pressed his lips together. "No idea, but whoever it

is does indeed sound like a potential problem if she's anything like the actual character."

"It would be amusing if this weren't so concerning. I don't know about any meeting on the sixth." Lucien was made aware of all Foreign Office meetings even if he didn't know the attendees or the purpose. That way, he could ensure none of the employees entered the meeting area. They didn't happen *that* often.

"We could just ask Kent if he knows anything about this," Dougal suggested.

"We could, but I'm inclined to keep it between us and see who shows up at the meeting."

"I am as well." Dougal held up his hand. "I haven't told you what Jess said about the letter."

"Don't leave me hanging," Lucien said drily.

"She felt there were similarities between this letter and the one she deciphered that was written by Giraud. Both required the use of another text to solve the code, but Giraud's letter was easier and used a common text—the Bible. She also thinks the hand that wrote both letters may have been the same."

"I assume the G in the note refers to Giraud."

"I do as well." Dougal crossed his arms over his chest. "I wish we still had the original letter from Giraud."

"Could we get it from Kent?"

"What reason would we give him without arousing suspicion? I don't think we can trust anyone at this point. What did the author of this note—and whomever it was intended for—do with 'G'?" Dougal gave him a dark stare. "I'm sure you're thinking what I'm thinking."

"That Lady Macbeth should perhaps watch her back." Lucien paced to the hearth. "Who are they, and why are they meeting? Also, how are they getting into the club? They have to be people who've been here before and can easily gain access."

"Indeed, since this letter was placed in the ladies' library. I think we have to assume the author is a woman."

"Or found a way to have it placed. Perhaps they used one of my employees." Lucien's blood began to heat. He didn't like not having full control of the club, but this was even worse. Someone had been using it to conduct business unknown to him. "What if this is the Foreign Office? The Phoenix Club is one of their conduits for conducting business."

"I think we have to presume it *is* them." Dougal gave him an ominous look. "Given the presence of this letter and its similarity to the one Giraud purportedly wrote, I think we can conclude that Giraud didn't actually write that first letter that Jess deciphered."

Lucien blew out a breath. "I think we can. This supports our theory that Giraud was innocent, that he was blamed for someone else's crimes. Finding that letter was a stroke of luck." He glanced toward the book in Dougal's hand. "What's it called?"

"*Diary of a Covent Garden Lady.*"

That sounded like something Kat would read. Lucien still couldn't believe *she'd* found this. "Does Kat know what the letter says?"

Dougal shook his head. "No, and Jess isn't going to tell her, at least not the truth. She'll say it was a silly love note."

"Does she plan to write up a decoy? Kat will probably ask to see it." Lucien would bet his life on it. She was nothing if not curious and thorough.

Dougal's eyes lit. "Brilliant. I'll make sure she does, if she hasn't thought of that already. She's not going to attend the assembly tonight, I'm afraid. Too many late nights working on this, and she's exhausted, especially carrying the babe."

"I understand. Please thank her for me." Lucien looked at the two pieces of parchment. "We ought to put this back the way Kat found it. Intact—with the letter folded inside. Did Jess perchance make a copy of the coded letter?"

"She did." Dougal flipped to a page in the book and handed it to Lucien. "The letter goes there."

Lucien folded the letter and tucked it into the book. "I'll return it to the library. Where does it belong?"

"Jess said Miss Shaughnessy found it while conducting research. She removed several books from the bottom shelf in a corner. You should be able to easily discern where it goes."

Lucien nodded. "I'll take care of it."

"What's our plan for this meeting?" Dougal asked.

"I don't know, but I don't like this." Lucien had begun to feel as though he were being used, and he was, really. He'd been put in place at this club to answer to the Foreign Office. Except Lucien had become attached to the enterprise and now he saw it as his. It *was* his.

"I don't either. There are things happening here that you haven't known about. I can only imagine how that makes you feel."

"Bloody angry. I have to wonder if there aren't people working at the club that have aided whatever is going on. People shouldn't be able to get into the club without someone knowing." Except it happened. Just a few nights ago, in fact, when Cass had smuggled Kat inside. It had also happened last year when Cass and Fiona had dressed up as maids to gain entrance. It suddenly seemed not only possible, but utterly expected that this sort of thing went on. Lucien tamped down his ire. He'd clearly been too lax with security.

Lucien scowled. "I have known and continue to be reminded that people are able to infiltrate the club using a variety of means."

"Apparently, because Miss Shaughnessy isn't even a member," Dougal said with a touch of hesitation, as if he hadn't wanted to point that out. "What was she doing in the ladies' library in the first place?"

"Cass helped her get in so she could conduct research as Jess told you she was doing." Lucien massaged his forehead. "Obviously, I need to increase security."

"Are there employees you can absolutely trust?" Dougal asked.

"A half hour ago, I would have said yes. But now? I don't know. As you said, I don't think we can trust anyone."

Dougal gave him a grim look. "Perhaps you and I will need to be security."

"Reynolds can stand guard. In fact, I could reassign him here indefinitely."

"But he's your butler."

"He's also completely trustworthy and wholly capable of handling any situation that may arise, if you recall."

Dougal had seen Reynolds in action in Spain. "Indeed I do. If you think it won't draw too much attention, it would be good to have him here. Would he be able to hire some lads to help him out? Perhaps he could organize shifts of men to keep watch."

"Brilliant idea, Dougal." Lucien would task Reynolds with recruiting men who would keep a watchful eye and report everything they saw. "What of people who walk in the front door as if they belong? What if these people coming to this meeting are members?"

Dougal exhaled, sounding beleaguered. "I suppose you could never leave the club and watch everyone who enters. I say that in jest. You absolutely can't do that. What about Arthur? He knows every member."

Arthur was the head footman and stood sentinel in the entrance hall when the club was in operation. On the rare occasion he wasn't there, his second-in-command, Fulton, took over.

"What if Arthur has been compromised?" Lucien couldn't believe he was saying it, let alone thinking it. Arthur had been with him since the club opened its doors. He was incredibly smart, organized, and he knew the club better than anyone besides Lucien, Evie, and Ada. "It would crush me if he were," Lucien said quietly.

"We don't know if he is," Dougal said reassuringly. "But you're right to be suspicious of everyone. I think it's best if we keep this between us and Reynolds, along with his hirelings."

"Agreed." Lucien felt a mild sense of relief as well as anticipation. "Please thank Jess for me and give her my best. I hope she gets all the rest she needs—and deserves. I'll see you later tonight?"

"Yes. I'll be here as much as possible, especially between now and Wednesday." Dougal gave him a nod, then turned and left.

Instead of taking the book to the library, Lucien decided he needed to speak with his butler immediately. They needed security in place that very night, if at all possible.

Reynolds wouldn't like leaving his post at Lucien's house on King Street, but he'd relish the opportunity to manage troops again. And there was no one better to do it.

Lucien hurried from his office. He hadn't a moment to lose with the assembly beginning in a few hours. He still needed to bathe and dress. Oh hell, Reynolds typically acted as his valet too. If the butler-valet was going to be at the Phoenix Club much of the time, Lucien would have to get his footman to take over.

For the first time, Lucien thought it might be nice to have a wife. She could play valet for the next fortnight or however

long Reynolds would be occupied here at the club. He immediately envisioned Kat in the role and smiled.

Then he nearly tripped down the bloody stairs.

He was *not* getting married. And certainly not to Kathleen
Shaughnessy of all people.

Perhaps the recent stress was finally getting to him.

CHAPTER 13

$\mathcal{K}$at and Cass entered the Phoenix Club by the ladies' side for the Leap Year assembly. They could have used the men's door, but since Ruark was already at the club, Cass had reasoned they should stick to their entrance.

The moment they stepped into the ballroom, Ruark came toward them, his gaze trained on Kat. "Kathleen Shaughnessy?" He let his jaw drop briefly—comically—then gave her an approving smile. "You look magnificent. One might think you actually are on the Marriage Mart."

"Oh, stop." Kat rolled her eyes and scoffed. She knew she looked different, and that was the point. Only, she wasn't trying to attract a husband. She was hoping to lure a certain club owner...

"It's one of the new gowns I ordered for her," Cass said. "I love that color on her—it looks like a flame."

Kat liked it too. The gown was unlike anything she'd ever seen, with a yellow-gold bodice and a skirt that went from a pale peach to a vivid red-orange. It really did look like a flame. Plus, Kat had allowed Cass's maid to style her hair in a more intricate fashion. There were probably a thousand pins along with ruby and gold combs that Cass had loaned her. She'd also decided to wear jewelry, which she only did on rare occasions. The dark coral earrings were a bit heavy and had taken getting used to. Kat was aware of their presence, but had at least stopped fidgeting with them.

Ruark grinned at Kat, his blue eyes sparkling with humor. "It's a good thing gentlemen are not allowed to ask you to dance, or you'd spend the entire evening on the dance floor."

"More likely, I'd spend my evening hiding in the garden or the library." Now that Kat knew the library's location and the treasures within it, she would likely spend much of her time there during any given assembly, including tonight.

Cass laughed. "Will you ask anyone to dance tonight?"

"Perhaps." She immediately thought of Lucien. There was no one else she wanted to dance with. And truthfully, she didn't even want to dance with him. But if that was the only way she could be in his arms, she'd take it.

Catching sight of Fallin nearby, Kat excused herself. She made her way to him, and he greeted her with a wide smile.

"Good evening, Miss Shaughnessy. You look splendid this evening."

"Thank you. I do think it's time you called me Kat since your wife is my dearest friend."

"Then you must call me Dougal. I'm still getting used to Fallin," he confided in a half-hushed tone.

"Where is Jess?" Kat asked, glancing about.

He gave her a sympathetic look. "I'm afraid she won't be here this evening. She was feeling too tired. It happens sometimes since she's been carrying the babe. She said to give you her best and that she wants a full report on the evening."

Kat wanted a report on the letter Jess was deciphering, but couldn't very well ask Dougal about it. Quashing her disappointment, she said she'd call on Jess soon. Then she took her leave and instead of returning to her brother and Cass, she skirted the edge of the ballroom—the side with refreshments and seating because the dancing and musicians were on the men's side of the room—and looked for Lucien. She lingered a few minutes to see if he appeared, then grew disappointed. Without him or Jess, Kat's enthusiasm for the evening waned.

Perhaps if she took a respite in the library, she'd improve her mood. Mayhap she'd even summon the interest to ask a gentleman to dance. Tonight would be the perfect opportunity to find a potential lover—there was no point in calling them research subjects at this point. She knew that what she wanted was a man to help her experience the things that lovers experienced. In fact, hadn't there been a book in the library about dancing? Skimming that might give her the courage, if not the desire, she needed to brave the dance floor.

Once she reached the library, she was pleased to find it empty. She closed the door until it was only slightly ajar in the hope that it would deter others from coming inside.

The dancing book was on the shelf above the naughty books. She'd read nearly everything she'd taken the other night, but thankfully, there were still some here since she hadn't been able to fit everything in the bag.

She picked up the book she thought was about dancing and nearly gasped when she opened it. Explicit drawings leapt from the page and into Kat's vivid imagination, along with descriptions of erotic acts. She'd seen other drawings, of course, but none of them had been as evocative as these. The expressions on the faces of the people in the sketches were so real, so *emotive*. Kat could practically feel what they were feeling.

Turning the page, she stared at a drawing of a woman standing against a wall. She held her skirts up around her waist while a man knelt before her, his face buried between her thighs. This sketch showed the woman deep in the throes of passion, her eyes closed and her lips parted. She clutched the man's head with the hand that wasn't holding her garments. On the next page was the same scene, but seemingly from the man's perspective. The drawing depicted the woman's sex, and the man used his hand to part her folds. His tongue was extended as if he were about to lick her—

"Kat?"

Snapping the book closed on her finger, Kat swung around. Did her face look as red hot as it felt? Her body was also flushed with heat. No, with desire. Her own sex had pulsed as she'd studied the drawing.

"Lucien, you surprised me."

He'd come into the room, nearly to where she stood in the corner. His gaze swept over her. "You look particularly beautiful this evening."

His use of the word *particularly* sent another wave of heat rushing through her along with that now-familiar pinch in her chest.

She took in his elegant evening clothes. Unrelenting black save the starched white of his shirt and the gleaming ivory of his cravat. He wore a small emerald pin amid the snowy folds. He was so handsome, it almost made her wince to look at him. Which was incredibly ridiculous. She was reacting like one of her sisters when they went on about Mr. Shiveley.

"Why aren't you downstairs?" he asked.

"Jess isn't here tonight, and I didn't see you, so there wasn't anything interesting keeping me down there. I did consider searching out potential gentlemen for dancing since it *is* a Leap Year ball."

He took a step toward her. "Just for dancing?"

"Are you asking if I plan to find a willing participant for

my research? That is always in the back of my mind." Whereas Lucien, the only participant she really wanted, occupied the rest of it.

"Promise me you won't go asking a gentleman to kiss you tonight."

"I'll do no such thing."

He came forward, standing next to her at the bookcase, his brow darkening. "Dammit, Kat, you can't steal away with a gentleman under your brother's nose."

A smile teased her lips, but she kept it in check. "Isn't that what I'm doing this very moment?"

Scowling, Lucien made that low growling sound in his throat that was equal parts amusing and enticing.

"Wouldn't it be nicer to stop being annoyed by your attraction to me? Nobody ever has to know what happens between us, least of all Ruark."

"I'm confident that's what he and Cass said when they were dallying together. All it took was a slight mistake—a footman saw her leaving a house party and told me—and their secret was no longer secret."

Kat edged closer to him, the bookcase grazing her right arm. "Does anyone know where you are?"

"No."

"No one knows where I am either. But no one would suspect we are together. You are typically busy on a night like this, aren't you?"

"Yes, especially the first assembly of the Season. And when attendance is not what it should be."

She saw the tension in his shoulders as he spoke. "It isn't?"

"It's too early to tell, but in general, fewer people have been visiting the club since Evie's past was made public."

"That is surely a temporary situation. The Phoenix Club is the most popular social destination in London." Not that Kat was an authority, but that was what she'd heard.

"I appreciate your confidence, even if I don't share it."

She realized he was carrying a book. Not just any book... "Where did you get that?" she asked.

"Dougal brought it. He asked me to return it to the library." He held it up. "Actually, it may be of interest to you."

"I've looked through it, actually. The other night when I was here borrowing books."

"And stealing into the men's side," he added with a roguish smile that made her heart skip, then beat even faster.

"It goes down there." Kat gestured to the half-empty shelf. "Have you read it?" Did he know about the letter? If he did, surely he'd say something. Had Jess finished translating the letter? Or had she not needed the book and asked Dougal to return it tonight? Kat definitely planned to call on her tomorrow.

"I haven't. I just came in to replace it." He inclined his head toward the book she held. "What are you reading now?"

"Er, not so much reading as studying. This has a great many illustrations." Again, she felt heat in her cheeks.

Lucien lowered himself to replace the prostitute's diary on the shelf. When he straightened, he was closer to her. Had he done that on purpose? Kat's pulse kicked up at his proximity.

"I think I've seen that book before."

"It's far more interesting—and educational—than the one you just replaced," Kat said. Did she sound strange? As if she were nine and about to be caught stealing paper from her father's study? "Have you seen this?" Tossing caution away, she opened the book in front of him, showing him the illustrations that she'd been studying when he'd arrived.

"Er, yes, I think so."

"You've certainly done it, haven't you?" She held her breath. Her entire body seemed to vibrate as the air between them thickened. Everything felt suddenly heavy, but deliciously so, like a pile of blankets on a frigid night.

"Ah, yes." Now he sounded strange. Strained.

"Does this activity bring a woman to completion?"

His gaze was fixed on the illustrations. "If the man is doing it right."

Kat had no doubt he would. "If you'd care to demonstrate, there's a secret passageway nearby…"

He closed his eyes, and she could hear him breathing. She could also see his chest rising and falling more rapidly than it would if he were calm. He seemed as affected as she was.

When he opened his eyes, they bore straight into her, a dark smolder that set her aflame with desire. "If there is anyone between here and the mezzanine, we will go our separate ways. Do you understand?"

Kat froze. He meant to take her? He meant to…show her? She couldn't form words, so she nodded.

He took the book from her and set it on the shelf. Then he clasped her hand and led her from the library. He moved quickly, so she had to take long strides to keep up.

Holding her breath again as they left the library and walked toward the mezzanine, she prayed they wouldn't encounter anyone. At last, fate was on her side, because they made it to the mezzanine without seeing a soul. Lucien opened the door and pulled her inside. Then he threw the latch.

"Did you lock it?" she asked.

"Yes, and I and Evie are the only ones with a key."

"Evie is not even in London."

"Which is precisely why I am allowing this one time. The time and location could not be more—"

"Perfect," she finished for him. Giddy anticipation swirled through her. At last, she would discover what her mind and then her body had been aching to learn.

It was nearly dark in the passageway, but there was a flame flickering farther along toward his office. "There's a light in here tonight," she said.

"I often use this to move back and forth during assemblies, so I light a sconce in the middle."

"How fortuitous." It really was perfect. As if it had been predetermined. They were to come together this very night in this exact manner.

"Did you hear me, Kat?" His question was dark and almost...desperate. "This is to be *one* time. I will show you completion."

She had to swallow in order to speak. "Like in the book?"

"Yes. That is the easiest in our current situation."

Kat had looked at the drawing and imagined Lucien doing that to her, but now that they were together, alone in this dark, small space, and he was telling her he would... She felt as if she had a fever. But there was no sickness. Just a pulsing, dire need for him to deliver her from torment. Still, she didn't want to think she'd pushed him to do this.

She looked up at his shadowed face, barely able to make out the tight set of his features. She couldn't at all tell how he was feeling. "I don't want you to if it isn't what you want."

He tugged her to the short set of stairs and gently pushed her against the wall. It was slightly brighter here. She could see the dark heat in his gaze.

Clutching her waist with one hand, he cupped her face with the other and looked into her eyes. "Kat, there is nothing I want more. Nothing I haven't thought more about in recent days—and God knows there are plenty of things to weigh my mind. But you..." He growled again. "You are torturing me, and I can't stand another moment." He lowered his head and kissed her.

She knew what to expect, recalled the slope of his lips, the stroke of his tongue, and the heat of his mouth. He kissed her long and hard, commanding her as he pressed his body to hers, pinning her against the wall. The weight of him against her was a delicious sensation, feeding what she craved.

He ground his pelvis against hers, sparking a tantalizing hunger in her sex. She arched against him, wanting what he said he'd give her—completion—whatever that was.

Dragging his mouth from hers, he held her by the nape and looked into her eyes, which she'd barely opened to see why he'd left her. "You didn't agree to my terms."

"You didn't state them."

"I said this will be one time and one time only. Do you agree?"

"That's one term. Are there more?"

"No, just the one."

Kat clutched his shoulder and his back. "I agree. Stop talking. Unless you're going to tell me what you plan to do. I do appreciate a good narrative."

Laughter bubbled from his mouth, and he kissed her again, swiftly but passionately. "You are unlike any woman I have ever known."

"I shall hope that is a good thing."

"Right now, it is the best thing," he whispered before he claimed her mouth once more and swept her away on a tide of arousal and longing. His hand moved down her neck and came around to her collarbone, his fingers skimming along her bare flesh.

"You want a narrative?" he asked softly, trailing his lips along her jaw and beneath her ear. "We must be careful with your gown. You'll need to hold it gently, so you don't wrinkle it. Can you do that? If you can't, we oughtn't continue."

"I can do that." Kat would have calmed the dogs of hell if it meant he wouldn't leave her. She dug her fingers into his back and shoulder. "Will you take off your coat?"

"Actually, that's a good idea." He released her to remove

the garment, and she had no idea what he did with it for she kept her eyes closed. Then she felt her skirt rise along her legs and cool air rushed over her bared flesh. Now, she opened her eyes to see him straightening. "Hold this. Remember, *gently*."

Kat curled her hand around the hem. "I'd rather hold you."

He chuckled. "We all have to make sacrifices, my sweet." His gaze lowered to her chest as he brought his hands up to cup her breasts through her clothing. "This is mine. I want desperately to loosen your clothing and suck on you here." He brushed his thumbs over her nipples. "Alas, that would cause too much upset to your appearance."

The words *next time* died on her tongue. There wouldn't be a next time. Just this one glorious, life-altering experience. She could already tell she would never be the same.

"Is that all you would do?" she asked, her voice low and thready. "Suck on me?"

"I would caress you, kiss you, lick you, pinch you." His hands closed around her as best they could, given her garments, and her breasts tingled with desire. Her nipples pulsed as if he were actually touching them. "Kat, you drive me nearly to mindless abandon."

In that moment, she wished she could witness him lose control. "I think it must be a wondrous sight to see you in complete surrender."

He looked into her eyes again and traced his thumb across her lips. Instinctively, she licked the pad. His eyes narrowed slightly. "Yes. Do it again."

She licked him again.

"Now suck."

Doing as he commanded, she drew his thumb into her mouth, all the way to the base. Curling her tongue around the bottom of the digit, she sucked on his flesh. His eyes closed, and his lips parted. It wasn't complete surrender, but it was ecstasy, and she was giving it to him. Kat felt a power she'd never expected. It made her even more aroused. She hoped she'd remember every detail of this encounter.

He withdrew his thumb and used it to moisten her lips, parting them just before he drove his tongue into her. A low moan filled the space, and Kat realized it came from her. She barely managed to hold on to her skirt as he ravished her mouth. Then he descended to her neck, feasting on her while his fingertips skimmed her thigh. He licked her flesh as low as he could go, his tongue dipping into her cleavage making her gasp. She wanted what he wanted so badly—to free her breasts so he could do what he said. For the rest of her life, she would dream of that.

She felt him move down her body and tensed as she felt his breath against her sex. He pressed a chaste kiss to her thigh.

"Don't be nervous," he said softly. "I think you will enjoy this. If at any moment, you don't, you must tell me. I suppose that is also a term. Do you agree?"

She nodded, her eyes still closed.

"Kat, look at me."

She opened her eyes and tipped her head down. Seeing him so close to her sex made her heart pound. So many strange sensations raced through her. Little quivers danced along her spine and her legs. Her breasts felt heavy and desperate for his touch. Her sex pulsed with need.

"Since you enjoy a good narrative, allow me to give you one. I'm going to pleasure you, and it will result in an orgasm —or completion as you are fond of saying." He gently traced his fingertip along the folds of her sex, and she sagged against the wall. "Hold on to my shoulder or my head, if you need to, but do not let go of your skirt, and for the love of God, try not to crumple it."

"I'll try. This is very intense, Lucien."

"Good. Intense is wonderful. At least, I think so. Now, I want you to put your foot up on this second step. That will open you to me." He clasped her calf just below her knee and guided her foot to the step. "There. All right?"

She definitely felt open now. It only increased her anticipation. "When are you going to touch me?"

"Now." He gripped her hip with his left hand, and with his right, moved his thumb up and down along her flesh, stroking and teasing her. "Does this feel good?"

"Yes, but I want more. It's as if something is just out of reach."

"That would be your orgasm. Some women can find it by being massaged here, on your clitoris." He swirled his thumb against the bead of flesh at the top of her sex.

Pleasure arced from the spot, moving through her abdomen and into her limbs. Kat whimpered like an animal and hoped that wasn't wrong. It was too bad if it was, because she was incapable of stopping herself. And her hips began to move, rotating with his touch, seeking friction.

"Other women," he continued, "come when they are penetrated. There's a spot inside that can trigger an orgasm."

"Come?"

"When you orgasm, you come."

That didn't make sense. "Why not arrive? If it's a completion, you wouldn't be coming, you'd be *arriving*."

He laughed again, his breath tickling her flesh. "Only you would debate this. Do you want to feel me inside?"

"Yes."

His hand skimmed from her hip to her sex, and now that thumb was stroking her sex. One of his fingers on his other hand pushed gently into her sheath. "Have you ever done this yourself?"

"No."

"Then I will go slowly." He entered her by degrees, his thumb moving up to caress her clitoris, until she was nearly panting with want.

When his finger was fully seated, he curled the digit toward him. "Is that the spot for you?"

It certainly felt good. White light danced behind her closed eyelids, and she did as he suggested, gripping his head with her free hand. But it wasn't enough. "I don't know. There has to be more."

"And there is." He withdrew his finger almost completely, then thrust in again, still going slowly, but faster than last time. "If we were actually coupling, this is what my cock would do to you." He pumped into her again and again, picking up speed with each stroke.

The thought of him doing this with his sex made her moan again, and she had to press herself against the wall to keep from crumpling. Everything was centered where he touched her, his thumb torturing her clitoris and his finger driving into her relentlessly.

"That excited you," he said, his voice deep and sensual.

"How do you know?" she sounded breathless.

"Your muscles clenched around my finger, and you got wetter. Do you feel how easily I move inside you now? The more aroused you are, the wetter you will be, and the better it will feel."

She never wanted him to stop. "Wetter is better, yes," she murmured, arching her neck as her body tightened with desire. There was something there, just out of reach. She just had to get there. *I'm coming,* she thought. *Aha.* Except she didn't think she was coming yet.

"When will I know if I'm complete?"

"You'll know, my sweet." He kissed her again, very close to her sex this time. "Now, I'm going to do what was in the book."

Her eyes flew open, and she looked down to see him watching her face. "You'll put your mouth...there?"

"Isn't that what you want?"

"Will it make me come?"

"I think so." He smiled, and her heart threatened to stop completely. "I hope so. I'm going to do my very best. Kat, I want nothing more than to bring you pleasure, to make you fall apart in my arms. Will you do that for me?"

She didn't think she could stop herself. "I feel something building. As if I'm moving toward something."

"Yes, move toward it. And do whatever you must. You won't hurt me. Make all the noise you want. No one will hear us in here."

"So it's all right if I mewl like a wounded animal?"

"It's fucking beautiful," he rasped. "I can't wait another moment, Kat."

She dug her fingers into his scalp. "I can't either."

He licked her sex, then he parted her folds and slid his tongue inside her. She watched as best she could, fascinated by his head between her legs. It was just like the book, but of course it was real.

Then he moved his mouth to her clitoris, and she stopped comparing anything. She closed her eyes again as her legs began to quiver. He kissed and sucked her, tormenting her flesh until she was both whimpering *and* moaning.

His finger entered her again while his mouth continued its ruthless attention. Her hips moved against him, and she prayed that was all right. She knew that was part of actual coupling, but was it acceptable for this? He'd told her to do whatever she liked, that she wouldn't hurt him.

Don't think, just feel.

Kat cried out as he buried his face against her, his tongue driving into her. She was so close, her body hurtling toward that light of bliss. Her legs wobbled, but before she could fall, he caught her, gripping her hips as he continued to lick and suck her flesh. When she was stable, he moved one hand back between her legs and positioned himself so that he was practically under her. He lifted her leg from the step and put it over his shoulder.

Good God, she was all but riding him. This wasn't the illustration, but it felt so bloody good. Then it started. Rapture uncurled inside her as her muscles tightened and pleasure cascaded through her. She cried out over and over, her thighs clenching.

Lucien didn't leave her. He held her and stroked her with his tongue and fingers until the release was complete.

"I have arrived," she croaked.

Somehow, his laughter broke through her addled state. He caressed her hip, her backside, her thigh as she put herself back together again. He had said she would fall apart, and that was precisely what it had felt like. And what a spectacular way to break.

"You can let go of your dress now." Lucien sounded as though he were standing, and she didn't feel him between her legs anymore. She could not have said when he stood.

"I seem to have gone somewhere," she said, opening her eyes to see him leaning against the opposite wall. It wasn't far away, for the corridor was quite narrow.

"I believe you said you arrived." A smile teased his mouth, and if she hadn't been so terribly weak from *arriving*, she would have moved to kiss him.

"Is my dress in good condition?" she asked, noticing he'd donned his coat while she was lost.

His gaze flicked downward. "Impeccable. It's a stunning gown. You look ravishing in it."

"So long as I don't look ravish*ed*."

"Your cheeks are flushed, but if you wait to go downstairs, you should look quite normal."

"I don't know what that is, but if you're saying no one will notice I am changed, then I suppose that's for the best. I, however, will *never* be the same, and I thank you most profusely."

He pushed away from the wall. "I'm going to my office. You go the way we came in. We can't risk leaving here together."

"That makes sense." She grabbed his hand. "Thank you. Truly. I know you were...hesitant."

He turned toward her and cupped her face. "Kat, I don't regret a moment, and I hope you won't either. But this is all there will be for us."

"I know." There was that breaking sensation again, but it was different. This was entirely emotional and not at all physical.

He kissed her cheek, and she felt his heat. It occurred to her that he had not found completion. "What will you do now?" she asked.

"What do you mean?"

"You'll just go down to the assembly without... I don't know...without satisfying yourself?"

He shook his head with a faint smile. "Do me a favor and do not ask me to dance. I couldn't bear it." He let go of her hand and walked up the stairs toward his office.

Kat's body sang with a satisfied bliss she could barely describe—but she would try. Later, when she returned home and probably stayed up all night reliving every moment so she could record it. For her research or posterity? How many times would she read it in the years to come?

She would make two copies, at least. For, she would like to reread them until they were in tatters. And then she would write them again.

Nothing would ever compare to this night. Nor did she want it to.

CHAPTER 14

*L*ucien stepped through the bookcase and pulled it closed, his gaze unfocused as he tried to make sense of the madness in which he'd just engaged. He managed to find the liquor cabinet and pour himself a glass of whisky. Swallowing all of it, he barely tasted the alcohol before it settled in his gut. Rather than pour another, he set the glass down and stumbled to the hearth.

He put his hand on the mantel and bent his head, taking deep breaths to calm his racing pulse. Unlike Kat, he hadn't reached a relaxed state following her orgasm. He was more agitated with lust than ever.

What will you do now?

Frig himself blind—that's what he *should* do. But that would be another surrender. Goddammit, he'd tried to withhold himself from her. He'd looked forward to tonight, thinking she might ask him to dance, that he'd at least be able to touch her in that way. God, had he really been that starved for her that he would anticipate such an unsatisfactory interaction?

Clearly, that was the case, because all she'd had to do was

show him an erotic illustration, and he'd lost his damned mind. That and the merest mention of the secret passageway. It was the one place he felt almost entirely confident they wouldn't ever be discovered.

Straightening, he took his hand from the mantel and scrubbed it over his face. He was angry at himself, but he didn't regret what he'd done. He'd meant it when he'd said it would just be the one time. That made it all right, didn't it? He laughed, a scratchy, hoarse sound that had nothing to do with humor.

No, it wasn't all right. She was Ruark's sister, and after Lucien's reaction to Ruark and Cass's relationship, it was beyond hypocritical. But it wouldn't happen again.

Except, if he could fetch her back here, he'd do it in the beat of a heart. One thing was certain: he couldn't just go down to the assembly with this raging erection and unfulfilled lust.

Exhaling a series of curse words, he threw himself in a chair near the hearth. He leaned his head back and closed his eyes, then unbuttoned his fall.

The scent and taste of Kat filled his senses as he pulled his cock from his garments and stroked the length. He imagined her hand around him, her inquisitive gaze, her lush lips as she licked them in anticipation. He groaned as his body galloped toward release.

"Can I help?"

Lucien's eyes flew open as if the club were on fire. He didn't immediately see her. She stood half in and half out of the passageway, her body pressed in the barely open bookcase. Had he not closed it all the way? She shouldn't have known how to work the mechanism to get in.

His hand stilled around the base of his shaft, but his cock didn't soften. If anything, more blood rushed to the organ, making him almost unbearably stiff. "You shouldn't be here," he rasped.

"I know, but I came to see if you were all right. I can't imagine you would be. If you'd left me before I arrived, I don't think I could face the rest of the evening. Or perhaps even the rest of my life." She laughed, and he would have smiled in return if he weren't in such agony.

"You are a treasure." And she was. He would forever think of coming as arriving now. As she'd said she was forever changed, so was he. He'd never shared an experience such as that with someone like her—someone so joyously inquisitive and so bloody honest.

She stepped fully into the office, her gaze moving to his rigid cock. "I could help you, if you like. You might have to guide me, but I'm eager to learn."

"Of course you are. This will get messy. Are you sure you wouldn't rather just watch?" God, that was perhaps worse. Moisture leaked from his tip as his cock twitched.

"That is incredibly tempting." She took a step toward him. "But as it's a Leap Year ball and I get to do the asking, I'm asking again if I may help. I suppose you can refuse, but really, it would be rude."

Now he did laugh. Only Kat would turn this into something he couldn't deny without losing face. "You're saying I won't be a gentleman if I don't let you frig me?"

"Is that what it's called? And yes, you'll be a cad."

"I am definitely a cad after what I did to you in the passageway." Another bolt of lust streaked through him. God, he could still taste her. "There are many names for it," he said, answering her question.

She tipped her head to the side. "What will you do to orgasm?"

"I'll stroke myself until I…arrive."

"You said it would be messy."

"A man's seed is far messier than a lady's...moisture. It will spew from the tip."

She gave a vague nod. "I imagine that's necessary to ensure the lady conceives, which was originally the point of coupling."

"I'm not sure that's the case. If so, why would it feel so damned good? *That's* what you should be studying." He could hardly believe he was able to have this discussion with her in this moment, but damn if there was anything else he'd rather be doing.

"You raise an interesting query. I will most definitely investigate that." She moved to stand in front of him, situating herself between his legs. "Show me how you stroke yourself."

"Weren't you watching from the doorway?"

"I was, but I want to see it again from this closer vantage point."

Lucien brought his hand up along his shaft and slid it down again to the base. Her gaze was locked on his movements, and he wondered how many strokes it would take. Two? Three? Not many.

"That's what I would do?" she asked.

"Yes." But it would feel so much better. He took his hand away. "Wrap your hand around the base."

She encircled him in her soft grip, and he closed his eyes briefly, letting out a low growl. "I like that sound," she said, surprising him. "Very animalistic. I'm learning that we are not so different from them."

"It's all very primal." Lucien could barely make words as she glided her hand up his length. He watched her, his body tightening with arousal and making him nearly incoherent.

She started to kneel. He grabbed her arm. "Don't. Your dress. What are you doing?"

"I wanted to put my mouth on you, as you did me. I know that's not unusual."

"No, it's not. But it's not usual at all for *you*. Dammit, Kat, I said what we did was a singular situation."

"This is a different situation," she argued. "I'm pleasuring *you*."

How could he find fault with that?

He gave up. And really, had he ever stood a chance? "Sit in the other chair, but try not to wrinkle your gown."

She hastened to obey, perching on the opposite chair. Lucien quickly went to make sure the office door was locked, something he should have done the moment he came in from the passageway.

When he returned to her, she was watching him with a heavy-lidded gaze, her lips parted, and the tip of her tongue just visible. It took everything he had to keep from thrusting into her mouth.

"Remember how you sucked my thumb?" he somehow managed to ask past the haze of lust in his brain. At her nod, he went on. "Do that to my cock."

"Lovely," she murmured, her expression one of hunger and desire. Yes, honesty. Nothing about her was artifice. She was completely and wholly with him in this moment, which made him completely and wholly in this moment in a way he perhaps had never been. "Come to me," she said huskily.

He moved to stand in front of her, gasping as she clasped his cock in both hands. She worked him slowly at first, using her thumb to caress the head. "Are you more sensitive here?"

"I'm sensitive everywhere."

Stroking down, she cupped his balls. "Here too?"

He leaned over her and gripped the back of the chair for support. "*Yes.* Please, Kat. Take me in your mouth."

She put her lips around him, and he jerked back. "Wait,"

he said, interrupting the most erotic moment of his life. "I said this is messy. There will be...semen—"

"Should I swallow it? That seems the tidiest. And isn't that what's typically done?" She didn't stop frigging him while she spoke, and he thought he might die.

"Typically, yes," he croaked. "But some women don't like it."

Lifting a shoulder, she licked her lips. "I'll let you know after I try."

Then she leaned forward and took him into her mouth, just as she'd done his thumb. Her tongue cradled the underside of his cock, and she sucked him to the back of her throat.

He nearly arrived right then. Digging his fingers into the chair, he resisted touching her, lest he wreck her elegant hairstyle. But when she began to move her head, delivering him into ecstasy, he clasped her collarbone, his fingers pressing into her nape.

One of her hands clutched his backside, her nails digging into his flesh as she worked her lips and tongue over and around him, doing things he couldn't even have thought to ask her. He'd been close for so long now, barely holding himself in check. He couldn't do it any longer. She had completely conquered him, and he wanted nothing but to give her his total surrender.

"Kat, I'm...arriving." He thrust into her mouth, unable to hold back. His balls tightened, and he cried out as his orgasm exploded over him.

He nearly shouted her name, but managed to stop himself. His office was not isolated like the passageway. Eyes closed, he held on to her as if he'd been cast into a wild sea. She was his anchor, the only thing keeping him from disappearing completely into the heavens.

Gradually, he slowed, his hips ceasing their thrusting. She

eased her mouth from him, and when he opened his eyes, she was just running her fingertips along her lips.

She looked up at him with an absolutely captivating smile. "I hope you arrived well."

"Never better." He realized that was true. The most erotic experience of his life in the passageway had somehow been surpassed right here.

"I must confess, the swallowing thing will take some getting used to."

Lucien froze. He was having a hard time gathering his wits, and that comment from her didn't help his situation. He managed to push his cock back into his garments and button his fall. "You needn't swallow if you'd prefer not to. I can spill myself elsewhere."

Her eyes lit with interest. "Where?"

"Your curiosity never fails to astonish me. Perhaps on your breasts."

Drawing in a breath, her mouth rounded. "Oh. Well. Next time, you can show me."

Lucien shook his head violently. "No. No, there will not be a next time. I was clear about this being a singular event, and you agreed."

She arched a brow at him. "Do you really want to attempt that feeble argument again? We have now had *two* singular events, and I, for one, am very much looking forward to the third. I do understand the care we must take, and as you said, this was a perfect opportunity of time and location. I am confident we will find such an occasion again, whether it's in a few days or a few weeks. I can be patient, particularly since I now understand completion and can perhaps even effect it for myself."

Damn it to hell, now he was going to be imagining that almost constantly. The notion of Kat in the throes of self-pleasure was enough to make his cock stir again. He stared at her, wondering how in the hell he'd become so bloody entangled. And why he wasn't running as far and fast as he could away from her.

Because he wanted her. He liked her. He *craved* her in a way he had never experienced before. And, God help him, this was just the beginning.

No, it couldn't be. He couldn't allow this to continue.

"What am I going to do with you?" he whispered.

She grinned. "A great many things, according to what you said recently. I'll make a list."

Instead of responding—because really what could he say?—Lucien wiped his hand down his face.

"I should probably go," Kat said, rising from the chair.

"You will take the passageway. I really need to get downstairs. I've been gone far too long." He would certainly have been missed. Excuses for his disappearance ran through his head. "You should go back to the library for ten minutes or so—we shouldn't return to the assembly at the same time."

She nodded. "I can do that. I'm keen to pick up that book from the library and take it home, though I probably oughtn't carry it around the assembly."

"God no, please don't."

"I'll fetch it before I leave, then. It will be most helpful as I make our list."

Our list. She fully intended them to be together again.

He feared he was helpless to stop it, for there was nothing he wanted more.

～

The day after the assembly, Kat called on Jess and learned the coded letter was indeed a love letter, though the author and intended recipient were not identified. Jess had given her a translated copy. While it was fascinating to learn how Jess had deciphered the letter, Kat had already moved on from that project. She was far more intrigued with cultivating her list of research topics to investigate with Lucien.

Though she'd considered sharing what had happened with Lucien with Jess, Kat had ultimately decided against it. The event was seared into her mind, probably because she'd stayed up most of the night recording every detail, in such a way that it had become a rather personal and private memory. No other research she'd conducted could compare, of course.

There was also the fact that Lucien was obsessed with no one finding out, which she understood. It would ruin Kat, not that she cared, but that would be detrimental to her family. It would also negatively affect Lucien, and he didn't need that right now with everything else going on. She did hope she'd relieved his agitation somewhat and wish she'd remembered to ask after their exciting encounters.

Three days later, her body was still thrumming with a satisfied bliss. Or perhaps it was anticipation. Both, she thought. She was most eager to see Lucien again, but didn't know when that would be.

Would he avoid her? She suspected he might. He'd been so reluctant to surrender to their mutual attraction. And she'd seen how affected he was—as much as she'd been.

"You're all ready?" Cass asked, sweeping into the entrance hall in her evening attire. "You look lovely."

"Thank you." Kat realized it was odd that she was waiting for Cass instead of the other way around, but she hoped Lucien would be at tonight's rout and was anxious to get there. He was also the reason she'd taken extra care with her preparations.

Cass's gaze fixed on Kat's head. "You let Eliza do your hair again."

Kat had been resisting the use of a ladies' maid despite Cass's efforts to give her one since she'd come to live with them. She accepted help to dress on occasion, but the rest of it seemed unnecessary and frankly intrusive. Kat appreciated her solitude and didn't care for people fussing about her. But when she recalled how Lucien had looked at her at the assembly, Kat had decided it was worth the trouble. "I did."

"Well, that's...nice." Cass was clearly surprised. "Shall we go, then?"

"Is Ruark not coming?"

"No, he's at the club with Lucien and Dougal and whoever else."

The hall suddenly grew more dim, and Kat had to keep her shoulders from drooping. "None of them are coming to the rout?"

"I don't think so. They're having some sort of strategy meeting about how to recruit some members or re-recruit." Cass waved her hand. "I'm not entirely certain." She walked to the door, and the butler opened it.

Kat, now without a hint of interest in attending the rout, grudgingly followed Cass from the house. When they were ensconced in the coach, she asked, "How long must we stay?"

Cass laughed. "You went to all that trouble and want to make it an abbreviated visit?"

Shrugging, Kat tried not to scowl. "I thought more people we knew would be there."

"It's entirely likely they will. Fiona will be there, and I'm hoping Prudence might be as well. She and Bennett returned to town with the baby on Saturday."

"I'm sure you're looking forward to seeing her," Kat murmured, her mind still fixed on the monotonous evening ahead.

"You don't sound very enthused." Cass, seated beside Kat

on the forward-facing seat, turned her head. "Who isn't coming that you'd hoped to see?"

Kat shrugged. "No one in particular, I suppose. It will be nice to see Prudence." Perhaps Jess would also come, but she'd told Kat on Saturday that she likely wouldn't attend.

Thankfully, Cass didn't press. A few minutes later, they arrived at their destination and departed the coach. The rout was hosted by Mr. and Mrs. Brightly. He was a man of import in the House of Commons.

Kat followed Cass inside, where there were more people in attendance than she would have liked. It could be that she'd need to beg off early anyway if she began to feel overwhelmed. Almost immediately, however, she saw Lady Pickering, who came directly toward her.

She took Kat's hand and surveyed her. "You look absolutely breathtaking. That gown is stunning." It was a dark orange, almost red, which was one of the hues of the gown she'd worn the other night.

"Thank you. The modiste said this color would make me glow."

"It does indeed." Lady Pickering exchanged pleasantries with Cass, and the three walked upstairs to the drawing room. "Is the new wardrobe catapulting you to the front of the Marriage Mart?"

"I hardly think so." Kat tried not to sound horrified at such a prospect. Lady Pickering didn't understand her desire to remain unwed, which seemed a trifle sanctimonious for a widow who clearly enjoyed her independence.

"Then let us attempt to rectify that this evening. You should be one of the most pursued young ladies this Season."

Before Kat could look to Cass for assistance, her sister-in-law had gone to speak with someone standing just outside the drawing room. It seemed Kat would need to manage this situation herself.

As she and Lady Pickering walked into the drawing room, Kat summoned what she hoped was a pleasant smile, but it felt rather fake. "Lady Pickering, I'm certain I've explained to you that I've no desire to wed. At least not at this time. I'm enjoying being in London without the responsibilities of marriage."

"Bah. Once you are wed, you can move about even more freely." Lady Pickering lowered her voice. "The trick is to marry an old, *wealthy* man. That's what I did, and I've been able to lead a magnificent life." She winked at Kat.

"I'm sure your parents demanded you marry," Kat said. "Mine have not." At least not yet, so she would take the time she had. Dammit, she didn't want to discuss this. Oh! She could talk about something else. "I found the most intriguing thing at the Phoenix Club the other night." She was vague about the timing since she could not admit to being there on Tuesday, but *was* there for the assembly on Friday.

"What could that be?" Lady Pickering asked with mild interest.

"I was in the ladies' library doing some research, and I found a coded letter tucked into one of the books. Since Jess is so good at solving puzzles and riddles, I gave it to her."

Lady Pickering's attention snapped to Kat. "Did you now? That *is* intriguing. Was she able to decipher it?"

"In fact, she was. It was just a love letter, and she has no idea who wrote it or who it was intended for. I have to think it was a missive between ladies given its location. It's no wonder they are communicating in secret."

"Did she—or you—put the letter back so the person could receive it?"

"Yes." Kat had asked Jess on Saturday if the letter had been replaced in the book. She hadn't thought to confirm that with Lucien in the library. Understandably, she'd been distracted by other things on her mind. Or by the man who'd interrupted her study. In the best possible way.

"Kathleen?"

Kat blinked upon hearing her name. The baroness refused to call her by the name of an animal, or so she said. She'd obviously missed something Lady Pickering had said. "Yes?"

"I asked how the assembly went. Since it was a Leap Year ball, I assume you took advantage of asking several gentlemen to dance?"

"I did." If two counted as several. Kat had wanted to ask Lucien, of course, but hadn't dared. Plus, he'd avoided her the rest of the evening after their encounters. If they were in any sort of proximity to one another, he retreated quickly. Instead, she'd asked two gentlemen she vaguely knew. In the not-too-distant past, she might have tried to lure one of them to the garden for a kissing experiment, but after her studies with Lucien, she couldn't remember why she'd deemed them worthy of kissing experimentation in the first place.

"Good evening, Lady Pickering, Kat." Sabrina Westbrook, the Countess of Aldington, who was married to Lucien's older brother Constantine, approached them. Her husband was nearby speaking with their host, and Kat vaguely recalled they were good friends.

Kat was relieved and glad to see Sabrina. Of all the people in her now extended family, Kat felt the closest kinship with the countess. "I'm pleased to see you here," Kat said, moving toward Sabrina.

"I decided to join Aldington," Sabrina said.

"How is your young son?" Lady Pickering asked.

"He's very well, thank you."

They chatted a few more minutes before Lady Pickering took her leave. Kat finally allowed her body to sag a bit.

"Did I rescue you from something?" Sabrina asked quietly.

"Why do you say that?"

"You look visibly lighter than a few moments ago. Or is it just that it's a crush?"

Kat appreciated Sabrina's perception. "Both, actually. Lady Pickering was asking about my efforts on the Marriage Mart. She actually encouraged me to find a rich, elderly husband."

"Well, I suppose that worked out well for her," Sabrina murmured. "But I don't think you're really in the market for a husband at present, are you?"

"No, and I thank you for noticing that. Sometimes I think Cass and Ruark would like to marry me off. With the baby coming, I'll be in the way."

"I don't believe they think that. However, if you ever feel as if you are in the way there somehow, I hope you know you are always welcome at Aldington House. Or at Hampton Lodge." That was their house not far from London in Middlesex, where Sabrina and Con spent much of their time. If Kat didn't love London so much, she might consider it. But she wasn't really being fair. Cass and Ruark were delighted to have her. "I think you are probably right, that *I* am the one thinking I might be imposing once the baby is born."

"You shouldn't. Cass loves you like a sister, and I can imagine she'd love for their child to have his auntie around."

That would be nice. Kat glanced around the drawing room and felt a bead of apprehension dash up her neck. It was very crowded. And loud. "How long are you staying?" she asked Sabrina.

"Probably not long. This is more people in a tighter space than I typically care for. However, I won't leave too soon because I don't want Mrs. Brightly to think I was uncomfortable. She's a dear friend. How about if we go downstairs? It's quieter down there."

"Yes, please." Kat started toward the doorway and just outside it paused to tell Cass where she was going with Sabrina.

"Wonderful." A small pleat formed between Cass's brows, perhaps indicating she realized this was potentially over-whelming to both of her sisters-in-law. "I'll come find you in a short while," conveying her understanding that they might need to leave soon.

Kat and Sabrina continued downstairs, where it was not only quieter but cooler. They walked from the staircase hall into another room—the library, probably.

And that was when the entire evening went to hell.

Kat came face-to-face with Mrs. Hickinbottom and her daughter. The mother was in her forties, with a round face and a small, dimpled chin. Her dark eyes focused sharply on Kat as her narrow nose wrinkled as if she'd smelled some-thing bad. "I was rather hoping we wouldn't have to suffer your presence here in town, Miss Shaughnessy."

"I beg your pardon, but I am the Countess of Aldington." Sabrina's tone and gaze were haughty and cool. Kat wanted to hug her. "There's no call for rudeness. It's likely Miss Shaughnessy doesn't want to suffer your presence either." She glanced toward Kat.

Kat suspected Sabrina didn't know who these people were, and why would she? "This is Mrs. Hickinbottom and her daughter, Delia, rather, Miss Hickinbottom." Kat had known Delia since they were children. Delia was the same age as Kat's younger sister Iona and had always preferred her company to Kat's.

"Ah, I see." Sabrina entwined her arm with Kat's, seem-ingly to indicate she now knew who these women were and would provide support.

"Just stay away from my daughter," Mrs. Hickinbottom said with a sneer. "Why you're permitted in Polite Society is beyond me."

"There's no call to air this here," Sabrina said quietly. She glanced about rather furtively, prompting Kat to wonder why.

Then Cass entered, and Kat felt Sabrina relax slightly. Cass came straight toward them, her features set with concern. But then she smiled brilliantly as soon as she arrived. "Good evening, Mrs. Hickinbottom, Miss Hickinbottom. How lovely to see you. I trust you're enjoying London? It's quite a change from Lechlade."

"You said you would keep this…strumpet away from us when we came to town." Mrs. Hickinbottom didn't try to keep her voice down, and even Kat recognized she was speaking rather loudly.

"I promised we would avoid you if at all possible, in part because you are incredibly disagreeable," Cass said through a wide smile. "However, if we encounter each other, it's best if we just continue on without engaging, don't you agree?"

Mrs. Hickinbottom pursed her lips.

"Mama, shouldn't we move on?" Delia asked in a soft voice. "You said I couldn't be in Miss Shaughnessy's company, that it would ruin me."

"As if we'd want to be in your sour company either." Kat hadn't meant to say that, but the words had somehow pushed their way forth. She knew better than to allow her impulses free rein, but sometimes she couldn't help it.

"Yes, yes, let us move on." Mrs. Hickinbottom gave Kat a dark glare.

"Have a good evening, Mrs. Hickinbottom," Sabrina said sweetly. "I'll let Mrs. Brightly, who is a very dear friend of mine, know how highly we think of you. We'll also be sure to give your best to Lady Wexford's father, *the Duke of Evesham.*"

Mrs. Hickinbottom's eyes widened just before she turned, dragging her daughter along with her.

"Let us depart," Cass said succinctly. "Are you coming, Sabrina?"

"I should tell Con." Sabrina gave Kat's arm a squeeze before walking back toward the staircase hall.

Cass turned to Kat. "Are you all right?"

"I should not have said what I did, but they were obnoxious."

"Yes, and hopefully the conversation was not overheard." Cass looked about the library, where there were fewer than ten people gathered in pairs or small groups. It was hard to tell if they'd heard what was said.

"Mrs. Hickinbottom was rather loud," Kat noted. "But hopefully everyone else was involved in their own conversations." Honestly, Kat didn't care about her reputation—what did she even need it for? The idea of becoming a hermit who could carry on a secret affair with Lucien was becoming more appealing by the moment.

"Yes, we will hope," Cass muttered. "I'm glad Sabrina was with you."

"Why, because I might have made things worse?"

Cass cast her a sideways glance as they moved toward the staircase hall. "No, because she's a countess and Mrs. Hickinbottom being rude in her presence will reflect poorly on Mrs. Hickinbottom."

"But it wouldn't have if it had just been me?" Kat shook her head. "I will never understand Society."

"Please talk more quietly," Cass said. "Oh look, Sabrina has met Con on the landing there." She gestured up the stairs.

Kat looked up to see that Con was frowning. Then he glanced toward Kat. The frown seemed to deepen. This wasn't her fault!

Well, tonight wasn't. However, she wasn't foolish

enough to think her actions a year ago hadn't caused this problem. Perhaps she should become a hermit for everyone's sakes. It wasn't as if she was any good at any of this nonsense.

"I'm going out to the coach," she announced to Cass.

"Wait." Cass tried to reach for her, but Kat moved too quickly. "You can't just—" She hurried after Kat.

The butler hastened to open the door for Kat before she bustled into the early March night. It was now drizzling, and the coach was nowhere to be seen, as there was a line of coaches of people coming and going. They should have sent a footman for it, of course, but Kat had simply barreled forward. *"Don't be so impulsive!"* her mother would admonish. *"You must learn to be patient."*

Hadn't Kat told Lucien that she could be patient? She'd learned to be, just as she'd learned to not act on impulse. Mostly.

Kat turned to Cass. "We should go back inside until the coach is here."

"Yes." Cass came to her and put her arm around her waist to walk back into the house. "I understand you're upset—and that you don't want to be. I know you find all this annoying."

"That is an apt description. I made a mistake a year ago. Must it continue to follow me?"

Cass pressed her lips together in a grim line. "Unfortunately, that is often the cost of mistakes."

They encountered Sabrina in the entrance hall. She told them a footman had already been dispatched to fetch Cass's coach. Con was also going to fetch their coach personally.

Kat must have missed seeing him dash out the door. She looked to Sabrina. "Will you please apologize to your husband for me?"

"There's no need for that."

"He frowned at me."

Sabrina's gaze widened with alarm. "What? Oh no, he was just concerned for you. Mrs. Hickinbottom was terrible."

"He's not worried I've caused problems for your family?"

"Not at all." Sabrina waved her hand. "He will crush Mrs. Hickinbottom like an errant fly. Well, he would, but I told him we needn't go to such extremes. I'd like to believe she'll leave you alone now that she's vented her spleen."

Kat hoped so, but wasn't sure she believed it. "How can you be sure that will happen?" Perhaps she wouldn't be able to go out in Society at all.

Would that be so terrible?

"Because I'm going to maintain a positive outlook," Sabrina said firmly. "You should too. In any case, we're not sorry we're leaving, are we?" She gave Kat a warm smile.

"Not in the slightest."

The coach arrived a moment later, and they took their leave. At least the evening had been short.

CHAPTER 15

$\mathcal{B}$etween anticipating today's meeting and continuing to think far too much about Kat, Lucien had barely slept last night. He'd been at the club particularly late, even for a Tuesday, but then he'd been spending even more time there. Especially in his office, where images of Kat filled his mind and tormented his body. Though it was torture, he liked being there where he'd last spent time with her. Because he had no idea when—or if—he'd ever see her like that again.

Of course he wouldn't. They'd risked a great deal and managed to escape notice. He'd lived long enough to know that eventually, they'd get caught. The more their passion consumed them, the less careful they would be. And Lucien was already in danger of completely losing his wits where she was concerned. He knew Ruark's house well and had mapped a dozen ways he could enter and find his way to Kat's room while evading detection. That was madness, but it didn't stop him from indulging his fantasies.

Those were all he had since he'd been avoiding seeing her and would continue to do so. It was for the best.

Except he'd just received a note from Cass inviting him to a family dinner on Sunday. Since Prudence and Bennett were back in town, she wanted to get everyone together. That more than likely included their father and would definitely include Kat. It would be the best and worst of times.

Lucien shook his head. He needed to clear his thoughts. The meeting would be happening today, and since it was now noon, he had to move into position to watch for their arrival. Who they would be was anyone's guess. Dougal hadn't been able to learn anything about a meeting, which wasn't surprising to Lucien. He was no longer an official part of the Foreign Office.

Reynolds had hired a team of men who'd been watching over the club since Friday night. So far, no one had entered the club who wasn't supposed to be there. Today, everyone was on high alert, watching carefully for who would enter and where. Lucien expected them to use the secret gate from Bury Street to the garden on the men's side. From there, they could take the private door that opened into the back staircase, which would take them up to the second or top floor where the "meeting cupboard" was located.

Because of that, Dougal was stationed on the second floor, and Lucien planned to sit behind a row of shrubbery in the garden where he could watch the gate and the door. Reynolds was on the street with his eyes on the gate's exterior. If anyone came in that way, Reynolds would shortly follow, just in case Lucien missed them. They weren't leaving anything to chance.

Lucien stood from his chair behind the desk and left his office. He went out to the back terrace and down the stairs to the garden. As soon as he took his spot behind the shrubbery, he realized he should at least have grabbed a hat. The March wind was brisk and cold.

It was more than an hour before someone finally came

through the gate. Lucien had allowed himself to fall into a half trance in which he peeled every piece of Kat's clothing from her body and worshipped every inch of her until she writhed and moaned and begged him to deliver her arrival. So when the two men stepped through the gate, Lucien had to blink to make sure he was actually seeing something real.

One of them was Oliver Kent. Yes, this was most definitely real. Lucien's gut clenched. Whoever showed up at this meeting had likely played a role in Giraud's death. Lucien was sorry to see the man he'd long looked up to had been involved, even if he wasn't surprised at this point. Especially since Kent had tasked Jess with determining if Dougal was working against the Foreign Office—which Dougal had specifically discovered was about whether he'd killed Giraud. To find out that Kent was involved would infuriate Dougal.

Lucien didn't recognize the other man, however. He waited until they'd gone into the club, then dashed across the garden to follow them inside.

Standing at the base of the stairs, Lucien worked to take deep, *quiet* breaths to calm his racing heart. He heard a door shut above him in the staircase, then carefully began his ascent. When he reached the landing of the second floor, he opened the door slowly and peered into the corridor. Dougal emerged from a small room at the other end.

Lucien hurried forward, keeping his feet as quiet as possible. Dougal met him midway, near the door to the meeting room.

"Did you see them?" Lucien asked, keeping his voice low.

"I was able to peer around the doorjamb and make out two men," Dougal whispered. "One of them looked like he could be Kent."

"Because he is."

Dougal's lips pressed together in distaste. "The son of a bitch. Ready?"

Lucien responded with a nod. A breath later, Dougal pushed open the door. Two candles flickered on the table, and Kent was just lighting the sconce on the wall.

"What's going on today, gentlemen?" Lucien asked affably. Dougal still looked mildly perturbed, or at least serious. Lucien was certain he was seething on the inside.

Kent turned from the sconce, appearing surprised. "Lucien, how did you know we were here?"

"It's my club. I like to know everything that happens here." Lucien didn't add that it seemed for too long he hadn't, and that he'd taken steps to rectify that shortcoming.

Kent smoothed his gray hair. He'd removed his hat and gloves and set them on the table. The other gentleman still wore his accessories, which Lucien found odd.

"This is Martin," Kent said, gesturing to the other gentleman who was at least a few years younger than Kent, which put him in his middle or late fifties. "He works directly for Lord Castlereagh."

Did he now? Lucien glanced toward Dougal to see if he recognized the man, but Dougal's features were utterly impassive.

"Welcome to the Phoenix Club," Lucien said. "To what do I owe the pleasure of your attendance today?"

"We came here to discuss a few things and to see you, Lord Lucien." Martin's accent was East London, if Lucien had to guess, but the man tried to cover that. It was possible he'd risen from some lowly rank over the course of his career and had been obliged to cultivate his speech. Martin flicked a glance toward Dougal, but didn't address him.

"Fallin, perhaps you'd give us a few minutes," Kent said with a faint smile. He seemed a trifle nervous. Which made Lucien anxious.

"He stays," Lucien said. "What do you want with me?" He addressed both Kent and the unknown Martin.

Kent grimaced. "This is rather delicate. I really would feel more comfortable if Fallin excused himself."

"I'm going to tell him whatever you tell me," Lucien said. "He's a key component of the Phoenix Club, and I assume your errand today involves the club."

"It does," Martin said. He stepped toward Lucien, his thin lips tightly pressed together. The man was much shorter than Lucien, but that was often true since he was a towering six feet and four inches. Martin had to tip his head back to meet Lucien's gaze. "I'll get right to the point. We know you killed Giraud, but we won't be punishing you for it since he was working against the cr—"

"That's not true." Outrage coupled with fear raced through Lucien prompting him to interrupt. "I barely knew the man." Giraud conducted a few meetings at the club, passing information while posing as a member. Dougal knew him far better.

"You can't know that," Dougal said softly.

Lucien turned his head to see his friend staring at Martin with unconcealed menace. If he hadn't known Dougal was his ally, he would be afraid.

"I *can* know that, and I do," Martin responded.

Dougal stepped toward Martin. "Lucien wasn't even near Bournemouth when Giraud was killed. I was, however."

"But you had nothing to do with his death," Kent broke in. "You've always maintained that you found him dead, and we've no reason to doubt that."

"Except you did," Dougal reminded him. "Or have you forgotten that you hired my wife to spy on me?"

"We resolved that you were innocent of any wrongdoing," Kent muttered. He didn't meet Dougal's eyes, which also bothered Lucien. Something was wrong with Kent. Probably, this was just an incredibly uncomfortable situation for him— he'd known Lucien for years.

"You can't believe I did that," Lucien said. "My position with the Foreign Office doesn't require that sort of...activity. I run this club, and that's the extent of my occupation."

Kent looked at Lucien now. "It's not as if you can't kill someone. You demonstrated that quite well in Spain. Furthermore, you could have hired someone to kill Giraud."

Was he referring to when Max had killed the soldiers who'd murdered his betrothed, and Lucien had aided him? "I will always defend my brothers-in-arms," Lucien said quietly, rage blistering his insides.

He would not apologize for what he'd done in Spain. Those men were barbarians. Yes, they should have been captured and tried for their crimes, but war didn't always work that way, particularly when unimaginable loss and grief were involved.

Martin cleared his throat and looked to Lucien. "The Foreign Office has decided it is time for you to retire. Completely. You'll 'sell' the Phoenix Club and walk away entirely."

Lucien stared at the man, barely keeping his anger in check. "I will not," he said softly, but with heat. Of all the things he might have suspected would happen at this meeting today, that was not one of them.

"You can't make him do that," Dougal said, looking between Martin and Kent, but settling on the latter.

"We can and we will. Lord Lucien has no choice but to do as he's told. He is not a principal owner of the club." Martin spoke in an utterly flat tone. "The Foreign Office will communicate the 'buyer' soon, and at that time, Lord Lucien will make the transaction public. Then he will go away, preferably *far* away from London."

Lucien's body had gone cold. It wasn't enough to take his club, they wanted to banish him from his home? He shook his head. "I won't do it. I'll go public with the Foreign Office's involvement and manipulation if I must."

Kent reached out as if he was going to grasp Lucien's arm, but ultimately decided to abandon the prospect, letting his hand fall to his side. "And how will that look—you turning on the Foreign Office? You will be the villain, Lucien. I'm afraid you have no choice. Since you do have some investment in the club, the Foreign Office will compensate you. It's not as if you'll walk away with nothing."

That was precisely what he would be doing. The Phoenix Club was everything to Lucien—his work, his livelihood, his friends, his bloody *family*. They, especially Kent, who'd been more of a father figure to Lucien than his own father, couldn't ask this of him.

Martin's mouth curled into a slight but irritating smirk. "Not to mention, if you cause difficulty, only consider what your father will think."

Lucien sucked in a breath and gritted his teeth. His father would make his life miserable—more than he already did. Was he aware of this current maneuver by the Foreign Office? Lucien sure as hell wasn't going to ask. The answer would almost certainly devastate him.

There had to be another way around this. Dougal would help him determine the right course.

"I must be off," Martin said, as if they'd just concluded a friendly meeting and not destroyed Lucien's life. "We'll send word regarding the transition." He glanced toward Kent, then started toward the door.

Given the size of the room, either Lucien or Dougal—or both—would have to step aside to allow him to pass. Though they didn't communicate, neither of them moved, which forced Martin to have to push between them. The door closed behind the officious bounder.

Again, as if they'd discussed their next move, Lucien and Dougal moved toward Kent in concert.

"What the bloody hell?" Dougal said furiously. "You know Lucien didn't kill Giraud, nor did he have him assassinated. What would be his motive?"

Kent looked nervously toward Lucien. "He was trying to protect the Foreign Office and by extension, the crown. He's already demonstrated that he's not opposed to taking matters into his own hands rather than following established procedures."

It seemed Kent was entirely aware of what had happened in Spain. And he was now using that to put the blame of Giraud's death on Lucien.

"I didn't do that with Giraud," Lucien said, somehow maintaining his calm. He speared Kent with a dark stare. "What Max and I did in Spain was celebrated. We've been lauded as heroes. Wasn't it just last spring that you supported his elevation to an earldom in recognition for his bravery?" Indeed, that was due to occur soon, according to Con.

"You were being considered for a title too. No small feat for a second son to earn his own peerage," Kent said, his dark blue eyes turning glacial. "But I suspect that won't be happening now."

Lucien's temper began to unspool. "As if I give a *fuck* about that."

Dougal advanced on Kent. "Goddammit, this makes no sense. Lucien has clearly been set up to take the blame for Giraud's murder. Why? You owe us that much."

"I don't know anything about Lucien being set up." Kent glowered at Lucien. "You can't think people didn't discover the truth of what happened in Spain, that you planted information on those dead soldiers to explain why Warfield—with your help—killed them."

Perhaps he'd been naïve, but Lucien couldn't imagine

how anyone could know. The only people who knew the truth, who'd walked away alive that day, were him and Max. And Lucien would bet his life that Max had never said anything. Unless…had the guilt overcome him? He'd been in a rage after finding his betrothed brutally murdered. The future he'd planned with her, with their babe, gone in a mindless instant. He'd lost his wits and attacked the man. Afterward, he'd been confused, almost untethered from reality. But he'd remembered what he'd done and had been horrified.

"If you can't tell me why, at least explain how you *think* you know about what happened in Spain. No one was there that day but me and Warfield."

Kent's expression remained cool. "Warfield spent considerable time healing before he was sent home. He was feverish a good many days, and he…talked."

Oh, God. Lucien hoped Max never learned he'd done that. He'd never forgive himself for jeopardizing Lucien. He'd already spent the last several years being angry with Lucien for inserting himself into the danger and covering up for Max's actions. Max believed he deserved punishment and had spent years hating and torturing himself. He'd come so far in his healing since he'd fallen in love with Ada. Lucien wouldn't let him tumble back into that sinister abyss.

"You can't take anything he said as truth." Lucien didn't care that he was still lying about it. He would do so until his dying breath to protect his friend. "He was incoherent."

"Except, it makes sense given what happened to that woman he wanted to marry."

Lucien growled as his hands closed into fists. "*That woman* was his betrothed and the mother of his child."

"Did you do it?" Dougal asked, interrupting their conversation. He leveled an icy stare on Kent. "Did you kill Giraud?"

Kent's eyes rounded and his nostrils flared. "How can you even suggest such a thing?"

"Your outrage after you first suspected me and now accuse Lucien is entirely laughable. Your guilt makes sense given how involved you've been in every aspect of this investigation. First you suspected me, then the matter was solved, and now you're confident it was Lucien. You've either somehow become really bad at your job or you're lying. I'm inclined to believe the latter. It serves your interest to keep assigning blame to others. That you would do so to both me and Lucien, whom you've mentored and who has cared for you as a dear friend, is sickening."

Kent had the decency to look embarrassed—if the redness in his face was any indication. Perhaps he was just angry. Either way, Lucien would never trust the man again. As if everything else wasn't bad enough, that particular betrayal hurt.

"Believe what you like," Kent said. "You've no standing in the Foreign Office any longer."

Dougal glowered at him, and Lucien was glad for his loyalty. "Perhaps not, but I have friends and contacts, and I am heir to the Earl of Stirling. I believe my *standing* is greater than you acknowledge."

Kent scrunched his eyes closed and wiped his hand over his face. When he opened his eyes and looked back at them, he nodded. "Please don't think I am unsympathetic to this situation. Lucien, if you really had nothing to do with Giraud's—"

"I didn't," Lucien ground out. "That you think I did is beyond the pale."

Pressing his lips together, Kent appeared pained. Still, he didn't acknowledge that he was behaving horribly, that his treatment of both Lucien and Dougal was both unfounded and repulsive. "I will do what I can to advocate for you. I don't know if there's anything I can do about the club, however. The Foreign Office is not pleased with the way you've managed things recently. You weren't able to get everyone back that we wanted."

"We tried." Lucien kept a tight rein on his temper so he wouldn't explode. "The ones who've refused simply can't be regained. Unless someone else from the Foreign Office would like to try?" It was a sarcastic question, but in truth, if they were so concerned with having those people on the membership roll, then they could employ other people, such as Kent or Lady Pickering—or hell, even Lucien's bloody father—to encourage them to rejoin.

Kent didn't respond to that. He grimaced and went to fetch his hat and gloves. "I'm afraid you're seen as a liability now, Lucien. You do what you wish, and you won't follow directives. The best you can hope for is to retain membership in the club when the new person takes over."

As if Lucien would remain in the club *he'd* built. "You've manipulated this entire situation for your own purposes." Lucien had to think Kent was only sharing information where and when it was necessary, likely to advance his own interests. And what were those? It was as if Lucien hadn't known the man at all.

"I'm sorry you think that." Kent looked at him sadly. "We've worked together well for years. I've often thought of you as the son I never had." He glanced at Dougal. "Along with you. It pains me to think you believe me capable of some malfeasance."

"And yet we're supposed to be fine with you believing the same of us," Dougal retorted.

Lucien fixed Kent with an icy glare. "I thought of you as the father I would have liked to have. Too bad you've turned out to be just as awful as my actual sire."

Distress flashed in Kent's gaze. "I'll do what I can, Lucien."

He inclined his head and left the room, closing the door firmly behind him.

"*Bloody fucking hell.*" Lucien wanted to punch the door Kent had just closed.

"What just happened?" Dougal pivoted to face Lucien. "Was this meeting compromised and they knew we were coming, or was it really planned for them to discuss you and then send for you to join them?"

"That is an excellent question. The latter is possible. But doesn't that make me Lady Macbeth?" Lucien combed his hand through his hair and paced to the other side of the compact space. "I wasn't plotting anything, and what else would such a designation mean?"

"I don't think you want me to answer that."

Lucien gave him a wry look. "Don't think my mind didn't already go there. If I am Lady Macbeth, I could be in danger of Giraud's fate."

"I think you need to put Reynolds back at your house," Dougal said darkly. "And one of his men should follow you at all times."

The first thing Lucien thought was that a shadow would mean he'd never get another stolen moment alone with Kat. He nearly laughed. *That* was what he was thinking of right now?

"What did you think of Martin?" Lucien asked. "I couldn't tell if you recognized him at all."

"Never seen him before. Or heard of him. But I suppose Martin could be an alias. Kent is fond of using them. He was Torrance when he recruited Jess." Dougal frowned. "I don't like *any* of this."

"I hate the lot of it. Especially Kent's role. He has never been on our side." Lucien exhaled, but the action did nothing to ease his ire or disappointment. "What do we do now?"

"As I told that blackguard Kent, I still have friends and contacts."

"But I didn't think any of them were sharing anything."

"Not yet. I suspect that will change when I tell them there are forces within the Foreign Office setting up innocents to cover for malfeasance. This may go beyond Giraud, and I'm more convinced than ever that he wasn't giving secrets to France." Dougal's expression was glacial. "He was set up too."

"I agree." Lucien felt so bloody helpless.

Dougal's features turned cautious, his gaze hesitant. "I know you're going to refuse, but I think we should consult your father."

"Absolutely not."

"We don't know how much time we have." Dougal stepped toward him. "Martin could initiate this club transition tomorrow for all we know."

Dammit, Lucien hated this. He wasn't going to don a white cravat and seek his father's assistance again. "He won't help me. He's already turned his back on me." Countless times.

Still, he should try. What other options did he have other than to wait and see if Dougal could discover what was really going on? Or wait to learn if Kent would actually be able to convince them to change their minds—or that he'd even try? Lucien had to think he wouldn't. He'd no idea whose interests Kent was serving, but it sure as hell wasn't Lucien's.

"We're going to get to the bottom of this, Lucien. I promise you."

"We'd better, or I'm going to meet Giraud's end."

Dougal's eyes glittered with a cold fury. "Not if I can bloody help it."

CHAPTER 16

*H*ad it really been a week since Kat had seen Lucien? Since he'd completely changed her world and given her a thousand reasons to smile?

Yes, and she was fairly certain he'd been avoiding her. He ought at least to have called on Cass at some point. Shouldn't he?

Well, Kat wasn't going to let him escape her tonight. She'd written a note and had it ready to slip into his hand or pocket, whatever was convenient. In it, she asked him to meet her in the passageway at nine, which meant she had less than an hour to execute her plan.

Tonight's assembly theme was the Frost Fair, an event that took place when the Thames occasionally froze over. The last time had been two years ago.

The ballroom had been made to look like the fair, with the dance floor being where people would skate. "Vendors" gave out lemonade, ratafia, cakes, and other confections. The atmosphere was particularly boisterous, and Kat wondered if she'd be able to endure the entire evening. She was glad she'd set the meeting time with Lucien for nine and not later.

"What a splendid affair," Cass remarked as they circuited the ladies' side of the ballroom. "The patronesses have outdone themselves. I must commend Ada. I'm only sorry Evie isn't here to see it."

"Is Lady Warfield here tonight, or has she already left for the wedding?" Kat had overheard Cass and Ruark discussing whether they would travel to Oxfordshire for Mrs. Renshaw's wedding to Lord Gregory. In the end, they'd decided not to as Cass was struggling with intermittent nausea and exhaustion from carrying.

Kat had decided that pregnancy sounded awful. Avoiding it altogether was yet another reason to recommend spinsterhood.

Lucien came from the men's side, his tall, athletic form drawing Kat's eye immediately. The pinch in her chest was now accompanied by a burst of heat through her whole body and an almost magnetic pull to go to him. She would have if he hadn't seen them and started in their direction.

Cass touched his arm when he joined them. "Lucien, this Frost Fair is the most extravagant assembly you've ever done. I can't imagine the expense." She immediately grimaced. "That is, of course, none of my affair."

"I just hope it draws more people than last Friday's Leap Year ball," he said, looking toward Kat.

"I'm sure it will. Attendance always goes up as the Season progresses," Cass assured him.

Lucien kept his attention on Kat. "You look very pretty tonight." Did he really think so or was he just trying to stop talking about the club with Cass?

"Thank you." Kat tried to think of how to give him the note, which was a small piece of parchment folded into an even smaller square. After withdrawing it from her pocket, she held it between her thumb and forefinger in the folds of her gown. From the corner of her eye, she saw Prudence and

Glastonbury enter the ballroom. "Cass, Prudence has arrived."

As Cass swung her head toward the door, Kat moved closer to Lucien. She pressed the note into his hand and gave him a pointed look.

His brow crinkled—just briefly—before he slid the note into the interior of his coat where there was likely a pocket.

"Don't wait long to read it," she murmured as Cass greeted Prudence and her husband.

Lucien welcomed them before moving on. Kat watched him for a few minutes hoping to see him read the note, but he did not. Well, she would be in the passageway at nine regardless. Hopefully, he would be too.

After a quarter hour of the noise and bustle—there was even bowling in the middle of the ladies' side of the ballroom, which had been a popular entertainment at the last Frost Fair—Kat excused herself. Cass had understood her need to find some peace and solitude for a while. Kat said she was going to the library.

Anticipation propelled her as much as her desire to leave the noisy ballroom. She made her way to the library, where she still had time to loiter before nine. Eagerness overcame her, and she made her way to the passageway ten minutes before nine. She sat on the stairs until it had to be nine, then stood. And paced. It was at least another ten minutes more before she finally heard footsteps coming along the passageway from Lucien's office.

At last, he came into view, and her body reacted in its usual manner upon seeing him, culminating in a smile she couldn't suppress. "I wasn't sure you were going to come."

"I should not have, but I heard you encountered the Hickinbottoms the other night, that there was a confrontation. Are you all right?"

A giddy warmth spread through her. "I appreciate your

concern. I am fine now. It was…irritating. Their son was as much to blame as I was. No one is harassing him about his behavior."

"Perhaps his wife is." Lucien smirked, and Kat laughed.

She gazed up at him. "You are so lovely." He never made her feel badly, not even by accident. But now she suddenly did feel badly, and it wasn't his fault. "I shouldn't have chosen to kiss him. It was unkind of me to do that to another woman's betrothed." Why hadn't she thought that sooner? It wasn't for lack of people, namely her sisters, pointing it out. Perhaps because Kat was beginning to understand the complexities and emotions of relationships. Was she having a relationship with Lucien? It didn't seem like it since she hadn't seen him in a week.

"Why are you avoiding me?" she asked.

He leaned his shoulder against the wall. "I should think it would be obvious. Besides, I've been busy with the club and…things."

"I can imagine. This assembly is quite lavish. You've gone to every length to make it almost exactly like an actual Frost Fair."

"All the credit is due to Ada and the other patronesses. Mostly Ada. She is the one who oversees the execution. I am sorry Evie isn't here to see it, but Ada will tell her all about it when she arrives in Oxfordshire for her wedding."

"Are you disappointed you can't be there?" Kat asked. She knew from Cass that he wasn't going. And she wasn't surprised. Lucien rarely left London. Did he ever, in fact?

"I am, but I can't leave now."

"Because of the club. But I suspect you'd find another reason. Why don't you ever leave town?"

He laughed. "You've noticed that? I've traveled to Max's estate on occasion."

"But can't you return the same day?"

"You've caught me. I don't like to be far from the club. I also like being here in the city. After I returned from Spain, I decided I didn't want to leave again."

Kat moved closer so that she stood against the wall just before him. "You never speak of your time there. Was it terrible? I imagine you could get quite bored too. *I* would get bored, I think."

He chuckled. "You would have plenty of animals to study there."

"Are you evading my question? I'd like to hear about your experience there."

"That's kind of you to be curious, but I don't like to talk about it very much. You were more right than you know when you imagined it was boring."

Kat knew that now wasn't the time to press him. They only had a brief interlude together. "Well, if you'd ever like to unburden yourself—about that or the club or anything else— I'd be happy to listen."

"Is that so you can record everything I saw for some future research?"

"And what research would that be?"

He lifted the shoulder that wasn't against the wall. "The mind of a former rogue?"

"That is an intriguing thought. You will only have yourself to blame if I shift my focus in that direction."

Grinning, he pushed away from the way. "I will flog myself. Now, why did you ask to meet?"

"I should think that would be obvious," she repeated back to him. "I wanted to see you."

"Just *see* me? After our last encounter here in the passageway, I have to think that's not all you wanted. But we can't do that. Or anything else on whatever list you've constructed."

"I have a marvelous list actually. Should I copy it for you?" She decided right then that she would whether he wanted it or not. On second thought, she'd send it to him one item at a time. Perhaps an incessant barrage of things they could do together would coax him to surrender to temptation.

"No. Though I admit to being curious." A small smile teased his lips, and the resulting pulse in Kat's sex was positively shameless. She hoped he would do it again. "However, I need to get back. I can't be gone like I was last week."

"The club *survived*," she said sardonically. Stepping even closer, so that they nearly touched, she put her hand on his coat, her fingers pressed against his lapel. "Why can't we plan to meet like this every week, here in the passageway, even for just ten minutes? You said this was the perfect time and place."

He groaned. "I regret that. The problem, my enchanting Kat, is that ten minutes isn't nearly enough time for anything worthwhile."

The hunger and disappointment in his tone were unmistakable. Kat felt a surge of delight—and power.

His eyes darkened. "The risk is still too great, I'm afraid."

She flattened her hand against him and slid it up to his neck so that she grazed her fingertips against the flesh above his cravat and collar. "Or, I could just drop out of Society altogether and become your paramour. We could—"

"That is *not* happening." He stared at her. "You can't be serious."

"Why not? I loathe the social requirements, and I don't wish to marry. I do, however, wish to complete every item on my list and add to it. There are thirty-three things, Lucien." She lowered her voice to a seductive purr. "*Thirty-three.*"

He closed his eyes briefly as if he were waging a battle inside himself. She hoped the part of him that demanded he return to the assembly was losing.

"Stop. You can't torture me. Well, you can, but I'm

begging you not to. In any case, you can't just become my paramour."

"Why not?"

"To begin with, I don't want one. I haven't had one since —never mind, I shouldn't discuss that with you either."

"Mrs. Renshaw?" she asked. "That's common knowledge."

"Not that she was my last mistress." He swore. "You are far too provocative. In every damned way. You can't leave Society. People know who you are. Your brother is an earl. Your sister-in-law is the daughter of a duke. You are *Somebody*, whether you like it or not. People will talk about you and what you do."

Kat swore, prompting Lucien's eyebrows to dash up. "You can't be shocked I would say such a thing."

"I shouldn't be." He did that devastating little teasing smile thing again, and she nearly tackled him to the floor. Sobering, he went on, "All that aside, your behavior affects your family. You can't be someone's paramour."

"It would be secret. Kathleen Shaughnessy would leave London and fade away into obscurity. I could be your mistress, and no one would know my identity."

"Good God, did you learn nothing from Evie's attempt at a secret identity? Which was entirely my fault, by the way. I convinced her to do it so she could work here." He swallowed. "I really am a selfish prick."

"Hardly. Ask anyone. You are the person who helps everyone."

"Not lately." His voice had gone hard, and now his gaze did too. "Nothing remains secret, Kat. I've been reminded of that too many times of late, particularly this week."

Again, she sensed his frustration, his…anguish and wished he would talk to her. It was interesting because she'd instigated this meeting to check something off her list. Instead, she just wanted to talk with him, to comfort him, to reassure him. It seemed their connection was more than physical. At least for her. Perhaps it wasn't the same for him, as kind as he was to her, and as understanding and supportive as he could be.

"I can see you'd rather withhold yourself from me in every way than take any solace in our attraction or friendship or whatever else we share. I'm sorry to have troubled you."

Kat spun on her heel and stalked from the passageway. Before she reached the door, she heard him call after her. She hesitated, almost turning around, but no, she wasn't going to throw herself at him or beg for his attention.

Perhaps it was indeed time for her to fade away—from Lucien most of all.

$\sim$

*T*he assembly was going very well. There were more people in attendance than last week, but the crush was still lacking when compared to last year. Lucien hoped the spectacle of the Frost Fair theme would buzz around London and lure people to next week's assembly.

But the success—or not—of tonight's assembly wasn't weighing on him as heavily as his interaction with Kat earlier. He'd allowed his frustration to show, to affect her, and it wasn't her fault he was torn up over the club, the Foreign Office, and, in truth, *her*. Keeping his hands from her had taken every bit of self-control he possessed, and he'd nearly lost the battle when she'd touched his chest. His entire body had sprung to awareness, and even now, nearly two hours later, he still wanted her with a ferocity that had kept his cock half-erect.

He'd tried to keep an eye on her as much as possible, but it had been difficult. He'd been busy, of course, and she hadn't been visible. He wondered how she'd spent her evening and found he was jealous of any time she danced or spoke with another man.

This growing fixation was going to get him into trouble.

Which was why he'd adopted that frigid tone with her. Her idea that she could become his mistress was preposterous, and she had to realize that. Ruark would take him out and beat him or challenge him to a duel. Or both. And Lucien would deserve all of it.

Lucien made a sweep through the men's club, which he did periodically during assemblies. There were plenty of gentlemen who escaped to the gaming room or members' den while their wives were busy displaying their daughters on the Marriage Mart.

As he climbed the stairs to the first floor, he encountered Dougal, who seemed pleased to see him. "I was just looking for you and hoped we could speak for a moment."

"Of course." Lucien motioned for him to accompany him back up the stairs, and they went into his office. "You have news?"

"No, unfortunately, but I think I'm wearing one of my former associates down. He's considering retirement. I can tell he's unsettled about something, but he's not divulging anything. I'm also not pressing as I don't want to scare him off. I'll keep at him, though." Dougal put a hand on his hip. "What about you? Have you given any thought to what you will do?"

"If you're asking whether I'll take whatever compensation the Foreign Office deigns to give me and skulk off into the night, the answer is no."

"You won't have a choice. I'm not sure I wouldn't put it past them to publicly name you as Giraud's killer and throw you in jail. I'm keeping my ears open for any mention of you, but so far, there's nothing."

Dougal's suggestion was rather upsetting, but Lucien didn't disagree it was possible. He expected almost anything at this point. "I appreciate your support in all this."

"You have it now and always. Are you sure I can't convince you to talk to your father about this?"

"Positive."

Nodding, Dougal started toward the door. "I should find Jess. Last I saw her, she was talking with Kat."

Lucien's gaze snapped toward Dougal. "I'll come with you. I need to get back downstairs."

They returned to the ground floor to the ballroom, entering on the dancing side. The dance floor was crowded, but before he could look for Kat, Jess approached them. She was with Cass and Ruark. But not Kat. Lucien tamped down his disappointment.

"What a wonderful assembly," Jess remarked. "It's absolutely inspired. People will be talking about it for weeks, probably the entire Season. I think you'll need to revisit this theme next year."

She was probably on to something there. "I'll pass that along to Ada and the patronesses."

"Oh, I already told Ada earlier," Jess said.

Lucien tried to think of a way to ask about Kat without seeming overly interested and settled on "I thought Miss Shaughnessy was with you."

"She was, but she's dancing now. I think Sir Rowland may be smitten with her, actually. This is the second time they've danced."

Cass's eyes widened. "Tonight? Doesn't she know not to do that?"

"Not tonight. They danced a week or so ago at a ball, I think." Jess cocked her head. "Or perhaps it was last week's assembly."

That distracted Lucien. And made his jealousy flare again. Last week's assembly belonged to him.

Jess turned to Dougal. "I'm glad you're here. I need a walk in the garden, where it's bound to be much cooler."

Dougal grinned at his wife and offered her his arm. "Happy to oblige."

They departed toward the doors leading to the garden, circling the dance floor.

"Lucien, don't forget the dinner on Sunday," Cass said.

He gave her a quizzical look. "Why would I forget?" He saw a flash of unease in her eyes just before she averted her gaze. Exhaling, he asked, "What aren't you telling me?"

"Papa is coming. He wants to see Prudence."

"Can't he just summon her for an audience as he does the rest of us?" That the duke had warmly accepted the illegitimate daughter of his sister into his family was still rather unbelievable to Lucien.

"Probably, and he may still. Please promise you'll behave." She gave him a pleading look.

"Perhaps I'll become ill before then. Or break my leg."

Ruark snorted, and Cass elbowed him in the side. Clearing his throat, Ruark said, "Just drink a glass of whiskey before you come. Or I can fill your gullet if you arrive early."

"It will take more than a glass," Lucien muttered. He looked out at the dance floor and was finally able to pick out Kat. She was on the other side, her dark gold skirts swirling across the floor as she moved. He couldn't, however, make out her expression. Was she enjoying herself?

"I'm going to have to ask Kat about Sir Rowland," Cass said. "I wonder if he's expressed interest in courting her."

Ruark made a face. "I hope not. He's at least ten years her senior."

Lucien was eight years older than she was. Did that disqualify him?

From *what*? Perhaps Lucien needed that gullet-full of whiskey *now*.

"That's not a terrible age difference," Cass said. "Plus, he's a trifle shy and may not mind avoiding social events after they are wed."

"You're marrying her off to him already?" Lucien asked, hoping he didn't sound outraged, which was precisely how he felt.

Cass waved her hand at him. "Just thinking."

Ruark looked to Lucien. "Cass is hoping—against hope, I keep telling her—that Kat will fall in love and wed soon. She's worried the Hickinbottoms may cause trouble, making it difficult, or impossible, for Kat to marry."

Lucien wanted to have words with the Hickinbottoms to ensure they left Kat alone. And how would that go? He'd threaten their social accessibility? He wasn't exactly the esteemed member of the ton he'd been a few weeks ago.

"Have they caused more problems?" Lucien asked. "Other than what you told me happened the other night at the rout."

"No, but I'm concerned I just haven't heard what else they've said," Cass responded. "I'm also worried Kat will do something to endanger herself, as she did in Gloucestershire. She just doesn't pay as close attention to her behavior as she ought. She's disappeared several times tonight for a quarter hour or more at a time."

Ruark touched Cass's back. "My love, she was feeling tired. Indeed, I'm surprised she's lasted this long. This is a heavy crush for her to tolerate."

Since Lucien now understood how Kat could be affected, he especially appreciated her brother's awareness and concern for her. "She's lucky to have you looking out for her," he said to Ruark.

Cass turned to Ruark. "I'm feeling tired, actually. Would you mind escorting me to the other side so I can sit—and then fetch me a glass of lemonade?" She batted her lashes at him.

Ruark laughed. "Anything for you." He looked to Lucien. "Will you let Kat know where we are? Or not. I know you're busy. She'll find us over there."

"Happy to," Lucien said. He would take the opportunity to make sure he hadn't upset her earlier. He hadn't meant to be such a jackass. He needed to stop doing that with her. And why did he? Was it because he didn't feel the need to hide his emotions from her?

Ruark escorted Cass to the other side of the ballroom, and Lucien watched the dancers. He walked slowly around so he was closer to where Kat was located. It was slightly cooler as the doors to the garden were open. Late winter air filtered in, but it was still quite warm in the ballroom. He caught sight of Kat and saw that she was flushed. She also looked bothered. Her brow was wrinkled and her jaw tight.

Then something terrible happened. She flung her arm, striking Sir Rowland in the chest. He wobbled but didn't fall. It was impossible to tell if she'd done it on purpose, but Lucien didn't think so. She brought her hand to her mouth, then dropped it to her side in a clenched fist. Next, she swept off the dance floor—and nearly collided with Lucien.

"Kat." He clutched her arm gently. "Are you all right?"

"I need to get out of here. *Now.*"

"Of course." Lucien moved quickly, ushering her out the doors into the cool night. "Better?"

She shook her head. "Too many people."

There weren't really. Most people preferred the ladies' garden. It had a larger reflecting pool and more benches with more than a dozen torches illuminating the space. This side was less populated. Darker. Far more places to hide.

But he wasn't going to hide her in the shadows out here. "Come with me." He led her to the door that was almost indiscernible next to the hedge, which hugged the outer wall separating the garden from Bury Street.

Finding the latch, he opened the door. "After you."

"Where are we going?"

"Somewhere quiet. Isn't that what you'd prefer?"

"Yes. Please. Or to go home." She stepped inside.

"You can do that too."

He closed the door behind them. "These are the back stairs that lead to the upper floors. We'll skip the first floor because that won't be quiet at all."

"Then where will we go?"

He moved to stand in front of her. There was a sconce on the wall halfway up the first flight of stairs, so there wasn't a great deal of light. Her face was shadowed, but he could see she was still flushed, and her eyes were fixed on some spot behind him.

"Do you trust me?" he asked softly.

She nodded, so he took her hand and started up the stairs. He moved slowly, giving her time to catch her breath or her wits—whatever she needed to do. When they reached the second landing, he opened the door into a corridor.

"What's up here?"

"Several bedchambers, actually. Most people don't realize gentlemen can lodge here, like at a hotel."

"Only gentlemen?"

"The ladies' side also has this capacity, but we've never had anyone stay. Ada's former apartment is over there. It's still her office, in fact."

"I didn't realize she lived here."

"Until she wed Max." Lucien was encouraged by Kat's even conversation. She'd seemed rather agitated in the ballroom. She'd certainly departed the dance floor in a manner that was bound to provoke gossip. He wouldn't mention that tonight.

Shit. If people did talk, Cass and Ruark would be worried sick. He'd send word downstairs that she was calming down upstairs and would then go home.

Lucien took her to the chamber directly above his office. His chamber. It was the smallest on the floor, but it was also entirely his. He didn't allow anyone else to use it.

Opening the door for her, he gestured for her to precede him. Then he closed them inside. "This is the bedchamber I use on occasion."

She surveyed the compact room, from the not terribly wide bed to the washstand to the small desk in the corner and the single chair situated in front of the cold hearth. Kat shivered calling attention to the fact that there was no fire.

Lucien hurried to rectify that problem. "I wasn't expecting to come up here tonight."

"When do you come up here? That is, what do you use it for?"

"Some nights, I'm too tired to go home, so I come up here and sleep for a few hours. On the rare occasion, I've taken a brief nap in the afternoon." He smiled at her over his shoulder as he built the fire.

"You don't meet women here?" she asked.

"Not until tonight." He stood and found the flint, then crouched to light the fire. When he was satisfied that it was going to blaze, he rose once more and faced her. "I'll go send word to Ruark and Cass that you're up here resting and will soon return home."

"Thank you. Please tell them not to come find me."

"I understand you'd rather be alone." Lucien wanted to know what had happened with Sir Rowland, but reasoned he could find out later. Perhaps when he saw her on Sunday. As if he'd have time alone with her at a family dinner. He started toward the door.

"No, I wouldn't. I want you to come back."

Lucien turned. The color had receded from her face, but not entirely. Small pink flags remained in her cheeks. And her gaze was still focused on something behind him. "Do you need anything?"

She shook her head. "Just you."

Her words rippled along his flesh as if she'd touched him. He left to find a footman or maid to convey the message to his sister and Ruark. And, if he were smart, he'd continue right back downstairs to the assembly.

It seemed that tonight, he wasn't smart.

CHAPTER 17

*A*fter giving the footman explicit instructions regarding Kat to deliver to Cass and Ruark, Lucien returned to the chamber. He hesitated outside, knowing that if he went in, anything could happen. Or not. Kat was likely upset and would want to go home soon. In fact, he should have sent for Ruark's coach to take her.

Lucien stepped inside, closing the door behind him. Kat was seated on the chair near the fireplace. Her hands were clasped in front of her chest, almost as if she were praying, and her face was now quite red—redder than it had been downstairs in the overheated ballroom. She didn't look at him.

"Kat…is everything all right?" He tried not to sound concerned, but was pretty sure he'd failed.

"Getting there." She kept her gaze on the fire as she stiffened, her hands squeezing together so that the knuckles turned white.

He grew alarmed and moved slowly toward her. "You don't look all right."

She blew out a breath and glanced up at him. "I'm sure I look like the aberration that I am."

"Stop saying that. You are not an aberration."

She tensed again, her face turning as red as a cherry. Then she abruptly released her hands, letting them fall to her lap. She exhaled and took several breaths. "You're looking at me as if I am."

"I'm looking at you because I'm concerned for your welfare. I don't know what happened downstairs, but you were very flustered. Cass and Ruark were concerned the club was too crowded and noisy for you tonight. I can go send for his coach to take you home."

"Yes, send me home. I'll stay there. I should have known better than to join Society to conduct research." She wiped her hand over her brow. "I don't even care about that anymore."

Lucien grabbed the small wooden chair from the desk and set it next to her. He lowered himself into it and rested his forearms on his legs as he leaned toward her. "I can't believe that's true. You'll feel better tomorrow, I'm sure."

"I will. I don't tend to hold on to negative emotions," she said somewhat flatly, as if she were in the process of doing that right now.

"Good." But Lucien wasn't convinced she'd be fine. Furthermore, he wanted to understand her and what was happening. "Why do you think you're an aberration?"

"Look at me. Is this normal behavior? I'm odd. I don't like the same things other people do, and when I try to talk to them about what I like, they find me boring or annoying. Or they laugh at me. Particularly when I can't dance as well as other young ladies. I know the steps, but sometimes the music is confusing."

"Is that what happened downstairs?" Lucien wanted to

know who'd laughed at her. He'd ensure they were never admitted to the Phoenix Club again.

She nodded. "I don't want to talk about it."

"You don't have to. But I maintain you are not an aberration. You are delightful and interesting, and I enjoy your company very much."

"Except when I'm pestering you about my research, trying to coax you to help me. Admit it—you found that annoying." She cut her hand through the air. "I know you did. I am always too focused on things that are important to me, and I expect others to focus on them too."

"I like your research," he said softly. "I wouldn't say I was ever annoyed. Perhaps frustrated. It's very difficult to listen to you discuss kissing and other mating behaviors and not want to shag you senseless, actually."

Her eyes widened as she finally turned her gaze on him. "Have you always felt that way?"

"Not always, but for some time. Indeed, I can't exactly tell you the precise moment that started." He fell silent. "On second thought, I am fairly certain it was when you asked me about finding a rake to help you with your studies. Honestly, your pestering me—if you want to call it that—about your research has been the only thing keeping me from losing hope about the club right now. You are the source of all my smiles and the thing I most look forward to."

"I am?"

He took her hand, which was surprisingly cool given her earlier activities. "Staying away from you, keeping my hands from you…it's all very difficult. The more I am with you, the more I want to know about you. I hope you don't mind, but Cass told me some of what you have dealt with throughout your life."

"So, you know I'm an aberration and are just being polite."

"Cass didn't describe you in that way, and neither would I."

"Not even after seeing what I was doing a few minutes ago? I used to do that all the time—whenever I needed to calm myself. It eases the tumult of whatever is bothering me. It's hard to explain."

He stroked the back of her hand with his thumb. "When I want to calm myself, I go for a brisk walk or a blistering ride. It doesn't sound very different."

"Except what you do is acceptable, and my behavior is seen as strange or alarming. My mother forbade me from doing it, but I couldn't stop. I did eventually manage to learn to only do it when I am alone."

His heart ached for her, for the girl who had to hide. "Like now? Except I noticed you didn't stop when I came in." He hoped she felt comfortable to be completely herself around him. But it wasn't enough to hope that she knew that. "I want you to know that I accept and appreciate exactly who you are. You don't ever have to hide yourself from me."

"I know that, which is why I didn't stop when you came in. Why do you think I became single-minded in my pursuit of having *you* help me with my studies?"

"Why?"

"At first, it was because you were the only person I've ever felt attracted to, but I realize that wasn't entirely due to physical attraction. I think the physical attraction followed the fact that I simply feel comfortable with you. I don't feel like I have to hide who I am."

Lucien smiled. "I'm glad. You seem to be feeling better."

"I am. You've helped immensely. As I said, I don't tend to hold on to negative emotions, especially when I can distract myself with something else. Or someone."

The air in the room shifted, becoming charged with a sensual current. "Should I send for Ruark's coach?"

She shook her head. "Not yet. Sometimes, when I'm feeling overwhelmed, it helps to remove my stays. They make me feel rather constricted, especially after I've done my squeezing."

"Is that what you call what you were doing?" At her nod, he stood and helped her up from the chair. "I can play ladies' maid. Unless you don't need me to?"

"I typically go without a maid, but these new gowns Cass ordered for me are more complicated than what I usually wear." Kat turned. "If you could unlace this, I can manage the rest."

Lucien took in the slope of her ivory neck where it met her collarbone and shoulder. She wore a simple pearl necklace, and he decided he wanted to see her wearing that and nothing else. But she was going home soon, and he ought to get back downstairs. Only, he didn't want to. All he wanted to do was strip her bare and show her she was not only *not* an aberration, but that she was beautiful and extraordinary, and he was the luckiest man to know her as he did.

His breath stuttered as it passed in and out of his lungs. His fingers tingled as he began to gently tug at the laces of her exquisite gown. Leaning forward slightly, he closed his eyes as her lavender scent filled his senses.

Too quickly, he was finished, and the gown gaped open. She pushed it off her arms so that the top pooled around her waist. He stood motionless behind her as she unlaced her corset, his body still, but teeming with energy.

She turned to face him as she loosened the corset enough to pull it over her head. Then she dropped it on the chair with a sigh. "Much better."

As she'd raised her arms, Lucien had focused on her breasts. The motion had lifted them, her flesh swelling above the edge of her chemise, the only garment covering her upper half.

"You're staring at me," she said, and he smiled at her utter and charming lack of guile.

"It's impossible not to."

"I remember everything you said to me about my breasts."

"Did you include that on your list?"

"There are several items involving them." She loosened the small tie that cinched the neck of the chemise, then tugged the garment down until her breasts were exposed. Not large and not small, they were tipped with dark, rose-colored nipples that stood erect with arousal. "That book in the library had a drawing of a man putting his cock between them while the woman held them around his shaft. Have you done that before?"

Lucien groaned. "It doesn't matter. Anything I've ever done means nothing because I didn't do it with you." He knew every experience he shared with her would be new and exciting, unlike anything he'd ever known.

"Well, aren't you going to touch them?"

He should not. But the time had passed for admonitions and caution. He was here with her, and there would be no better time. He simply couldn't deny her. Or himself.

She held the edge of her chemise, and he put his hands over hers, lifting them to cup herself. "Have you ever touched them?" he asked, holding her hands in place. "They feel quite wonderful filling your hands. See how the nipples are hard and eager?"

"For what?" she breathed.

"For a touch." He brushed his thumbs over them. "Or a pinch." He carefully pressed his thumbs and forefingers around each. "Or perhaps even a tug." He pulled gently until she gasped. Or moaned. Or both, actually.

"I've never done that, and now I'm rather disappointed."

Lucien laughed. "Perhaps they want a kiss instead. That you cannot do." He dipped his head and held her left breast to his mouth for a soft, reverent kiss. "Hmm, a lick may be in order." He tongued her nipple with languid strokes.

"Can I let go and touch you?" She sounded rather desperate.

"If you must," he said, greatly enjoying this play.

"I need to get my arms free." She pulled them from the chemise, and he helped by pushing the garment down to her waist. "Much better," she murmured, putting her hands on his shoulders. "Didn't you mention sucking?"

"Probably. You want that? Always feel free to tell me what you want, Kat. Though, I don't think you'll have trouble with that." He smiled against her flesh.

"I do want that. I want everything."

He immediately complied since he desperately wanted that too. He closed his mouth around her and sucked, gently squeezing her. Her hands moved up to his neck, one of them curling around his nape.

Pulling back slightly, he blew over her nipple and felt her shiver. She moaned softly. "Again," she urged.

He licked and sucked and blew. Over and over until her body quivered. Then he moved to her other breast and performed the same dance, all while massaging and teasing the first breast.

"I don't understand how this is making my sex so desperate for your touch," she said. "And I'm sure it's wet, which means I must be quite ready to find my completion. Is it possible that will happen if you continue in this manner?"

Always the researcher... Lucien chuckled. He lifted his head to look at her face. "I think it may be possible, but it hasn't happened in my experience. Does this mean you don't want me to send for the coach yet?"

She narrowed her clever eyes at him. "If you think I'm going to leave before I arrive, you don't know me very well at all."

Laughing, he bent his head to kiss her. She met him eagerly, her lips and tongue gliding against his as they clung to each other. Lucien pivoted with her and guided her toward the bed. When they reached it, he lifted her to sit atop the mattress and pushed the skirts of her gown and petticoat up to her waist. He slid his hand beneath her chemise, which hit her midthigh, and stroked along her flesh until he found her sex. She was indeed quite wet, and his erection throbbed against his garments.

He teased her clitoris as she wriggled her hips against him. "More?" he asked against her mouth.

"Much more." She squeezed his nape as she opened her thighs.

Sliding his finger into her sheath, he felt her muscles constrict eagerly around him. How he longed for that to be his cock. He thrust deep and found the spot that would make her twitch in his arms. He was not disappointed.

Kat whimpered and begged him to continue. He kissed her while he gave her what she wanted.

After several strokes, she pulled her head back. "No, stop."

Lucien withdrew his finger and stilled his hand. "What's wrong?"

"I want more than that." She brought her hand down his abdomen until it met his stiff shaft. Placing her palm over him, she pressed. "I want *this*. Inside me."

"Kat, I can't take your virginity."

"Why not? That's such a load of nonsense. What is virginity? Innocence? Ignorance? I am neither innocent nor ignorant, nor do I subscribe to some notion that I need to save all my sexual education for my husband."

"Chances are he wouldn't conduct it very well anyway," Lucien murmured, thinking she was the most amazing woman he'd ever met. "But you aren't getting married, or so you've repeatedly said."

"If you're aware of that, then why are you hesitating? There is no reason we can't fully consummate this…companionship."

Lucien groaned. The temptation was overwhelming. If she were anyone else, he would have tupped her already. Probably many times. Certainly tonight. They were alone in a bedchamber and would not be disturbed. Still, she would be expected to return home soon. What if Cass and Ruark left to meet her, and she wasn't there?

"This is not what I would choose," he said softly, brushing his lips against her temple. "I would keep you all night so we would have plenty of time to check many things off your list."

"You've already checked off three."

"Have I? Then it seems I should at least be able to attempt a few more, but we can't afford to take all night. You'll be expected at home."

"I know." She sounded disappointed. "But I will take when I can get and be more than grateful for it. *Please* don't send me away just yet."

He imagined a night where they explored each other, giving and receiving pleasure, dozing, talking, and finally waking together to greet the day. For the first time in his life, that potential filled him with a joy that took his breath away.

"Lucien?" she prompted.

Shaking his head, he looked into her eyes and smiled. "Just thinking of what I'd like to do to—and with you. Do you have any requests?"

"Just that I feel you—all of you—inside me. I want to arrive just like that."

He put his lips on hers again as he stroked his finger into her sex. "Then we'd best begin the journey."

∽

*A*nticipation and joy swirled through Kat as they kissed. She'd hoped Lucien would agree to her request, but wasn't at all certain he would.

He pumped his finger into her, stirring her arousal until she was panting with need. She wanted to feel more of him, so she pushed his coat off his shoulders. He shrugged it away, and then she started unbuttoning his waistcoat.

"We can't take the time to fully disrobe," he said.

"Can I at least remove this?" She finished unfastening the buttons and pushed it open, flattening her palms against him and reveling in the heat of his flesh through the single layer of his shirt.

Lucien sent the waistcoat the same way as the coat. "Leave the cravat, please. I'm rubbish at tying them, and I have to return to the assembly."

She let out a low sigh of disappointment. "Someday, I shall see you without clothing. Until then, I will use my imagination."

"I shall do the same. We don't have time to take everything off, unfortunately. But that gives us something to look forward to."

Kat's heart skipped. Had he just referred to a future coupling?

He lowered his head to her breast again, and she lost coherent thought for a moment. She'd never imagined the sensations that would provoke, or how keenly she'd feel them in her sex. Pleasure arced through her, and she could glimpse her orgasm if he kept up what he was doing.

"Shouldn't you stop?" she asked breathlessly. "I want to arrive with you inside me."

"My darling, you can arrive now and hopefully again with my cock in you."

"Can I? You're certain?"

"Well, no. But in my experience, it's more than likely."

She trusted him, and in truth, she was so close to arriving, she wasn't sure she could face the frustration of not finding completion. He seemed to know this because he applied more and faster pressure to her clitoris. Then he sucked hard on her nipple, and that was all it took to push her completely into oblivion.

Crying out, she clasped his head as her thighs quivered. Her body tensed as wave after wave of rapture carried her deeper into the darkness. When she finally began to fall back into herself, she realized he'd pulled her slippers off and was moving her fully onto the bed.

He climbed on with her and quickly situated himself between her legs. She pulled her garments up to her waist while he unbuttoned his fall. Watching him, she licked her lips as he pulled his cock free.

"Kat, you're going to make me spill, and I haven't even got close to you yet."

She reached for him, curling her hand around his shaft and stroking him several times. "Well, you can arrive now and again shortly."

He laughed, the sound short and harsh. "It's not quite the same for men. We need more time for recovery."

"How long do you need?"

"Longer than we have tonight, I'm afraid." He situated his cock at her sex. "I'll go slow."

"Must you? I rather like the speed of your hand when you coax me to arrive."

"I'll go slow at first." He barely breathed the last word as he slid into her. "God, this is…you are…I can't—"

"I fear you've been robbed of your senses, Lucien."

"Most definitely. And if it feels this good, I don't want them back." He pushed into her, filling and stretching her. It wasn't painful, but it wasn't exactly comfortable either. "Lift your legs and put them around my waist."

She did, and that made things better. Her pelvis tilted so he seemed to fit more comfortably. And he pressed against that internal spot that made her want to coo with delight.

He began to move, and the friction was a wondrous pleasure. She clutched his back, pulling at his shirt. Next time, there would be nothing between them. At least this time, they were joined in the best possible way.

Each time he thrust into her, he moved a little faster. She loved the feel of him filling her and the press of him against her clitoris. When he drove deep, she arched up, grinding her hips against his. *This* was unparalleled ecstasy.

Then he nipped her breast, using his teeth and lips to make her moan. No, *that* was unparalleled ecstasy. She hoped she remembered everything he did so she could cross it off the list. She was certain she'd have to add several more things.

Such as the way he now sucked at her neck. Why did everything he did feel *so* good?

He pulled almost completely out of her and drove in again. She dug her heels into his backside, wanting him deeper and harder.

"Can you go faster?" She copied what he did and sucked the underside of his chin—it was the best she could do since his cravat was still tied around his neck.

He tipped his head down and kissed her, his tongue driving into her mouth with the same penetrating strokes as his cock into her sex. His body picked up speed, thrusting into her with a relentless passion that prompted lights to dance behind her eyelids. Her orgasm was there, just beyond reach. It didn't seem quite as accessible as the others.

His hand closed around her shoulder, then cupped her neck briefly before he dragged his palm down to her breast where he pinched and pulled the nipple. This shot a jolt of pleasure directly to her core, propelling her to the edge. But his hand didn't stop there. He skimmed down over her abdomen until he reached her clitoris. With a series of strokes, he sent her where she wanted to go, right back to where the ultimate satisfaction dwelled.

As her body shuddered with release, Lucien continued to thrust. She squeezed her legs around him and held him tightly.

"Kat, I need to—"

His backside clenched. His entire body went taut, and she knew he was arriving. She kissed his jaw and cupped the back of his head.

Suddenly, he pulled her legs from his hips and withdrew his cock. He swore.

"I can't tell if that was good or bad," she said.

He pushed up as if she'd caught fire and rolled to his back. Then he swore again. Several times. In increasingly colorful ways.

"What's wrong?" Kat reached to smooth down her dress and immediately put her hand in something wet. "Oh, you spilled."

"On purpose, but not soon enough. *Shit.* Sorry." He got up from the other side of the bed and went to the washstand. She heard a drawer open, but couldn't see what he was doing because his back was to her.

When he turned, which was rather quickly, he was buttoning his fall. Moving swiftly, he came around the bed with a cloth. He frowned at her. "I completely messed that up. I meant to leave you before I started to arrive. To prevent a child."

Of course, his seed was necessary to do that. "Well, it feels as if you spilled on me and my gown."

He handed her the cloth. "Not all of it, I'm afraid."

Kat sat up and dabbed at the mess. It wasn't a terrible amount, but it was good she didn't plan to return to the assembly. "I'm sure this will wash out."

"Unless you want the maids to know what you were doing, you should wash it yourself. Say something was spilled on you."

Laughing, she gave him a wry look. "That's precisely what happened. But I shall be vague. Why do you look so distressed?"

"Because I didn't leave you soon enough. What if you get with child?"

That was not something she'd considered, and that was foolish of her. She didn't want children any more than she wanted to be married—at least not now. "I'm sure I won't." She ignored the troubling sense of unease at the back of her mind.

"You must be vigilant for your courses," he said with a grim expression. "Promise to let me know immediately. If you are with child, I will get a special license and we will wed."

While the thought of spending a lifetime in Lucien's arms was more than tempting, Kat hadn't ever been seeking a proposal. "I haven't changed my mind about marriage."

"You can't have a child out of wedlock."

"Plenty of women do."

He bent to pick up his waistcoat and drew it on. "My God, Kat, sometimes you are infuriating in your lack of concern. If you won't think of yourself, think of the child and what it would mean for them. And think of your family and how it would affect them."

"If I had to have a child, I wouldn't do so here in London. I'd go somewhere else and either find a home for it, or mayhap I'd decide to mother it myself. No one would ever need to know."

"Those kinds of secrets never seem to stay secret," he muttered. He stared at her. "This is another of your fade-into-obscurity plans?"

"Slightly different from what I proposed to you earlier because I would actually go away. Unless I gave the child away to someone else to raise, then I suppose I could come back after taking an extended 'trip.'"

He'd put his shoes back on, which he'd apparently removed at some point, while she spoke. "What about *me*? What if *I* want to raise my child?"

"Do you?"

Jaw clenching, he averted his gaze.

Kat set the soiled cloth beside her and pulled her chemise back up over her arms and breasts and cinched the neckline. "You don't want a child any more than I do, nor do you want to wed. The last thing I want is you marrying me because you feel you must." She shook her head vehemently.

"I—"

She slid from the bed and adjusted her gown so she could pull it back up over her torso. There was no point in putting her corset back on, nor would she need to explain not wearing it. She always discarded it when she became over-wrought. "You what?" She turned her back to him so he could lace her dress.

"I don't know." He tugged at the laces and drew the garment closed.

"No need to do it tightly. It won't fit quite right without the stays anyway."

He finished, and she found her slippers. Moving her corset aside, she sat down on the chair she'd occupied earlier and slid her feet into her shoes. "Are you going to fetch Ruark's coach?"

"I'll send you home in mine. That way, Ruark's coachman can't say how long you took to leave."

She waved her hand. "Don't overthink this. It won't matter if I was up here for as long as we were. It's not unusual for me to take a great deal of time to recover."

"But I've been gone too, and I'd just as soon people not make any presumptions."

"Do what you will. Where shall I wait?"

"Go down to the bottom of the back stairs when you're ready. A man will see you out to the coach."

"You're not worried this man will tell tales?" she asked. He seemed terribly concerned with every detail.

"He won't."

"Your footmen are that trustworthy?" she asked.

"He isn't a footman, and he won't be in Phoenix Club livery. I'm going now." He went to the door.

Kat stood, smoothing her hands down her horribly rumpled gown. She'd have no problem explaining that away too. "You're not even going to kiss me before you leave?"

Exhaling, he came toward her. He took her hands. "Promise you'll tell me if there's a babe. There are…options, and I would be honored if you'd discuss them with me."

He was also incredibly fixated on the potential of a child. But she appreciated his concern and his support, particularly for discussing options. "I promise," she said softly.

He kissed her forehead, then her lips. "Don't worry," he whispered. "We will handle anything together."

Together. She'd never had a partner before. Jess was the closest friend she'd ever had, and while Ruark and Cass were wonderful, it wasn't the same as this. Whatever this "together" with Lucien meant.

His mouth met hers again, and he briefly clutched her to him. Very briefly, because he abruptly stepped away with a laugh. "Unless I want to finish the evening smelling like fornication, I should stay away from your dress." He grimaced. "I am so sorry about that."

"It will be fine—all of it," she assured him. "Now go."

She pushed the specter of a child from her mind in favor of reliving the joy of having Lucien in her arms. Plus, he'd mentioned next time. Yes, she'd focus on that. In the meantime, she needed to add *several* things to her list.

CHAPTER 18

*W*hen Lucien arrived at the Wexfords' house on Sunday for the family dinner, he was already feeling brittle. Between waiting for the Foreign Office's next move regarding the club and his deepening connection to Kat, he wasn't sleeping as much as he needed to, and he was on edge, which seemed to be the norm of late. Add the fact that he was going to spend the evening in his father's company, and Lucien wished he'd drunk at least a half bottle of whisky beforehand. Perhaps then he could have some hope of relaxing.

The time spent before dinner in the drawing room was thankfully brief, and Cass was smart—and kind—enough to seat Lucien at the opposite end of the table from his father. While it was generally required that the highest-ranking guest be seated next to the host, Cass knew her father would prefer to sit beside her instead of the "Irishman." That meant Lucien got to sit next to Ruark, and Kat was seated on the other side of him.

During the first course, Lucien tipped his head toward

her. "Are you behind this seating arrangement?" he whispered.

"No. It's entirely luck." Kat flashed him a smile, and the brilliance of it struck him like a bolt of lightning. Had she ever looked so cheerful, so…happy?

Lucien glanced down the table toward his sister and hoped she hadn't picked up on anything between them. Or worse, that she was randomly playing matchmaker.

No, she wouldn't do that. Not to Kat. To Lucien however…he'd meddled in enough pairings to acknowledge that he likely deserved someone trying to match him.

"I trust you were well after leaving the club on Friday?" Lucien asked softly.

"Quite. You entirely cured my agitation. I think I've found something that soothes me even better than squeezing." She kept her voice low, but it wasn't quite a whisper. Lucien feared Sabrina, who sat on her other side, might hear. And so he stopped talking to her. At least about anything to do with *them.*

Throughout dinner, he was aware of her presence, her lavender scent teasing him. He'd been tempted to touch her. Finally, when the final course was served, he let his hand stray to her chair, where he barely caressed her hip.

Her gaze snapped to his, her lips parting. He immediately regretted his action because now he wanted to kiss her. And his cock was swelling.

To tame his lust, he reminded himself that she could already be carrying his child. That had the effect of being tossed into an icy lake. In truth, that possibility had been part of why he hadn't been sleeping much.

It wasn't as if he hadn't bungled things before. He'd been late pulling out—or had simply not done it, particularly in his youth—on many occasions. To date, though, he wasn't aware of any by-blows. He supposed that didn't mean there weren't any, and damn if that didn't trouble him from time to time.

Was that why he was so agitated about the possibility of Kat carrying? Perhaps, but it was also the way he felt about her. She was not like any other woman he'd taken to bed. Hell, he hadn't even really taken her to bed yet. How he wanted to. He glanced over at her, hoping his longing didn't show on his face.

There was also the simple question of the child. He'd suggested to Kat that he might want to raise it. She'd seen right through him though, prodding him for the truth. The real truth was that he didn't know how he felt. He'd never imagined having children because he'd never imagined getting married.

But that wasn't entirely true. There had been times when he was in Spain, when he'd felt alone and afraid. He'd had comrades to talk with, to avoid the stress of war with, but it wasn't the same as someone to whom he could bare his soul. He'd never had a person like that.

Kat, he realized, could be that person. She made him say and do things he normally wouldn't. She made him think about possibilities he'd never entertained—children, for heaven's sake. It wasn't just that. He'd begun to wonder if it would be terrible if he walked away from the club...and straight into her arms.

He also acknowledged that part of the reason he was so drawn to her was her view that she was an aberration. No, it wasn't her view. It was the opinion and judgment of others. And it had burrowed deep within her, despite her ability to cover up her feelings nearly all the time.

Whatever had happened Friday at the assembly had upset her greatly. When he'd returned to the ballroom, he'd tried to determine what had happened. Cass had told him that people were saying Kat had fumbled while dancing and that another young lady had said something to her, which had caused her to flail and strike Sir Rowland. No one had known what the young lady said. Apparently, the young lady wasn't providing the information either.

Lucien could imagine, but he wanted to know for sure. He *had* been able to identify her and would ensure she didn't return to any future assemblies. He'd also put it out that night that gossip about his sister's sister-in-law at the club would not be tolerated. He didn't like any sort of nasty gossip. That wasn't what the Phoenix Club was about. It was a haven for people who were too often the butt of such malice.

As dinner concluded, Lucien held Kat's chair. She turned her head toward him. "Why did you do that? When you touched me?"

He gave her a faint smile. "Couldn't resist. Don't worry, I'll keep my hands to myself for the remainder of the evening."

She gave him a brief pout. "That's unfortunate. Perhaps I won't," she added saucily as she grazed her hand against his.

Then she spun on her heel and preceded him from the dining room. Lucien smiled faintly as he walked toward the door. He made eye contact with his father, who was watching him with a peculiar look. He hadn't seen Kat touch his hand, had he? No, the chair would have been in the way.

Before Lucien could make his escape, the duke came toward him. They were the only two left in the dining room. "You and Miss Shaughnessy are the only unwed people in attendance."

Lucien bristled in the man's close presence. "Not by design. This is a family gathering. We are simply the only ones who aren't married. Actually, that isn't true. You aren't married."

"She would make you a good wife. She's smart and

focused on enriching tasks. Cassandra says she likes to conduct research and spends a good deal of time reading. She's not flighty or silly."

"She is, however, Irish. That can't recommend her to you."

"It's not ideal, especially since your sister already married one of those. However, Miss Shaughnessy doesn't have an accent since she was raised in Gloucestershire, nor does she seem to practice That Religion."

"Because her mother married her deceased husband's steward and fled Ireland. *That* can't recommend her to you either." Lucien narrowed his eyes at the duke. "Why are you playing matchmaker?"

When Lucien was younger, his father had suggested a handful of potential brides, but had abandoned the prospect upon Lucien's disinterest. He'd never made a secret, however, of his disappointment that Lucien preferred to remain unwed.

"I'm making conversation more than anything. I thought I saw something between the two of you when you stood up from the table, but perhaps I was mistaken. Come, I need to speak with you. We'll use Wexford's study." The duke pivoted and departed the dining room without waiting to see if Lucien would agree to accompany him.

Lucien had half a mind to ignore him and go up to the drawing room instead. Or perhaps leave entirely. But no, curiosity and a perverted sense of obedience drove him to follow the man.

The duke stood near the hearth, facing the doorway when Lucien walked in. "Close the door," he said.

Lucien did so, but didn't move farther into the room. "To what do I owe this honor?"

"I'm aware of what the Foreign Office is demanding of you." The duke clasped his hands behind his back and lifted his chin. His gaze didn't quite meet Lucien's. "I can help you, if you'll allow it."

"They told you?" Fury twisted Lucien's insides. "I thought you had retired."

"Fallin told me."

Lucien vowed to punch Dougal. Twice. "He should not have done that."

"He said you were being stubborn. Fallin knows, as do I, that you can't win this battle. Just walk away from the club and take whatever compensation they're offering. It may be enough to start a new club. If it's not, I'll give you whatever you need."

If the house had fallen down around Lucien, he would have been less shocked. "*Now* you're offering me help?"

"You need it," the duke said with great exasperation.

Lucien gritted his teeth. "I needed it before, when I came to see you asking for money weeks ago."

"The Foreign Office won't take your money. They want the club and what it affords them."

"I would still give them what they want—the access and the secrecy. They just wouldn't be able to dictate my membership."

"That isn't giving them what they want. You took your little experiment with inviting outcasts and pariahs too far."

"It wasn't an experiment. That is the Phoenix Club, and the Foreign Office *liked* that aspect when I explained how it would ensure a variety of people frequented the club."

Unclasping his hands and tugging at the hem of his waistcoat, the duke exhaled. "Just take the damn compensation, Lucien. Your pride will recover."

"This isn't my pride! This is my work. Which you've never valued."

"Then why am I offering to help you found a new club?"

the duke asked softly, his dark eyes—which were like looking into a mirror of Lucien's future—glittering.

"I haven't the faintest fucking idea. What else did Dougal tell you?" Lucien feared the duke also knew that the Foreign Office was blaming him for an assassination he didn't commit.

"Nothing." The duke's eyes narrowed almost imperceptibly, but Lucien could see the wheels of his mind turning. "What else is there?"

For a moment, Lucien considered telling him the truth, but to what end? Did he really expect the man to help him, or that he could? It seemed there was nothing even the duke could do to change the Foreign Office's mind about forcing Lucien from the club.

"Tell me," his father pressed.

Lucien cocked his head and gave him a humorless smile. "Though you're retired, I'm confident you can probably find out what you need to from the Foreign Office. Indeed, I'm sure they'd welcome your help in getting me to do their bidding."

"Dammit, Lucien. I'm trying to help *you*, not them."

Now, Lucien took two steps forward, propelled by anger and hurt. "And until you explain why, I can't believe that to be true. You've never helped me, and I certainly wouldn't expect you to put me over your sense of duty. I know there is little more important to you than that. Perhaps nothing."

Spinning about, Lucien threw open the door. It hit the wall given the force he'd used, but he didn't pause. He stalked from the office, then went to the entrance hall, where he asked Bartholomew for his hat and gloves.

Briefly, Lucien considered staying. He hated leaving without saying good night to Kat. But he had to get away from his father. Perhaps Dougal would be at the club and Lucien could take out his aggression on him.

Or, he could find a quiet place in or around the house to sit and wait until everyone went to bed and he could lose himself in Kat's arms. His ire diminished to be replaced by a consuming need.

Bartholomew returned with his hat and gloves. Lucien walked out into the night and realized there wasn't really a choice to make.

~

*K*at had suffered grave disappointment when Lucien hadn't come up to the drawing room with his father. She wondered what the duke had said to drive him away and was not the only one. Con and Cass pulled their father aside, and while the conversation could not be heard, the anger on the siblings' faces was unmistakable.

The duke departed just after that.

"What happened?" Kat asked Cass.

"I don't know exactly, but my father met with Lucien in Ruark's study and Lucien left."

"You didn't look pleased with His Grace," Kat said.

Cass frowned. "As far as I can tell, he ruined a lovely family evening by provoking Lucien somehow."

Ruark came and put his arm around Cass's waist, then brushed a kiss against her temple. "I'm sorry, my love. Don't let him ruin things."

"I wish Lucien hadn't gone," Cass said. "He's been under such strain lately, and this should have lightened his mood. He seemed to enjoy himself at dinner."

"He did." Ruark looked to Kat. "Don't you agree?"

"Yes." And now that he was gone, Kat didn't want to participate in whatever activities Cass had planned. "Do you mind if I retire?"

"Of course not." Cass's brow creased. "You aren't over-taxed, are you?"

"Not at all. I just have some reading I'd like to do." Kat bade them good night and did the same with the rest of the guests because it was the polite thing to do. It was a good ten minutes before she was able to finally quit the drawing room and go upstairs to her chamber.

Kat was especially glad she didn't require a maid's assistance this evening. As soon as she entered her chamber, she kicked off her slippers and closed the door behind her. Always tidy, she picked up one shoe, but had to look for the other. The toe peeked from under the bed.

Muttering, she crouched to retrieve it, then froze when she caught sight of another shoe—a Wellington. Her heart hammered and she fought to draw a quiet breath. As if whoever was hiding under her bed didn't know she was there!

But wait, who would be underneath her bed? Only one name came to mind.

She knelt and lowered her head to peer into the shadows. "Lucien?"

"Are you alone?" he whispered.

"Would I have addressed you if I wasn't?"

As he slid out from under the bed, Kat set her shoes together neatly. She straightened just as he did. "What are you doing under my bed?"

"Waiting for you. What else would I be doing?"

"I can't imagine," she murmured as a heady desire raced through her. Her joy was tempered by the creases in his expression and the darkness in his gaze. "What happened with your father?" She also wanted to ask how'd managed to get up here undetected, but would save that question for another time. She was far more concerned with his seemingly ominous mood.

"I don't want to talk about that. Or him."

"I'm sorry he upset you. I wish I could kick him."

Lucien smiled, but it wasn't his usual face-splitting grin. He was troubled.

Kat went to him and put her hands on his chest. "Then why are you here? Were you hoping we might play chess? Or discuss animals? I still owe you a drawing for your study at your house."

"Do you?"

"Cass said I should give you one. I have several you can choose from." She started to turn toward her desk, but he closed his hand around her wrist and drew her back to face him.

"Don't go," he rasped.

"Just to my desk."

"No." He brought her hand back to his chest. "I came because I need you. May I stay?"

She saw the hunger in his gaze, and her body responded with a desperate longing. "Always."

"Good." He let out his Lucien growl and lowered his head to kiss her. The touch of his lips seared through her as if she stood beside a roaring flame.

Kat gripped his lapels, holding on to him as if it would keep her on the ground instead of floating into the heavens, which was where his kisses typically threatened to send her. But these kisses were different. They were harsh and deep, fueled by a passionate need.

Lucien shrugged out of his coat and tossed it past Kat. His hands went to the buttons of his waistcoat and began unfastening the garment.

"Do I get to remove your cravat tonight?"

"You can burn the damn thing." He claimed her mouth once more, his tongue driving against hers.

Giddy with anticipation, Kat untied his cravat as Lucien

began to pluck pins from her hair. "Don't let them fall to the floor," she said. "I may not find them all, and that will distract me endlessly."

"Then I shall keep them all safe here in my hand." He kissed her cheek, then trailed his lips back to her ear, where he licked and sucked at her flesh.

Kat shivered as she finally got his cravat loose. "Huzzah!" With a flourish, she swept the silk from his neck before carefully tossing it onto the bench at the end of her bed.

His gaze met hers with an intensity she'd never seen. "Please don't ever change. You are the purest, most honest person I've ever known. Being with you is a balm to my soul."

Words escaped her for a moment while her insides cartwheeled, and her heart felt as though it may burst. "Oh," was all she could manage. "That is so lovely."

"*You* are lovely." He finished removing the pins from her hair, and the mass fell down to the middle of her back.

She took the pins from him and deposited them on her desk, which was the closest surface. "You know what's lovely? You without a cravat. I'd like to see if you're even lovelier without a shirt." She tugged the garment from his waistband.

"Don't let me hinder your investigation." He raised his arms, and she pushed the shirt up until he caught the hem and drew it over his head. At least, she assumed he did. Her focus was entirely captured by the gorgeous expanse of his chest and abdomen. Muscles rippled beneath two red-brown nipples, and dark hair covered the space between them as well as provided a helpful trail down to his cock. Well, she assumed it went all the way to his cock. He was still wearing too many clothes.

Kat spread her hands out over his flesh and explored

every inch of him from his shoulders to his waist. Impatient, she began to unbutton his fall. "You don't mind?"

"I would beg if you weren't doing it already."

His words somehow enflamed her further. She wasn't sure she'd ever been this aroused, and he hadn't even really touched her yet.

When his fall was open, she pushed the garment down over his hips, her gaze moving slowly and exactingly over each new inch of exposed flesh. He was so beautifully formed. She just wanted to stare at him. No, she wanted to draw him. But she'd never get him right. Her frustration would only mount as she restarted her sketch a hundred times.

"Why do you look upset?" He brushed his thumb between her brows.

"I was thinking I'd like to draw you, but that I wouldn't be able to do justice to how splendid you are in reality." She stripped his pantaloons down his thighs, holding her breath as she revealed the thick length of his cock.

Licking her lips, she planned to take him in her mouth as soon as she bared his legs. She wanted him entirely naked. Working quickly, she pulled his boots off, which took more effort than she would have supposed, then tugged the pantaloons from his legs. He helped by lifting his feet. Lastly, she peeled his stockings away. Kneeling before him, she swept her gaze up to his shaft.

"Your turn." He grabbed her upper arms and hauled her to stand before him.

"But I was going to take you in my mouth."

"First, you're going to be naked like me. I've waited far too long to look at you the way you're devouring me."

"You do look good enough to eat."

"Don't think I didn't see you licking your lips. You are such a temptress." He kissed her hard and fast. "Does this gown unfasten in the front? Shit, I should have asked if you were expecting a maid."

"Have some faith in me. I would have told you. And yes, it's a round gown." She loosened the cinched neckline and unhooked the front of the bodice just below her shoulders. Then she untied the dress at her waist before pulling her arms from the sleeves. "Help me take it over my head, please."

"Nothing would make me happier," he murmured.

"Be careful." She grasped the gown from him. "I'll take it." She laid it across the bench at the foot of her bed. Next, she loosened the laces of her stays. She felt him move behind her and sweep her hair from her neck. His lips fell against her nape and conducted an erotic expedition of her flesh from the base of her scalp to the top of her clothing.

She hurried to pull the corset over her head. Lucien helped her again, and this time, she didn't care what he did with the garment. Her body quivered with need. She just wanted his mouth on her again. Pushing the straps of her petticoat from her shoulders, she untied the waist and shoved it down her legs so it pooled at her feet.

Lucien put his arms around her and cupped her breasts through her chemise while he kissed and sucked her neck. She cast her head back, moaning, as he caressed and stroked her, bringing her nipples to hard, stiff points.

His cock pressed against the top of her backside, and she was desperate to remove the last bit of clothing between them. Wriggling, she worked the garment up. Thankfully, he took over and swept it from her body. Except, she wasn't naked, for she was still wearing her stockings.

But he was already sliding the right one down her leg, his lips and tongue following the path of the silk as he stripped it away. Kat's knees were weak by the time he finished with the second stocking. Now, they were bare to each other.

But before she could turn around to face him, he came

behind her once more, his tongue trailing up her spine. She groaned with need, desperate for his touch. "Lucien, I want—"

"Shhh." He kissed beneath her ear. "In a moment." He guided her to the bench. "Kneel on that and put your elbows on the bed."

What was he doing? This wasn't on her list.

She didn't protest, however. She would do anything he asked. She trusted him completely.

When she had positioned herself as he'd directed, he tapped the inside of her thigh. "Move your knees wider apart."

Again, she complied. She began to suspect what he intended, and that *was* on her list. Her sex pulsed, and she snagged her lip between her teeth lest she whimper.

"Just like that." His voice was a sensual rasp from deep in his throat, and it only escalated her desire. His hands closed over her backside, gently caressing her and then squeezing. "You are so exquisite. I would lick every part of you." He licked her backside—one side and then the other. Then his tongue dipped lower, sliding against her sex just before his finger slipped into her. "And you are so wet. Does this excite you? Do you want me to take you from behind?"

"Yes. Yes." She clutched the coverlet. "Please, Lucien, I want you to come inside me—hard and fast."

"I can't resist, but only for a moment. I want to take you in the bed, face-to-face." He clutched her hip as he pressed his cock into her.

Kat gasped as he filled her. An astounding flood of pleasure washed over her. She pressed back against him until her backside met his pelvis. He ground into her, and she thought she might arrive at that very moment. But then he withdrew, and she felt utterly bereft.

He leaned over her back and grasped her hair, pulling her

head up. He nipped her earlobe. "I need you to arrive before I'll put you on the bed. Can you do that for me?"

She was already so close, but she couldn't convey that. Only garbled sounds left her mouth. She nodded and whimpered as she wriggled her backside against him.

"Good." He released her hair and wrapped his arm around her to fondle her breast. He thrust deep into her as he tugged her nipple, and she knew she was lost. She cried out over and over as he barreled into her, filling and stretching her with a rapturous splendor. His hand left her breast and moved lower. The moment he stroked her clitoris, she flew apart into a thousand pieces.

She dropped her head to the bed and made a series of very loud unladylike noises into the coverlet. Before she'd regained her senses, he left her. He swept her up and deposited her gently onto the bed.

Her body tingled everywhere from the orgasm he'd just given her. But she was nowhere near satisfied. He stood beside the bed with his eyes closed, his breathing rapid.

"Lucien?"

He opened his eyes, looking a little lost.

Kat sat up and touched his cheek. "Are you all right?"

"I'm just..." He shook his head. "I'm fine. Because of you." He kissed her softly, his hand tangling in her hair as he lowered her down to the bed.

"Let's make you more than fine," she whispered with a smile.

CHAPTER 19

*L*ucien hadn't meant to come up to her chamber. He'd decided to go to the club, to seek out Dougal and unleash his wrath. But his body had made a different decision. He'd found himself stealing into the entrance to the kitchens, then risked ascending the back stairs to the second floor. From there, it was a short dash to Kat's room where he'd concealed himself beneath her bed, prepared to wait for hours if necessary.

Except it had only been minutes. She could not have stayed in the drawing room very long. Had she learned that he'd left and opted to abandon the party as well? The thought made him smile.

Or it had. At this moment, he was overcome with her sensuality, her beauty, her generosity her absolute…joy. Being with her was far better than letting his father provoke his emotions.

No. The duke was not allowed here. With her.

As Lucien climbed onto the bed, she wrapped her hand around his cock, stroking him with a now-expert skill. It was as if she'd been made for him, and he for her. He was surprised that he'd told her to kneel on the bench, but even more shocked that she'd done it. But the absolute wonder had been her reaction. She was wholly eager for anything he suggested, trusting him in a way he wasn't sure anyone ever had. Plus, she somehow teased and comforted him at the same time.

He raked his gaze over her body, moving slowly and meticulously to study each swell and crevice. He tried not to think of her hand on his shaft as he caressed her neck and shoulders, her biceps, her breasts. She sucked in a breath as he swirled his fingertip around each nipple, then dragged it between them, moving down over her abdomen. Her belly went concave as she inhaled sharply and held her breath. He skimmed his hand down to her hip and thigh, lower still to her knee and calf. She had to let go of him, but as he moved from her left foot to her right and back up the other leg, she kept her hand poised to receive him once more.

When she curled her fingers around him again, he closed his eyes for a brief moment, willing himself not to pump his hips into her hand. Shortly, he was going to thrust into her glorious body and take them both where they wanted to go.

He situated himself between her legs, and she lifted her hips, planting her feet on the mattress. Locking his eyes with hers, he thumbed her clitoris. Her lids drooped, and he put his hand over hers, guiding his cock to her sex. She helped him slide the tip inside but then put her hand on his hip.

She was so tight and warm around him, so wonderfully perfect. He tried to go slow, but ultimately thrust deep into her until he was fully seated. Her eyes widened, then narrowed. Then she purred. Like a cat. Which seemed fitting.

"Why are you laughing?"

Was he? Apparently so. He leaned down and kissed her, plying his lips upon hers with soft teasing strokes. "You bring me joy, my wild Kat."

"You think I'm wild?" She put her cheek to his and gently bit his earlobe. "How's that?" She moved her lips down his neck and nipped him again. "Or that?"

"Yes, and don't ever stop." Lucien began to move, withdrawing, then thrusting, gradually building speed. She wrapped her legs around him, squeezing him as he gave himself over to the bliss of being inside her.

But he couldn't lose his senses this time. He had to pull out before it was too late. Slowing his pace, he kissed her again, letting himself bask in the glory of sharing this with her—finally—in a bed, without clothing.

"Why are you going slowly?"

"Because I don't want this to end." He kissed her jaw, her cheek, her neck.

"It does feel rather nice. I love feeling you against me like this. I liked feeling you behind me too." She wriggled her hips as he drove deep.

He envisioned them together in a variety of positions, their bare bodies entwined as they entangled themselves in the bedclothes. It was such a breathtaking image, he felt as if his chest might burst.

Burying his face in her neck, he sped up again, needing the friction along with her sex tightening around him. He kissed her, trailing his lips down to her breast, where he sucked her nipple into his mouth.

She arched up as her muscles clenched around him. She lifted her legs higher so her heels dug into his lower back. Lucien surrendered to her and drove into her again and again, reveling in her orgasm. His balls squeezed, and he knew he had to leave her. One more stroke…

He reared back and pulled his cock from her, fisting the shaft to begin his orgasm. He started to move away, but she put her hand over his, stroking him hard and fast.

"How did you…?"

"I want to make sure you arrive. Don't leave me. You may spill yourself wherever you like. I think you suggested my breasts?"

She urged him up her body as she scooted down to meet him, never stopping the movement of her hand. He cupped the sides of her breasts, pushing them together as blood rushed to his cock. His body went rigid as he pumped relentlessly into her hand. He had to bite the inside of his cheek lest he shout and alert the entire household to his presence. His seed pulsed forth onto her flesh. Watching her finish him like this brought him to a pinnacle of rapture he'd never reached before.

He had to close his eyes. He couldn't withstand another moment. Down he fell, into a deep and dark, satisfying release.

After some minutes, he returned to himself. She continued to stroke him, and he realized he was holding her too tightly. He abruptly released her, hoping he hadn't marked her flesh. "Sorry," he murmured.

"For what?"

"Did I hurt you?"

"Not at all. Did I hurt you?" she asked. "You looked rather pained."

"Arrivals are like that," he said with a smirk, his hips finally slowing from their frenetic pace. "They are not our most attractive moments."

She laughed softly. "Perhaps not, but they feel better than just about anything else, do they not?"

Just about anything. The only thing that felt better was simply holding Kat in his arms. Or so he thought. He hadn't really got to do that. He realized that was what he wanted, that was why he'd come tonight. This, what they'd just shared, had been an extra bounty.

"Let's get you cleaned up." He moved away from her and

off the bed.

"There are cloths over in the washstand in the corner." She gestured across the bed.

Lucien returned to give her a cloth as she sat up, then went to tidy himself. When he turned back toward the bed, she was watching him.

"You shouldn't go now," she said. "I don't know how you got up here, but I doubt everyone has left yet. It's best if you wait to leave until the house is quiet."

"Would you mind?"

"Not at all." She pushed the bedclothes down beneath her and slipped between them. "Come lie with me."

No request had ever been more inviting.

He climbed into the bed and faced her. "Thank you."

She turned on her side toward him. "Thank *you*." She smiled. "Is that typical? Thanking each other after sex?"

"You want to know for your research, I assume."

"My curiosity is rarely satisfied."

He chuckled, thinking that was the truest thing ever. "No, it's not typical." He pulled her against him and kissed her head. "But then, *you* are not typical."

"I know. I'm strange."

He put his hand beneath her chin and tipped her head up. "*No.* You are not strange You are absolutely unique, and it's goddamned spectacular. Everyone should envy you. *I* envy you."

"You do?"

"You are honest and guileless, and you're bloody clever. You're also very, very good at this."

"Sex, you mean?"

"Yes."

"That's rather flattering." She kissed his jaw. "So are you. I think we're rather good at it together."

Yes, they were. Lucien closed his eyes and fell asleep thinking it—with her—might just be the thing he was best at.

~

*I*t had been dark when Lucien had left Kat's bed. She'd heard him dress, though he'd worked hard to do so quietly. He'd returned to the bed to kiss her cheek, but she'd turned her head and met his lips. Then he'd tucked her in, and she'd smiled as she'd fallen back asleep.

The joy of his visit was still with her, but along with it had come a realization. She didn't want to continue as she had been. As she walked into the park with Cass the following afternoon, she took a deep breath as she planned to make her confession.

"I'm still so annoyed with my father," Cass said. She'd already mentioned her lingering irritation once before they'd left the house and once more since.

"I gathered," Kat murmured.

"I wish I knew what he said or did to Lucien."

So did Kat, and she hoped Lucien would tell her. She'd understood his need to not discuss it last night. He'd seemed so out of sorts when she'd found him beneath her bed. "Perhaps it wasn't anything specific," Kat said. "Isn't the duke's mere presence enough to sour Lucien's evening?"

"Normally, I would say yes, but he made it through the dinner and seemed to be enjoying himself."

"The duke was at the opposite end of the table," Kat said wryly. "We should have ensured one of them left the drawing room right away so that they weren't left alone."

Cass scowled. "I should have known better. But I must confess that things seem even worse between them, as if something has happened."

"Do you have any hint what that could be?"

"Not really, but I'm sure it's related to the club. Lucien has been completely devoured by it since the scandal about Evie. Oh my goodness, she and Lord Gregory are getting married today." Cass's sudden smile was almost as quickly replaced by a frown. "I wish Lucien had gone. Evie is one of his dearest friends."

"He seems to rarely leave town, and given everything going on at the club, I'm not surprised he chose to remain here."

"You've been very observant about Lucien."

"We do see him a great deal," Kat said, hoping Cass wouldn't leap to any assumptions.

"That's true. He likely also thought attending Evie's wedding would only feed the flames of the scandal—because they used to be lovers."

"I suppose that makes sense." It also made Kat feel a blast of jealousy, which was absurd since Lucien and Mrs. Renshaw had been friends instead of lovers for years now.

Cass sent her a quick, almost hesitant look. "I wanted to ask you about the assembly. Do you want to talk about what happened?"

"Not particularly. I would, however, like to discuss the Season." It was time for the confession. "I've made a mistake trying to participate. I'm just not enjoying it."

"I understand. Why not take a respite for a while? You can stay home for a week or a fortnight even. Read, sketch, do whatever makes you happy." She gave Kat an encouraging smile.

"That's the problem I'm struggling with. I'm not entirely sure what will make me happy." Kat had always been incredibly focused on whatever topic or project interested her. Right now, that was Lucien. She couldn't exactly spend all her energy and time on him, as much as she wanted to.

Perhaps that was something to investigate on its own. She

recalled what Lucien had said to her, that she wasn't concerned with others. He was right. Kat didn't always think about those around her. She was typically too locked up with whatever *she* was doing.

Kat looked about the park, wondering how she could alter her perspective. What could she do that would help her friends and family instead of focusing on herself?

She noticed people looking at her. And talking to one another. The moment her gaze drifted in their direction, they diverted their attention. "I think people are talking about me," she said quietly. There she went putting the focus on her again. "Or perhaps they're talking about you."

Glancing over at Cass, Kat noted her slight grimace. She didn't want to upset Kat. People *were* talking about Kat, then.

"Definitely me. But that's not unusual." Except there were an awful lot of them.

They passed a pair of ladies on the path who made a point of bending their heads together and talking in a low tone. It wasn't the cut direct, but it was close.

Cass twitched beside Kat. "I am so angry. This is likely due to whatever happened at the Phoenix Club the other night. Or perhaps the Hickinbottoms are to blame."

Kat touched her sister-in-law's arm. "It's all right. I'm used to people talking about me." Even in her own family.

"I'm not," Cass said sharply. "It's rude and awful."

"It is, but there's nothing to be done, so why allow yourself to be agitated?"

Cass looked at her with incredulity. "How can you not be?"

"I decided long ago that there was no point in worrying about such things. I can't change people's reactions or judgment. Worrying about or being upset by their behavior doesn't help me at all." Kat paused on the path. Perhaps that was why she'd always been so inwardly focused. It was easier and far less painful.

Stopping alongside her, Cass asked, "What's wrong?"

"Nothing." Kat shook her head. "I think I've just made a realization. As I said, I don't want to participate in the Season, and that includes walking in the park during the fashionable hour." Which was what they were doing. It was too bad because Kat adored the park. She'd just come earlier in the day.

If she stayed in London. "I'm thinking of going to Hampton Lodge. Sabrina invited me to visit whenever I wanted."

"Oh." Cass sounded disappointed. "You should go if that is what you want. A change of scenery might be good. But please, don't let these horrible gossipmongers drive you away."

"It isn't them. It's me," Kat assured her. "Though, I suppose they make the decision easier," she added with a laugh.

"How do you manage to remain so positive? I don't know what happened at the assembly, but I have to imagine it wasn't pleasant for you."

"No, it wasn't. And you must remember that I didn't remain positive. I fled the ballroom and had to calm myself before going home." That wasn't precisely what had happened of course, but Cass didn't need to know that.

"I wish I could have helped you. Why do you always isolate yourself? Don't you get lonely?"

"No. Solitude helps me...resituate myself, to regain my equilibrium. It's difficult to explain." However, she realized that Lucien had helped her do that at the assembly. And right now, in this moment of feeling stares and knowing people were discussing her, she wished he were with her. She wasn't lonely, but she craved his company.

"Oh blast." Cass put her arm through Kat's. "Let's turn."

"Why?" Kat asked just before she caught sight of the Hickinbottoms farther along the path. Mrs. Hickinbottom was sneering in their direction.

Now, Kat wanted to escape. Perhaps she wasn't completely immune to other people's treatment of her. "Let's go home," she said, pulling her arm tight to her side, which brought Cass closer to her.

"Yes, let's." Cass turned with her and gave her hand a pat. "I hope you know how much you are loved—by me and the whole family. I wished you'd stayed in the drawing room last night. You could have seen that for yourself."

While Kat appreciated hearing that, there was only one person's love she really wanted, and acknowledging that was absolutely terrifying.

CHAPTER 20

*L*ucien walked into the small sitting room on the ground floor of Wexford House, answering the summons he'd received from Kat earlier that day. Summons? She'd sent a short but lovely note inviting him to call today so she could give him a drawing for his study. He welcomed the opportunity to see her—and not just so he could be in her presence, though that was enticement enough. He ought to explain to her what had happened with the duke the other night since it had prompted him to seek solace in her arms.

And what solace that had been. Lucien had felt as though he were on a cloud the past day and a half. Not even the troubles of the club had weighed him down.

Kat came into the sitting room looking so lovely that it was actually painful to not go to her and take her in his arms. Her dark hair wasn't atop her head. It was just pulled back from her face and hung down her back. The style made her look younger, probably because it wasn't how ladies of the ton wore their hair. But then Kat was different, and she embraced that.

He smiled at her. "I like your hair."

She touched it briefly. "Do you? I prefer it because it requires fewer pins. I've been making myself wear it up more since I decided to do the Season, but now that I've abandoned that, I can go back to my more comfortable ways—hair down and the least constricting corset I own."

"What do you mean you've abandoned the Season?"

"I'll get to that in a moment." She moved farther into the room and put a large piece of parchment on a round tea table. "This is for you."

Lucien joined her and surveyed the stunning drawing. "A peacock." In full mating mode with his feathers extended and his head high. "Is this a commentary on me?" he asked drily.

Kat laughed. "Perhaps. Not that you regale yourself in ostentatious costumes, but you do tend to strut."

After studying the sketch a moment longer, he shifted his gaze to Kat. "I thought we might talk as well. I'd like to know what happened at the assembly to provoke your...difficulty. And I thought I would share what prompted me to leave the dinner party on Sunday."

Kat made a face. "I'd rather not revisit the assembly, at least not that part of it, but since I'd like to know what happened with your father, I'll agree to the trade."

Lucien did laugh now. "I'm glad to hear it. Shall we sit?" He gestured toward the settee, which faced the doorway. With the door open, Lucien wanted to know if they were about to be interrupted.

"Yes." She took his hand, which was not appropriate, but he didn't care, and led him to the red-and-beige-covered settee. Sitting down with him, she situated herself so she was angled toward him, and their knees touched. She also didn't release his hand.

He glanced down at their entwined fingers on the cushion. "Is that wise?"

She shrugged. "We can see the door and move apart if we need to."

He couldn't argue with that, so he allowed himself to enjoy being close to her, touching her. "Who should go first?"

"I will." She exhaled. "I was dancing with Sir Rowland—badly, if I'm to be honest."

"When are you not? Honest, I mean."

A brief smile flashed across her lush mouth, and he was nearly overcome with the need to kiss her. He managed not to. "As I've told you, I struggle with dancing. My body and the music don't always get along."

"Is that what happened at the assembly?"

"Yes, and one of the young ladies in our square decided it would be amusing to draw attention to it. She said I would benefit from more time with a dancing master. She added that she was only teasing, but it sounded mean-spirited to me."

Lucien knew the identity of the young women thanks to Cass and would ensure she paid for her malice. Lady Pickering would most certainly help him in this endeavor. She would hate that someone had sought to embarrass Kat. "She won't ever be at the Phoenix Club again," he told her.

Kat's gaze flashed with surprise. "Indeed? Well, that's very nice. However, I won't be there either."

"Are you referring to your comment earlier about abandoning the Season?" He held up his free hand. "First, finish with the assembly story."

"There isn't much left to tell. She said something snide, I lost focus on the dance, and nearly caused a fracas. I suppose I *did* cause a fracas since I smacked Sir Rowland in the chest. I did murmur an apology to him before I fled the dance floor. I do hope he heard me." She looked at Lucien. "Do you think I should send a note of apology? Perhaps that would cool the gossip. I hate how it's affecting Cass."

Lucien narrowed his eyes. "It's affecting Cass?"

"Only because she possesses such a kind heart and worries about me. We were walking in the park yesterday, and it was clear I was the topic of many conversations." She spoke of the gossip about her as if it were an ordinary occurrence completely lacking in import.

"Bloody hell, Kat, I'd say it's affecting you."

"Bah, only if I let it, and I refuse to do so. I told you that I'm an aberration, and perhaps my ability to ignore others is part of that."

"Except you weren't able to ignore it on Friday," he said quietly. "You don't have to put on a show of bravado for me. I'd rather know how you really feel, even if you're trying not to feel it. *Especially* if you're trying not to feel it." He had a great deal of experience with that, particularly when it came to his experiences in the war in Spain.

Her eyes rounded slightly. It took her a moment to respond. "I am not always able to ignore it, particularly in environments when I am already overwhelmed by what's happening around me. The sound and the dancing put me in a state where I am less capable of managing my emotions. Think of it like juggling. I can keep the items aloft until that one I'm not expecting is thrown in. Then I drop them all."

Lucien thought he understood. "What an excellent analogy."

"But since you are asking how I really feel...I am bothered by it, actually. Not for me, you understand, but I don't want it to affect Cass. I have thought a great deal about what you said to me, about me not concerning myself with others as much as I ought. I'm trying to change my perspective. That is one of the reasons I've decided to abandon the Season and leave London."

"Leave London?" He felt as if his stomach had dropped beneath the floor. "You can't leave London. You love it here."

"Bath is probably similar, isn't it? In the meantime, I'm thinking of going to Hampton Lodge. Sabrina has extended an invitation for me to visit whenever I like. I can go there for a time, then ultimately settle in Bath, where I can fade into spinsterhood."

Lucien vehemently shook his head. "Absolutely not. You can't run away."

"I'm not running away. I'm putting others first. It's better for everyone if I leave. There won't be any more gossip about my strange behavior, I won't risk my reputation with you or anyone else, and I won't have to fear running afoul of the Hickinbottoms, who, I think, are out to discredit me in any way that they can."

Lucien made a note to inform Lady Pickering about the Hickinbottoms as well. They needed to be reminded that their son was part of the "scandal" and if he could be allowed to get on with his life, Kat should be given the same benefit.

"I hope you aren't going to be risking your reputation with anyone other than me. And I will take care of the Hick-inbottoms," he added in a more serious tone.

"Are you going to work your Lucien magic and bend them to your will?"

"Something like that. In any case, you shouldn't leave town. Stay here and do what you like, be who you are. Hold your head high and know you are supported by many who care about and love you."

Including me.

That thought made him freeze. He definitely cared about her, but did he love her? The possibility made him a little unsteady. He was glad he was sitting down.

She surprised him by laughing. "What does that even look like? I don't enjoy Society or most of the social obligations, and I certainly can't be bothered with all the rules that don't make sense to me. Why torture myself and everyone else with my presence?"

Her argument was compelling, but dammit, he didn't want her to leave. "Your presence isn't a torture to Ruark, to Cass, to me, or to a number of other people I could name. You think of London as your home, do you not?"

Her blue eyes were clear with confidence and her persistent honesty. "I do."

"Then you can't let anyone drive you away. This is precisely what's happening to me at the Phoenix Club."

She leaned toward him, her gaze darkening with concern. "It is?"

He hadn't meant to tell her this, but if it would help her make a different decision—if it would persuade her to stay—then it would be worth it. "Not many people know this, including your brother and my sister, but I don't own the Phoenix Club. I run it, of course, but the primary owners are unhappy with how I've managed things regarding the departure of the Hargroves and what happened with Evie—because I wouldn't expel her." He refused to call it a scandal.

"Didn't you expel the Hargroves?"

"Lady Hargrove, yes. Her husband left of his own accord."

"I can't imagine he wanted to stay after you tossed his wife out," Kat muttered. "And good riddance to him. So, they're making you leave the club? They can't do that. The Phoenix Club is nothing without you." She spoke with great fervor, gesticulating with her free hand while squeezing his hand with the other.

"I did try to tell them that," he said with a smile, appreciating her loyalty. "I'm not going to let them do it. That's what my father and I argued about the other night. He wants me to leave the club, which shouldn't have surprised me."

Kat scowled. "He's completely wrongheaded. No wonder you left the party. But why did you come to my room?"

Lucien opened his mouth, but paused. What if he could leave the club and not be devastated by the loss? What if there could be more to his life than that? He heard his father telling him to take the compensation, that Kat would make him a good wife...

Fuck, was he considering his father's advice? He was past unsteady now. He felt downright ill.

"Lucien?" Cass's voice carried over the sitting room.

Lucien cursed inwardly. For all that they'd positioned themselves to watch for intruders, they'd completely missed Cass's arrival.

Kat released his hand and leapt up from the settee, moving to the table with the sketch. "I was just giving Lucien this peacock drawing for his study."

"Excellent choice." Cass swept into the room and joined Kat. "Isn't this marvelous, Lucien?"

"It's exceptional. I am eager to have it framed and mounted on the wall." He picked it up. "I must be on my way. Thank you again, Kat." He wanted to tell her to consider what he'd said. No, he wanted to make her promise she wouldn't leave. However, he did neither. He simply bowed and took his leave, wondering how the hell his father's counsel had worked its way into his brain.

$\sim$

Finally, Kat had an objective that had nothing to do with herself or her own interests. She was going to help Lucien get his club back.

She'd lain awake last night thinking of how best to aid him. It seemed obvious that she should talk to Mrs. Renshaw, but since she was not currently in London, Kat decided Lady Warfield was the next best person.

So it was that Kat found herself waiting in a sparsely

furnished drawing room at the Warfields' new house on Bruton Street. Lady Warfield entered wearing her usual cheerful smile. "Good afternoon, Miss Shaughnessy. What a pleasant surprise."

Kat clutched her reticule. "I hope you don't mind my calling on you like this, but I need your help."

"This sounds important." Lady Warfield gestured to the only seating area in the large room, save a lone chair situated near the hearth on the opposite side. "Forgive our rather Spartan décor. We just moved into the house recently, and we're still filling the rooms. I suspect it will take a while. Max is woefully uninterested in such matters."

"Aren't men usually?"

Lady Warfield laughed. "Yes, but Max is actually grumpy about it. He can be grumpy about many things. It's the basis of his charm."

Kat wasn't sure how grumpiness could be charming, but she determined he must be a good sort since Lady Warfield clearly adored him, and he was also a good friend of Lucien's.

"Let me get right to the point, Lady Warfield."

"Ada, if you please. I insist."

"Then you must call me Kat. I've come to you seeking help for Lucien. He is being forced out of the Phoenix Club."

Ada's eyes nearly popped from her head. "How can that be? It's *his* club?"

"It isn't, though. At least, he doesn't *own* it. Those who do want him to leave. They don't like how he's handled the recent scandal."

Ada grumbled, and Kat could have sworn she'd cursed. "I know he's been under strain, but I had no idea it was this dire. I can't believe he's going to just leave the club. I suppose that means I'll be leaving too. Drat, I really enjoy my work there." Her brow puckered as she frowned deeply. "Who are these horrid owners?"

"I don't know, but it shouldn't be too difficult to find out. First, however, we need the means to buy them out so that Lucien can be the rightful owner."

Ada's features lit. "But of course! Everyone will want to help Lucien after all he's done for so many. I daresay we could put out a collection plate, and it would fill by morning."

Kat smiled and allowed some of the stress to flow away from her body. "I was hoping you would say that."

"You can't put out a collection plate." The masculine voice came from the other side of the room, from the vicinity of the chair near the hearth.

Ada adjusted herself on the settee. "Max?"

The viscount stood, his large form unfolding from the chair, which was situated so the back was facing them.

"We didn't see you there," Ada said. "Nor did you alert us to your presence." She gave him a wry look. "Come and join us, then, if you want to participate."

He ambled toward them, looking rather fierce with the scars on his face. Kat thought they made him look far more interesting than any London dandy.

"Why not a collection plate?" Kat asked.

"You'll need to be more covert than that," the viscount said. "I suspect Lucien doesn't want anyone to know he's in need. Otherwise, this wouldn't be a surprise to any of us."

That was true. He'd told Kat that almost no one knew about the true ownership of the club. "Then what should we do?"

"We'll give him what he needs to buy it." His gaze flicked to Ada. "Not 'we' as in us. I wish we could give him what he needs. I certainly owe him that and so much more."

Kat was intrigued to know more about this perceived debt, but now was not the time to pursue that.

"I wish we could too," Ada murmured. "However, we are still rebuilding the Warfield estate."

"When I said 'we,' I meant Lucien's friends and family," Warfield clarified. "There are many of us who will help. What does your brother say about this?" he asked Kat.

"I haven't told Ruark yet. I wanted to speak with Ada since she is more closely involved with the club than pretty much anyone, save Mrs. Renshaw, who isn't here." Kat looked toward Ada, whose features were drawn into a contemplative expression.

"I know where we can get most, if not all, of the funds, actually," Ada said. "Evie and Gregory are thinking of opening a ladies-only club, and Evie's sister and her husband are planning to invest. I'm sure we could persuade them all to invest in Lucien instead."

"I doubt persuasion will be necessary." Warfield turned his gaze on Kat. "You don't know who these owners are?"

Kat shook her head. "I wish I did."

He gave a subtle nod. "We'll secure the funds, then we'll go to Lucien so he can conduct the transaction."

"If he would be offended by a collection plate, will he accept this financial support from his friends and family?" Kat was glad she'd decided to speak with them before alerting anyone else.

"He bloody well better." Warfield grunted. "I'll make sure he does."

Ada gave him a pert stare. "No more fisticuffs with Lucien, dear."

Fisticuffs? There was most definitely a story here, and Kat would endeavor to hear it. But first, they needed to help Lucien. She looked from Ada to her husband and back. "How shall we approach this?"

"I will speak with Evie and Gregory as soon as they return, which should be by Sunday," Ada said. "Max and I can also talk to Prudence and Bennet, though I'm not sure how much they'll be able to give." Glastonbury's father had left a great deal of debt when he died. "Can you speak with your brother and Cass?"

"Certainly. I can also speak with Jess and Dougal." Indeed, Kat would call on Jess next. "They will most definitely want to help."

"I'll talk with Overton," Warfield offered. "He'll demand to be involved."

"Of course he will," Ada agreed. "We have a plan, then."

Kat clasped her hands together. "Yes, and we must act quickly. I do wish Mrs. Renshaw were here."

"I'll speak with her as soon as she arrives in town. Don't worry, Kat, it will all work out." Ada tilted her head to the side. "How is it that you came to know about this anyway?"

"I, ah, Lucien told me. I suppose he needed to unburden himself, and I seemed a safe person to tell."

"How's that?" Warfield asked.

"Well, we aren't close friends like all of you are. Perhaps he didn't think I would tell anyone or involve myself." Was that true? Kat didn't think so, but now she would wonder.

"I think you're closer friends than he realizes," Ada said with a smile. "I'm so glad you came to me—to us. You're a wonderful friend."

"Actually, to me, Lucien is family." Kat realized she definitely thought of him that way, but not in the related-by-marriage manner. She felt closer to him than anyone, even her beloved brother.

Ada nodded. "I suppose he would be. How splendid."

It was most splendid indeed.

~

*J*ess greeted Kat in her private sitting room and had the maid bring tea and cakes. Kat was anxious to tell Jess about the club, but she somehow held her tongue until the tea had been poured and the maid had departed.

"You seem impatient," Jess noted with a laugh.

"I am, and I'm sorry. I'm here on a dire errand. Dougal may even want to join us."

"Unfortunately, he's not here. He's at the Phoenix Club with Lucien."

"That is precisely why I'm here," Kat said. "For Lucien and the Phoenix Club."

Jess blinked in curiosity. "Has something happened?"

"Not yet, but it will. Lucien confided in me that he does not actually own the club, and that the owners are forcing him out."

"Lucien confided this to you?" Jess hesitated the barest moment. "Have things between the two of you progressed? I've wondered since the day we schemed to get you alone with him and you kissed, but I haven't wanted to pry."

Kat was now glad for the refreshments as she busied herself taking a bite of cake so she could think of how to answer. After swallowing she said, "We've become...closer."

"Confidants are quite close." Jess smiled. "I shall take that as welcome news. It is, isn't it?"

"Er, yes. But that really isn't why I'm here."

Jess straightened. "Of course not. If he doesn't own the Phoenix Club, who does?" Her gaze seemed almost intense but then she picked up her teacup to take a drink, and Kat was certain she'd imagined Jess's expression.

"I don't know, but I've spoken with Ada and—"

Setting her cup down with a clack, Jess rounded her eyes at Kat. "You told Ada about this?"

"Yes. And Warfield because he was there."

"Who else have you told?"

Kat frowned at the alarm in Jess's tone. "Why are you so agitated? I went to Ada because she is a patroness *and* an employee, and Mrs. Renshaw isn't here. Ada and Warfield said that Lucien's friends and family would come together to raise the money for him to purchase the club."

"I don't doubt that they would, but it won't be that easy," Jess murmured. She wiped her hands over her eyes and exhaled. "I think you need to understand why this is complicated. If Lucien told you about not owning the club, he can't mind if I reveal the rest, at least as it pertains to me. I didn't tell you the truth about that letter you found in the ladies' library."

"What do you mean?" A chill tripped down Kat's spine.

"It wasn't a love letter. It was about a meeting at the club and referenced an agent of the Foreign Office—a man who was killed and found to be secretly working for the French."

If Kat had made a thousand guesses as to what that letter might be, espionage wasn't one of them. "How do you know all this?"

"Because I worked for the Foreign Office. They recruited me when I was staying with Lady Pickering. Remember that man who was sending me puzzles to solve?" At Kat's nod, Jess went on. "He works for the Foreign Office. He was testing my skill. They brought me on to decipher coded documents, specifically on a mission that I undertook with Dougal. We met at Lady Pickering's house in Hampshire and then masqueraded as husband and wife while we investigated another couple in Dorset."

With each revelation, Kat's mouth opened a little more until she was gaping at Jess. "You're a spy?"

"Shh, not so loud," Jess said with a laugh. "Not anymore. I didn't particularly enjoy it, and Dougal left his position after his brother died. He needed to focus on being heir to the earldom."

"What does all this have to do with the club? And with Lucien?" Kat leaned forward and spoke in a hushed tone. "Does he work for the Foreign Office too?"

"Yes, actually. He can explain the specifics to you since you've apparently grown close."

"Not *that* close or he would have told me all this." Kat was mildly hurt, but reasoned there was a good explanation since he worked for the bloody Foreign Office. She could hardly countenance it.

"Not necessarily," Jess argued. "He told you more than I would have suspected. Barely anyone knows that he doesn't own the club, and I'm fairly certain that only Dougal and I know who the owner is."

"It's the Foreign Office," Kat said, seeing how it all came together—why Jess had revealed the truth.

"Yes," Jess said. "And they had certain member requirements for the club. They don't like that Lucien expelled Lady Hargrove—they wanted Hargrove in the club, apparently—and they don't appreciate the cloud of scandal that retaining Evie will cause."

It was no wonder Lucien had been under such stress lately. His worry over the club went far deeper than attendance. Since the Foreign Office was involved, he couldn't really discuss it either. Except, he'd told her part of it—enough that she felt glad he'd trusted her.

"I was just hoping to help him, the way he's helped others. But now I can see that I shouldn't have told anyone." Kat shook her head. "What do I do now?"

"I don't know. I'll talk to Dougal when he returns. I don't think Lucien will be allowed to buy the club, however." Jess gave her an apologetic look. "So, there's no need to raise any money."

"We have to find a way to stop them from forcing him out." Kat recalled what he'd told her yesterday, that she couldn't give up and leave London. She wouldn't let him do that either, not that she thought he would. He was prepared to fight, and she would do anything to help him. Kat looked intently at Jess. "Since you worked for the Foreign Office, you know people there. Can you talk to someone about this? Persuade them not to make Lucien leave the club that he built?"

"I wish I could, but I'm afraid my time there was short. I only communicated with two people besides Dougal. I suppose I could try to speak with them."

Kat remembered what Jess had said a short while ago, that she'd met Dougal at Lady Pickering's house in Hampshire. Jess had also been recruited while staying with Lady Pickering. "Does Lady Pickering work for the Foreign Office?" Kat asked.

"I think I should not answer that," Jess said with a lift of her eyebrows that seemed to communicate Lady Pickering was indeed a part of the Foreign Office.

"It makes sense that she does since you were staying with her when you were recruited, and she was aware of your penchant for solving riddles. Indeed, I mentioned finding the coded letter in the library and that I gave it to you to solve."

Once more, Jess seemed alarmed, her expression growing tense. "When did you tell her this?"

"Last week. Monday, perhaps? Why does that matter?" If it *was* a secret message to do with Foreign Office affairs and Lady Pickering was associated with them, there shouldn't be a concern.

Jess lifted a shoulder. "It may not. I just want to be able to tell Dougal every detail. He's much better at this sort of thing than I am. He conducted investigations for the Foreign Office here in England for several years."

Kat heard the pride in her voice. "I'd love to hear more about that. What a fascinating occupation. Does he miss it?"

"Somewhat, but he says he prefers being married to me." A sly smile curled Jess's lips.

"Of course he does. Will you let me know if you learn anything about how we can help Lucien?"

"Yes. Right away. What will you tell Ada, since you've already spoken to her about this?"

"I'll think of something, since I can't tell her all you've told me."

"Thank you. It's very important that this stays between us, though I'll tell Lucien what I've told you. Or you can, if you prefer."

"He and I have much to discuss." Kat wasn't going to allow him to be pushed out. She was going to fight for him.

CHAPTER 21

"*A*fternoon, Lucien."

Lucien looked up from the open ledger on his desk in his office at the Phoenix Club and scowled vaguely at Dougal.

"Still angry with me that I told your father about the Foreign Office asking you to leave the club?" Dougal came to sit in the chair beside Lucien's desk.

Lucien only grunted. Or growled. However one wanted to describe it, he made a disgruntled sound and bent his head back to his ledger.

"I won't apologize," Dougal said.

"So, you've told me." Lucien exhaled, then sat back in his chair to look at his friend. "What do you want?"

"I don't know anything specific, but it seems as if the Foreign Office will be making their move soon. Tomorrow, even, or perhaps the day after."

Swearing, Lucien tipped his head back and frowned at the ceiling.

"You need to decide what to do," Dougal prompted after a moment.

Lucien lowered his gaze to Dougal's. "I have already decided. I'm not going anywhere."

Dougal pressed his lips together and stared at him. "How is that going to be possible? Dammit, Lucien, I know you don't want to walk away, but you're out of options. Unless you want to remove Evie and see if they'll let you stay."

"I refuse to consider that." He had, however, despite what he said, begun to consider leaving. Because Dougal was right. In the end, Lucien wouldn't have a choice. "Perhaps if they'd communicated the compensation they plan to offer, I might have accepted it."

"Would you really?" Dougal seemed skeptical.

"My father said I should take whatever financial settlement they give me and start a new club." Lucien curled his lip. "He even offered to provide whatever else I needed to get started."

"You didn't tell me that," Dougal said. "Why are you hesitating?"

Lucien glowered at him. Before he could remind Dougal of the myriad reasons he would never accept—or more importantly trust—help from his father, there was a knock on the door, which stood ajar.

Both of them looked toward the doorway as Jess poked her head into the office. "May I interrupt?" she asked.

"Yes, especially if it means taking your husband away," Lucien said grumpily.

Jess slipped inside, closing the door behind her.

Dougal jumped up from his chair and went to her. "What's wrong?" He took her hand, his features etched with concern.

She gave him a warm, reassuring smile. "I'm fine. Everyone is fine. I just needed to speak with you—and Lucien—right away." Jess's gaze found Lucien, and he knew immediately that even if she was fine, *something* was wrong.

He stood and walked around the desk. "What's happened?"

"Kat came to see me. She, ah, she's launched a crusade to help you buy the club."

Dougal snapped his head toward Lucien. "How the hell does she know about that?"

Lucien lifted a shoulder. "I might have mentioned it."

Jess tugged on her husband's hand. "We don't have time for admonitions. Lucien and Kat have become close. If he wanted to confide things to her, it's none of our business."

"Did you tell her about the Foreign Office's involvement?" Dougal asked, still seeming cross.

"Of course not," Lucien responded. Though, he wanted to. He wanted to share everything with her.

"I did," Jess said, drawing Lucien and Dougal to stare at her.

Dougal frowned. "You didn't."

"I wish you hadn't," Lucien added. Not because he didn't want Kat to know, but because he would have liked to tell her himself.

"I felt I must. She'd already gone to Ada to come up with a plan to buy the club for Lucien." She glanced toward Lucien, who felt a burst of warmth that Kat would do that. She hadn't wasted any time in leaping to his defense. He wanted to thank her. "I had to tell her there was no point in raising money to buy the club," Jess continued. "If she did obtain the funds and then nothing happened...well, I thought it best to avoid that scenario."

Lucien wanted to do more than thank Kat. He wanted to kiss her. "I should go see her and explain everything."

Jess released Dougal's hand and held hers up. "Before you do that, you may want to investigate another matter." She looked between Lucien and Dougal. "Kat said she told Lady Pickering about the coded letter. Kat, of course, didn't realize it was anything to keep secret—we purposely told her it was a love letter so that it would appear innocuous. Nor did we tell her to not say anything."

"That would only have aroused her curiosity." Lucien couldn't help smiling. It really was amusing that her name was Kat since actual cats were incurably curious.

"Precisely," Jess agreed. "The important part is that Kat told Lady Pickering about it last Monday. Which was *before* the meeting mentioned in the note."

Dougal's brows drew together. "You think she's involved in this?"

"Don't you think it's possible?" Jess responded.

"Bloody hell," Lucien muttered. "I would have a hard time believing that. She doesn't have anything to do with the transport of messages. She wouldn't have had reason to even know who Giraud was." He looked to Dougal. "Unless she did, and I'm simply not aware of it." There was a question there for Dougal, and he didn't disappoint.

"That makes two of us who are unaware," Dougal said. "I too would be shocked if she was involved, but she is close with Kent. Perhaps she's been a pawn?"

Lucien supposed that was possible. "In what way?"

"Kent could be manipulating her. I don't trust him anymore."

"I think it's time we confront him."

Dougal nodded. "Agreed. Send him a note telling him you're ready to surrender. That will get him here in a trice."

Lucien couldn't argue with that. He walked back around his desk and sat down to draft a short note. He glanced up at Dougal, who'd come to stand in front of the desk. Jess stood at his side. "Where do you think he'll be?"

"I've a few ideas. Write three identical notes so we can send men to each place."

"Brilliant," Lucien murmured as he scratched the first one

out. "Jess, I must thank you for bringing this to our immediate attention. It's past time we get to the bottom of Giraud's assassination."

"I'm quite annoyed with myself for not pressing this sooner," Dougal said.

Lucien heard the frustration in Dougal's voice as he wrote the second note. "There's no sense in castigating yourself now."

"What are you going to do about Kat?" Jess asked.

Just the thought of her made Lucien's hand pause. He wished he could go to her immediately, to thank her for her support. But they needed to interrogate Kent and solve this puzzle once and for all. Then, after Lucien had demonstrated his skill in solving Giraud's murder, perhaps the Foreign Office would change their mind about forcing him out.

It was unlikely, but Lucien would cling to any hope he could find.

~

*N*ervous energy thrummed through Kat as she stood in Lady Pickering's library awaiting the baroness's arrival. Kat looked out at the back garden, where she'd spent many afternoons reading last summer.

After several minutes, Lady Pickering joined her. Kat looked at the woman as if seeing her for the first time. She'd no doubt the baroness worked for the Foreign Office, even if Jess wouldn't confirm it.

Kat had noted Jess's reaction to hearing that Kat had told Lady Pickering about the letter. Jess had seemed alarmed, then she'd asked more questions. It seemed clear to Kat that Lady Pickering was involved somehow. Kat hoped she could help plead Lucien's cause to the Foreign Office.

"Good afternoon, Kathleen. How lovely to see you. Shall we sit?"

In response, Kat perched on a settee while Lady Pickering took her favorite chair where she liked to read in the evenings. Now that she was here, Kat's mind went blank as she tried to think of what to say. She couldn't exactly blurt out, *"I think you work for the Foreign Office, and I need you to convince...someone there that Lucien should stay and continue managing the club. Furthermore, you also need to convince them that Lucien should buy their stake so that he is the sole owner."*

Why couldn't she say all that?

Because this Foreign Office business was *secret*, and she wasn't supposed to know.

Lady Pickering's brow wrinkled ever so slightly as she studied Kat. "Did you call for a reason?"

"Er, no. I mean, yes. I'm just... I am not very good at social engagements."

"Nonsense. You can be quite engaging when you want to be. Is that why you've come? To seek help with your social interactions?"

Kat gritted her teeth. Wanting to be engaging was not the issue. People always assumed it was a simple choice to just blithely go anywhere with anyone and...engage. It wasn't that simple. Sometimes, it was just too hard. Sabrina understood that.

But her visit didn't have anything to do with that, and she couldn't allow herself to be distracted. It was going to be difficult, she realized, because she'd already had several interactions today and she was starting to feel socially fatigued. Or perhaps it was Lady Pickering's comments that had made her that way.

Kat forged ahead, not entirely sure what she would say. "If you could help someone with something very important, something that would make all the difference to them, would you?"

Lady Pickering cocked her head to the side, contemplating Kat as if she'd asked a ridiculous question. "Of course I would."

"What if that something was secret?"

"I'm afraid I don't follow what you're saying. Is there something specific you'd like to ask me about?" She began to sound exasperated.

Oh hell. Kat didn't want to dance around the issue. Helping Lucien was too important. "I think that you perhaps work for the Foreign Office, and they are forcing Lucien out of the Phoenix Club. It's not fair. He built that club, and he should be able to buy it from them so they can no longer dictate to him."

Lady Pickering straightened in the chair, her shoulders squaring. "Why do you think that?"

"I just...do." Kat realized that sounded flimsy.

"That can't be. You must have some reason for thinking that." Lady Pickering laughed. "You think they'd employ a woman?"

"They employed Jess." Kat noted the slight flare of Lady Pickering's nostrils. Too late, Kat recognized she ought not have said that. She had never been very successful at keeping secrets, though she did try.

"You seem confident of that fact," Lady Pickering said with a sigh. "What did Jessamine tell you?"

"Only that she was recruited for her decoding skills."

The baroness rested her elbow on the arm of the chair, her hand poised just off the edge as if she were about to direct something. "Does she know you told me about the coded letter from the Phoenix Club?"

The question surprised Kat. "Yes."

"Hmmm." Lady Pickering turned her head, frowning. The

fingers on her extended hand moved slightly, almost as if she were counting. She looked back to Kat. "When did you tell her?"

Why was everyone so concerned with the timing of these things? "This very afternoon."

Lady Pickering clasped her hands together in her lap and gave Kat a flat-lipped smile. "Let me see if I understand. You've been told that Jessamine works for the Foreign Office, and you *think* I do too. Do I have that right?"

"Yes."

"And Lord Lucien wishes to purchase the Phoenix Club from the Foreign Office, which I suppose must mean he doesn't own it as all of London has been led to believe."

Shouldn't she already know that? Did this mean she didn't work for the Foreign Office? Kat had been so certain. She crumpled back against the settee.

"Did Lucien tell you this?" Lady Pickering asked.

"Yes, and before you ask, he told me yesterday."

The baroness put a finger to her lips, then tapped several times as she stared toward the windows. When she returned her attention to Kat, she smiled. "I do wish I could help you, but I'm afraid I'm not associated with the Foreign Office. Such a shame that Lucien is in trouble. It sounds as though he should have done what they said."

"He isn't going to expel one of his dearest friends. Lucien would never be so cruel." Kat froze. She hadn't said anything to Lady Pickering about why he was being forced out. Kat was more confident than ever that the baroness was somehow involved. Why was she hiding her connection? Was she just trying to maintain secrecy?

Kat pursed her lips. "Let us forgo the prevarication, Lady Pickering. I should like to think we are friendly enough to be honest. I don't believe that you aren't associated with the Foreign Office. I didn't mention that Lucien had failed to do what he was directed. You clearly know more than you are willing to admit. Just please tell me why you won't help Lucien? He's such a kind and generous man. He helps everyone."

Lady Pickering's gaze cooled. "You can't think you know him that well. You've no idea what he's done in his work for the Foreign Office. If you did, you wouldn't think him so kind or generous."

"What are you talking about?" Kat didn't want to hear anything bad about him. "You'll never convince me he isn't the best sort. He's proved it time and again."

Arching a dark brow, Lady Pickering asked, "Would it shock you to know he's killed?"

"No. I'm aware he was a soldier." Kat folded her arms over her chest.

"Not in Spain, but here in England." Lady Pickering sniffed. "Nasty business. He's lucky the Foreign Office is only taking the club away. Anyone else might have been imprisoned. Or hanged."

Kat couldn't help the gasp that slipped past her lips. "There has to be a reasonable explanation."

"There is. He was taking care of a problem. However, it seems he may have been *part* of the problem. If he walks away, he may be able to avoid further scrutiny...or punishment."

None of this made sense. The man she'd come to know would never have killed anyone, unless it was in his own defense. Since Lady Pickering had used the word "seems," perhaps they didn't really know for certain. Which might explain why Lucien was being pushed out of the club instead of the other things she'd mentioned.

She was anxious to speak with him. This was all far more convoluted—and potentially dangerous—than she could have imagined.

Standing, Kat adopted a businesslike tone in the hope that it would mask her urgent desire to leave. "Well, since you are not able to help me, I will be on my way."

Lady Pickering stood. "I'm afraid I can't let you go. You know a great many things you should not."

Kat swallowed against a wave of unease. "I'm good at keeping secrets," she lied. "Especially when it means protecting someone I care about. I wouldn't wish to cause any more...trouble for Lucien." She just needed to get to him. He would explain everything, and she would feel better.

"Lucien is in enough trouble. He doesn't need your help, sadly. But I also don't want you going to him to tell him what we discussed." Her lips stretched in a humorless, almost sinister smile. "I just need to talk with someone before I can let you go." She rang the bell, and the butler came in. "Will you send for Hudson, please?"

The butler departed, leaving Kat to wonder who Hudson was. She didn't remember anyone in the household with that name from when she was Lady Pickering's guest.

Before I can let you go.

The words echoed in Kat's brain, turning her unease into fear. "Are you telling me I can't leave?"

"Not just yet. Find a book and settle yourself in your favorite chair over there." The baroness inclined her head toward the windows where Kat used to curl up with a book.

A large man came into the library, and Kat understood why he'd been summoned. "Is he to ensure I don't leave?"

"He's going to keep you safe," Lady Pickering said with another fake smile. "I'll be back soon."

After the baroness left, Kat surveyed the hulking figure who now stood just inside the closed doors. He was tall and wide enough to resemble a tree, and Kat was certain if he fell on someone, he'd crush them just the same as one.

Pray, who was Hudson keeping her safe from?

CHAPTER 22

*L*ucien and Dougal had waited in Lucien's study for one of the men to return with Kent. It was just under two hours since they'd dispatched the men when a footman entered to say their delivery had arrived. This was code for Kent having been delivered to the meeting room on the second floor.

After the footman departed, Lucien and Dougal sprinted from the office up to the second floor. Arriving at the meeting room, they found Kent seated in one of the chairs and Reynolds a mere foot away from him.

"Thank you, Reynolds," Lucien said.

"You don't want me to stay, my lord?"

"If you could stand just outside, that will be sufficient."

Reynolds inclined his head and left, closing the door behind him.

Kent frowned at them, looking from Lucien to Dougal and back again. "Why does it seem as though you aren't really going to surrender to the Foreign Office's demands?"

"I may yet, actually, but first we need to settle some

matters." Lucien picked up another of the wooden chairs and set it directly in front of Kent.

Dougal moved to stand behind Kent. He remained silent. They'd planned how they would do this.

Kent swung his head around to look at Dougal. "What are you doing back there?"

Still staying nothing, Dougal merely stared at him with a blank expression.

When Kent returned his attention to Lucien, who'd sat in the chair he'd moved, there was a glint of fear in his eyes. Good.

"The meeting you had here a week ago did not go as planned, did it?" Lucien asked.

"Of course it did," Kent said, scoffing. "Martin came to deliver a message to you, and it was delivered."

Lucien looked at Kent intently. "Am I Lady Macbeth?"

Kent sputtered then. "I don't know what you're talking about."

"I think you do. I think you know all about the letter we found in the ladies' library. Did you put it there?"

"I...no."

Studying Kent closely for any sign of fear or tension, Lucien detected a tic in his jaw. "I don't think that's true." He sat back in the chair, exhaling as he crossed his arms. "I am disappointed in you. When you greeted me upon my return from Spain, I felt as though I'd met the father I never had. Now, you are setting me up to take the blame for Giraud's murder. After you considered laying the fault at Dougal's feet. We both looked up to you, *admired* you."

"I'm very proud of you and Dougal." Small beads of sweat appeared on Kent's brow near his hairline. "I'm not setting anyone up for anything."

Dougal put his hand on the back of Kent's chair, making the older man flinch.

"I wish you wouldn't lie." Lucien kept his temper in check. They would break him. He leaned forward, adopting a tone of interest. "Did *you* do it? Or are you covering for someone else?"

Kent didn't immediately answer. He wiped his hand across his brow.

Dougal bent down and spoke softly near the man's ear. "Lucien and I are not going to play your or the Foreign Office's games. Tell us the truth. You owe us that much."

Still, Kent said nothing. But the sweat began to trickle down his left temple.

"Let's review what we know," Lucien said. "Some months ago, you gave Lady Fallin a letter to decode. This letter indicated that Giraud was working for the French. That solved the question of who was giving information to the enemy. However, the matter of who had killed him was unsolved. Lady Fallin is a very clever woman, which I'm sure you know since you recruited her to work for the Foreign Office. She is confident the letter she decoded for you and the letter she decoded that we found in the library were written by the same hand. Now, Dougal and I didn't compare the letter from the library with anything written by you because we, of course, haven't kept anything you've written. Still, we both believe the hand who wrote both letters belongs to you." While Lucien was speaking, Kent paled, and the sweat on his forehead was now a glossy sheen.

Lucien looked at Dougal. "I think I have the answer as to whether he was working for the Foreign Office in all this or if he was a rogue operative. If he had the backing of the Foreign Office, he would not be this agitated." Returning his gaze to Kent, Lucien asked, "Who was that man who came here with you last week, Martin? He doesn't actually work for the Foreign Office, does he?"

While they'd waited for someone to find Kent, Lucien and

Dougal had talked through a number of scenarios. In one, they concluded that Martin had been hired by Kent.

When Kent still said nothing, Dougal said, "I'm growing weary of his silence." Dougal slid a baton from his sleeve and hit it against the back of Kent's chair.

Kent leapt forward and lost his balance. Lucien caught him.

"It wasn't me! I didn't kill Giraud. I knew about the letters, and I distracted those in charge from what was really happening."

Lucien set the man back on his chair with a stern frown. "What was really happening?"

Kent glanced back at Dougal. "Will you move where I can see you, at least?"

Dougal took two steps forward, but held the baton in front of him, gripping the base while the end rested in his other hand. "Talk."

"Lady Pickering was siphoning information and selling it to the French. When it became clear that someone was leaking information, she convinced me that it was Giraud. She arranged to have him killed."

Lucien and Dougal exchanged looks of shock. "Lady Pickering?" Lucien wiped his hand over his mouth. "Why should we believe you? It's even harder for us to conceive of her doing such a thing than that it was you. And you've proven that you're a liar willing to deflect blame toward anyone but yourself."

"I'm sure you know that she and I have a...special friendship."

"I have long suspected you were at least occasional lovers," Dougal said. "That doesn't prove anything."

"She made some poor investments and was perhaps too fond of spending her late husband's fortune. It became necessary for her to...augment her income. If you investigate her financial situation, you'll find that she was in need of funds. She got them working for the French."

Lucien and Dougal exchanged a dubious look. While they didn't trust Kent, his story was at least plausible. She certainly acted and looked as if she had plenty of money to spend.

Dougal leveled an expectant stare at Kent. "When did you find out she was the one actually working against the crown?"

"Frances—Lady Pickering—tried to convince me it was you. That's when we hired Lady Fallin to investigate you. I didn't believe it, and when Lady Fallin found no proof, I insisted that Frances was mistaken. Shortly after that, she excitedly presented me with a coded letter. That was the one Lady Fallin deciphered regarding Giraud selling information." Kent looked them both in the eye in succession. "You were right that those letters were written by the same hand, but it wasn't mine."

"It was Lady Pickering," Dougal said. "When did you put that together?"

Kent's shoulders sagged. "Almost as soon as I saw the letter. She tried to make it look unlike her own writing, but that is a difficult skill to master."

Despite his anger, Lucien felt pity for Kent. "It wasn't a great leap to determine she was covering her own misdeeds, that she had blamed Giraud for her own crimes, then killed him to wrap it up all tidy, like a message to be delivered. But you didn't turn her in."

Shaking his head, Kent sniffed as he bent his head. "I love her."

"Still?" Dougal's contempt was evident in his tone.

Kent turned toward Dougal. "You know what it's like to fall in love, to want to do anything for that person."

"I do, but I wouldn't look the other way while my beloved

committed murder, then went on to see that someone else paid for the crime. Lucien and I have been good, loyal agents of the crown. You would have seen Lucien's very lifeblood—this club—stripped away, and worst of all, you would have let Lucien potentially dangle at the end of a rope, all to ensure a corrupt woman gets away with her crimes. You're despicable." Dougal sneered at him. "I feel as if I never knew you."

Wilting in the chair, Kent swung his gaze back to Lucien. "What do you want me to do? I'll do my best to make this right."

"You were going to let Lucien pay for *your* crimes." Dougal shook his head. "There is no way to make that right."

"I will name Lady Pickering," Kent said quietly, his head tipping down in defeat.

"And admit to your own malfeasance," Dougal said. "We won't cover for you."

Kent nodded.

"We'll go to the Foreign Office now, and you'll tell them everything." Lucien stood.

"Wait." Kent thrust his hand into his coat.

Dougal lifted his baton. "Take your hand out of there."

"I received a note." Kent pulled a very small folded piece of parchment from the garment and held it out to Lucien. "It's from Frances. She says you probably know the truth—and yes, she calls you Lady Macbeth."

"Why is that?" Lucien asked as he opened the missive.

"Because she would do anything to achieve her own ends. It fit her story for you to be a villain, so she gave you the name of one. She chose a woman to make it harder to discover your identity."

Lucien read the note aloud to Dougal:

The cat has learned too much and I fear will alert Lady Macbeth, who will no doubt determine the truth. The end has come, and we must complete the mission.

"What does she mean by 'complete the mission'?" Dougal asked.

Kent grimaced. "Eliminate Lady Macbeth."

Lucien reread the note. "Who is the cat who will alert me?" As soon as he said the words aloud, he knew. "Kat? Kathleen Shaughnessy?"

"I'm not sure." Kent sputtered. "Frances hasn't used that name before."

Dougal's gaze snapped to Lucien. "Kat knows enough. What if she went to see Lady Pickering?"

Lucien swore violently. "She might have—she thinks they're friends."

Dougal gave him a sympathetic look. "We all thought we were friends."

Anger tearing through him, Lucien grabbed Kent by the arms and hauled him out of the chair. He put his face within an inch of Kent's. "If anything happens to Miss Shaughnessy, you and Lady Pickering will be eternally sorry."

"Let's go." Dougal was already opening the door.

Lucien shoved Kent into the corridor. "Reynolds, don't let this man out of your sight. We're all going on an errand."

"My coach is outside," Dougal called over his shoulder as they made their way to the stairs. He held the door for Lucien and looked him in the eye. "She'll be fine. Lady Pickering isn't going to do anything—she hires others to do it for her."

"What if she already has?" Lucien dashed down the stairs. By the time they were settled in the coach, he felt as though he was going to explode. If anything happened to Kat, Lucien feared his actions would make Max's in Spain look tame.

~

*a*fter dispatching one of Reynolds's men to Wexford House to ascertain that Kat was there—and safe—Lucien and the others took Dougal's coach to Hanover Square. The coachman parked at the opposite end of the square from Lady Pickering's house. Lucien quickly reviewed the plan they'd developed on the drive from the Phoenix Club.

"Kent, you will go inside and find out what Lady Pickering is up to as well as if she's seen Miss Shaughnessy."

Kent nodded. While he was upset that he was going to betray the woman he loved, he was resolved to help ensure Kat was safe. "And if she *has* seen Miss Shaughnessy, I'll determine her location."

"Reynolds and I will assume our positions at the front of the house and the entrance to the scullery." Dougal exchanged a nod with Reynolds.

A nervous energy careered through Lucien. He was eager to get on with it. "I'll be at the back of the house." He'd chosen that location because Kent had said that Lady Pickering would likely greet him in the library, which had a large window looking out to the back garden. Lucien would be able to see what was going on inside, provided the curtains were open.

They climbed out of the coach. Reynolds had been tasked with sticking to Kent until the man walked up the steps to Lady Pickering's house lest he lose his sense of duty and try to run off. Lucien would be leaving the square to access the alley that ran behind the house.

Dougal clasped Lucien's forearm just before they split up. "Try to keep a calm head."

Lucien grunted in response, then broke off at a run since he had farther to travel. Several minutes later, breathing heavily, he slipped through a gate into Lady Pickering's garden. The sun was just setting, and he prayed the curtains would still be open.

Crouching down and keeping to the side of the garden, he hurried to the house, where he crept along the back until he reached the window. Thankfully, the curtains were open, and the interior was bright with candlelight.

Lucien swept off his hat and clutched it in one hand, taking deep breaths to slow his racing heart. He lifted his head just enough to peer through the bottom of the window. Right away, he made out Lady Pickering standing near the center of the room. Kent stood just inside the doorway.

Movement near the hearth drew Lucien's eye. There was a second gentleman, his back to the window. He stood a few feet from Lady Pickering and seemed to be addressing Kent. Then the man pivoted slightly toward Lady Pickering, making just enough of his profile visible that Lucien could determine his identity.

Bloody fucking hell. It was his father.

What in the name of the sun and moon was he doing here? Now? There was only one explanation—he was somehow involved.

Lucien abandoned their carefully constructed plan and found an exterior door that led into a breakfast room next to the library. Pulse pounding with rage, he made his way to the library and stepped inside behind Kent. His gaze went directly to his father.

"What are *you* doing here?"

"Lucien, I could ask the same of you," the duke said affably. Affably? Since when was he ever cordial with his least favorite child?

Kent turned. "Lucien, you weren't supposed to—"

Lady Pickering cut him off. "Oliver, you know what we must do." She pulled a pistol from her pocket and aimed it at

Lucien. "I'm sorry it's come to this, for I've always liked you very much."

Before Lucien could say a word, she pulled the hammer. Everything after that was a blur. There was a dark movement in front of Lucien, blocking his view of the baroness. Then a thud, followed by another flash of a body moving across his frame of vision. A second thud sounded.

Why hadn't Lucien moved? And why wasn't he in pain? Hadn't he been shot?

Lucien put his hand to his chest and blinked. The room came back into sharp focus, and he was immediately aware of Lady Pickering making noises. Looking down, he saw three shapes—Kent atop Lady Pickering and, separate from them, the duke. The latter was closest to Lucien. In fact, he was lying at Lucien's feet.

The scene that had happened so quickly and so vaguely was suddenly devastatingly clear. Lucien dropped to his knees just as his father rolled to his back, his face pale and sweating. A quick assessment revealed he'd been shot in the shoulder—and had fallen on it.

Lucien pulled off his cravat and pressed it to the wound. "We'll send for a physician."

His father grunted. "Take me home first."

"Not bloody likely."

The duke hissed as Lucien applied greater pressure. "Must you do that so hard?"

"Yes." Lucien turned his head to see that Kent was hauling Lady Pickering to her feet.

"Oliver, there is still time to save ourselves. Finish them, and we will be on our way to France."

Kent looked so sad that Lucien actually felt sorry for him. "Frances, we aren't going anywhere."

Dougal and Reynolds burst in wielding pistols. The butler

followed on their heels and immediately gasped as he sagged back against the doorframe.

"I heard a gunshot," Reynolds said. "I fetched Lord Fallin."

Lucien looked to the butler. "Send for a physician immediately. Tell him the Duke of Evesham has been shot." The butler blinked, fear evident in his gaze. "Go!" Lucien pushed inadvertently harder on his father's shoulder as he shouted the order.

"Lucien, not so hard." The duke coughed.

"There's a chaise in the corner," Kent said. "Perhaps you should move him there."

Lucien moved around above his father's head. "Help me, Reynolds. Dougal, keep your pistol on Lady Pickering. If she has her way, she'll be on a boat to France by morning."

"She's not going anywhere," Dougal said. "We've got her right where we want her."

Reynolds positioned himself at the duke's feet, and on the count of three, they lifted him from the floor. The duke moaned but then clamped his jaw shut, his face going paler, as they carried him to the chaise.

He was bleeding quite a bit, and Lucien felt true fear. Perhaps he didn't hate the man as much as he thought. Had he really thrown himself in front of Lucien to save him from Lady Pickering's bullet? It was that, or he'd chosen that moment to leave.

They situated him on the chaise. Lucien looked to Reynolds. "Perhaps you should go fetch the physician personally."

"I can do that, but what about Lady Pickering and Kent? Can you and Lord Fallin manage them?"

"I think so." Though Lucien also wanted to keep an eye on his father. And Kat. *Shit.* Where was Kat?

Lucien looked to Kent. "Did you find out what happened to Kat—rather, Miss Shaughnessy?"

"Not before you rushed in." Kent had kept a strong grip on Lady Pickering since lifting her from the floor. "Frances, where is Miss Shaughnessy?"

"Why would I know that?"

"Because your note mentioned a cat. If you weren't referring to her, who were you talking about?"

The butler returned. "I've sent three footmen—all that we have—to summon a physician. I wanted to make sure they'd find someone to come right away."

Before Lucien could thank the man, Dougal addressed him. "Was Miss Shaughnessy here earlier?"

"Yes, my lord," the butler answered.

Lady Pickering scowled and tried to break free of Kent's grip. Dougal moved to grab her and steered her to a small, wooden-backed chair. "Sit." He shoved her down, then trained his pistol on her. "Don't move. Kent, we need something to bind her with."

"Painter, don't you help them," Lady Pickering snarled.

Painter must be her butler's name.

Lucien needed to know what happened with Kat. Hopefully, she was just at home. "Painter, where did Miss Shaughnessy go? I encourage you to answer me. Lady Pickering shot my father, and if you do her bidding, you will be aiding her criminality."

The butler's eyes widened, and his face lost most of its ruddy color. "She left over an hour ago with Hudson. He's Lady Pickering's personal footman."

A tremor ran through Lucien, making him lighten the pressure on his father's shoulder. The cravat nearly slipped away, and he renewed his attention. He couldn't afford to lose focus now. But dammit, he needed to go after Kat.

"Is Hudson a hireling?" Dougal asked Lady Pickering.

She pressed her lips together and said nothing.

The butler responded with "Hudson often accompanied

Lady Pickering on errands, and always when she travels to her house in Hampshire."

"Painter, do you know where they went?" Lucien asked with barely restrained rage.

"I'm afraid I don't." The poor man looked genuinely sorry. He wrung his hands, and color had come back to his face.

"Thank you," Dougal said. "Please fetch something with which we can bind the baroness, and be quick."

"And send a maid," Lucien added. "To tend the duke."

"Right away, my lords." Painter took himself off.

Dougal pointed the pistol at Lady Pickering's chest. "Where did your man take Miss Shaughnessy? And why?"

"You may as well tell them the truth," Kent urged her. "I've already told them everything I know. There's no escape now."

Lady Pickering's eyes flashed with vitriol. "You fool! I thought I could depend on you. You said you loved me."

"I did," Kent said, sounded utterly brokenhearted. "I do."

"Well, I do not return the sentiment," she said coldly. "You were a means to an end, and I should have realized you would fail me."

"Just tell us where Hudson is taking Miss Shaughnessy," Dougal said. "Perhaps that will save you from a worse punishment."

"He wasn't going to hurt her," the baroness said defensively. "Once Lady Macbeth over there was out of the way, everything would have gone back to normal."

"Then why take her anywhere?" Lucien demanded.

"For insurance," Kent said. "I'm sure she wanted to make sure she could manipulate you if that became necessary." He gave Lucien a sad smile. "I'm afraid I've learned rather well how her warped mind works."

"Warped indeed because I also know the truth," Dougal

said softly, narrowing his eyes at Lady Pickering. "Or were you planning to kill me too?"

Lucien was losing patience. Reynolds seemed to realize this, for he came and inserted his hand beneath Lucien's, taking over the pressure on the duke's wound.

His hand covered in blood, Lucien stalked to the baroness and bent to put his face in front of hers. *"Where is Kat?"*

He wiped his hand down the side of her face, coating her flesh in his father's blood. "You already have the blood of the Duke of Evesham on you. Will you have Miss Shaughnessy's too?" Saying the words filled Lucien with an icy dread. He couldn't lose her.

A maid came in carrying a tray with steaming water and a stack of folded muslin. She stopped short upon seeing the pistol pointed at her employer. She looked at Dougal, her eyes wide. But Dougal's focus on Lady Pickering never wavered.

"What happened to Miss Shaughnessy?" the maid asked, appearing terrified.

Lucien straightened as he turned to face her. "Did you see her when she was here?"

"No, but I heard she was."

"Did you hear anything else, such as where she might have gone with Hudson?" He was desperate for any kernel of information.

The maid glanced toward Lady Pickering.

"It's all right," Lucien said, trying to be soothing while his insides were twisting with fear for Kat. "You are not in any trouble, but I'm afraid your employer is. She sent Miss Shaughnessy away, and we're afraid for her safety."

"Because she left with that brute, Hudson?" The maid shivered. "None of us like him. I did hear that the coach was being prepared for the usual trip to Hampshire. I was surprised her ladyship wasn't going." She clutched the tray to her chest as she looked up at Lucien. "I took care of Miss Shaughnessy and Miss Goodfellow last summer when they stayed here. They were lovely ladies. I would feel just awful if something happened to her."

"Then you must be Dove," Dougal said, still watching Lady Pickering. "We appreciate your assistance. Knowing Miss Shaughnessy is on her way to Hampshire is very helpful."

"Yes, thank you." Lucien wanted to bolt out the door, but he needed to see to his father first. "Dove, if you would come this way. I need you to tend my father, the Duke of Evesham. Reynolds here will help you if you need anything."

"I should go with you to Hampshire," Reynolds said.

Perhaps he should. Before Lucien could determine what to do, Ruark ran into the room with the man they'd sent looking for Kat.

"Where is my sister?" Ruark looked as terrified and tense as Lucien felt.

"On her way to Hampshire," Lucien said. "You can come with me." He looked back to Reynolds. "We'll be fine. You stay here and help Dougal keep an eye on the baroness and Kent."

Reynolds nodded. "I'll make sure His Grace is taken care of."

Lucien looked down at his father, whose eyes were closed. His pallor was concerning, but Lucien was sure the duke was too stubborn to die in this manner.

"Father?"

The duke opened one eye and looked up at him. "You're going to Hampshire. The physician will be here shortly. I'll be fine."

"Yes, all those things."

"Go to the Hanover mews and ask for Beasley. He tends

the Marquess of Frome's horses. Tell him it's an emergency and that Evesham sent you. Be on your way, then."

Suddenly overwhelmed with emotion at his father's act of selflessness—had he really stepped between Lucien and a bullet?—Lucien clenched his fists to keep a rein on himself. "Thank you."

The duke waved the hand of his uninjured side. "Later." He tipped his head down slightly as if to see his wound. Wincing, he cast it back and closed his eye once more. "Shame you weren't wearing one of your hideous colored cravats. I wouldn't feel bad about ruining one of those."

Miraculously, a smile flitted across Lucien's lips. "Never fear. I shall have this one dyed so that I can wear it and remind you of the time you had to let me get close to you." Lucien touched his father's hand, then turned to go, but not before he heard him mutter:

"Then it shall be my favorite cravat."

Lucien nearly stumbled on his way to the door.

"My lord," Dove called. "I believe they usually stop for supper in Chessington."

Turning to send a grateful look to the maid, Lucien thanked her.

"Good luck," Dougal called as Lucien tugged on Ruark's arm.

"What the devil is going on?" Ruark demanded, his Irish accent so thick with emotion as to be barely understandable, as they left the house.

Lucien sped up so that he was nearly running. "I'll explain on the way, but we need to hurry. Kat is in danger, and we need to get on the road to Hampshire as quickly as possible. They have over an hour lead on us, but they're in a coach, so we'll make up time."

Ruark kept pace with him. "Why is my sister on her way to bloody Hampshire with what sounds like a miscreant?

And why in God's name was Dougal holding a pistol on Lady Pickering? Furthermore, what happened to your father?"

"I'll explain everything in detail when we have more time, but Kat's eagerness to help me put her in danger—from Lady Pickering. She's a French agent who was working against the crown." Lucien cut his hand through the air. "She had her hireling take Kat to Hampshire, probably to ensure everyone would go along with her plans."

"And what the hell were those?"

"To kill me, and I'm not entirely sure what else." Lucien reasoned she would have had to kill Dougal to in order to protect herself. And Jess.

Upon reaching the mews, Lucien found Beasley, a spry, gangly fellow in his forties. Lucien repeated what his father said and requested two horses be saddled with the utmost haste. Beasley didn't question anything and quickly set to work, drafting several grooms to help.

Ruark gripped Lucien's arm. "Why would Lady Pickering use my sister?"

"Kat, ah, knew more than she should have. Your sister is exceedingly clever."

"She is indeed." Ruark's brow furrowed. "But what does she know? It seems to involve you. I am struggling to see how Kat is involved."

"I, ah, Kat and I have become close friends. I confided some information to her that ultimately led her to seek Lady Pickering's help. Then she must have unraveled the baroness's lies and determined what was happening. Your sister is incredibly clever." Lucien felt a surge of admiration for her along with a much stronger emotion that clouded his eyes and made his heart clench and then swell.

"'Close friends'?"

"Actually, I'm in love with her." Now that Lucien recognized the emotion, he was eager to name it, to share it, to claim it for all time. But none of that mattered if he couldn't get to her.

Ruark stared at him in shock. "Does she love you?"

"Honestly, I don't know. I think I've loved her for some time, but I didn't realize it until this moment." How could he not have seen it? Looking back, it seemed incredibly obvious. There was no person on this earth that he wanted to be with more, whose very presence made everything just *better*.

"You realize the irony here?" Ruark asked

"That I had such a problem with you and Cass?" Lucien nodded. "I'm more than aware. Don't think that wasn't part of my hesitation in developing an attachment for Kat." He'd held her at arm's length for far too long.

Beasley brought the horses. "Ready, my lords. They are quite fast."

"Thank you." Lucien mounted one and Ruark took the other. "We'll have them back tomorrow." He hoped. If he didn't, Lucien had no idea how he would live.

CHAPTER 23

At least the hulking brute had allowed her the forward-facing seat. Kat despised riding backward in a coach or any sort of equipage. It upset her belly and made her feel as she did when she was in a crowded social event with too much noise and heat. Despite not riding backward, she still felt her agitation rising with each mile.

How far from London had they come? It had been light when they'd left, but now it was full dark. Her stomach groaned.

"We'll be stopping for food shortly," he said. His speech was surprisingly polished. Kat supposed she expected him to be an uneducated barbarian.

"I would also like to relieve myself." She didn't really need to, but if she could get away from him, perhaps she could, well, get away from him permanently.

He grunted in response. Not entirely polished.

His nonverbal reaction reminded her of Lucien's growls. What a mess she'd walked into! All because she wanted to help him. She still did. And she didn't regret doing what she'd done. For too long, she'd been focused on herself.

Lucien had been upset for weeks. Instead of pressing him to confide in her, she'd yammered on and on about *her* research. She should have asked him about his problems, his worries. She should have been a better friend.

That made her think back to all the times she'd ignored her sisters and their woes—even if they did seem silly to Kat. Was a stained dress really a reason to cry for two days? It was to Abigail, and Kat should have given her comfort.

She silently admonished herself again. If she'd learned anything in recent days, it was that she needed to think of others beyond herself. Not that she didn't, but she needed to do it *more*, and not after the fact of something important.

If she managed to get back to London, and she absolutely planned to, she'd make sure Lucien knew how much he meant to her, how important his concerns were to her, how much she loved him.

Loved him?

Kat sat up straight and blinked. She loved him? How could she know?

Because she just did. He made her want to do better, *be* better. He always made her feel important and that he cared for her. She'd found his concern over her reputation annoying, but in hindsight, it was incredibly endearing. Most gentlemen would have run far away from her—or taken complete advantage. He'd done neither.

Settling back against the squab, she fidgeted with the cloak Lady Pickering had wrapped around her before she'd left. What did it matter that she loved him? It wasn't as if they would marry and live a lifetime of happiness with a brood of children.

He had the Phoenix Club, and by God, she'd make sure he kept it. And she had…her interests. Along with her desire to remain unwed so she could be precisely who she wanted to be.

The coach came to a stop, and she pulled aside the curtain on the window. They'd pulled into the yard of an inn.

"Time for supper," Hudson said, opening the door and climbing down. "You'll stay with me at all times, or you won't get any food. Understand?"

"What about using the privy?"

"There's one behind the inn. I'll stand outside while you use it."

So much for her plan to escape. There had to be another way, and she would find it.

They went into the inn, and she stood silently while Hudson asked for two plates of whatever they were serving. The innkeeper looked like a kindly sort, with gold wired spectacles and a cheerful smile.

"I've a place near the fire. Spring is nearly upon us, but it's a cold night to be sure! Will you need a room?"

"No. Our destination isn't much farther."

Kat knew that wasn't true. They were on their way to Winchester—or near it anyway—which was a two-day ride. They couldn't run the horses that far without resting or changing them. So there had to be another stop along the way.

The innkeeper nodded in response, still smiling. "Take a seat, then, and I'll have your dinner served momentarily. Would you care for ale or wine?"

"Ale," Hudson said.

"Wine, please." Kat didn't really care, but just wanted to be contrary. She gave the innkeeper a worried look as if she could silently convey that she was here against her will. Perhaps she could write him a note. If only she had paper...

But she did! She had her small notebook and pencil, which she'd been carrying nearly everywhere since that day she'd gone to Jess's and maneuvered Lucien into kissing her in Dougal's study.

That had been so lovely… Remorse tainted the memory. She shouldn't have lured him like that.

She followed Hudson to the table near the hearth and was surprised when he held her chair. "You seem well-mannered for a brigand."

"I am not a brigand. And keep your voice down." He glanced about, but there were only three other people in the common room. Granted, they were sitting rather nearby.

"I'm afraid I've a penchant for speaking in a loud tone." She unclasped the cloak beneath her throat and folded it over the back of the chair to have her arms free to eat. "Some people find it annoying."

"I noticed that in the coach."

"Did you? How clever of you since we barely spoke." She lowered her voice, but not too much. She had no problem with anyone overhearing what she said. In fact, it would be bloody helpful. "If you aren't a brigand, what are you?"

"Please be quiet." He tossed her a dark glower.

"Well, at least you said please." Kat watched the other three patrons rise from their table. She looked longingly at them, but they didn't even glance in her direction. Dammit!

The innkeeper brought their food and drink. Kat wanted to slip a note into his hand or perhaps his pocket, but how was she to write it if the brute was always watching her?

He reached across the table and picked up the knife that had been delivered with her stew and bread. "You won't be needing this."

"How am I to spread the butter on my bread?" she asked.

"You don't need butter. Dip it in your stew." He tore a piece of bread from his small loaf and dipped it into the thick meat broth.

"I'm allowed a spoon? What if I use it to carve out your heart?" She smacked her forehead. "Not possible since you *don't have one*."

He didn't react at all, just picked up his ale and took a long drink. Too late, Kat realized she could have reached over and tipped it so that it poured down his chin and front. Then she could grab the tankard and bludgeon him over the head with it.

Goodness, she was thinking rather violent thoughts. But how else was she to get away?

Write the note.

If she could, what would happen next? The innkeeper would take on this huge brigand? Kat didn't care what Hudson said. He was absolutely a brigand.

Kat put her hand into her pocket and touched the notebook, as if it would give her comfort. Then her fingers closed around the pencil. Wait. This was a weapon! She'd sharpened it earlier that day. If she could plunge it into his neck... God, that would be gruesome. Ah well, needs must.

A rush of anxiety swept over her. She felt shaky and uncertain. But she had to take advantage of this moment. If she waited until they were in the coach, it would be much more difficult with the darkness and the motion. Plus, what would she do trapped in there with a bleeding brigand?

Just the thought of that made her shiver.

Kat took a drink of wine to fortify her courage. Hudson was bent over his food, his attention completely on eating. The neck was a difficult target because of his cravat and shirt collar. But bent over like that, she could perhaps move behind him and stab him in the nape. She'd have to move quickly...

What if she killed him? Could she live with that?

The sweat dappling her body turned cold.

Why couldn't she just stab him in the hand and flee to the kitchen? Surely the innkeeper wasn't alone here. They could outnumber the brigand. It was the only chance she had.

Heart racing, she watched him eat. When he picked up his

tankard again, she made her move. Swiping her hand across the table, she sank the pencil into the back of his hand.

He yowled with pain, dropping the tankard into his stew so that ale and food splashed on him and the table. Kat jumped up and raced toward where the innkeeper had gone after delivering their food.

But she didn't make it. A hand gripped the back of her gown and pulled. She feared she'd soon be exposed as well as recaptured.

"Let go of her!"

A familiar voice thundered through the common room.

Hudson did indeed let Kat go, which sent her sprawling forward. She got her hands out in front of her and mitigated the damage as she struck the floor. Behind her, she heard a tussle.

Scrambling to roll over and get to her feet, Kat saw Lucien and Ruark wrestling the brigand. "Find something to bind him!" Lucien yelled.

Kat stared at them for a moment before springing into action. She didn't have to go in search of the innkeeper, for he had entered the common room, his expression stricken. A woman and a young man stood behind him.

"I was kidnapped by that brigand," she said in a rush, her voice high and sounding not at all like herself. "They need to bind him so he won't escape. Do you have rope or…something?"

"I'll fetch some," the young man said before turning and hastening away.

The woman came forward and put her arm around Kat. "I'm so sorry, dear."

The innkeeper shook his head, his face pale. "I had no idea. I should have helped you."

"You're helping now," Kat managed. She was shaking, and while she appreciated the woman's concern, she didn't want to be touched. Stepping away from the innkeeper's wife, she gave her a feeble smile. "May I have a blanket?"

"Yes, of course." The woman hurried the same way the young man had gone.

Lucien and Ruark had successfully subdued Hudson. They hauled him back into his chair, which they'd pulled away from the table. And Lucien held a pistol toward the brigand. It was odd seeing him in that situation. He was the charming membership club owner and Society darling, not a violent man who would kill. Lady Pickering's words came back to her. Had Lucien actually killed someone?

Ruark came to Kat and tried to hug her. She stiffened, and he immediately stepped back. "You must be terribly overwhelmed," he said softly. "But are you all right?"

She nodded. "Yes, to both of those things," she whispered, her mind clogging with everything that had happened. She could hardly believe what Lady Pickering had done.

The young man came back with some rope. Ruark went to bind Hudson's hands and feet while Lucien kept the pistol trained on him. Once Hudson was secure, Lucien relaxed. He glanced toward Kat. "You're safe now."

"Did you kill someone?" she asked, fixated on what Lady Pickering had told her.

Lucien blinked. "Tonight? No. Ever? Yes. I was a soldier."

"But that's all? Lady Pickering said you killed someone."

"She was trying to make it look as if I did, but no, I did not."

Kat exhaled, feeling marginally better. "Good. I didn't think you had, but watching you wield that pistol…I had to ask."

"I understand." Lucien moved toward her. "I'm so sorry you got involved with this."

The woman returned with a blanket and gave it to Kat. She immediately wrapped it around her shoulders and shuddered as she squeezed herself smaller to generate heat and to calm herself. When she felt overwhelmed like this, both emotionally and physically, it was as if her entire body was silently screaming. "I'll fetch some tea," the woman offered before disappearing once more.

Lucien came to stand in front of Kat. He gently touched her face, his dark eyes weighty with concern. "I was so worried."

"What are you doing?" she whispered, incredulous at his behavior. "My brother is *right there*."

"I know you think you're being quiet," Ruark said, "but I can hear you. I know all about you and Lucien."

Kat stared at Lucien. "You told him we had sex?"

Lucien's eyes closed, and his nose scrunched up. Ruark stalked toward them. He grabbed Lucien's shoulder, spun him around, and planted him a facer.

Gasping, Kat moved to catch Lucien—not that she could have stopped him from falling. Thankfully, he just stumbled backward a few steps.

She let go of Lucien and turned to glare at her brother. "What was that for?"

"You're a pompous, hypocritical son of a bitch." Ruark sneered at Lucien. "I suppose you left that part out when you were confessing your love for her to me."

Lucien loved her?

Rubbing his cheek, Lucien narrowed his eyes at Ruark. "Well, thank you, for that's precisely how I was hoping she would find out that I am in love with her. Remind me to come to you for all my matchmaking needs."

Ruark glared at Lucien. "That's rich too! You've meddled with practically everyone!"

"Not with you, because you and Cass kept it secret," Lucien said tersely.

"As did you and Kat." Ruark looked to her. "What were you thinking?"

"That Lucien was an excellent person with whom to conduct research on mating rituals. I'm happy to report I was quite right."

"I deserved that punch," Lucien said.

Ruark crossed his arms over his chest. "You sure as hell did. When is the wedding?"

Wedding? Kat froze. Why would they get married? Neither of them wanted to wed. She shivered again and drew the blanket tighter around her shoulders. But it didn't help. The silent screaming was still there. As was a growing urge to flee into solitude.

"As soon as possible." Lucien returned to Kat. He took her hand and brought it to his lips, pressing a kiss to the back. "I do love you. And I would like to marry you." He sank to one knee. "Will you do me the great honor of becoming my wife?"

This wasn't the plan. She wasn't ever going to get married. Or fall in love. Or get kidnapped. Or stab a brigand with a pencil. She glanced toward Hudson and saw the blood caked all over his hand.

She couldn't do this right now. It was all too much. She couldn't...think. Or feel. She felt the storm coming. She was going to lose her barely held control if she didn't get away. She shook her head. "I...can't. Did you know I stabbed him in the hand with my pencil?" Where had her pencil gone?

"Did you?" Ruark went to the table and held up the writing instrument. "This? Yes, it's rather bloody. Well done, Kat."

"I'm not surprised," Lucien said, and she could hear the pride in his voice. "You are quite capable."

"Until I'm not," she snapped. She just wanted to be alone.

She wanted to squeeze her fear and anxiety away. If she could. "Can I go back to London? Alone?"

Ruark frowned. "You shouldn't be alone."

Lucien stood and let go of her hand. "But she needs to be. This has been a harrowing experience. She needs time to manage it all, and she does that best on her own." He looked into her eyes. "I'll have the coachman drive you back in Lady Pickering's coach. He didn't realize you'd been kidnapped. He thought he was driving you to Hampshire for a respite. You'll be safe with him. You can leave now. Is that acceptable?"

She nodded, so grateful that he understood. But also ashamed that she couldn't contemplate marrying him. Not now anyway. "Yes. Thank you."

Ruark moved toward her. "I'm sorry this happened, Kat. Everything will be all right."

"I know." But it didn't feel that way right now. She desperately wanted to get out of there before she completely lost control. "Just take me to the coach, please."

Lucien inclined his head toward Ruark. "Go ahead. I'll need to secure another coach to transport Hudson."

Kat walked to the door, and Ruark hurried to open it for her. She wanted to say something to assure them that she'd be fine, but she didn't have the words or strength. She was completely spent.

"I'll see you tomorrow," Lucien called after her.

She wasn't sure she'd feel better by then. She couldn't guess when she'd feel better at all.

CHAPTER 24

*B*ender admitted Lucien to Evesham House and informed him the duke was resting in his chamber. "He'll be delighted you're here," the butler added.

Delighted? Despite the astonishing events of the previous day, Lucien still thought that was probably a stretch.

He climbed the stairs, memories of running up and down them with Con in their youth flitting through his mind. He'd been feeling particularly reflective and even nostalgic since yesterday, especially on the long ride back to London with Ruark and Hudson.

They'd tied the horses to the back of the coach and returned them to the Hanover mews. But first, they'd taken Hudson to Bow Street, where he was currently imprisoned, as were Lady Pickering and Oliver Kent. Lucien didn't know what the Foreign Office had planned for any of them, and at the moment, he couldn't spare much concern over it.

He was too worried about Kat. She'd been incredibly upset last night—and understandably so. He knew she needed time to work through things in her own way. He just hoped that when she was ready, she'd want to see him. After her reaction to his marriage proposal, he was not encouraged.

Lucien hesitated as he neared his father's suite. He knew the duke would likely be fine. Con and Cass had been with him last night, and Cass had spent the night here to keep watch over him. The physician had removed the ball from his shoulder and stitched him up, saying the damage was fortunately minimal. If there was no infection, all would be well.

He knocked softly on the door in case the duke was sleeping.

"Enter."

Not sleeping, then. Which meant Lucien had to see him. Why was he so bloody nervous? He'd come to meet his father countless times and had expected his disdain or disinterest. He hadn't felt anxious about any of those encounters in a very long time. So why now?

Because of what the duke had done yesterday and that thing he'd said about the cravat Lucien had used to stanch the flow of blood from his wound being his favorite. It hadn't been just what he'd said, but the way he'd said it, as if he really and truly appreciated not the cravat, but Lucien.

A maid sat in the corner stitching something as Lucien walked in. The duke was propped up against several pillows in the bed. He wore a thick blue dressing gown, and the bedclothes were pulled up to his chest. A book lay beside him on the bed.

"Leave us," the duke said, and the maid departed, closing the door after her.

"You're looking better," Lucien said.

"Hardly."

"I should hope you'd present a better appearance than you did after just being shot. Your color is far better."

"I suppose taking a ball to the shoulder might make one look rather gray. Did I?"

"Gray is a good description. I'm glad you will be all right." Lucien meant that.

"Unless there's an infection, so you may be rid of me yet."

Lucien resisted the urge to roll his eyes. He moved closer to the bed, but didn't go around to the side where his father was situated. "I am not eager for your death."

The duke narrowed one eye at Lucien as if assessing whether he spoke the truth. "Why not? Our relationship is contentious at best. You must hate me."

"I do not." Lucien might have thought the word with regard to him, but in truth, he didn't hate him. "I am rather certain, however, that you at least loathe me, so I am trying to puzzle out why you would put yourself between me and a bullet."

The duke folded his hands on his lap and looked at his feet. Or in the direction of his feet anyway. He certainly wasn't looking at Lucien. "I don't loathe you. If anything, I loathe myself. Would you sit for a moment? It's past time I explain something to you."

Lucien's heart began to beat faster as a ribbon of anxiety unfurled inside him. "You don't owe me any explanations, Father."

Now, the duke swung his gaze to Lucien's. In the dark depths, Lucien saw a swell of emotion he'd never seen before: regret, fear, and things he couldn't name. Forcing himself to move, he perched on the other side of the bed from the duke.

"Thank you." His father took a deep breath. "There is a reason we have always been at odds." He grimaced, but before Lucien could ask if he was in pain, the duke said. "That's not right. There's a reason I've always treated you differently from your siblings. It's because they are your half siblings."

The room tilted. Lucien had been born on the wrong side of the blanket, and he wasn't his father's son. Everything made sense now.

Except for the way their eyes were identical.

"I'll take that explanation now," Lucien said, his voice sounding thin.

"You are my son, of course. We are far more alike than not, something I have purposely ignored and you likely haven't realized."

"But my mother?"

"I had an affair. It was brief—at a house party over a few nights."

Hell, who was Lucien's mother? Some woman in Society he'd met countless times who'd looked at him with affection? No, that didn't make sense. She would have raised Lucien as her son, not given him to the duke.

"She was a maid in the household. It was, without question, the thing I am most ashamed of in my life. I loved your mother. I was young and stupid." He waved his hand with a scowl. "None of that excuses anything. The maid was let go, of course, and she came to me for a settlement. I was so distraught, and your mother—the woman who raised you, bless her—provoked the truth from me. I'd been acting strangely since the house party. I was completely overridden with guilt, which only became magnified when the maid informed me that she was carrying. I wanted to give her money and send her to America."

Lucien tried to imagine the life he might have had as a completely different person. No "Lord" Lucien. Hell, he wouldn't even have been called Lucien. "Why didn't you?"

"Because as soon as your mother found out, she wanted to give the maid a choice—she could take a sum of money and raise the illegitimate child as her own, or she could retire to the country with your mother for the duration of her pregnancy, at the end of which the duchess would become the child's mother."

Their mother had been beloved by all three of her children. But for Lucien, she'd been a bright spot against the darkness of his father's expectations and disappointment. That she'd fought for him before he'd even been born aroused an emotion so stark and so terribly wonderful, that Lucien feared he would sob.

He swallowed, hoping to keep himself in check. He did not want to dissemble in front of the duke. "The maid chose the second option obviously."

"She did. She was intrigued with the idea of starting a new life in America. I agreed to pay for her voyage and give her enough money to get settled as a seamstress."

"Where is she now?" Lucien asked, wondering why it mattered.

The duke met his gaze. "I don't know. She left a week after you were born, and we never saw or heard from her again."

Though Lucien loved his mother now even more than he had before, he felt an ache in his chest for this unknown woman who'd given him life, who'd chosen a future that would benefit him. "Was it...hard for her?"

"I confess I don't know that either," the duke said. "I wanted nothing to do with her. I never saw her after she and your mother went to Cornwall. We leased a house for your mother—and for Con. He accompanied them."

Con wouldn't remember that, of course. But it raised a question Lucien had to ask. "Does anyone else know this?"

Lucien shook his head. "Not a soul. Just your mother, of course, and the midwife and the few retainers that took care of them at the house. They were all well compensated to keep the secret."

Perhaps irrationally, Lucien wondered if he could find any of them, to ask them about this woman who'd carried and given birth to him. To what end? Nothing in his life would change, including the way his father had treated him his entire life.

"This is why you've never liked me," Lucien said softly.

"Yes. But the truth is that it has never been about you. It's me. I hate myself for what I did to your mother, and damn me to hell, but every time I look at you, I remember my betrayal and your mother's generosity and grace, and I want to rail at God for taking her instead of me."

Lucien put his hand to his mouth. It was that, or the emotions would escape. His heart was racing, his throat burning.

"Sometimes I try to do better, to treat you as you deserve to be treated—as my beloved son—but I always seem to fail. That, my dear boy, is why I stepped between you and the bullet. And I would do it again and again if it would save you." He turned his body slightly, wincing as he moved. "The reason you were offered a position with the Foreign Office in Spain was because I insisted. I knew you would be an excellent asset, but more than that, I wanted you out of battle. You are right that I am incredibly selfish."

Lucien didn't know what to say. What could he? His entire life had been upended. As if yesterday hadn't been overwhelming enough.

Lowering his hand to his lap, Lucien said, "I have to wonder how much of my life you've been manipulating. The Foreign Office's involvement in the Phoenix Club? Was that your direction?"

"I told them you were—are—a valuable resource, and

they said they were looking for someone to manage certain things in London."

The Phoenix Club existed because of his father's influence. Lucien couldn't wrap his head around that. The mission of the club with regard to its members was all Lucien, but the part that was managed by the Foreign Office was due to his father.

"You've never hidden your disdain for the membership I've cultivated there—inviting those who aren't included at White's or Brooks's. You also haven't appreciated the environment I've created, that it's a place many prefer to those other clubs."

"I confess I don't care for it, but that doesn't make me any less proud of all that you've done."

Lucien stood from the bed as anger swept the other emotions away. "Proud? You told me to walk away from the club. You did nothing to help me, and yet you claim we have so much in common. If telling yourself such horseshit alleviates your guilt for five minutes, then I pity you."

His father didn't flinch in the face of Lucien's ire. "Nothing alleviates my guilt. Not even your mother's forgiveness."

"That's pathetic. You've squandered a lifetime. *My* lifetime."

"I know. You said you didn't hate me, but I suspect you do now. As well you should. Before you go, the Foreign Office is relinquishing their control of the club. You will have sole ownership. They would, however, like to continue your arrangement for allowing certain things to happen there— after they investigate what went wrong with Lady Pickering and Kent."

Lucien realized he never asked why his father was at her house. Since she'd shot him, it appeared he wasn't working with them. "Why were you there last night?"

"I took your advice and learned what I could from the Foreign Office. I heard a few things that made me want to ask her some questions. They were closing in on her and Kent. You and Fallin—and Miss Shaughnessy—simply helped them along. They are quite grateful, by the way."

"I know. A gentleman called on me this morning, but I didn't see him. He left word with my butler, thanking me." Lucien shook his head. "You actually took my advice?"

"I have much to learn from you, and I've been trying to do that. You're the reason I worked with that group to reunite French prisoners with their families here."

"I thought you said you owed Witney a favor."

"I did, but I also realized it was something you would do without hesitation. So, I thought I should participate. I admit it was satisfying to bring people together."

Lucien moved around the bed to stand beside him. "This is what I don't understand. You look down your nose at Evie and are repulsed by my giving her a position of prominence in the club, then you work to reunite her with her long-lost father. I can't make sense of you."

"Your mother used to say the same thing. I am my own worst enemy, Lucien. There is no greater battle that I fight than with myself."

The sadness in his father's eyes pulled at Lucien's heart. "I don't hate you. You make me very angry, but I'm glad you finally told me the truth at least. I will need time to come to terms with everything."

"Of course."

"And you'll need to tell Cass and Con. I won't keep it secret from them."

The duke's nose wrinkled slightly. "As you wish."

Lucien realized something very important. "Your unexpected acceptance of Prudence makes sense. No one could understand why you so readily embraced your sister's illegitimate child. It's because you had one too. Does Aunt Christina know that?"

"No, but I suppose you think I should tell her too. I'll consider it. What of Miss Shaughnessy? Will you be marrying soon?"

"I don't know. She hasn't accepted my proposal." Lucien ignored the swell of unease in his chest.

"You made one, then?"

"Last night. However, she was overwhelmed by all that happened."

"That's to be expected."

"You still advocate for the match?" It seemed impossible that the duke would approve of an Irish-blooded girl who talked too loudly and preferred to avoid social gatherings.

"Wholeheartedly." The duke actually *smiled*. Lucien nearly fell over.

"Does this mean you want me to be happy in marriage? Con said you preferred we all avoided that."

"I did, but I've revised that opinion due to your brother. I watched you and Miss Shaughnessy at dinner the other night. There's a light in your eyes when you look at each other, and I don't think your smiles ever fully faded throughout all the courses."

"I'm surprised you noticed. I love her very much, and I do hope she'll say yes."

His father's brow creased. "Perhaps I should call on her."

"You want to play matchmaker?" Lucien laughed. "We are *much* too alike. Please stop."

He looked Lucien in the eye. "I want you to be happy."

Emotion rose in Lucien's throat, and he had to wait a moment to respond. "Thank you. Things will be different now, then?"

"Yes, but I am still me. You have permission to remind me not to fall into the abyss of my self-loathing."

Lucien grinned. "That will give me great pleasure." He took his father's hand and gave it a squeeze before letting him go.

As Lucien started toward the door, the duke said, "You'll send word when she accepts?"

"Yes. And I'll expect you to invite Con, Cass, and me for a meeting when you're feeling up to it. In the meantime, should I extend you an invitation to the Phoenix Club?" Lucien turned to look at his father.

The duke stared at him. Then they both laughed.

Leaving his father's chamber, Lucien felt both heavy and light. His mother would always be his mother, but knowing the truth helped. No, knowing that his father's treatment of him was never about him *helped*.

It made all the difference.

~

*I*t was just before noon on Friday when the butler informed Kat that Lucien had called to see her. "What shall I tell him?"

"I'll meet him in the drawing room," Kat replied.

She'd spent most of yesterday in her room, but had surprised Cass and Ruark when she'd joined them for dinner. She'd been shocked to hear all that had transpired at Lady Pickering's, which had led to Lucien and Ruark coming after her, particularly the duke throwing himself in front of Lucien when Lady Pickering had tried to shoot him. Kat had almost gone to Lucien right then, but she hadn't been ready to answer his proposal. She didn't think it was fair to see him if she couldn't respond.

She'd spent a great deal of time contemplating his proposal. It was *all* she could think about, really. Part of it was adjusting to a future that was different from what she'd planned. How would it feel to live with him? To share a bed with him? And she wasn't just thinking about the obviously wonderful physical rewards of doing so. She liked her own space.

You also like snuggling with him. His weight feels really nice.

She couldn't argue with that.

Realizing she needed to get to the drawing room, she hurried from her chamber and went down the stairs. He was standing in the center of the room when she entered.

He smiled, and she was reminded of how wonderful it was to see him—every single time. That was love, apparently.

"Good morning," he said. "I'm afraid I couldn't wait any longer to call on you. Since you didn't send me away, I will take that to mean I'm not being a nuisance."

"You could never be a nuisance." Kat walked into the room until she stood about a foot away from him. "How is the duke? I heard what happened. Actually, how are *you*?"

"Trying to cope with what he did." Lucien shook his head as if he still couldn't believe it. "Will you come sit with me? It's the most astonishing story."

"What is?" Kat was glad for the distraction. She could put off addressing his proposal while he talked.

They sat together on the settee, their bodies angled toward one another, but not touching. It was the same way they'd sat the day she'd given him the peacock drawing. Kat felt hesitant, uncertain.

He looked at her intently. "I should preface this with the fact that no one else knows this but me—and my father, of course. He will tell Cass and Con soon, when he's feeling better. Until then, I should like you to keep this between us. I realize I should have said this to you when I shared the secret of not owning the Phoenix Club."

Kat felt a wave of remorse. "I'm sorry about that. I'm not very good at keeping secrets, especially if I'm not explicitly told to do so. I just wanted to help you the way you help everyone else."

"I'm incredibly glad you did, for it led to the exposure of Oliver Kent and Lady Pickering and, frankly, saved me from losing everything."

Excitement vibrated through her. "You won't lose the club?"

He smiled. "I was saving that bit for later, but no, I am to be the full owner."

She touched his hand, and their eyes locked for a moment. "That's so wonderful. I couldn't be happier for you."

"Thank you, and I truly do owe you for setting everything in motion." His brow darkened. "Though, I would have greatly preferred that you weren't put in harm's way."

"I'm all right."

"You were beyond resourceful. I didn't think my admiration for you could increase, but I was quite wrong." He took her hand then, and she let him entwine his fingers with hers. "I couldn't reconcile my father's actions—him stepping between me and Lady Pickering—until he made a startling confession." Lucien paused to take a deep breath. "My mother was not my mother, as it happens. My father went to a house party and got a maid with child. When my mother found out, she offered to take the maid to Cornwall to have the baby, at which time the maid would give the child to her and my father to raise. The maid accepted that, and from then on, I've been a daily reminder of my father's worst mistake and biggest shame."

Kat had tightened her grip on his hand while he'd spoken. "Oh, Lucien. I don't know what to say. That's...shocking."

"As I said, I'm still trying to sort it out. The most important part is that my father doesn't hate *me*, though it always felt as though he did. He said that every time he looked at me, he hated himself more. I suppose all that negativity spreads. It was impossible for him to treat me as he should. And he knows it."

"You must be angry." Kat put her other hand over his. "I would be."

"I was. I still am, but I'm also grateful to know that it wasn't really ever about me."

"It doesn't forgive the way he's treated you."

"No, but forgiveness is for me, not him. I can continue with our mutually antagonistic relationship, or I can accept his olive branch and strive for something better. I'd prefer the latter."

Kat smiled and took her hand from his to cup his cheek. "You are the kindest, most generous man."

"I want to be. And in the spirit of generosity, you should know that I want to share everything with you. There isn't a thing I don't want to talk to you about or a day I don't want to spend with you."

Oh no, was he going to propose again?

Before she could stop him, he went on. "I specifically wanted to tell you about my time in Spain. You asked me the other night if I'd killed anyone, and I said that I had as a soldier. The truth is that I did kill a couple of men outside battle." He blew out a breath. "Outside an official battle, anyway. My dear friend Max—the Viscount Warfield—had fallen in love with a local woman. She was carrying his child, and they were to be wed. A small squadron of enemy soldiers found her one day. They violated her and killed her." He paused as Kat sucked in a breath. "Max fell into a rage and went after them. I realized what he had done and followed him, but he'd already killed several of them. I wanted to stop further bloodshed, but they were going to kill Max, who was wounded at that point. I had to defend him—and myself."

"That is completely justifiable. Those men were despicable. Evil."

"Yes, and I don't regret what I had to do to survive and to protect Max. But that went past just saving his life. I had to ensure he didn't suffer any consequences for what he'd done, so I planted a letter on one of the dead soldiers to make it look like they'd stolen information and we were retrieving it. I worked as a spy at the time, so it was easy to concoct this scheme."

"Do you regret doing that?"

"No. But I don't know if it was the most moral choice." He looked past her, his eyes taking on the fog of memory. "One of them begged me to let him live, but he was already too far gone. I can still hear his voice some nights."

Kat threw her arms around him and held him tightly for several minutes.

"Thank you," he murmured. "It will probably always haunt me, but I stand by what I did."

"I'm glad you told me."

"It's a part of who I am, and a part I haven't ever shared with anyone. Max and I don't really discuss it. For a long time, he was angry with me for saving him. I think he attacked those men thinking he would die and that he wanted to after losing his love."

"That's so sad. But he's happy now. At least he seems to be. Honestly, how can he not be with Ada? She's the most cheerful person I've ever met."

Lucien chuckled. "When I sent her to help with Max's estate, I wasn't even thinking of a match between them, but they are perfectly suited to one another. She truly saved him, and in some ways, I think he saved her too."

"That's lovely."

They were silent a moment before Lucien spoke again. "I was wounded in that incident in Spain, and though it wasn't serious, they sent me home. I learned from my father yesterday that he arranged for that to happen. Apparently, I get my penchant for meddling from him."

"It's nice to know that, isn't it?"

He nodded. "Surprisingly, yes. What about you? Would you like to share anything with me?"

There it was. Words stuck in her mouth as if it were a quagmire. "How would this work?" she blurted.

Confusion danced in his gaze. "How would what work?"

"Marriage. I have recently learned that I am somewhat selfish, or at least inwardly focused, which is pretty much the opposite of you and your ability to constantly think of how you might help others. But I've also realized that I am perhaps that way as a sort of defense against people who don't understand or accept me." She released his hand. "In any case, I don't see how we could be married to one another. You will be at the club socializing and generally being the most adored man in London, while I am that awkward woman who can't dance and would rather curl up alone in a library than swan about the Phoenix Club."

Lucien pressed his lips together. Then he smiled faintly. Finally, he took her hand once more and brought it to his lap. "First, I am rather enamored of the idea of you sitting in my office at the club reading a book while I *swan* about the common areas. Second, on the occasion you are feeling social—and I know that happens—you can come to the library, which is usually populated by our family and close friends and isn't crowded. I think you'd feel quite comfortable there. Third, there is an exceedingly lovely bedchamber on the second floor, with which I think you are acquainted. I should think that would be a delightful place for you to sit and read. I would, of course, need to come and check on you from time to time..."

Kat tried not to smile and mostly failed. Straightening her

face, she asked, "Can I come to your office any time or only on Tuesdays?"

"Any time. Remember, we have our secret passageway. Or, if you'd rather, I will simply spend more time at home with you."

Vehemently shaking her head, Kat clutched his hand more tightly. "I won't let you do that. The club is your lifeblood."

"*You* are my lifeblood." He released her hand and cupped her cheeks as he gazed into her eyes. "Don't you know by now that I would do anything for you?"

She felt exactly the same way about him. "I would be quite comfortable in your office. Or the library. Or the bedchamber. Or the passageway. And when I am not—feeling comfortable, that is—I'll stay home by myself, and I'll be quite content to do so. If you're going to worry about me, this won't work." But she knew it would. He was the one who'd sent her home alone from Chessington the other night. He'd seen that she needed solitude and had given her precisely that without argument. Indeed, he'd done it with gentle care and an indelible kindness. She had never known another soul like his, and she expected she never would again.

"I would be a fool to refuse you," she said softly.

He pulled his hands from her face. "Not at all. Only you can decide what is right for you. Just know that I love you, and I will do everything in my power to make you happy. The real question is, do you love me?"

Emotion gathered and expanded within her until she felt she might burst. "More than I ever dreamed I could. I think... I think my answer is yes."

Lucien's brows arched, and he held his breath. "You'll marry me?"

"If you're still asking."

"I was prepared to ask you every day until the end of time." He touched her face once more and kissed her.

Kat put her arms around his neck and kissed him back. When they broke apart, they were both laughing. She clutched his shoulder. "I love you so very much."

"I love you more."

She shook her head. "Impossible. This is not a debate you will win."

"I've a lifetime to try," he said before kissing her again. Soon, he'd pushed her back on the settee, and they'd stretched out as much as they were able. If they weren't careful, he'd be lifting her skirts soon.

"We should tell Cass and Ruark the good news," she said. "Lest we get carried away here."

"I would very much like to carry you away. Right up to your chamber." He kissed her neck and licked her.

"They'll be thrilled. And Ruark won't have to kill you."

Lucien laughed. "Everyone else will be shocked. We are two people who were never expected to marry, let alone to each other." He looked at her with mirth lighting his eyes. "Even my father is in favor."

"Oh dear, I hope that doesn't bode ill."

"On the contrary, I think it signifies a wonderful future—for all of us." He lowered his head and kissed her again until she was breathless, his hand stroking her breast through her clothing.

"We really do need to stop before we're caught," she said. "But perhaps you can find your way back into my chamber tonight. I still have many things on my list for us to do. Plus, I've added several more."

"Have you? Well, I've drafted my own list. Perhaps we should begin by comparing them and striking any duplicate items."

"Or we could just do them twice?" She nibbled his ear. "I fear I will never stop being curious—or eager."

"I don't fear that. I welcome it." He looked into her eyes with so much love that Kat was glad she was lying down because she might have swooned again. "Don't ever change, my insatiable darling."

EPILOGUE

Five Days Later

$\mathcal{L}$ucien looked around the dining room at the Phoenix Club and couldn't quite believe what he saw: his wife speaking with his father, who was *smiling*. That Lucien was both married and on friendly terms with the duke—his father—was astonishing. Indeed, he wasn't sure when he would be able to believe it.

After obtaining a special license, Lucien had asked Kat if she minded waiting to wed until his father was feeling up to attending. She hadn't minded at all, particularly because she was able to confirm that she was, in fact, not carrying a child, and preferred to delay the wedding for at least a few days for…reasons. Lucien had been relieved by the news as he didn't think he could deal with another massive, unexpected shift in his life at the moment.

Still, he hoped they would have children someday. And that alone was a great change.

"Where did you go?" Evie asked from beside him. She and Gregory had returned the previous Saturday, and no one had been more surprised by the announcement of his and Kat's betrothal than she was.

Or Con.

Or Max.

Or...hell, they'd all been flabbergasted by the news. Except for Jess, who'd apparently aided Kat in her kissing scheme in Dougal's office, just as Lucien had speculated.

"I was just marveling at this occasion," Lucien replied.

"We all are. I still can't decide what is most shocking— your marriage or the sudden and complete change in your relationship with the duke." She shook her head.

Lucien had told her the truth behind his father's treatment of him. He wouldn't share it with everyone here, but he'd wanted her to know. She really was one of his dearest friends.

"Can't they be equally devastating in their unpredictability?" he asked.

"I suppose so." Evie regarded him intently. "I can't get used to you like this."

He pulled his attention from Kat, who was talking rather animatedly to his father, her hands gesticulating. "Like what?"

"Utterly smitten."

He laughed. "That's precisely what I've been thinking about you." His gaze darted toward Gregory, who stood somewhat nearby with Dougal and Jess. "You and Gregory seem quite happy."

"We are." She touched his arm. "How wonderful for us both. Especially since things with the club seem to be on the upswing."

She was right. Attendance at the Welcome Spring assembly had exceeded any of last year's assemblies, due in part to the fact that Lucien and the membership committee had issued a flurry of invitations a few days before. "It's so bloody fantastic not to have to garner anyone's approval for membership invitations anymore."

"Oh, yes, that is quite nice." Evie smiled, but quickly sobered. "I will never be able to thank you for allowing me to stay, for fighting for me even when you were pushed into a corner." She knew everything that had happened with the Foreign Office. Lucien wanted her to know the truth, particularly since the Foreign Office might occasionally conduct business at the club. He'd thought it important that the entire membership committee be aware of their involvement—both past and future—so he'd held a meeting with everyone to share the details.

"I will never abandon you," Lucien said. "Or any of my friends and family."

"And that is what makes you the second-most wonderful man I've ever met." Her brow puckered briefly. "Perhaps third now that my father has returned."

"I will happily take third. Now, let us congratulate Max on his elevation to earldom." That had happened a few days ago, much to Max's eternal disgruntlement. He hadn't liked being a viscount at all, and he looked forward to being an earl even less.

As they walked toward Max and Ada, Kat joined them, sidling close to Lucien so that he could put his hand on her lower back. "What were you talking to my father about?" he murmured.

"Peacocks. He said there are several mated pairs at Wood-break. You never mentioned that."

"Probably because I haven't been to my father's ancestral pile in years." Which was too bad because it was beautiful. "I'll take you there after the Season. Then you can demonstrate your peacock dance for me, and I'll judge whether it's accurate."

Kat swatted him in the arm as she chuckled.

They reached Max and Ada, and Lucien looked to his friend. "I know you don't want me to, but I'm going to propose a toast to you becoming earl."

Max grunted in response. Ada grinned widely. "How thoughtful of you."

"Not before I make a toast to you and Kat," Con said, apparently overhearing since he stood nearby.

"I'll instruct the footmen to serve the champagne," Sabrina offered.

Fiona and Tobias came toward them—slowly. Poor Fiona was having a difficult time getting around, but she'd insisted on coming today.

"Oh dear, that will be me in a matter of months," Ada said. She looked up at her husband. "Perhaps you'll have to carry me."

"I will do whatever you ask." Max's eyes glowed with love as he returned her gaze.

"My goodness, but we're a love-struck bunch," Lucien mused.

"Pardon us," Tobias said, appearing strained if truth be told. "Fiona and I must take our leave. It seems the babe has decided that your wedding day is an excellent time to make an appearance."

"Oh!" Ada exclaimed. "Do you need to go upstairs? We have several bedchambers at the club. You could use mine. The bed is very comfortable."

"It is indeed," Max agreed.

Lucien stifled a smile. He turned his attention to Fiona, whose features were tightly drawn and her face pink. "We do have many bedchambers."

Fiona exhaled as if she'd been holding her breath. "I'm actually well aware of that, and yes, the beds are most pleasant."

Lucien wondered if everyone had used the Phoenix Club for an assignation. "Then, let us get you upstairs."

"No. I would like to go home and give birth in *my* bed. But I think we'd best hurry." Her eyes widened. "I think...my waters..." She swung her head to Tobias. "Yes, take me upstairs, please. Our room, if you can."

"I'll send for maids from the ladies' side," Ada said quickly, already moving. "Evie, have the footmen carry warm water up."

"The doctor," Tobias said, his face going pale. "Someone fetch the doctor."

"I'll dispatch Arthur," Lucien said.

"I'll take care of it." Max took off after his wife.

"What is happening?" Kat's mother had come toward them while Lucien wasn't paying attention. Because the wedding had been delayed so his father could attend, they'd had time to send word to Kat's family so they could rush to London. It was a good thing, because Mrs. Shaughnessy would have been *very* hard to appease if they'd held the wedding without her.

"Lady Overton is going to have her baby," Kat said. "Isn't that wonderful?"

Tobias began to guide Fiona toward the doorway. When she paused after a few steps and hunched over slightly, he swept her into his arms and hurried out of the dining room.

"Does this mean the breakfast is over?" Iona, Kat's younger sister by two years, asked. She sounded disappointed.

"Not at all," Kat said.

Prudence and Bennet approached them. She addressed

Lucien. "I hope you don't mind if I go up and help. I think Fiona might like that." Since Prudence had been her companion when she'd come to town a year ago, that seemed fitting.

"Of course not. Take Cass with you." His sister would want to go since Fiona was one of her closest friends.

"I will." Prudence touched her husband's sleeve before going to meet Cass, who was, in fact, on her way to join them. Everyone seemed to be congregating in the center of the room. But then Prudence and Cass departed just as Sabrina came back in. She was trailed by footmen carrying trays of champagne.

"Is it true that Fiona has gone upstairs to have her baby?" Sabrina asked.

Lucien nodded. "Yes. We have many reasons to toast today, it seems."

"We do indeed," Lucien's father chimed in as the footmen distributed the glasses of champagne. "I meant to tell you that the Hickinbottoms won't be bothering you anymore. They realized it wasn't in their best interest to denigrate my daughter-in-law."

"That is a relief!" Mrs. Shaughnessy exclaimed as she took a glass of champagne from a tray. "Thank you, Your Grace."

Lucien handed a glass to Kat and took one for himself. They exchanged a look of joy and promise, and he was suddenly eager for the breakfast to be over.

"Let us drink to my brother, Lucien," Con said loudly. "And his brilliant bride, Kat. I think I can speak for all of us when I say this is a union no one expected, but that we all wholeheartedly approve."

"We don't need that," Lucien said with a dry laugh.

"No, you don't," Lucien's father said. "But you have it nonetheless. Perhaps what Con should have said is that we all endorse your marriage, for there are no two people who are better suited to each other."

This was met with several people mumbling at once, causing Lucien to laugh again.

"Why are you laughing?" Kat asked, somewhat quietly. Well, quietly for her.

"Because every married couple in this room would likely argue that they are the couple who are best suited to one another." It was then that Lucien realized everyone was a married couple, save Kat's three sisters, Lucien's aunt, who although married certainly couldn't be described as half of a *couple*, and his father. Lucien glanced toward him and wondered if he might wed again. Stranger things had happened, and he certainly deserved happiness—if he could allow himself to have it.

"They are all wrong," Kat said, sipping her champagne.

Lucien had just taken a drink too and nearly choked on it. After swallowing the wine down, he tipped his head toward her. "I completely agree."

Con frowned as he tapped his glass with the ring he'd started wearing when Robert was born. It had been a gift from their father to commemorate the birth of his heir. "That was not the toast I'd hoped for. May we try again? Without the commentary?" He looked around the room, but narrowed his eyes at Lucien, who'd started everything with his rejoinder about approval.

"Please," Lucien said, putting his hand around Kat's waist.

Taking a deep breath, Con started anew. "To my brother and Kat, we all love you and are so glad you found one another." He fixed his gaze on Kat. "Kat, we welcome you to the family and hope you can endure our foibles, for they are great and often frustrating. You have already improved it immensely." Smiling, Con looked to Lucien. "Lu, I think we are all especially delighted to see you fall in love and find an everlasting happiness, for you certainly deserve it. I would say it ought to cure you of your matchmaking tendencies, but it would seem we are all matched." Con addressed them both, his gaze moving between them. "May your love be a comfort, a beacon, and the greatest adventure you will ever have." He lifted his glass and everyone joined him with cheers of "Huzzah!"

"That's easy," Lucien whispered to Kat. "It already is."

"Later, you can show me just how adventuresome you can be," she responded huskily. "If you please."

He looked into her eyes with heat and promise. "*Nothing* would please me more."

Don't miss my next series, LORDS IN LOVE, which I'm writing with my bestie, Erica Ridley! Book one, BEGUILING THE DUKE, written by me, is coming March 7, 2023!

When a duke is stranded in a small town during its matchmaking festival, he offers to help his host's daughter find a husband...until he wonders if he is the match she's destined to make...

*N*eed to go back and catch up with all eight books in the **Phoenix Club** series? Start with book one, **Improper**! Want to check out my other series? Read on to discover what to dive into next!

Would you like to know when my next book is available and to hear about sales and deals? **Sign up for my VIP newsletter** which is the only place you can get bonus books and material such as the short prequel to the Phoenix Club series, INVITATION, and the exciting prequel to Legendary Rogues, THE LEGEND OF A ROGUE.

Join me on social media!

Facebook: https://facebook.com/DarcyBurkeFans
Twitter at @darcyburke
Instagram at darcyburkeauthor
Pinterest at darcyburkewrite

And follow me on Bookbub to receive updates on pre-orders, new releases, and deals!

Need more Regency romance? Check out my other historical series:

The Untouchables
Swoon over twelve of Society's most eligible and elusive bachelor peers and the bluestockings, wallflowers, and outcasts who bring them to their knees!

The Untouchables: The Spitfire Society
Meet the smart, independent women who've decided they don't need Society's rules, their families' expectations, or, most importantly, a husband. But just because they don't need a man doesn't mean they might not *want* one…

The Untouchables: The Pretenders
Set in the captivating world of The Untouchables, follow the saga of a trio of siblings who excel at being something they're

not. Can a dauntless Bow Street Runner, a devastated viscount, and a disillusioned Society miss unravel their secrets?

The Matchmaking Chronicles
The course of true love never runs smooth. Sometimes a little matchmaking is required. When couples meet at a house party, what could go wrong?

Wicked Dukes Club
Six books written by me and my BFF, NYT Bestselling Author Erica Ridley. Meet the unforgettable men of London's most notorious tavern, The Wicked Duke. Seductively handsome, with charm and wit to spare, one night with these rakes and rogues will never be enough...

Love is All Around
Heartwarming Regency-set retellings of classic Christmas stories (written after the Regency!) featuring a cozy village, three siblings, and the best gift of all: love.

Secrets and Scandals
Six epic stories set in London's glittering ballrooms and England's lush countryside.

Legendary Rogues
Five intrepid heroines and adventurous heroes embark on exciting quests across the Georgian Highlands and Regency England and Wales!

If you like contemporary romance, I hope you'll check out my **Ribbon Ridge** series available from Avon Impulse, and the continuation of Ribbon Ridge in **So Hot**.

I hope you'll consider leaving a review at your favorite online vendor or networking site!

I appreciate my readers so much. Thank you, thank you, *thank you*.

ALSO BY DARCY BURKE

Historical Romance

The Phoenix Club

Improper

Impassioned

Intolerable

Indecent

Impossible

Irresistible

Impeccable

Insatiable

The Matchmaking Chronicles

The Rigid Duke

The Bachelor Earl (also prequel to *The Untouchables*)

The Runaway Viscount

The Make-Believe Widow

The Unexpected Rogue

The Never Duchess

Lords in Love

Beguiling the Duke by Darcy Burke

Taming the Rake by Erica Ridley

Romancing the Heiress by Darcy Burke

Defying the Earl by Erica Ridley

Matching the Marquess by Darcy Burke

Chasing the Bride by Erica Ridley

The Gift of the Marquess

Joy to the Duke

Wicked Dukes Club

One Night for Seduction by Erica Ridley

One Night of Surrender by Darcy Burke

One Night of Passion by Erica Ridley

One Night of Scandal by Darcy Burke

One Night to Remember by Erica Ridley

One Night of Temptation by Darcy Burke

Secrets and Scandals

Her Wicked Ways

His Wicked Heart

To Seduce a Scoundrel

To Love a Thief (a novella)

Never Love a Scoundrel

Scoundrel Ever After

Legendary Rogues

Lady of Desire

Romancing the Earl

Lord of Fortune

Captivating the Scoundrel

Contemporary Romance

Ribbon Ridge

Where the Heart Is (a prequel novella)

Only in My Dreams

Yours to Hold

When Love Happens

The Idea of You

When We Kiss

You're Still the One

Ribbon Ridge: So Hot

So Good

So Right

So Wrong

ABOUT THE AUTHOR

Darcy Burke is the USA Today Bestselling Author of sexy, emotional historical and contemporary romance. Darcy wrote her first book at age 11, a happily ever after about a swan addicted to magic and the female swan who loved him, with exceedingly poor illustrations. Join her Reader Club newsletter for the latest updates from Darcy.

A native Oregonian, Darcy lives on the edge of wine country with her guitar-strumming husband, incredibly talented artist daughter, and imaginative son who will almost certainly out-write her one day (that may be tomorrow). They're a crazy cat family with two Bengal cats, a small, fame-seeking cat named after a fruit, an older rescue Maine Coon with attitude to spare, an adorable former stray who wandered onto their deck and into their hearts, and two bonded boys who used to belong to (separate) neighbors but chose them instead. You can find Darcy at a winery, in her comfy writing chair, folding laundry (which she loves), or binge-watching TV with the family. Her happy places are Disneyland, Labor Day weekend at the Gorge, Denmark, and anywhere in the UK—so long as her family is there too. Visit Darcy online at www.darcyburke.com and follow her on social media.

facebook.com/DarcyBurkeFans

twitter.com/darcyburke

instagram.com/darcyburkeauthor

pinterest.com/darcyburkewrites

goodreads.com/darcyburke

bookbub.com/authors/darcy-burke

amazon.com/author/darcyburke

Made in the USA
Monee, IL
27 February 2023

28797656R00213